# FAVERSHAM DREAM

# ANTHONY DUNCAN

This edition published in Great Britain in 2011 by Skylight Press, 210 Brooklyn Road, Cheltenham, Glos GL51 8EA

First published in 2001 by Sun Chalice Books, Oceanside, USA.

Design, typesetting and cover photography by Rebsie Fairholm
Publisher: Daniel Staniforth

Printed and bound in Great Britain by Lightning Source, Milton Keynes

www.skylightpress.co.uk

ISBN 978-1-908011-11-4

**Author's Note**
All the characters in the twentieth century part of the story are figments of the author's imagination entirely and bear no resemblance whatever to any person, living or dead. The village of Fairloe is likewise a figment of the author's imagination and the topography of Gloucestershire has been slightly modified to contain it. Fairloe Court, together with its inhabitants in the late fifteenth and sixteenth centuries, is likewise fictional.

# FAVERSHAM'S DREAM

# CHAPTER ONE

NEEDLESS TO SAY, she wasn't there.

John peered into such corners as he could see from where he was standing, but no; she wasn't there. He was not particularly surprised, nor was he very much put out by the discovery. He and Jane had been married quite long enough for him to have learned that she was seldom where she said she would be at any appointed hour. Sometimes she would not be at the appointed place either. If he showed signs of petulance at being kept waiting, or at the discovery that he had been waiting at the wrong place, it was made plain to him that he "ought to have known!"

John was a patient man and he was devoted to his wife. No, he was not altogether surprised that she wasn't there.

But she probably would be there, at whatever the last possible moment would turn out to be. John closed the door behind him and smiled at the girl who was selling the catalogues. Caroline? Was that her name? Old Thingummy's daughter. John had never been adept at fitting names to faces, but he seldom forgot a face.

"Catalogue, Mr Faversham?" She gave him a pretty smile and offered one.

"No thanks, I'm not bidding. I'm looking for my wife – as usual!"

"I haven't seen her. If you're staying, have a catalogue on the house. There can't be many lots left. These are almost waste paper by now, I couldn't possibly charge you."

"Thanks."

John settled down, as quietly as he could manage, on a remarkably uncomfortable chair about a third of the way down into the audience. But no! It wasn't an audience was it? What was it? How did one describe a gathering of morose and preoccupied bidders at an auction? A congregation perhaps? He looked about him.

Well, the congregation was getting a bit thin by now and they were all slumped into their uncomfortable chairs. But there was a vigilance apparent in their slumping. One eye of the pair might be closed but the other was still glittering with avarice, ever alert for the main chance.

Dealers!

The world of auctions and antiques was a closed book to John Faversham and he was content to let it remain that way. He had picked up scraps of knowledge from Jane's Aunt Sarah who knew about these things. Aunt Sarah knew about most things, but her inner encyclopedia appeared to operate as much by intuition as by reason and the two faculties could add up to a startling combination. Jane was meeting Aunt Sarah here – that had been the confidently stated intention at the breakfast-table – and he had arranged to meet the pair of them here after his own meeting in Cheltenham because it wouldn't be worth going back to the office afterwards. The combination of Jane and Aunt Sarah was so unpredictable, however, that for all he knew they were by now at the top of Blackpool Tower, entirely convinced that their own brand of remorseless logic must infallibly lead him thence from Gloucestershire.

The trouble was that there always was a remorseless logic in it, but it was curiously different from his own brand.

Dealers!

John had heard dark stories of dealers; of rings of dealers, fixing things, holding second auctions in the backs of vans, of items changing hands a dozen times between their actual purchase and their departure from the hall. And there could be big money in it too!

John's mind could not rise to such dizzy heights. He had a good and deservedly well-paid job, he loved his work and was fiercely loyal to the firm in a way which was quite out of date and which they never quite understood. And he really wasn't very interested in money as such. All he wanted was to be able to pay the bills, and with Rosemary graduated from University and working in London, and Jane teaching part-time, money was not too much of a problem for them – at the moment. John was never a man for taking things too much for granted.

Dealers!

John took another glance round the congregation in the Tythe Barn and came to the conclusion that he was the only non-dealer present. He consulted his catalogue, found the place in the order of service and looked up.

The Liturgy was going on up front. Yes, it was rather like being in an odd sort of church. The god was Mammon with a vengeance! And there was the clergyman, immaculately suited, smooth, well-spoken, smiling and very nearly deferential. He would commence his Litany and glance pleasantly round the congregation, eliciting Responses. His acolyte would meanwhile reveal the icon of the moment to the gaze of the Faithful. He would elevate it with reverence, self-effacingly. The whole business was hushed, polite, gentlemanly. In a word: "Nice!"

All except the congregation, who looked positively nasty! Steading and Barnard were a very old-established and well-respected firm. They were all delightful to meet and to deal with and they made a great deal of money in a very gentlemanly sort of way. They used the Tythe Barn quite often for sales of this sort. Still no sign of Jane and Aunt Sarah! John fervently hoped they would succeed in arriving before the end and that he would not have to cudgel his brains to discern where they might be found, waiting impatiently for him. He glanced at the catalogue. Books. Not many lots, eight or nine perhaps. Where the hell were they? A slumped figure to John's left showed signs of animation. He nodded and twitched by turns and some three or four lots went down to "Terrace Titles." John turned to survey "Terrace Titles" and decided that "Vampire Volumes" would suit him better. There were not a few like him in Cheltenham! Another couple of lots went for next to nothing and they were down to the penultimate lot of the day. Where the hell was Jane? Where the hell was Aunt Sarah? Lot 428 was described in the catalogue as "Assorted Poetry." The High Priest of Avarice smiled sweetly at his congregation. "Now, who will give me five pounds?" There was a total silence.

"Four?" He beamed, but the silence was as of the tomb.

"Three?" The smile was sad, almost reproachful.

"Two?" A note, almost of despair, was in his voice.

"One?"

To his absolute astonishment, John discovered himself making a gesture with his catalogue.

"Thank you Sir!" The auctioneer clearly regarded him as a close personal friend.

"Sold for one pound to Mr … ?"

"Faversham," said John, rather self-consciously.

At that moment Jane and Aunt Sarah came breathlessly through the door and began an intense three-way whispering session with Caroline, old Thingummy's daughter.

"Sold to Mr Faversham for one pound!" Said the auctioneer in ringing tones and the intense three-way whispering stopped in full flow.

Jane and Aunt Sarah both stared at him, aghast, as if he had just done something very naughty indeed, and rather embarrassing to boot.

Lot 429 was a ragged collection of nothing in particular. The auctioneer wound resignedly down from five pounds to one pound without a bidder.

"Could you possibly help us out, Mr Faversham?" He smiled. John returned his smile and sadly shook his head.

"What have you done? What have you bought?"

An urgent whisper assailed him. Jane and Aunt Sarah had done what John liked to describe as a bumwise sidle along the row of empty chairs and were now sat beside him, fizzing with interrogation. "Culture," he replied.

"Yes, but what?"

"Literature," he said.

"Yes, but what have you bought? What have you bought?"

"Like I said," he said.

Exasperation was setting in next door. His answers were clearly unsatisfactory. The sale was over and the congregation was dispersing. "Come and see!" he said.

They came, and they saw. And John parted with a pound to a tall, rather wispily pretty girl at the cash-box whom Aunt Sarah seemed to have known since infancy. It was altogether extraordinary how many people Aunt Sarah did seem to have known since infancy. It didn't seem to matter where you went.

A little bundle of books, tied together with string, passed into the possession of Mr John Faversham of Fairloe Court near Gloucester and, with noddings and smilings, and sudden zig-zaggings and delays, John finally shepherded his womenfolk into the open air of a nearly empty car-park.

A steady drizzle was falling.

It was no more than a mile and a half from the Tythe Barn to Aunt Sarah's house in Prestbury. Hers was a very ordinary, redbrick house with a very ordinary tiled roof, but Aunt Sarah had somehow succeeded in investing it with the aura of a half-timbered cottage, deeply thatched. The small front garden was a very traditional cottage garden, somewhat over-stuffed, and the roses that adorned the front of the house looked curiously old-fashioned. John walked round to the rear passenger's door to open it for Aunt Sarah. As he did so, Jane emerged awkwardly from the front seat and reassembled herself on the pavement. Jane was a tall, graceful woman but getting out of motor-cars was not her most ladylike accomplishment. She seemed always to be carrying three things too many.

"A nice cup of tea!" Aunt Sarah dumped a collection of very large handbags and exotic scarves on to the hall chair. In reality there was only one large handbag and one exotic scarf, but with her, things always seemed to exist in the plural.

"Or gin?" Aunt Sarah looked over her shoulder at John with an eager-to-please expression on her face.

"No thanks, darling. We're driving!" Jane took any words that might have been in John's mouth right out of it and gave him one of her "don't be a naughty boy" looks.

The two women decided that it had suddenly turned chilly and made great slappings and clutchings of their own upper arms as if to emphasise the point. They huddled over a coal-effect electric fire in the drawing room, leaving John far out in the middle of the room, on the settee. Men did not feel the cold.

John, temporarily sidelined, glanced round the familiar room and his eye fell upon the silver framed photograph on the bookcase, with the smaller silver frame beside it enshrining a medal, the Air Force Cross. He was very fond of his wife's eccentric aunt and these two silver frames, and their contents, never failed to touch him. They touched him again now.

Sarah Redmayne had been born in 1920, the very much younger half-sister of Jane's father. Old William Redmayne had had two boys, Edward, killed at the Somme in 1916, and Charles, who had inherited the estate.

Charlie Redmayne had been born in 1897, had enlisted in the Royal Engineers on the first day of the First World War, was commissioned a year later and transferred to the Royal Flying Corps just before his brother's death. He had survived the war with a DSO and some rather nasty wounds which gave him trouble in later life and probably shortened it by a year or two.

Old William Redmayne, widowed not long after Edward's death, had married again after the war. He was more than old enough to be his second wife's father and the marriage had caused raised eyebrows in Worcestershire. Eyebrows were raised again when Sarah was born, twenty-three years younger than her half-brother. Sarah's had been an odd childhood. She had been educated at Cheltenham, had gone on to Oxford in 1938 to read History and had entered the Women's Auxiliary Air Force immediately upon graduation. She met and married Flight Lieutenant Martin Gregson, of Bomber Command, and was widowed within the year, in 1942. There were no children and she never married again.

Martin, a nice-looking fellow, had smiled from his photograph upon thirty-five years of Sarah's teaching History at a Girls' School, and upon some five or six years of retirement thereafter. She had never looked seriously at another man.

"By the way – how did you get here, darling? I didn't notice your car." A lull in the conversation brought John back from his customary communion with Uncle Martin. He rejoined the ladies. "I hitched a lift in with Susan, and then Lucy dropped us both off at the Tythe Barn on her way to Winchcombe. Lucy has joined a new Group." Jane's voice betrayed a hint of fascination. John's heart sank. Lucy was one of Aunt Sarah's odder friends, deeply committed to the esoteric and was, John feared, a less than satisfactory influence …

"She wouldn't stop talking!" Aunt Sarah was inclined to be apologetic. "That's why we were late."

John wondered who wouldn't stop talking. He could imagine the periodic exclamations about the time and the urgent protestations that they must be off – followed by fresh bursts of conversation on completely disconnected subjects.

If the truth were to be told, John, who had a deep and genuine fondness for womankind, was more than a little in awe of them and sought to conceal the fact, to himself at least, by indulging in amused and supposedly detached observation, with a hint of male chauvinism to set it off. Needless to say it concealed nothing whatsoever from women, all of whom could read him like a book. "Well! Where are they? Let's have a look!"

John obediently picked up the little parcel of books from beside him and began, painstakingly, to pick at the knot in the string that bound them. He could feel his wife's mounting agitation. There was nothing Jane liked better than unpacking parcels, but this was *his parcel!* He had paid a whole pound for it and he would unpack it himself.

"You're making heavy weather of that string, darling! Why don't you just cut it?"

John thought that pretty rich from one who seemed to value wrapping paper more than its contents. She would always cry out and scold him when, man-like, he tore the wrappings from his own birthday presents.

"Good piece of string this! Might come in handy."

Jane snorted in imperial disdain, but just in time the knot gave way and the little pile of books was released to await detailed discovery. "You've got a Palgrave!" Aunt Sarah could not restrain herself. "I peeked at it in the car. I wonder if it has those lovely wishywashy illustrations, all in pink and green?"

John up-ended the pile and extracted from the middle of it a shiny, brown leather-covered volume with gilt edges. "Golden Treasury," he said, and opened it at random.

"Yes, There's a picture here of an old gaffer in a smock, leaning on a rather prim young woman. All rather pink and green, just as you say."

Aunt Sarah became animated.

*"O could I feel as I have felt*

*"Or be what I have been!"*

John glanced at the caption and blinked in astonishment. She had quoted it word for word! Well, that was Aunt Sarah all over! "Youth and Age," she said. "All about a withered waste of life. Very Byron!"

It occurred to John that he had done well for his pound, and there was more to come.

"Poems and Songs for the Open Air," he looked inside, "compiled by Edward Thomas." He turned the pages. "Tunes in it too." Jane gave a whoop of glee and plucked it from his hand. "You can sing and recite while you're digging the garden!" She giggled. "It'll frighten all the neighbours. They'll think you've gone dotty. What's a Bullgine?" She enquired, suddenly.

"Something to do with ships," said Aunt Jane.

"Let the Bullgine go ..." Jane attempted to sing a snatch of an unfamiliar sea-shanty, and then gave up.

John picked up the third book of the four. He liked the feel of the soft leather. He squinted at the spine and then found the title page. "Goethe," he said. "Über allen Gipfeln." He turned a few pages.

"Gothic script and pictures. Nice!"

"Sally's youngest can have that!" Jane was good at disposing of other people's property. "She's doing O-Levels next summer. I'm sure she's doing German."

John regarded the exotic script with a curious delight. It might be worth learning German for this. He smiled lovingly at his wife. "Did you buy anything, darling? In Cheltenham."

"Yes, I bought two pairs of pants and a bra, in Marks and Sparks."

John beamed at her. "Well, Sally can have the pants and Molly, the Vicar's wife, can have the bra. She looks as though she could do with a new one."

There was a hasty interjection from Aunt Sarah. "Why don't you just dispose of your own things, darlings? Can I have a look at the Goethe?"

John handed it over and watched with interest as Aunt Sarah devoured the contents.

"Its almost worth you learning German, you know." Aunt Sarah looked up at him with one of her enthusiastic looks. "Goethe knew a thing or two. He was Rudolf Steiner's great inspiration, Steiner really got going after editing the definitive edition of Goethe. It really turned him on!"

John felt something inside him kick for touch. There was a strong "alternative" streak in Aunt Sarah. She was as encyclopedic about things esoteric as she was about things ordinary and normal. Some of her friends he found decidedly odd. John felt he had quite enough on his plate, keeping his head above water in engineering in the 1980s, without going dotty on the inner planes as well. "You haven't done badly for a pound, darling. What's the last one?" Jane was eying another brown leather volume with an almost obsessional interest. "It looks as though it might be interesting." John picked it up and looked at the title page. He frowned. "James Hasfield," he said. "Poetical Works."

"Never heard of him!" said Jane, in a tone almost of reproach. "What did you want to buy that for?"

"James Hasfield?" Aunt Sarah sat bolt upright and gazed into a private middle-distance. "James Hasfield! He used to live in your house! Yes, he did!" She regarded her guests with triumph.

"Who was he?" John was interested in anyone who might have lived in their funny old house. Perhaps this unpromising brown leather book was going to be interesting after all.

"Local poet," said Aunt Sarah. "Very minor! Died about eighteen-ninety-something. Old – *you know!*" She racked her brains. The result was, as ever, unpredictable. "The boy stood on the burning deck – what's his name?"

"Mrs Hemans," said Jane.

"No darling! Not the author, the battle!"

John observed in fascination. The retrieval processes from Aunt Sarah's memory-bank were singular to say the least.

"Battle of the Nile!" Aunt Sarah was triumphant. "Well old Jimmy Nile who used to have that shoe-shop in Thingummy-street in Gloucester – his grandfather used to know James Hasfield very well." She beamed at John and Jane. "Yes, James Hasfield of Fairloe Court. I'm sure it's mentioned somewhere."

This pound had been well spent indeed! John opened the book. "Pages are uncut," he said. "Nobody has ever read it! Do you think they were wise?"

Jane giggled. "The very minor Victorians can be a bit heavy going, can't they Sarah? They are always being 'thrid' or 'furled,' and they go 'wonning' about all over the place!"

*"Thro' God's own heather we wonn'd together,*
*"I and my Willie (O Love my love);"*

Aunt Sarah was always good for a quote, but Jane was seldom far behind.

*"I need hardly remark it was glorious weather,*
*"And flitter-bats waver'd alow, above."*

The two women collapsed in helpless giggles.

"C. S. Calverley," explained Aunt Sarah. "A wicked send-up."

"Well, what is this bloke Hasfield like? Any idea?"

John felt a curious reluctance to open the book in the presence of these Philistines. He found himself suddenly protective about the Poetical Works of James Hasfield. After all, the chap had lived in their house! He didn't want him giggled into the waste paper basket before he, John Faversham, had given him a decent innings and made his own mind up about him.

"Can I have a look, darling?"

Something about the book had excited Jane's urgent curiosity.

And so John reached out and put it into her hand.

John Faversham had a long-established dislike of driving in Cheltenham. He liked the town itself, but it had never been the easiest place for the motorist and the Council's successive attempts to improve the traffic flow had only succeeded in confusing him. It was always the previous system that seemed to engage his consciousness, not the current one.

Had they not been travelling home in John's company car, Jane would have been in the driving seat. She enjoyed driving, and her husband, unlike many men, quite enjoyed being driven. She was a skilful and determined driver and had no problems with Cheltenham whatsoever. Theirs were very different personalities. Herbert Faversham, born in 1890, had been all his life a schoolmaster at various boys' public schools. He was almost a caricature of the Senior Classics Master; tall, slightly stooping, possessed of a quiet but keen wit and altogether wrapped up in his subject. At the age of thirty-eight he had married Constance Hawkins, the daughter of another schoolmaster, and two years later, in 1930, she was delivered of their only child, John.

When John was seven years old they moved from Sussex to Somerset, Herbert having secured a senior post in one of the boys' public schools in the county. There they stayed for the rest of their lives. Herbert died in 1970 at the age of eighty and Constance followed him seven years later at the age of eighty-two.

From a local preparatory school John moved on to study as a day boy at his father's school. He was an only child, and the slightly semi-detached status of a day boy at a boarding school, combined with his father being one of its senior masters, made his a somewhat lonely adolescence. The one thing that might have bridged all the gaps, ability at games, was denied him. He hated organised games and showed no aptitude for them whatsoever. John was an able scholar, but in the wrong subjects. His father was heartbroken by the boy's indifference to the classics and slightly incredulous at his ability at mathematics and the sciences. This he inherited, not from his father, who was incapable of changing a light bulb, but from his somewhat eccentric mother. Connie Faversham had the appearance of a perpetual schoolgirl, she was capable of wearing a gym-slip into her sixties, she usually wore sandals and her grey hair was rather inefficiently gathered into an untidy bun from which it escaped perpetually, to her irritation and bewilderment.

Connie mended everything that broke and made everything that needed making. Having dismantled and then successfully reassembled a malfunctioning grandfather clock, she announced that some of its little wheels had been "Suffering from ingrowing toenails." She was thus an untaught mechanic and a natural engineer, innocent of all the appropriate terminology. She encouraged her son in the construction of model aeroplanes and was a perpetual astonishment to her devoted husband. She was however a less than gifted cook and her housekeeping was always a trifle haphazard. John therefore had had a curious childhood but not by any means an unhappy one. He began to come into his own when he left school for he elected, much against his parents' wishes, to complete his National Service before going on to University.

Two years in the Royal Artillery were the making of John Faversham. He was commissioned 2nd Lieutenant, seriously considered applying for a Regular Commission, and finally chose to read Engineering at Durham University instead. He did well, added a Doctorate to his BSc and joined the firm in 1957.

John Faversham enjoyed a placid disposition. Everything about his upbringing had conditioned him to be rationalistic and suspicious of the intuition. Underneath his conditioning, however, he was a very intuitive man, and also a sensitive one. He was, as Aunt Sarah had spotted at once, insecure in many ways, and he needed to retreat, often, to his little workshop at the back of the house and make things – more, if the truth be known, for the retreating than for the making.

Quiet he might be, and placid, but John was nevertheless well able to cope with his wife's more overtly strong character and those who knew them best knew them to be well matched, and the more happily married because of it.

Once through Cheltenham and on the dual-carriageway to Gloucester, John's motoring troubles were over. He glanced at Jane. "You went all funny over that last book. So did Aunt Sarah. I thought for a moment we were going to have tears. What was up?" John sensed an awkwardness beside him, a reluctance, almost, to give a straight answer. For an unpleasant instant he felt threatened. Something odd had happened as soon as he had given Hasfield's *Poetical Works* to Jane. She had opened it, stared at what she saw in apparent disbelief, and handed it immediately to Aunt Sarah without a word.

Aunt Sarah had said, "Oh!" and handed it back to Jane. Then she had produced a handkerchief and had begun to dab her eyes. And then she had tried to conceal the fact by a vigorous cleaning of her spectacles.

"Come on! Out with it! What was the matter?"

"Oh! Nothing really. I … I just got a bit of a shock, that's all."

"What kind of a shock?"

"Did you see the photograph of Hasfield in the front of the book?"

"Yes. Sepia-tinted. They used to go in for that."

"Did you notice anything about it?"

John frowned. He tried to remember what he had seen, but he had not really attended to the photograph.

"He looked, sort of … what? Late fifties, early sixties? A bit older than me perhaps. Why?"

Jane hesitated. She felt a great reluctance to say what was in her mind.

"It was … well, it was almost as if it was you! Not an exact likeness of course, but it was *you*! If you know what I mean? The eyes! They were your eyes! That's what gave me the shock."

John looked at his wife, one eyebrow in the air. But his outward appearance belied what was going on within. One never knew what Jane would produce by way of reactions to things. She and Aunt Sarah were birds of a feather. Sometimes their reactions seemed bizarre to him but they were very seldom found to be actually wrong. "What about Aunt Sarah? She was trying to hide an emotional spasm behind a vigorous cleaning of spectacles."

Jane glanced at her husband. He didn't miss much! And he was a bit rattled by what she said. She knew he would be. He made a great thing of being ordinary and normal, without any flights of psychic fancy to trouble him, but Jane knew him better than that. There was a whole dimension to John Faversham that he had not yet come to terms with. She wondered what he would make of the photograph when he looked at it properly.

"She had exactly the same reaction as I did."

"Well! What do you make of it?"

"I don't know. I don't suppose it matters – if you know what I mean. But it did give me a shock. I'll be interested to see if it says anything to you when you look at it again."

"Well … Yes … Hmm!" John was mentally kicking for touch again. "Odd to think we are taking Hasfield's poems back to the house in which they were written! I'll cut the pages tonight, when I get back from the PCC I hope the damned thing doesn't go on all night!"

"Darling … " Jane's voice betrayed a trace of anxiety.

"Hmm?"

"Do you think we might be … well, invoking something?"

"By taking it back home again?" John laughed. "I'm sure Lucy would think so!"

"Don't be beastly about Lucy! She's a bit dotty I know; what you would call dotty at any rate. Full of half-digested 'teachings' from half a dozen esoteric Gurus, but she's no fool! And she is really rather a dear. But she can talk!"

By this time they were clear of the outskirts of Gloucester and were crossing the marshy glumness of Alney Island, between the canal and the River Severn. Just short of the bridge at Over they turned right, drove up between the river and the Maisemore Ham, crossed the Maisemore bridge and drove a mile or two through the village and out the other side. Then John slowed the car, turned left and ran down a steep little lane towards the reedy banks of the little River Leadon. Some two thirds of the way down he slowed almost to a halt and turned into a drive. There, framed in the car's windscreen was the half-timbered façade of Fairloe Court, their home. "I'll leave the car out. I'll want it this evening."

The drizzle had cleared and a shaft of early-evening sunlight was making the tower of Gloucester Cathedral, some three miles distant, shine like a great candle. John put an arm round his wife's waist.

"Lucky to live here, aren't we?"

And he kissed her.

"That must have gone on for a long time! Or did you go on to the pub?"

There was a grunt from an invisible John and sounds, in the hall, as of a man divesting himself of coat and cap. Jane looked up just as her husband's face came round the door. He looked weary.

"Pub? You must be joking! The bloody meeting went on and on. I thought it was never going to end."

"Parochial Church Councils are all the same, aren't they?" Jane had skilfully sidestepped a proposal to elect her to the PCC a few years back. She was happy, she had said, to do the flowers, make tea, help with church cleaning – anything at all – but committees of any description: No! John had been elected instead. She was occasionally tempted to feel guilty about it but she managed to resist the temptation.

Charlie Redmayne had married Cecily Matthews in 1928 and the marriage had caused quite a stir in Worcestershire, for Cecily was then regarded as a Great Beauty. She was ten years younger than her husband, high spirited and somewhat of a handful. They had had to wait seven years for their first child, and then two daughters were born to them in fairly quick succession.

Jane was the eldest, born in 1935, and Barbara followed two years later. The two girls inherited characteristics from both parents; Jane inherited much of her mother's looks and figure, but a good deal of her father's nature. It was from her father that her intuitive gifts came, as well as her love for music and for literature. Barbara inherited more of her father's looks and her mother's nature. Her first marriage had ended in a noisy and highly publicised divorce and she was now married to a wealthy stockbroker and lived in some opulence not far from Horsham. The two sisters had little in common and the two brothers-in-law even less.

The girls had been educated at one of the girls' public schools near Malvern. Jane had proved to be a good all-rounder, she was good at games, she was a competent pianist and possessed a fine soprano voice. She went up to Oxford in 1953 to read English, toyed with the idea of a career in publishing but, after graduation, took a Post-Graduate Diploma in Education instead, rather to her mother's scorn.

It was her interest in music that brought her and John together. They met at the Three Choirs Festival in 1957 and, after what they liked to describe as a whirlwind romance, they were married in the December of that same year.

Charlie and John had taken to each other at once, but there was trouble from Cecily. As soon as she knew that her will would not prevail, however, she had bowed to the inevitable with great good grace and appeared at the wedding in triumph as the most attractive Bride's Mother Worcestershire had seen in twenty years. Jane taught English at a Gloucester girl's school for a few years after her marriage, and then resumed when her own children's education began to become, first expensive, and then very expensive in the inflation years of the 1970s. She enjoyed teaching, but now Rosemary was graduated and launched upon her own career, Jane had taken to teaching part-time, as much to keep her hand in as for any other reason.

Jane was bossy and impulsive, sometimes wilful. She could be moody and was conservative in most things. A nature less placid than John's might have found her difficult to live with, and a weaker character would soon have been ridden down. But she was the soul of kindness and much loved by her many friends. None loved her more than her husband, and that love was entirely mutual. John slumped into his chair by the huge fireplace. Logs were burning merrily on a deep pile of ash. He closed his eyes for a minute, then he opened them and smiled at his wife.

"Its hard to be businesslike when the chairman can't chair to save his life! They wouldn't let him anyway; any hint of normal committee discipline and they'd all be mortally offended." John gave a short, grunt-like laugh. "Twenty minutes work, and we took two and a half hours over it. Poor Walter looked shattered when it was all over."

"Were they getting at him again?"

"Not really. But we make such a meal over the inevitables. I mean – the Diocesan Quota is going up again next year. It was bound to, but anybody would think it was a personal affront, unique to St Mary's, Fairloe, instead of something that happens to every parish, inexorably, every year."

John paused and gazed at the fire.

"And old George kept rabbiting on about pre-war and how the whole parish used to be run on eighty-five pounds, seven shillings and tuppence a year – year after year. We've heard it all before. We hear it at every meeting, but Walter hasn't the heart to tell him to shut up. You can't. So that was a full thirty minutes wasted."

"Poor George! Poor Walter!"

"Poor everybody!" John shook his head and sighed. "And of course the organ is packing up. Only about a third of it ever gets used because nobody knows how to play it properly. I stuck my neck out and suggested we got rid of it! I suggested getting an electronic keyboard that almost anybody can play – they could play it from where they are siting in a pew! We could get a new one every year for what we are having to fork out, tuning and patching up an overblown contraption that nobody wants."

"What did they say to that?"

"Oddly enough it didn't provoke any outcry at all. But Walter was quick to point out that we would have to get a Faculty to make that kind of a change and he thought the Diocesan Advisory Committee would have a fit. It just isn't done to replace pipe organs with something electronic. *Status quo* rules, however expensive, however inappropriate. I hope he is wrong. Anyway we've deferred the matter until the next meeting – having taken forty minutes to decide to arrive at no decision at all."

"Oh dear! Was that all?"

"Some hope! The Architect is coming to do the Quinquennial inspection of the church fabric next month and we all got the jitters about what he might find wrong. Then George suggested finding a cheaper architect! He reckoned the poor chap's fees were too high! Nothing would persuade him that the whole thing was being done more for love than for money – and probably at a thumping loss to his firm too. In normal commercial terms the fee is peanuts!" There was another pause, and a prolonged gaze into the fire. "Oh yes! Then Annie burst forth under Any Other Business to tell us that 'People' were getting very upset by the state of the churchyard. Poor Walter's patience was wearing a bit thin by then and he suggested – quite pleasantly I thought – that instead of griping in corners, 'People' might like to lend a hand to keep it tidy."

"Don't tell me. Annie is now officially upset!"

"How did you guess?"

"Darling, would you like a drink? I could do with a nightcap myself. No! You sit tight, I'll get them."

John sat back in his chair and stretched himself. He loved his little parish church and he was very fond of its amiably cantankerous congregation. He liked Walter too. Walter was priest-in-charge of the parish; he was a non-stipendary clergyman who had entered holy orders in middle age and continued to hold down quite a demanding secular job in Cheltenham.

The parish was tiny and could neither justify nor support a full-time Vicar. Fairloe was lucky to have Walter, and when he reached retirement age they were almost certain to be joined up with another parish or group of small country parishes. But for the time being, the miniscule parish of Fairloe retained its proud independence.

"There you are, darling! And there is your homework!"

John opened his eyes and discovered a tot of whisky on the occasional table beside him. Beside it lay the *Poetical Works* of James Hasfield, and his own best pen-knife.

"Thanks, darling! But I don't think I can get into all this now. I can't take it in after that meeting."

"No, but you can cut the pages, and then Mr Hasfield will have come home properly, won't he?"

"You mean that when I've cut the pages all his thoughts can start leaking out all over the place?" John grinned. "Cheers!" He took a welcome sip from his glass and then, with great care, he set about his task.

"Its funny how they used to sell books uncut like this. Quite a voyage of discovery to get into the thing. A creative experience, you have to actually do something to get to the next bit." Something stirred in John's memory and he turned to the front of the book. He moved aside the tissue-like page which protected the photograph of its author, and then he gazed upon the countenance of a man who had probably sat where he was sitting now, and who had written the contents of this book one hundred years before.

"Hmm! A bit like me I suppose. Funny the way he looks straight at one. Interesting!"

So saying, he resumed his painstaking cutting of the pages.

"Are you going to read something?" Jane watched him close up his pen-knife and put it down on the table.

John shook his head. "Not tonight. I want to come to him fresh. Curious business! I hadn't the slightest intention of bidding for that pile of books. And look what we've got! And all for one pound! I want to find out a bit about this chap and read him properly. But right now, I'm going to bed."

The nightly routine of door and window fastening, of putting the heavy iron guard in front of the fire, and the turning out of lights was finally accomplished.

As he gave one last glance into the drawing room before going up to bed, John saw the flicker of the dying fire reflect on the shiny leather of the book which he had left on the little table by his chair.

"I wonder what we have started by bringing you home again, old chap?" His mind lingered on the curiosities of a long day. "I'll attend to you in the morning," he said.

And following his wife up the creaking, uneven stairs, he went to bed.

# CHAPTER TWO

"A IL, MARY, full o' Grace. The Lord be with thee. Blest art thou that art 'ighly favoured, and blest be the fruit o' thy womb, Jesus." Walter de Furlowe knelt on the rush-strewn floor of the tiny chapel in the South aisle of the church. Tears ran down his rough cheeks, unchecked. Walter was quite without inhibitions, he would laugh until he cried and, when he was sorrowful, he would weep openly like any other man. And at this moment his heart was breaking within him.

Was he to be widowed again? His beloved Kate had died in childbirth when they were both but twenty, and his little son had been born dead. Was he to be widowed again?

The light had gone out of Walter's life when his pretty Kate had died. He would gladly have died himself and was careless of his life for many a long year afterwards. He would gladly have died fighting for King Richard at Bosworth Field. But it was his own father, William de Farlo, who had died that day and Walter had lived to bear the dread news to his mother.

William had died with his King. Richard had led a furious charge against the Battle commanded by the Steward of his own Royal Household, Thomas, Lord Stanley. The Stanleys had stood back from the fight until they had made sure who was going to win it. When the tide turned in favour of Henry Tudor they joined in with him and deserted their King.

King Richard had gone down fighting, and so had William de Farlo, fighting beside him.

Walter's mother had lasted but twelve months into her widowhood and, by the time of the rebellion in Yorkshire and the uprising nearer to hand in Worcestershire, Walter was master of his own modest estate.

Aye! And he wanted to keep it! And he wanted to keep his head on his shoulders at the same time! King Henry the Seventh was a hard, sharp-eyed man whose old opponents were beginning to disappear. So Walter had thrown in his lot with the Tudors and he had fought for King Henry at Stoke Field.

Walter had served his new master well and had caught the King's eye. He was safe enough now, but the wound he had received at Stoke Field left him lame – he accepted it as a penance for turning his coat – and kneeling on a stone floor was an agony! "Ail, Mary, full o' Grace. The Lord be with thee. Blest art thou that art 'ighly favoured, and blest be the fruit o' thy womb, Jesus." Kate, dead in childbirth. And now Meg? His whole heart reached out to the Holy Mother of God, our Lady Saint Mary. Would she not add her prayers to his for poor Meg? Would she not see Meg safely through?

But meantime, where the plague was the priest? A pox on him! Walter had married Meg when he was rising thirty and she a young widow of twenty-five. On their wedding night, Sir Richard, the Vicar, had come with holy water to bless their bed-chamber, their bed, and themselves in it.

"God bless your bodies and souls, and bestow his blessings upon you as he blessed Abraham, Isaac and Jacob."

They had said *Amen*! And the priest had closed the door behind him and commanded that they be left in peace.

Nine months later, to the very day, young William had been born. He had been baptised in this very church and, within a fortnight, he had been buried in this very churchyard.

Five long years later, in 1497, young Meg had been born. She had been the light of Walter's life but, at the age of two, she had died and left them childless again.

Was there a curse on him? Or on Meg? No! The wise woman he had consulted in the Forest had said not. And she had promised that he should have a son to succeed him. Aye! But would he lose his wife in the process? She had said nothing about that!

A pox on that priest! Where was he run to?

Where was Sir Richard? Walter had sent his two lads to find him and tell him to make haste and get his armour on, for there was a Mass to be said.

Old Harry, the Parish Clerk, was gone to Flaxley in the Forest of Dean, to the Cistercian Abbey of the Blessed Virgin Mary which held the Great Tythe of this parish. Sir Richard was but a Vicar, a stipendary priest put in and paid for by the Abbot. He was godly enough, in his way, and he cared for his people faithfully. Sir Richard had his wench of course, like a good many of the parish clergy, but Walter did not grudge him that. As long as she wasn't his wife, mind! For t'was a mortal sin for a priest to marry! But where the plague was he?

Walter had spent all night and half the day walking up and down in the hall which adjoined his house, cursing and praying by turns. He had thrown logs on the hearth in the middle of the hall floor and he had watched the smoke trying to find its way out through the hole in the blackened roof above.

He had been kind and cruel by turns to everyone who dared to enter. He had shouted in fury at the mawkins in the kitchen when she made a clatter with her pots, and he had both thanked her tenderly and then growled at her when she had set food in front of him. He had fondled his favourite hound, and then he had cursed it and kicked it when it relieved itself among the rushes on the floor, as it usually did. And then frightened, white faces had appeared at the house door and had told him that if he loved his wife he would get a Mass said for her, and the sooner the better!

He had sent the two lads hot-foot to find Sir Richard and he had limped painfully and furiously to church as fast as his bad leg would carry him. Was a man to ride a horse to church, to throw himself at the feet of the Almighty and weep for the life of his wife?

The sound of hurrying feet made Walter pause in his *Hail Marys* and turn anxiously, almost angrily around. Young James ran up to him, made the sign of the cross and knelt beside him. "I did find un, Master. 'im were a-diggin of 'im's Glebe. 'im's acomin as fast as a can. I did tell un t'were the Mistress, look. 'er bein bad wi' child, like. And 'im did say as 'ow a would be a-sayin a Mass o' the Virgin, for women a-labourin wi' child. I was to tell 'ee to 'ave faith, Master. 'im did say as all 'ud be well."

Walter reached out, put his arm about the lad's shoulders and kissed him.

"Now to thy 'ail Marys, young James! Tis bad wi' the Mistress, and I can't be a-losin of 'er! No, Lord Christ!" He cried aloud, "I can't be a-losin of 'er!" And with that, he broke down and wept uncontrollably.

More footsteps sounded. Young Harry, the Parish Clerk's son, came into the chapel through the wooden screen that separated it from the nave.

"'im's come, Master! 'im's a-puttin on of 'im's armour. My father's awoy, so I'll be answerin o' the Mass, look!"

Walter nodded gratefully at young Harry through a sea of tears. He was a good lad, was Harry. The old chantry priest had done well with him. Harry could read and write more Latin by far than he, Walter, could. Harry got up from his knees and slipped out of the chapel. A minute later a little bell sounded and Harry reappeared, leading Sir Richard, armoured in white and gold for a Mass of the Virgin.

The priest touched Walter on the shoulder as he passed and stood at the foot of the altar step with young Harry kneeling beside him.

*Emitte Spiritum tuum et creabuntur.*

Sir Richard's voice rose into audibility and sank back into near silence, as it would do throughout the Mass.

*Et renovabis faciem terrae.*

Young Harry's response was slow, deliberate, and rich in its Gloucestershire overtones.

The Mass followed its course, praying that a merciful Father would hear the entreaty of his servant on behalf of his handmaiden now in labour. And that he would, of his blessing, go before them and bring matters to a speedy and successful issue, to the honour of his Holy Name, and at the intercession of the glorious Virgin. The tiny congregation, kneeling on the dusty floor, made their responses and said their *Amens* with all the devotion of which simple and uncluttered hearts are capable.

"O Mary, handmaid of Christ, mother of God, hear a poor sinner truly sighing after thee, lest infants be in peril in their mother's womb."

Sir Richard had a fine voice, and the plainsong Sequence echoed in the little church, timeless and haunting.

"To whom, therefore, shall desolate women with child flee save to thee, O spotless Virgin."

And as the Sequence was sung, Walter looked up, craning his neck to see through the nearby arch to the painting above the opposite arcade. There, our Lady Saint Mary was being crowned Queen of Heaven by God the Father and God the Son, with God the Holy Spirit fluttering above her head in the form of a dove. They wouldn't let him down! Meg would be delivered and safe when he got home! In his heart he knew it, and he was at peace.

The dread and most holy Sacrifice was offered and the Mass was ended. Sir Richard, still in his armour, met Walter as he emerged, tear-stained and exhausted, through the screen into the nave. Without a word, he and Walter embraced each other.

"T'will be all right now!"

Walter could speak at last. There was peace in his tired eyes.

The priest nodded.

"I da come, presently," he said.

# CHAPTER THREE

"**N**OT THAT TIE with that shirt, darling!"
The tone suggested an heroic patience sorely tried. "Didn't you look in the mirror?" She added.

John sighed inwardly. It was obviously going to be one of those mornings and the sooner he got away to the office the better. He returned to his little dressing-room, peered in the mirror, shrugged his shoulders and changed his tie to the one he had worn yesterday. No great matter of principle was involved and he was a man who preferred quietude, especially at the breakfast table.

He had been alerted. With her morning cup of tea he had enquired of his wife: "Sleep well, darling?"

By way of response he had received the single word:

"Odd!"

She was preoccupied now, and scowling, and he had a curious sense that, in some arcane fashion, it was all his fault.

And now Jane's preoccupation was absolute. She was glaring into the looking-glass, poking fiercely at her hair and, snatching up lipsticks and eye-shadow, jabbing them furiously at her countenance. He, John Faversham, had altogether lapsed from existence and so he slipped from the room and sought the sanctuary of the kitchen. A plaintive mewing assailed his ears. Philomena was howling at the back door.

John was very fond of the little cat. She was archetypally feminine, she was as pretty as a picture, she had fur like a powder-puff and she was relentlessly wicked. He unbolted the back door and opened it. "Come on, Sweetheart! Poor little soul! Do you want your breakfast?" Philomena spat at him and darted under the old settle by the kitchen window. John opened the refrigerator, found the half-used tin of cat-food, tightly sealed with its plastic top, and forked its contents into a saucer. He put it down by the Aga, together with a dish of fresh water.

Philomena emerged from beneath the settle and approached her breakfast. She sniffed and drew back, a picture of disdain. "Come on, Sweetheart!"

John put a hand out to stroke her, by way of encouragement. As quick as lightning she lashed out with her claws.

"Little beast!"

John regarded the back of his hand. She had drawn blood. He thought of his wife, and he looked at the cat, now oblivious to him and biting, urgently but daintily, at her breakfast. "Bloody women!" he said.

John and Jane breakfasted frugally. Jane periodically did the round of the Health Food Shops and produced varieties of odd-looking muesli which she would devour in silence with an almost religious intensity. John stuck to old-fashioned toast and marmalade. As it seemed to take longer to prepare

Jane to confront the world at large, John usually saw to the preparation of breakfasts. It didn't take a lot of preparation when all was said and done, and it was difficult to make mistakes.

"No darling! Not that milk!"

Difficult, but not impossible. John replaced one jug and rummaged for the other one. He found it, hidden behind everything else in the refrigerator, but thought better of the comment that came, almost, to his lips.

Breakfast was silent, ominously silent. John saw his wife's eyes darting about the room. She was evidently looking for trouble. She glared at him as he ate. Any minute now he was going to receive a sharp lecture on how toast and marmalade ought properly to be eaten. The lecture was pre-empted in mid-formation, however, by the totally unscheduled arrival of Philomena into the middle of Jane's lap.

"Oh! Darling! Why on earth did you let the cat in? You knew I was going to wear my navy-blue! Now look at it! Cat hairs all over it!"

With outrage all over her countenance, Jane dumped the cat unceremoniously on the floor and swept furiously from the room.

"Come here, little Sweetheart! Daddy loves you!"

John was long accustomed to his wife's periodically sulphurous breakfast-times and was seldom seriously ruffled by them. If the truth be known he took very little notice. As he stroked a purring Philomena and finished his second cup of coffee he wondered just how psychic he would have to be – having left his wife in the bedroom, clad in nothing but pants and a bra – to predict the style of her arrival at the breakfast-table, she having changed her mind totally at least once in the meantime.

The mathematician in John found it an interesting exercise in probabilities but he had never attempted it. There were altogether too many improbables.

"And wouldn't I have got into trouble if I hadn't let you in and given you your breakfast, Sweetheart?"

Philomena purringly agreed with him. And then, for good measure, she bit him.

It was one of Jane's teaching days at the School. Well, the poor kids were in for a rough time and no mistake, but she would return full of sweetness and light. She nearly always did. John gathered up the crockery and put it in the dishwasher. He tidied up the other breakfast bits and pieces and he went into the hall to collect his coat. At the foot of the stairs he called, affectionately, to his wife. "I'm off, darling. Have a lovely day! Give 'em hell!"

The response from above was incoherent.


"Cecily!"

John saw the metallic grey Volvo standing by the front door as he turned into the drive. "Ma-in-Law! What is she up to now?"

It wasn't that John had anything against his Mother-in Law, but her unscheduled arrival was usually charged with significance of one sort or another and he wondered what it might be this time. Whatever it was it would involve him in endless complications, it always did. John liked Cecily, but at the end of what had been an unusually taxing day, his heart sank in spite of him.

But no, it wasn't Cecily! The right kind of car but the wrong number-plate. John's spirits rose. He felt rather mean about it. What was it about these small Volvos? What did they remind him of?

"A ladies motor-car!"

The phrase jumped out of his pre-war, schoolboy memory, and at once he had a mental image of the old Lanchester; black, heavy, with rather small, dark-looking windows. That had always been described to him as "a ladies motor-car," and in some strange way the mantle of the old Lanchester had fallen upon the small Volvo – at least in the mind of John Faversham.

Hadn't the Lanchester been a pup of a Daimler? John couldn't remember, but he passed the visiting motor-car with interest. No, it wasn't Cecily's. Whose might it be?

John dumped his briefcase in the hall and hung up his coat. Voices were coming from the drawing-room. Women's voices. He pushed open the door and entered the room.

"Darling! We think you are an incarnation!"

Jane was regarding him with glee. John's startled gaze took in two more women, turning to look at him from the settee. One was Aunt Sarah and the other? Damn! It was that mad woman, Lucy! All the weight of a heavy day at the office returned and hung about John's shoulders like a laden yoke. He smiled. "A what?"

"An incarnation. Isn't he, Sarah?"

Aunt Sarah looked at him, almost guiltily, he thought.

"Do you mind?" she asked.

"Oh! Not a bit, really."

John saw the tall, slightly scraggy figure of Lucy sitting alert and almost triumphant beside Aunt Sarah. She had an intelligent face, framed by rather wispy, greying hair. Hers was the face of an enthusiast, a convert, an evangelist. He winced inwardly.

"It will have been your *Karma*," she said, pleasantly.

"Very likely! I'm sure we've all got lots."

Something inside of him was desperate to kick for touch, but he had a horrid feeling that he wasn't going to be allowed to.

"So you accept Reincarnation, then?"

Lucy's countenance had taken on a vaguely Himalayan cast. She was aloft in Eternal Wisdom. John's heart sank.

"No, Lucy. I don't. I respect it as a venerable and a quite often plausible speculation. It seems to make a lot of things tidy and suggests explanations for the otherwise inexplicable. But it doesn't have a place in my own system of belief – not as a part of The Faith at any rate."

"But do you regard it as incompatible with Christian belief?"

"I don't know, Lucy. And I have never felt the need to ask myself the question; seriously, that is. I'm an engineer, not a theologian. I'm conscious of my limitations, I suppose."

John smiled at his interrogator, hoping profoundly that the interrogation would lapse and that someone would offer him a cup of tea without him having to ask for one.

"I should have thought *Samsara* might have appealed to the engineer in you!"

John looked desperately for an escape route. The obvious one occurred to him.

"Whose incarnation am I supposed to be?"

"Hasfield's of course!" Jane looked at him, mischief all over her face.

"Oh!" he said.

"Oh! Do give poor John a cup of tea!" Aunt Sarah was, he thought, a little uncomfortable at the turn things were taking. "Poor John! Fancy coming home to discover you are somebody else! – Or used to be!"

"We were all looking at your photograph before you came in," explained Jane as she handed him a tea-cup and a plate with a slice of fruit cake on it. "Hasfield's photograph I mean, and we've all decided you are a reincarnation of Hasfield!" She bent down and kissed him.

"I'll do my best," he said.

"But, John dear, we weren't spending all our time talking about you! Honestly!" Aunt Sarah was anxious to re-establish equilibrium.

"No, darling. We were talking knitting patterns if you must know!" Jane giggled. "Lucy has taken a fancy to my red pullover and I managed to dig out the pattern for her."

"Yes, I'm quite normal really!"

Lucy's eyes were twinkling at John. The thought struck him that she wasn't a mad woman after all. In fact he rather liked Lucy. John drank his tea and had his cup refilled. The conversation had reverted to knitting patterns and allied subjects, John's immediate entertainment value having been exhausted.

He excused himself, left the room, went upstairs and washed and changed into casual clothes. The sound of intense conversation was still coming from the drawing-room so he retreated from the scene into his private sanctuary, a lean-to workshop at the back of the house. And there was the dining chair in pieces, awaiting reassembly. It had been there in pieces for a fortnight and Jane had become somewhat importunate about it. Goodness knows how many decades of use had caused the joints to begin to work and he had finally been prevailed upon to do something about it.

John preferred doing things he had thought of rather than the multitude of "little jobs" Jane might think of, given half a chance. But this had become an urgent matter and so, with infinite patience, he had eased the joints apart, cleaned them up and prepared the whole job for reassembly. He just hadn't got round to reassembling it, that was all.

Reincarnation! He searched in the drawers for the wood adhesive. *Samsara* ought to appeal to the engineer in him! He found the glue and stood up to think.

Yes, it ought! He could imagine, in principle at least, quite a tidy "people re-processing plant," on a rotating principle with an upward spiral delivering an end-product. He stood there for ten minutes, speculating about the various inputs and quality-control systems that might be needed, about automatic returns for reprocessing and a dozen other refinements.

He began to look about him for pencil and paper to sketch something out – he would give it to Lucy as an outline in "dense manifestation" of a *Samsara-plant*, then he snapped out of his frivolity. No! It would be a great discourtesy, it would be an impertinent trivialisation of sincerely-held and most venerable beliefs. Beliefs in which he did not happen to share ...

The joints fitted together very nicely. He had done a lot of painstaking work on them, packing with great care those which had worn, and managing not to mark the polished surfaces.

Now all he needed was something by way of a clamp ... Was reincarnation incompatible with Christian belief? John supposed that a lot depended upon how one approached the subject. It was, after all, the approach that mattered. Nobody, neither Lucy nor the Archbishop of Canterbury *knew* what the form was. It was all opinion, speculation. John remembered Marcus Aurelius: "Remember, all is opinion!"

It was the approach that mattered, surely.

What was he going to use for a clamp? The obvious thing was a piece of string, ringing the newly-glued joints, and tightened up by twisting round a stick. But string might bite into the wood and leave marks. He needed something flat ...

Yes, it was the approach. There was something abhorrent to John about the almost mechanistic image that doctrines of reincarnation presented one with. He stood up straight as an idea came to him. They knew nothing of forgiveness! Indeed, in some cultures, the Christian belief in Divine Forgiveness and Restoration was considered immoral!

Bias binding! Jane would have some in her workbox! He slipped out of his workshop and rummaged in the kitchen. Yes, she did have some! Well, he wouldn't disturb the party in the drawing-room and the glue would soon be beginning to harden so he would help himself now and explain later.

Love is the fulfilment of the Law, both of Torah and of Karma, surely? In the life of Grace, obligations are those of Love, not of law. This would put a different complexion on things altogether. Now, if he, John Faversham, was indeed the reincarnation of James Hasfield – he grinned to himself – it would have been Love which demanded it of him, not a process of mechanics. That approach he could live with – as long as he remembered that it was pure speculation from first to last!

Yes! Bias Binding would do it nicely!

John flattened out the tape, then he returned it to its normal, folded state.

It would be wide enough folded and it would need the extra strength. He cut off two generous lengths with a Stanley knife, ringed the four chair legs, at the top joints and at the lower, and inserting two pieces of half-inch dowel, tightened up first one and then the other.

One had to get it just right. Not too slack, and not so tight as to tear the binding or mark the wood.

What was it that made people like Lucy chase off after all kinds of esoteric speculations and eclectic odds and ends of oriental religion? John made the pieces of dowel fast against unwinding.

"School religion! Enough to turn anyone Hindu!"

John made a wry face. He had reacted violently against it himself. In his case, away from "Establishment Mattins" into the parentally frowned upon "High Church" extravagances of incense, confession, and a positive sense of the numinous in worship. He had never consciously perceived the extent to which this was a reaction against a relentless conditioning which had denied him the knowledge of quite half his own nature.

"That's better! Now I had better rejoin the ladies."

John washed his hands in the kitchen sink, dried them on a tea-towel, glancing over his shoulder lest Jane appear, loud with rebukes, and squaring his shoulders, advanced upon the drawing-room door.

John's reappearance in the drawing-room precipitated the very thing he had been waiting for.

"Oh Lord! Look at the time!" Aunt Sarah looked up from her wristwatch with a look of shocked disbelief all over her face.

Aunt Sarah invariably displayed shocked disbelief at the time of day. Her steadfast incomprehension of the passage of time was one of John's delights, as were the departure rituals that followed the discovery. It must not be supposed that John was in any hurry to see the back of his visitors; he simply enjoyed naughtily observing their departure rituals and making his own estimates as to their likely duration.

The three women all jumped up from their seats in great urgency. Then they settled down again, but perched on the edges of their chairs. First one and then another made a discreet departure from the room, followed by an equally discreet re-entry. And then, all restored to comfort but still very temporarily perched, a wholly new subject of conversation was embarked upon.

There was a second horrified discovery of the time. They all jumped up again, talked very quickly and perched again.

At the third horrified discovery they departed in a body into the hall, still talking. John followed.

Between the final jumping up and the final departure, having left the house, and having re-entered in order to search for Aunt Sarah's spectacle-case, they embarked briefly upon three fresh subjects of conversation.

These, in turn, concerned the health of two mutual acquaintances and their uncertain prognoses, and the intimate domestic tribulations of a third.

As John held open the driver's door of the Volvo for Lucy to enter, she paused, looked at him, and said:

"I hope we didn't threaten you!"

Damn the woman! They had, and she knew!

John grinned and shook his head.

"Not too seriously," he said.

"Keep an open mind," said Lucy.

"I'll try."

As the car backed out of the drive, John glanced at his watch. Not a bad guess! Twenty minutes!

Jane, waving frantically, gave a little sigh of relief when the car vanished from sight and she could stop. She looked sideways at her husband.

"Pig!" she said.

"Par for the course," he replied.

Jane gave her husband's arm a little squeeze.

"Sorry about the reincarnation thing," she said. "But it flashed into my mind as soon as I saw that photograph. And Sarah had the same reaction. We were talking about Hasfield and his book and we had another look and showed Lucy."

"And Lucy defined the doctrine! I thought as much. But she isn't as dotty as I thought she was. I rather took to the woman to tell you the truth."

"Oh Lucy is all right. She used to be into just about every psychic group in Cheltenham at one time. But ever since Deirdre has taken her in hand she has become much more normal."

"The Earth-Mother!"

John was more than somewhat in awe of Deirdre. He regarded her as the doyenne of all Aunt Sarah's more "alternative" acquaintances. He had an uneasy feeling that Deirdre was probably a witch of some sort or another. He winced.

"Has the Earth-Mother been consulted about the Hasfield affair? Has she vouchsafed an opinion?"

"You're very naughty, darling!"

"I know. It passes the time. And I have to keep my end up somehow. When do we eat?"

"Sorry we're so late, darling. I wasn't expecting them. I'll rustle something up quickly."

"Well, thank God its Friday, and thank God it will be too late to get the mower out by the time we've eaten!"

John wondered how unbelievably dull an all-male departure ritual would seem, detachedly observed by a woman.

"Vive la différence!" he thought.

"Well! You can have a look at your book now, can't you? I've been very good, I haven't been peeking into it in advance."

John sank into his chair, to the right of the great chimney-piece in the drawing-room. He grinned at his wife.

"Only at the photograph!" he said.

He picked up the brown leather volume from the occasional table by his chair. He opened it, moved the tissue from the face of his predecessor, and looked at him thoughtfully. The eyes bothered him. They looked straight at him and had an urgent, preoccupied look about them as if they were trying to tell him something. His eyes? Surely not! He hoped he didn't look like that! He consulted the contents page.

John Faversham was not one for opening a book at random and reading the first thing that caught his gaze. Jane would do that, but not John. He liked to study the contents as described and start from there. Jane found this one of his more maddening traits. "Why don't you read something?" she asked.

"I'm coming to that. I want to see what there is to read first." He sensed her fidgeting in her chair. "The Victorians loved being pompous, didn't they? I think they used to find it funny – or something. Hmm!"

"Can't you just choose something and *read* it?"

Jane was having to restrain herself from snatching the book from him.

"We could try *Animadversions concerning an unsuitable courtship* if you like."

John painstakingly found the page, opened it and scanned its contents thoughtfully.

"*Read it*, darling!"

"In a minute! Dialect! Funny how the Victorians loved writing dialect poems. Like Tennyson. He is completely unintelligible in dialect. Hmm!"

"What does it *say*, darling?" Jane wanted to scream.

"Lots of old dialect words in it. I shall have to put on my best 'Glaster' if I'm going to read this!"

"Darling! I don't care a damn what you put on – or take off! Just read the bloody thing!"

John looked up at his wife's exasperated countenance and gave her a beatific smile. Then, clearing his throat and adjusting his dialect, he read the poem.

I seed 'em by the flip-flap gate;
And I 'ad 'alf a mind to 'ide,
But bein as t'was gettin late
I just goes on and lets un bide.

A-kyollopin with 'im's silly grin
Back 'ome 'im came, back to the farm.
'im knew I knowed just where a'd bin
And kep 'isself way out o' 'arm!

Right Molly Mawkins in 'er place!
And 'im too mombly for to see,
A-kyawin' at 'er's silly face!
A proper yawny that 'un be!

"Read it again, darling."

And so, with slightly enhanced dialect assurance, John read it again. He looked up and grinned.

"Better than its title!" he said.

"I haven't heard some of those words since I was a child." Jane was rapt in recollections. "Isn't it ghastly what radio and television, and everybody dashing about in cars, seems to have done to things?" She frowned. "What was he doing to her silly face? Clawing?"

"A-kyawin'" said John. "Gawping, we would say."

"I love Molly Mawkins!" Jane grinned. "It says it all! And I love the Proper Yawny too! You can see him, all goofy with his mouth wide open. Why can't people talk like that now? What's happened to England?"

"Usual English mixture: snobbery and urban dilution I suppose. It hasn't been fashionable to speak with a regional accent for decades, and the big cities spread their horrid accents, diluted, for miles in every direction."

John gave a sad little laugh.

"Do you know why I shall never run off with my secretary, darling?"

"Oh! Poor Vera! Why won't you run off with her? She adores you!"

A look of sadness came over John's face.

"Because she always says 'Yass' instead of 'Yes!' Diluted Brum washing against the gates of Cheltenham. Am I an awful snob?"

Jane giggled. "You mean to say that if you propositioned Vera and she went all eager and said 'Yass!' you'd be turned right off?"

John nodded, glumly.

"Yes darling! You are an awful snob and quite absurd, and I love you! Read something else."

John returned to the contents page and consulted it with great intensity. Jane resigned herself to a long wait.

"What about *Prospect of the River Leadon from its Source to its Confluence with the River Severn at Over*?" A weariness was in John's voice. "Little wonder nobody cut the pages!"

"Go on, darling!" Jane was tired of waiting. "It might not be quite as dreadful as its title."

There was another painstaking finding of the right page, a long consideration of its contents and a clearing of the throat.

By Evesbatch and by Halmond's Frome
Springs rise to serve thy reedy rill
And set thee on to, winding, roam.
Steen's Bridge bestrides thee, Beacon Hill

O'erlooks and guards thy spreading power
And hands thee on to Bosbury Tower.
Thy waters move through Earth's own land,
Brown-stained and sluggish. Mire and pond

Both fed and feeding, stagnant stand
Until the hills, once far beyond,
Begin to close. Thou runnest by
Where Lesbury Spire sharp stabs the sky.

From Marcle and the Preston Brook
Thy floods are swelled. Dark Dymock Spire
Stands squat and brooding since was shook
By Gethyn Goch with sword and fire.

Then Ketford, Cutmill, loop and bend
To Pauntley round, by Murrell's End.
Upleadon and its timbered Tower
Salute thee! Hartpury, lost beside.

Let Rudford bless thy closing hour
As from my step I see thy tide
Under the Druid's Oak now run
To Severn and the setting sun.

There was a long silence. Both John and Jane were lost in mental pictures of the familiar countryside and of the little river which flowed at the foot of the slope upon which their old house stood.

"Mmm!" said Jane, "I feel cosy!"

"We've got an old One-Inch map," said John, "I must check him out!"

"I love the bit about the step. Its our own doorstep! We must have a look before it gets too dark. Any more doorstep ones?"

John Faversham then did something completely out of character.

He opened a page at random and read it.

"The Dream," he said. And mumbled to himself as he read it.

"Doorstep in this one too …"

He put the book down suddenly and stood up.

"What are you doing? What's the matter?"

Jane sensed that something had smitten her husband. He was tense and on edge.

"I'm going to the doorstep! Coming?"

And with that, he marched determinedly out of the room.

They stood side by side on their front doorstep. John put his arm round his wife's shoulders as much, she sensed, for his own comfort as for hers. Something had him badly rattled.

"There's Rudford over there," he said. "About a mile and a half as the crow flies; South-South-West I should think. There it is, busy blessing Leadon's final hour!"

Jane peered along her husband's arm.

"I think I can see the bell-turret," she said. "I adore Rudford Church, it's one of my favourites."

*"As from my step I see thy tide*
*Under the Druid's Oak now run."*

John had a gift for instant memorisation, when his interest was sufficiently aroused.

"There's Lassington Wood, on that bluff, about a couple of miles due South of here. The old Oak would still have been standing in Hasfield's day." He frowned. "Severn and the setting sun are due South! Poetic licence I suppose!"

Jane leapt to Hasfield's defence.

"No darling! The Severn Estuary faces pretty well straight into the setting sun. I think that's fair enough."

John nodded. "Fair enough!" he said.

"Darling!" Jane was curious about the other doorstep poem. "What was that poem you didn't want to read out? What was it about?"

John looked ill at ease.

"Oh! The chap had a nightmare and ended up on his doorstep:
*... And a shell*
*Upon the threshold stood of hell.*
And then he woke up! Gave me the creeps!"

John peered, anxiously, in the direction of Gloucester, as if he was looking for something. He was looking for something but he couldn't remember what it was. He didn't want to remember either.

"The phone!" An urgent and incessant tremolo sounded from within. "Shall I answer it?"

"Yes ... Well, no! I'll answer it if you like."

And like a man shaking himself out of a dream, John Faversham returned to the real world of trivialities and arbitrary interruptions, and Jane followed him back into the house.


"Darling?"

They were lying in bed. The light had just been put out. It was the time for intimacies.

"Hmm?"

"Something really stirred you up, didn't it? That poem. The one you didn't want to read."

There was a prolonged silence. Then:

"Yes. Quite extraordinary. Hasfield was describing, in exact detail, a rather nasty dream I had about a fortnight ago!"

"You mean – the same dream?"

"Yes! In every detail."

"What do you think it means?"

"I haven't the faintest idea. But it does give a new twist to things. I really must find out about Hasfield, it suddenly seems important."

"Do you think it can have anything to do with – well – the things we were talking about at tea-time?"

"Reincarnation? No idea. It hadn't occurred to me. I don't know, but that seems a bit too easy an answer if you know what I mean."

"What was the dream?" Jane hesitated. "Can you talk about it?"

"Not at this time of night! Its all in the book, in fullest detail. Read it in the clear light of day! And by the way …"

"Yes, darling?"

"I love you!"

"I love you too!"

# CHAPTER FOUR

WALTER DE FURLOWE sat on his stool to the right of the great chimneypiece in his house, his bad leg thrust out in front of him. His great barrel chest and huge shoulders gave him a curiously topheavy look, and he was brooding; turning over in his mind news lately come from London, and also another matter more pressing and much closer to home.

"What ails thee, Walter?"

Meg had been carefully mending a small shirt, her eyes squinting in the flickering light of the fire. She put it down, her eyes could no longer see what they were doing.

"'Tis Master Poynz, Meg. 'im's come from London and 'im da say as Prince Arthur be took proper bad. 'im says as 'ow that Spanish Princess'll be a widow afore she's a bride, likely!"

Walter stirred on his stool, which creaked under his weight. "And 'tis all over London as 'ow the King'll be a-marryin of 'er to Prince 'enry if Prince Arthur da die. 'im's that set on a-marryin of 'im's childen off to foreign kings and queens! Princess Margaret be Queen o' Scotland, look; to kep 'em quiet, likely!"

Meg shook her head in profound disapproval.

"'im can't be a-doin o' that, Walter! 'im can't be a-marryin o' Prince Arthur's widow to Prince 'enry. 'tis agin the law, a man a-marryin of 'is brother's wife."

"'im'll get Pope ta change un for un! 'im's King, look!"

"Right, Walter! But 'im's not God, look!"

Walter held his peace. There was no profit in having an argument with Meg. She could argue the hind leg off a horse and she was usually right. Walter did not approve of many of the doings of Kings, but he was a pragmatist, and he recognised the pragmatism of the Papacy. And in any case, who was he to approve or disapprove? He could only risk a critical discussion of such matters in the privacy of his own house – not even in his hall beyond that very door! The King had ears everywhere.

"'tis said King 'isself is beginnin to fail. But Master Poynz wouldn't be drawn on't. 'im kep a-lookin round about un, case anyone was a-listenin!" Walter laughed a short, grim laugh. "Master Poynz wants to be a-keepin of a's 'ead, look!"

"What's King's age, then?" Meg frowned as she tried to remember how much older he was than her Walter.

"Five year older than me. Ten year older than thou. That da make un fifty-one."

Meg nodded and grunted. Walter could see by her face that she was speculating upon the succession.

"Prince 'enry be sixteen," she announced. "Eight years older than young John. Walter! I never did think as England ud 'ave a King Arthur on the throne! 'twas ill done, a-baptisin of un wi that name! 'twas a-temptin o' Providence, look! 'twas presumption!" The great Arthurian epic, with the *Quest of the Holy Grail* in its midst, turning all the worldly values upside down, was the very foundation of English lay spirituality. To baptise a King's eldest son Arthur was to make presumptuous suggestions indeed as to his future reign.

Walter fell silent and enjoyed the comforts of his fireside. He had built the great chimneypiece into the middle of the wall of his house, on the opposite side to the hall, the year after young John had been born. Now logs blazed in the hearth and the smoke went obediently up the chimney instead of swirling about under the roof. It was a fine thing for an English yeoman to be able to sit alone with his wife, in warmth and comfort by his private fireside, without having to be all hugger-mugger in the hall, sharing the central hearth with the lads, the maids and the dogs.

Walter had a more immediate matter on his mind than the doings of Kings and Princes, however. The time was fast approaching when he was going to have to do something about young John's education. The boy was rising eight years of age and some said that Walter had delayed long enough already.

The boy could read and he could write. His mother had seen to that. She was of gentler upbringing than Walter and having been an intelligent and determined girl, with an enlightened father, she had acquired a passable education. She was sufficiently proficient in Latin to be able to use parts of *The Little Office of our Lady Saint Mary* in her private devotions and she was, like her husband, deeply devout.

But what of the boy?

There was nothing resembling universal education in England, but literacy was widespread and, with the invention of printing, it was becoming more so and more important. Any boy whose father was determined enough could be educated after a fashion. All the cathedrals had schools attached to them. Most of the monasteries, and certainly the larger ones had schools and, in the towns and villages, chantries abounded. Wherever a chantry had been established, the chantry priest would usually teach such boys as came to him the rudiments of reading and writing and Latin enough to answer the Mass.

Old Sir Gilbert, the chantry priest, kept a tiny school for village lads in the North aisle of the church, behind his chantry chapel. Should young John go to him for his schooling?

No! The boy was intelligent and he was a thinker. He knew as much Latin as his father already. Walter must do better for him than the little village chantry.

"Meg!"

Walter had arrived at a decision. He wanted to share it with Meg at once.

"Meg! I'll be a-sendin o' young John to the Monastery o' St Peter in Gloucester." (He pronounced it Glaster.) "Th'Abbot's school is good, they da say, and t'will set un on 'is woy."

He sat back, relieved, like a man who has been bearing a burden for a long time and has at last set it down.

"If a can do well, look, them'll send un on t'Oxford!" The Benedictines were good schoolmasters, and the wealthier abbeys would often send a bright boy of modest means on to one of the Universities and maintain him there in one of their own houses. Most of the Bishops were the sons of yeomen, or of tradespeople. Very few came from the great families.

"Now I be glad ye did say that, Walter."

Meg looked across at her husband. He was a typical Gloucestershire yeoman and she was proud of him and had come to love him dearly. They had shared great sorrows together over their two lost children.

John was the last and, thank God, he was strong and healthy. There would be no more, the years were beginning to show on both of them.

"I be glad ye did say that," she repeated. "For I bin a-thinkin much on't. But now, Walter! I would be a-sendin of 'im to Glastonbury, not Gloucester. Tis ever so much the best for schoolin. They da send ever so many of the likes of our John to Oxford or to Cambridge." She paused, and she looked Walter straight in the eye as she did whenever she had a trump card to play.

"And Walter! My cousin, Sir Hugh! 'im's a monk at Glastonbury, and tis 'im as da teach the young lads! Send our John to 'is own kinsman, Walter. T'will be the best as you can do for un!" Walter de Furlowe sat up, wide-eyed. He laughed out loud and he smote his thigh.

"Meg! T'were 'eaven's doin! T'was our Lady Saint Mary 'erself as did send thou to I! What would poor Walter be a-doin if t'weren't for Meg?"

And he gazed adoringly at his wife with her lined face and her greying hair. And then he got up and peered through the house door into the hall.

James was asleep. Young Harry was teasing the pretty mawkins who cleaned the pots and helped with preparing the food. Two hounds were curled up by the fire in the middle of the floor, and young John was fast asleep in his corner. This was Walter's household and he was proud of it. And one day it would be John's.

"Glastonbury 'tis, my Love!"

He closed the house door and limped back to his stool. "I'll be a-ridin there tomorrow! No! Tis all right, look! I'll take young Harry wi' me, and young James can look after you 'ere." He knew Meg would fret and imagine nameless horrors all the time he was away. A week or ten days would suffice, he knew the roads and there were monasteries with guest houses to give them safe lodgings on the way.

"If tis to be, Meg! If tis to be, then a can go as soon as a can!"

The horses were saddled bright and early the next morning. Meg and the mawkins fussed about, bringing provisions and endless advice, for the mawkins was as anxious for young Harry as Meg was for Walter. At length all was ready, and the two men set off, amid a cackling of hens and a barking of dogs, for the three or four day ride to Glastonbury.

There was much waving and weeping from the two women, standing at the door of Walter's hall. Meg was much comforted to see the powerful figure of young Harry riding beside his master. It was a long journey through strange country. The Mendips were said still to be a stronghold of the ancient religion of witches and warlocks, and who could tell what might befall a lone traveller on that road? It was ten long days later that they returned, tired, travel-stained, but triumphant. Walter swung stiffly from his horse and embraced a Meg who was near-delirious with relief at seeing him alive and safe again.

"Young John'll be at Glastonbury for Michaelmass!" He looked round for the boy, but he was off somewhere, at games with his friends.

"Thy cousin, Sir Hugh'll see to un, and all shall be well, look!" Meg could not speak for tears. Tears of relief at her Walter's safe homecoming; tears of joy that the best they could hope for for young John would be accomplished, and tears of grief at his impending departure. For John, her last and only living child, was shortly to go from her to begin his long and painful pilgrimage to manhood. Harry led the horses away and Walter and Meg went into the hall.

Walter looked about him, as he always did upon a homecoming. Times were changing and new fashions were abroad. He had been much inspired by a yeoman's house he had visited in Somerset. Walter looked up at the smoke-filled roof and he looked down to contemplate the hearth in the middle of the hall floor. Next summer, when the days were beginning to be warm, he would begin a mighty work in this hall! It was too late to think of it this year and his ideas had not yet matured. But Meg would be mightily pleased with what he was planning to do! Of that he had no doubt. At that moment, young John appeared at the door, saw his father and came running towards him. Walter swept him up into his arms and kissed him.

"John, my son!" he said. "Come Michaelmass, and thou'rt to go to thy kinsman, Sir Hugh, at th'Abbey o' St Peter and St Paul at Glastonbury! Tis an 'oly place, mind! And thou shall be a scholar there, and the best scholar as ever they did see! And thou shall go on t'Oxford, look! And thou shall end up Lord Chancellor o' England! What da thou say to that?"

"Better I be King o' England!"

John had no idea what his father was talking about and for some weeks to come was completely unable to take it all in. Why! He had been the three and a half miles to Gloucester but once in his whole life! Glastonbury? It was as remote to his imagination as a journey to the moon.

# CHAPTER FIVE

PHILOMENA was coiling and uncoiling herself, with unbridled sensuality, in a patch of bright sunlight on the old settle by the kitchen window. At length she settled down and, observant as always, regarded her humanfolk with amused indulgence.

Philomena would stay with them now for the rest of her life. They needed her. And she had them well trained and they were fulfilling their part of the relationship very satisfactorily. She had grown very fond of them and it was possible, almost, to treat them as equals. Philomena was an intelligent cat and she had taken interested note of all manner of human rituals by which their very different lives seemed to be bound. She knew that, at any moment now, an invariable Saturday morning breakfast ritual would be enacted. Like a great many human rituals it was conversational, that seemed to be the way with them.

It began, invariably, with a wholly unexpected disclosure. It was always the same wholly unexpected disclosure.

"Darling! I must rush into Gloucester straight after breakfast! We are out of nearly everything! I haven't had a chance of doing any shopping this week!"

The response was equally invariable, and John obediently made it.

"Would you like me to come with you? You know! Push a trolley round Sainsbury's? Carry things?"

"No darling. Thank you very much, but I'll get on much quicker on my own."

This, Philomena had observed, concluded the first measure of the conversational dance. It was followed by a second, equally invariable.

"Back in time for coffee, darling? When shall I put the coffee on? About eleven?"

"Oh! I don't know, darling. Don't bother about coffee for me. I don't want to feel rushed."

Philomena settled down in the patch of sunlight. She tucked her front paws under her chin, her tail was tucked in round one side and her eyes were tightly shut. The ghost of a smile played about her lips. She trained her ears forward so as to catch the next exchange which was also invariable in principle if not in actual detail of content.

"What are you going to do, darling?"

There was something in Jane that could not possibly depart for Gloucester and Sainsbury's upon a Saturday morning without first being sure that her husband would be satisfactorily occupied. The slightest hesitation on his part would immediately produce from her a list of "little jobs." There was nothing more untidy to a mind as organising as Jane's than the thought of a husband standing idle, doing nothing.

"I'm going to do some research. I want to grope about in the churchyard and see if I can find Hasfield's grave. He must have been buried in the parish if he lived in this house."

"Don't be silly, darling! Look in the Burial Register first and find out. You could waste hours in all the brambles and Old Man's Beard!" Jane liked nothing better than organising other peoples' activities. She always did it so much better than they could! "Ring Walter now!" she commanded. "Ask if you can look in the Registers."

John smiled sweetly at his wife. Why, he asked himself, had he allowed himself to be thus caught off his guard after nearly thirty years of marriage? He would have to manoeuvre himself out of the corner of relentless common sense into which he had unwittingly allowed Jane to push him. Once she had, mentally, taken over the management of his activities she had a tendency to be exceedingly put out by recalcitrance on his part. If he did not agree immediately he was in danger of being called silly and obstinate. Jane was quite likely to rush off to Sainsbury's in a huff. When she returned, having forgotten something obvious and vital, she would blame him for being so stupid as to make her forget.

"Walter is away for the day. I thought of that!" he lied. It was a white lie or, perhaps, in that diplomatic phrase, he was just being economical with the truth.

"And it isn't just Hasfield and his gravestone – if he's got one – I want to hunt about for a few other things as well, while I'm about it. You'll see when you read that poem."

"Oh! The nightmare one?" Jane was preoccupied and inclined to be dismissive. "I haven't had time to read that! I've been far too busy getting ready."

She finished her coffee and jumped up from the table to continue with the serious business of getting ready. It involved, as John had so often observed, a great deal of running about and several seemingly unconnected dashes from one part of the house to another. John had often wondered what a Time-and-Motion Study would have to say about Jane's "getting ready" routine but he saw neither hope nor purpose in any such exercise.

At length the process was complete and, clutching a handbag and two large shopping bags, and with a wheeled shopping trolley in tow, she swept cheerfully from the house in the direction of her waiting Mini.

"Don't spend all morning flirting with the Dean and Chapter!" John's sense of the absurd was stimulated by the frequency with which his wife would return from her Saturday forays to Sainsbury's having had one gentle trolley collision after another with a succession of dignitaries from the Cathedral. The entire Close evidently rushed wildly into Sainsbury's as soon as its doors opened upon a Saturday morning.

John tidied away the breakfast things and stacked the crockery in the dish-washer. It was full now, so he filled up the little hatch which held the detergent, closed the door and selected a programme which seemed appropriate to the contents.

Then, tickling Philomena between the ears, he left the kitchen and crossed the long hall into the drawing-room. There, still on the occasional table by his chair, was Hasfield's book. He picked it up and consulted the contents page. Then he opened it at the page containing *The Dream* and studied the text, frowning and mumbling to himself as he did so.

John replaced the book on the table and returned to the kitchen. He locked the back door, checked in his pocket for his front door key, said "Won't be long, Sweetheart!" to an indifferent cat and went out through the front door, dropping the latch behind him. Philomena, left in sole charge of Fairloe Court, relished the solitude. Well, the comparative solitude. She opened one eye and surveyed her domain, noting this thing and that thing, and dwelling briefly upon another. Then she closed her eye, content that all was as it should be.

She had wondered, quite often, how it was that humankind were so limited in their perceptions. But then, having breakfasted well and having supervised the breakfasts of John and Jane to her satisfaction, she fell, most contentedly, asleep.


It was a fine, sunny morning with plenty of blue sky. The weather forecast had been tentative and had hinted at trouble to come, but John suspected the forecasters of hedging their bets. No! There would be no rain today!

The sun shone on Gloucester, but the bluff of Lassington hill with its untidy-looking wood, and the fallen relic of its ancient oak, obscured the view due South. A little to the West of South John had a glimpse of the Saxon tower of Lassington Church, less than a mile away on the other side of the Leadon.

John thought sadly of Lassington and its little church. The tower was all that was left of it. For some reason, now forgotten, a Norman church had been demolished and rebuilt in neo-Norman style in 1875. But the foundations had been faulty and the chancel had begun to part company with the nave.

The end had come at a Harvest Thanksgiving service in the early 1960s. A sudden downpour in the middle of the service had deluged the visiting preacher in his stall. The church, used only occasionally by that time, had finally been abandoned, for the parish had long been united with that of Highnam, a mile down the road. John stood on his doorstep and thought of the wealth of ancient churches, all within a mile or two of each other and all within five miles of where he was standing. Maisemore, a mile away to the East. Fairloe, half a mile up the lane behind the house. Hartpury, about a mile beyond, separated from the present village of that name by a couple of miles of twisty lane.

And to the West there was Rudford. And a little further to the West, beyond Lassington and Rudford, there was a great half-moon of small and medium-sized churches, most of them ancient. Minsterworth on the Severn; Churcham on its little hill; Tibberton and the ruin of Taynton old church.

Then there were more recent ones like Bulley, and that dark and beautiful Victorian extravaganza, the Church of the Holy Innocents at Highnam.

John wondered what the mediaeval communities had been like, to build and maintain so many enduring stone buildings, so close together. For most originated from the thirteenth century, some on earlier foundations. Like Fairloe, most of them had been reduced to a consummate ugliness after the Reformation and had then been restored in the nineteenth century to a style of mock-mediaevalism which accorded more with romantic Victorian fantasy than with the slightest historical reality.

Pipe organs, robed choirs in chancels and crowded acres of pitchpine pews providing seating for the hoped-for or the imaginary! John wondered how many rural communities, in the late nineteenth century, had far more church and chapel seats than ever the population could provide bottoms to put on them! These poor little over-restored country churches had all to pretend to be miniature cathedrals and had been fitted out accordingly by their wealthy-younger-son parsons and their squirearchy. All curiously inappropriate to the needs of the present moment, John could not help but think. John Faversham loved old churches. He shook himself from his reverie and set off down the lane towards the River Leadon. Just short of the river bank the lane turned sharp right and ran the half mile or so upstream to the tiny village of Fairloe, and the mile or so beyond to Hartpury church and Highleadon.

At the bend in the lane, John began to poke about in the long grass between the lane and the river. He was looking for something. Looking for traces. The grass was long and obscured the ground beneath it. John shook his head and shrugged his shoulders. Then he waded through the long grass until he reached the river bank. He looked, this way and that, along some fifty yards of muddy bank. Then he returned to the bend in the road and scratched his head in puzzlement.

John Faversham resumed his morning walk. He set off upstream towards the village, the river parting company with the road and curving away to the West. Just short of the village he paused in his stride, closed his eyes as if in recollection, and then peered intently at the first two half-timbered cottages on the left hand side of the road.

There were not more than a dozen old cottages in the village altogether, with a few more modern houses beyond. A tiny estate of council houses, in blocks of four, lay along an old track which led West in the direction of Rudford. The Church lay to the right, and behind it, and up the bank behind the churchyard, a few more houses stood, including the new Vicarage, built in the 1950s. John was trying to recall something to mind. It had not occurred to him to do so when he set out, and he was not fully aware of the significance of what he was doing now. At the churchyard gate he paused and stared intently at the South front of the little church of St Mary, Fairloe.

It was very ordinary, 13th Century for the most part. There was a modest West Tower, a nave with both North and South aisles, and the chancel had, in

Victorian times, been adorned on the North side with both an organ chamber and a small, damp vestry, with a mouldering boiler-house beneath them.

As he walked up the church path, John decided that he would try an experiment of a kind he had never attempted before. He would do all in his power to close off his immediate sense perceptions and to bring out of his subconscious what he had *seen*.

The possible implications of such an attempt did not occur to him and so he passed through the South porch and into the church with his eyes practically closed. And he stood at the back of the church and tried, with all the intensity of which he was capable, to recall. To invoke …

He had a flash of the most vivid recollection. And then there burst upon him that utterly terrible …

John snapped himself out of his nightmare and back into normal consciousness in something very close to panic. He opened his eyes and discovered that he was wholly disorientated by the familiar interior furnishings of St Mary's, Fairloe. He could not relate to them at all! All that was familiar to him looked totally alien and out of place.

He went outside into the sunlit churchyard and sat down on a convenient stone. He found his hands wandering reassuringly over its rough surface. He stamped his feet to somehow come back to earth again. He made himself be conscious of the warmth of the sun. But traces of the nightmare were still lingering in odd corners of his mind. Whose nightmare, for God's sake? His, or Hasfield's? John stood up, stamped his feet determinedly and looked at the church door. Dare he go in again?

He recollected himself and quietly and deliberately recited the Lord's Prayer. Then he braced his shoulders and marched determinedly into the church.

Yes! Everything was normal and as he had always known it. But he spent some time looking at the pillars on both sides of the nave, looking at their bases as well as their capitals, seeing things he had not noticed before.

He would return to this, but not now. Sunshine and fresh air beckoned him and so John returned to the churchyard and made as if to search among the nearby gravestones. But he abandoned his search after a minute or two. He felt drained and exhausted. He must go home.

John retraced his steps through an apparently deserted village. It occurred to him that, most unusually, he had not caught sight of a living soul this morning. Perhaps they were all ransacking Sainsbury's, with Jane and the Dean and Chapter.

As he regained his doorstep, John turned and gazed towards Gloucester. He was looking for something. What the hell was it? He unlocked the front door – Jane obviously wasn't back yet – and entering the kitchen he filled the kettle at the cold tap, put it on the Aga, and sat down on the settle beside Philomena.

All of a sudden he felt utterly drained.

"Hello Sweetheart!" He stroked the cat, feeling more than slightly sick. "Daddy has given himself a bit of a fright."

Philomena had sensed trouble as soon as her man had entered the house. It was emanating from him powerfully; he was in trouble! Without a sound, she raised herself and climbed on to his lap. She purred lovingly all round his hand as he stroked her.

"What a little sweetheart you are! I feel better already!"

What, Philomena wondered, did the damned fool expect?

"Darling! Whatever's the matter? You look ghastly!" John opened his eyes with a start. He found his wife crouched in front of him, her face a picture of alarm.

"Yeah … OK … Yes." He gave her a wan smile. "I think I may have done something damned silly!"

"Oh God! You haven't given yourself a heart-do? You haven't ruptured yourself? Oh you are silly! You're not fit to be left alone!" John began to remember where he was. Philomena uttered a deep-throated purr and dug her claws into his thigh. He was awake at once.

Jane sat beside him on the settle and put her arms round him.

"Darling, what have you been doing? Shall I get the doctor?"

"Get the psychiatrist if you like! I have been trying to call up a nightmare, on site you might say. And I seem to have succeeded. In fact the damned thing won't go away. I've been dreaming bits of it all over again on this settle."

John shook himself.

"What's the time?"

"Ten to eleven. Shall I make some coffee? The kettle is boiling its head off on the Aga!"

"Good idea. I can't have been asleep long. I put the kettle on just before I sat down. Philomena has been a great comfort. Haven't you, Sweetheart?"

John stroked the side of the cat's face. She purred and slowly extended her claws.

Two cups of strong coffee restored John to normal consciousness. He sat, collecting himself, while Jane whirled about the kitchen, putting things away and straightening things up to her satisfaction.

"Meet anyone in Sainsbury's? Dean and Chapter, perhaps?"

"I bumped into Deirdre in Woolworth's."

"The Earth-Mother! Was she full of the Perennial Philosophy? Eternal Wisdom and all that?"

"More than you, you chump! Fancy trying to invoke a nightmare! What on earth did you think you were doing?"

"Archeology!" John thought for a moment and added, "Of a sort!"

"Darling! Where is that wretched poem? I can't bear it any longer. I don't know what you are up to."

"The book is on the table by my chair in the drawing-room. Shall I get it?"

"No! You just sit tight, I don't trust you with it. I'm beginning to wish we'd never been to that wretched sale."

Jane swept from the room and returned with Hasfield's book in her hand. She hesitated.

"I'll read it on my own if you like. I don't want to set you off again."

John looked up and smiled at her. God bless her! She was really bothered about him! Even after nearly thirty years of marriage the realisation touched him deeply.

He reached out his hand and she gave him the book and sat down at the kitchen table, opposite him. He found the page, looked up at her, and then he read the poem.

I out from my smoke-laden hall.
The rutted lane made sudden fall
To rude cot-bowsen, three or four,
Each with its hovel. By the shore

A rough-made jetty, and afloat,
The timbers of an antique boat.
I turned and wandered up the stream
Enchanted, fearful in my dream,

To where the village stood around
Rough-timbered, some thatched to the ground,
Off-shuts adjoining. To one side
A tallet door hung open wide.

The church seemed altered back in years.
I looked to calm my mounting fears,
But screened and shrined and strange within
It smote me with colossal sin.

As I fled back to gain my door,
Of mortal souls, not one I saw.
And at my doorstep, gazing down
Upon an ancient Gloucester town,

All hope departed. And a shell
Upon the threshold stood of hell.
A wisp of smoke hung in the air –
I woke – locked fast in dark despair.

John shut the book and put it down on the kitchen table. There was a long silence.

"Oh God! I can see it all!" Jane's eyes were shut and she was tense. "It's so vivid!" She opened her eyes and shook her head violently. "What on earth does it all mean?"

45

"Its almost as if it is describing a flash-back in time. That is how the dream felt to me. And then came the terrible nightmare – real dread! The *colossal sin* bit, I suppose. That is what hit me again this morning, in church."

"You mean that you were actually going over the ground? Physically?"

"Yes. I fished about in the long grass at the foot of the lane, looking for traces of old buildings. Couldn't find anything. Couldn't find any trace of an old jetty either."

"Darling. What are cot-bowsen?"

"Its an old Cotswold word for cottages."

"What about the village? Did you recognise anything?"

"I'm not sure."

"What about the church?"

"That's the key to the whole thing. I'm sure of it. In the dream the interior was different and more primitive-looking. It was very vivid, just for an instant, before the nightmare bit broke in upon it. I must have been stark raving mad!"

"What did it look like? But don't go and bring the nightmare back whatever you do!"

"*Screened and shrined and strange within.* I can't put it better than that. The aisles seemed to be screened off. There was a big rood-screen, and I'm sure the walls above the arcades and round the chancel arch were covered with paintings. Oh yes! And there were no pews. But it was just a flash, I had no time to really take anything in …"

John shook his head and paused for a moment.

"And when I opened my eyes I couldn't relate to the way it is now at all!"

He looked up with a start, his eyes wide open.

"*As I fled back to gain my door,*
*Of mortal souls not one I saw.*"

"And I didn't either! I thought they must all be in Sainsbury's! The place was deserted, like a tomb!"

Jane suddenly reached across the table and took her husband's hand.

"Darling! This isn't just a silly coincidence! You go to an auction you had no intention of going to. You buy a pile of books you had no intention of buying. You find among them a book of poems by a former occupant of this house, and you discover that he had – and exactly described – the same dream that you had three weeks ago. Now don't tell me that all this is just random chance! I don't believe it!"

"Neither do I! But I'm damned if I know what to make of it either."

Jane could contain herself no longer.

"Darling! You are much more sensitive than you will ever admit! You are a highly intuitive man, but you have been positively conditioned not to believe it. I know what you are like, full well. So does Sarah. So does Lucy, come to that! It sticks out like a sore thumb, but you won't have it, will you?"

John gave his wife a very odd look.

"Well, I might have to, mightn't I?" he said.

# CHAPTER SIX

**W**ALTER DE FURLOWE had no intention of setting out upon his journey with young John to Glastonbury until the Autumnal Equinox was past. The journey would be hazardous enough for the lad without the uncertainties that attended those strange days before the Equinox. In the Church Calendar, the Equinox fell upon the Feast of the Exaltation of the Holy Cross; the 14th of September. The Dog Days ended on that day, and so they would set forth upon the day following.

It must be understood that the Julian Calendar was still in use and that it would be seventy-four years yet before Pope Gregory XIII, acting on the advice of his astronomers, altered the calendar. He then decreed that October the 5th 1582 should be October 15th instead, thus re-aligning the calendar with the progress of the seasons. And to ensure that this alignment was retained he instituted the Leap Year, with an extra day at the end of the month of February every fourth year.

This calendar reform, of an astonishing accuracy, was not accepted universally, however. In lands where the Pope's writ no longer ran it was long in being introduced. England would wait until 1752. But of all this, Walter was entirely innocent. He and John would both be in their graves before any of these things came to pass. The entire family heard Mass on Holy Cross Day and the following morning – auspiciously the Octave of the Nativity of our Lady Saint Mary – Walter and John, with young Harry as companion and escort, set out upon their journey not long after first light. They would have to travel more slowly with the young boy with them, and the horses would be laden.

John, now embarked upon the first great adventure of his life, gave but one glance back after a tearful leave-taking. He saw his mother and mop-headed Ann supporting each other, with young James standing behind them in the door of the hall. The mawkins was weeping uncontrollably; she adored John and she was deeply in love with young Harry. She had quite convinced herself that she would never see either of them alive again.

They crossed the Severn and entered Gloucester by the West Gate and began to pick their way up the long hill to the Cross at the centre of the City, where its four main roads met. John had been but once to Gloucester and features he could see from the step of the hall loomed enormous as they came into his field of vision, peering as he did on either side from behind his father's broad back. The narrow lane with its crowded, overhanging houses, stank powerfully. Filth ran down the middle of the street. A church tower, topped with a crooked-looking spire, jutted into the street ahead of them.

"That un's St Nicholas," explained Walter. "And be'ind un be another; tis called St Mary de Lode, but I can't be a-tellin of thou why!"

He chuckled to himself. Town churches often seemed to have their names all garbled up, their origins long forgotten. They passed the opening of a broad lane to their left. A fine gatehouse came into view, and behind it a church of immense proportions with a tower which seemed to John to reach half way to very heaven itself.

"And that un's th'Abbey o' St Peter," explained Walter. "A King be a-buried in there! And ever so many folk da go there on pilgrimage, because 'im were murdered. Tis said 'im's tomb be some kind o' 'oly place, look."

Walter regretted that he had mentioned the King's tomb. The view was widely held that the tomb of the murdered King Edward II had been a vast financial boon to the Abbey. Had they not rebuilt the tower and the choir on the proceeds of pilgrimages? Had they not, perhaps, made more of the holiness of poor murdered King Edward than his life might seem to have justified?

Walter was a deeply devout man and devoted to the Church because it was Christ's Church. But he was neither blind nor stupid. A great deal was not at all as it should be and much needed putting right. Walter had his opinions but he seldom gave them expression, and then only with the greatest restraint. A man could come to a terrible end if he opened his mouth too wide on that kind of subject! Fortunately John had not reacted to the idea of a King's tomb in Gloucester. His attention was being claimed by one wonder after another. Bells were ringing all over town for it was still very early and Masses were beginning to be said.

"Grey Friars be over there, be'ind all them 'ouses."

Walter pointed to the right as they rode on up the hill.

"And there be Black Friars too! And that un's St Michael's Church, and there be the Cross. Now we be at the very 'eart o' Gloucester!"

"Father! Why da they build churches so big?"

"Tis the Glory o' God as them's built for. And they da make un o' stone so as they da last for ever, look. Just like 'eaven itself! And Christ's Mass is what they be for, so – in a kind o' way, look – they is 'eaven!"

Yes, John saw. It made complete sense to him. His father went on:

"Our li'l cot-bowsen; they da come and they da go – just like we. They's for we to live in, that's all. They da keep the rain off the likes o' we! But a church is different."

He didn't say how or why it was different. He didn't try to explain further. He couldn't. And if anybody asked him – well, they couldn't possibly know what they were asking, could they?

They turned right at the Cross and began a gentle downhill ride towards the South Gate, passing the church of St Mary de Crypt on their way.

"Now, son John! Tis the open road for we from now on, and for many a long mile. We've to be at th'Abbey o' Saint Mary at Kingswood before dark. There's time enough, but I don't want thou a-fallin asleep and a-fallin off th'orse!! Thy mother'd give thy father a cruel scoldin if that did 'appen!"

"Then we byunt a-stayin at Berkeley, Master?"

Harry was surprised at the route Walter had chosen.

"No 'arry, we byunt! I byunt a-takin a son o' mine to stay wi' folks as did kill their King! And 'im a prisoner under their roof!"

"Killed the King?" There was awe in John's voice. "What they be a-doin o' that for?"

"T'was a long, long time ago. Them 'ad King a prisoner in that great castle o' theirn. And they was a-doin of 'im to death most 'orrible. T'was all rivalries and 'atreds, and folks was all a-grabbin at power, like the barons used to. Like they always does when King byunt King enough!"

"Father! What be that church?"

They were clear of Gloucester now and riding down the ancient Roman road which led to Bristol. John pointed to a church tower on a little knoll, a half a mile or so to the West.

"Tis St Swithun's, John. And the village be 'empstead." Walter enjoyed airing his knowledge. "T'was rebuilt by Prior 'enry of Llanthony St Mary, 'bout the time I were born. Tis served by th'Augustinians, and Prior 'enry, 'im went to be Archbishop o' Canterbury!"

"Did a?" John was deeply impressed.

"A did!" Walter laughed. "And the very next church as we da see, St James at Quedgeley, that un belongs Llanthony St Mary too."

"Why be they a-callin of un Llanthony St Mary, father?"

"Cos t'were first founded in Wales, in the Black Mountains. But tis ever so wild there, and tis dark too, and strange. So they be fled from there and they da call this un Llanthony St Mary to be different from Llanthony St John as they be fled from."

The horses bore them South at a steady walk. Harry's horse was laden with provisions and all manner of other things that Meg and the mawkins had put together for John to take with him to the Abbey. Walter was determined not to hurry. He could take no chances with young John, perched up behind him and clinging on for dear life. And being a kindly and thoughtful man, Walter wanted his son to enjoy his first great adventure to the full.

Some five miles out of Gloucester, John pointed to a church tower, half a mile to the West, with another just visible a couple of miles or so beyond.

"What be them two?" he asked.

"St Nicholas. And beyond un, St Lawrence. 'ardwick and Longney be the villages. Tis flat down by the river. But John! Thou da see them 'ills beyond?"

"Yes, father."

"Tis the Forest!" Walter's voice changed tone. He grew solemn. "Tis the Royal Forest o' Dean. Only the King 'isself can be a-'untin o' the deer in there. And tis dark! Tis strange!"

There was no Forest blood in Walter. His forefathers had been Cotswold men and he had, in full measure, the inbred Gloucestershire sense of unease about the Forest of Dean.

They rode steadily on, the boy gazing now at the dark line of the Forest, away to the West beyond the Severn, and now at the great escarpment of the

Cotswolds, drawing steadily nearer and thrusting a great spur out ahead of them as if to cut them off from their destination. They would have to round that spur and climb up the far side of it. John took to spotting church towers and quizzing his father about them. Walter was a mine of information so far, but once beyond the spur his knowledge grew more scanty. The tower of our Lady Saint Mary at Frampton caught John's eye, as did the spire of St John, Slimbridge, a few miles on. Then he dozed off, still clinging to his father's belt, and he woke to find them halted in a spinney some little way East of the old road. Walter was well pleased with their progress so far and so they lingered an hour or so, eating what Meg had provided, before setting off again. This time their path took them up into the hills and they worked their way along the West flank of that great spur whose foot they had rounded when John was dozing on the horse's back. It was harder work now, much harder. The tracks were rougher and less well defined and they wound up and down and in and out of woods for mile after mile. John was tired and spent more time dozing than waking. Harry rode close behind his Master and kept a close eye on the boy lest his grip should loosen and he be in danger of falling. Like John, Harry was beginning to feel stiff and sore and wondered how much longer their first day's journey would go on. They passed through a large village. Ahead of them was a fine church tower, but they turned off well short of it, sharply down towards the South once more.

"One more mile ta go!"

There was relief in Walter's voice. In a very little while they would be at the Cistercian Abbey of the Blessed Virgin Mary at Kingswood. A fine gatehouse hove into view. Walter noticed that it had been partially rebuilt, and quite recently. A window of the most modern style had been inserted into it which, to Walter's taste, seemed incongruous. A fine vault arched over the roadway which was closed by a great gate. They had arrived!

Walter swung stiffly from his horse and stamped life back into his feet. His bad leg was paining him. There was an hour or two of daylight left and John had stood up magnificently to his first long day on the back of a horse. He lifted the exhausted boy down and embraced him before setting him on his unsteady feet, blinking and looking about him in wonder.

Harry dismounted and held the two horses as Walter advanced to the wicket in the great gate. He would knock and ask for food and shelter for the night. For they were two pilgrims on their way to Glastonbury, and with them was a little boy, bound for the Monastery School. They would be kindly received. They would be safe here from robbers, horse thieves and evil company. They would hear the Mass of St Edith in the morning and be set safely upon the next leg of their journey.

Walter had given this next stage much thought. His first plan had been to make for the great Abbey of St Augustine in Bristol itself. But Bristol was a sea-port and an evil place for strangers unacquainted with it. Walter had therefore decided upon a different route entirely. It led more directly to Glastonbury and the following night would therefore be spent at the

Augustinian Abbey of St Mary, St Peter and St Paul at Keynsham, some few miles to the East and a little to the South of Bristol.

"Father! What did thou mean, 'bout King when 'im byunt King enough?"

They had made an early start from Kingswood and now they were approaching Wickwar. John, who missed little and forgot nothing, had his mind full of kings, and of knights, and of the battles in which his father and his grandfather had fought. And there had come into his mind the reason why they had avoided Berkeley the previous day.

Walter thought long and hard before he answered, for the boy would remember what he said and invest it with a terrible authority. "Tis terrible 'ard to be King, look," he said. "all depends on un. Now if 'im be strong, and if 'im 'ave the respect of 'is barons, then there be peace all over England. But if 'im don't … ."

Walter paused, his head full of memories.

"Now see, son John! King must keep the law and see there be justice. And 'im must be the rightful King. And if there be any as da think they've a better claim … well, 'im must be strong enough to kep 'em quiet!"

"King 'ave to be a good man, then?"

Walter didn't answer for a full minute. How was he to impart worldly wisdom to a boy of eight when it seemed to be turning all true Christian values on their head?

"Now tis ever so fine if King be a good man, John," he said. "But tis almost better if 'im be strong. If 'im be strong and good, why! Tis best o'all! But 'im 'ave to be strong or there be no peace in England. I da know that!"

Walter remembered his own father's death in battle.

"If King 'enry vi ud bin as strong as a were good, then thy grandfather'd be an old man yet, and thy father'd be a-walkin on two good legs!"

"'im were a bad King, then?"

"'im were a mortal bad King, but tis said as 'ow 'im were a Saint! Better if they'd let un be a monk, as a wanted to be." Walter thought ruefully of what might have been if the great King Henry V had not died prematurely, leaving a ten-month old baby to succeed him.

"'is father ud well-nigh conquered France. They were to be acrownin of 'im King o' France. Then 'im died sudden. And then there weren't no King to lead th'army, and armies byunt no good wi' no King. And that were th'end o' King of England a-bein King o' France!"

Walter shook his head, sadly.

"They was a-marryin of 'im to Margaret of Anjou, when 'im were twenty-two and 'er were but thirteen. Proper she-devil that un! But 'im were weak and this un, and that un, thought as 'ow they 'ad better right to be King than 'im. And then the wars did start! And then King Richard were killed at Bosworth, and thy grandfather alongside of un. And then it did stop. And why? King 'enry vii be a strong King! I don't know as 'im's a good man, but 'im's a strong King, and we be 'avin peace these twenty years."

"It don't matter if King be bad, then?"

Walter winced. That was not what he had meant. He tried again. "See 'ere, son John! Best is when 'im's both good and strong, look. Next best is when 'im's strong. Worst is when 'im's weak. See?"

"I da think so."

Walter breathed a sigh of relief. Encouraged in his task of schoolmaster, he continued the lesson.

"Now King must be strong. But King must also 'ave a son to succed un. King must 'ave a son, look! Cos if 'im don't, why! Barons'll start a-fightin agin. 'im *must* 'ave a son!"

"What if 'im don't?"

Walter thought very hard before he gave his answer. It would be so easy to confuse – even to corrupt – the boy's understanding. Walter, like everybody else, recognised that different rules applied to kings, because they had to! The maintenance of peace and order demanded it. Holy Church recognised this and bent the rules accordingly. What should Walter tell John about this?

"Now, son John!" he began. "If 'im's Queen can't be a-givin of 'im a son, then … well, sometimes … *just sometimes, mind!* Pope'll be a lettin of un marry another! 'cos 'im's King, mind! Not 'cos 'im do fancy it! See?"

"If 'im's got no son," said John, grasping the difficult point that Walter was trying to make, "then there be battles and folks be a-gettin killed and that. So tis better 'im gets a new Queen and gets on wi' a-gettin of a son."

"That's right, son John. But mind! Tis only for Kings! Byunt for the likes o' we!"

"Do Popes be often a-doin o' that?"

"No! Them 'ates a-doin of it! But t'as bin done. Not in England, mind! Nor never t'will! Tis for foreigners, look!"

They were well beyond Wickwar and were at the outskirts of Yate. There they halted briefly. The tall, thin tower of the parish church looked out of proportion with the squat, crushed-looking nave and chancel. They did not stay long; they were making excellent time and would be at Keynsham well before dark.

As they journeyed on, Walter looked ahead to the following day's ride. Could they do it in one day? Could they cross the Mendips and reach Glastonbury by nightfall?

They could surely reach Wells. If it was too late they could spend the night there and ride the six miles to Glastonbury the following morning. But it were better to do it in one day.

They would go by Midsomer Norton, Walter's mind was made up.

The roads were better and Walter had no great liking for the Mendips. He wanted to give Priddy a wide berth, with its nine ancient barrows and its three great magic circles.

Walter was proud of his son. That first day had been hard for him. Today was easier and tomorrow would be no worse than the first day. They were over half way by now. Over half way to the Abbey of St Mary, St Peter and St Paul at Keynsham. Over half way, too, to the great Abbey of St Peter and St

Paul at Glastonbury where John must be left at the School, and from where Walter and Harry must begin their sad journey home again without him, back to Gloucestershire and to Meg.

The Augustinians at Keynsham had received Walter and his little party with great kindness and the Guest-Master had made a tremendous fuss of John. They were sent on their way bright and early and, the weather staying fair and the roads being good, they covered the ground in fine style. Walter was soon persuaded that, barring accidents, they must surely reach Glastonbury by nightfall. The talk on the road was of the distinction between monks, canons and friars. How did the Cistercians of Kingswood differ from the Benedictines of Glastonbury? And what of the Augustinians whom they had just left? And what other orders of canons were there? And how did black friars differ from white friars? And what of the grey friars? Walter's head began to spin with it all.

"I be fair boffled wi' all thy questions, John!" He said at last. "Now there be five miles o' peace afore thy next!"

Five miles had barely passed before John was at his interrogations again. But this time he touched on deeper matters altogether.

"Father! Do Popes 'ave to be strong, same as kings?"

Walter's heart sank within him. How was he going to explain to a boy of eight the vexed and tangled relationship between the Pope at Rome and the King of England? He must do his best.

"Now, son John," he began. "Popes is different agin. Them byunt kings. The Pope be Bishop o' Rome, and that da make un chief Bishop, look!"

Walter decided against making any reference to the Great Schism between the Eastern Church and the Western, or of that other Pope who ruled over the Eastern Church, even though he was now a prisoner of the Turks in Constantinople.

"'im's chief Bishop," Walter repeated, "and so 'im's th'ead o' the Church. That's 'im's job, look. But 'im byunt no king. Tis different ..."

Yes, but the Pope behaved like a king for all that! The Papacy had been playing politics ever since the time of Hildebrand. And the Pope and the Holy Roman Emperor, instead of being each complementary to the other, were deadly rivals. For generations, Popes and Emperors had played each other's games with hideous consequences for thousands of poor people who had been butchered or burned in rival excesses of ostentatious enforcements of doctrinal orthodoxy. And how could Walter tell young John of the Babylonish Captivity of the Popes at Avignon? Or of all the rival Popes and Antipopes? How could he tell him of the blatant corruption, the filling of English prebends – even Sees – with foreigners who took the money but never appeared to fulfil their pastoral duties?

Could Walter tell John of the massive universal indifference – even contempt – in which the whole Papal apparatus was held by the vast majority of Englishmen, devout Churchmen or otherwise? Walter de Furlowe, like the great majority of believers, had arrived at a *Modus Vivendi* in which a very few things mattered exceedingly and were not subject to human sin and corruption. As for the rest – well, some things were necessary, however fallible! It was better to leave the work of reformation to those whose business it was. A man could come to a hideous end if he waxed too eloquent about corruptions in faith and order according to his own lights. "Now, son John! Tis a terrible job, a-bein King, but tis ever so much worse a-bein Pope! And sometimes Popes byunt as they should be – bein sinners, look! But they's still Pope for all that. Sometimes they be rotten bad, but they's still Pope! God's a-judgin of 'em!"

"Be they rotten bad then?" John's voice betrayed astonishment. Even alarm.

"No! No they byunt!" Walter was alarmed himself at what his words might have conveyed. "But now and then, some byunt as they should be. They be sinners; mortal men, same as we! And sometimes they do play at bein kings. Then they gets a-meddlin in things as byunt their business. *Sometimes*, look!"

"What do King do if Pope be a-meddlin?"

"'im do tell un to stop! And 'm do get Parliament to pass laws of *Praemunire*, which is Latin for: 'don't be a-meddlin in the King o' England's business!' They do generally stop then. They gets no money, else!"

Walter was ill at ease. He was having to articulate things he would rather have left unformed in his mind. He would have to be careful! He could easily be misunderstood, and not only by John. And that could be a very dangerous business for any man.

"Like I do say, John. Tis ever so 'ard to be Pope. Tis th'ardest job in the world! Tis no wonder they do get un wrong, now and then." John was silent for a while and Walter was glad of it. But, all of a sudden, the questions began again.

"'ow be they a-meddlin, then?"

Walter cast about for some examples.

"Well now! King o' England be Emperor in 'im's own right, look. 'im don't owe allegiance anywhere. Byunt Pope or th'oly Roman Emperor as do give un the crown. 'im's Emperor 'isself, see? But now and then, Pope's bin a-sayin as 'im byunt Emperor! 'im owes is crown to Pope! But 'im don't!"

Walter paused. A more difficult example came into his mind.

"Ever since Saxon times, John, King o' England's bin known as *Vicar o' Christ*. Now, 'im 'ave to be, look! 'im's responsible! 'im's people are Christians, look! And that do mean that King o' England's always bin 'ead o' the Church in England. Stands to reason! Now, 'im's King, mind; 'im byunt Pope! Tis different! 'im's the Christian King o' Christian people, so 'im's *Vicar o' Christ*, in England, see?"

Walter chose his words carefully. This was a difficult matter and he almost wished he had not thought of it. He would have to do his best.

"Now Pope's bin a-sayin that 'im's th'only Vicar o' Christ. Well, 'im's Vicar o' Christ in 'im's Pope kind o' woy, but 'im's not th'only one!"

"So they be rivals, then?"

Walter sighed. He wanted to draw this lesson to an end. "If Pope ud just be Pope, and if Emperor ud just be Emperor, and if King ud just be King, then t'would all be well, John. But see! They's only men! They's all sinners, same as we. And they gets ameddlin!" There was a long silence from John. He was clearly taking it all in and making what he could of it. Then he broke his long silence with the only sensible question that he could have possibly come out with.

"What's us do about un, then?"

"If thou's any sense, son John," said Walter. "Leave all them things to the folk as business tis to be a-sortin of 'em out. There's but two things, John, as do matter. And they do matter for thy dear life! Shall I tell ee what?"

"Yes, father."

"First is Lord Christ and 'is Mass. Second is our Lady Saint Mary and all the Saints in 'eaven. They two's beyond all corruption and meddlin, and tis only the devil 'isself as ud try! Now, what are they, John?"

"Our Lord Christ and 'is Mass, father. And our Lady Saint Mary and all the Saints in 'eaven."

"Tis all as we do need, John! And thou do leave the rest to them as business tis!"


They came to Glastonbury before nightfall and the Guest Master made them welcome. Sir Hugh was sent for and came hurrying across to greet them. Walter had loved his wife's cousin on sight and the Guest Master had already confided in Walter that he must surely be Abbot one day! Walter had enjoyed the look on Meg's face when he had told her that!

Now it was John's turn to meet his schoolmaster and his kinsman, and he too loved Sir Hugh as soon as he set eyes on him. They were to become the firmest of friends. The parting, when it came, would be a little less painful for all of them because of that. Walter and Harry stayed until the Feast of St Matthew the Apostle and Evangelist. They heard Mass with John and then, with remarkably few tears, they set off on their long ride home. They arrived on the eve of Michaelmas, to a rapturous but tearful welcome from Meg and mawkins Ann.

John never forgot his father's little catechism on the long road to Glastonbury. It stayed with him for the rest of his life.

# CHAPTER SEVEN

S T MARY'S CHURCH, Fairloe, was one of the many Gloucestershire churches that had been energetically restored in the 1860s by the prominent local firm of Fulljames and Waller. They had practically rebuilt Maisemore, just down the road, but by happy chance funds were more limited in the case of Fairloe and their zeal had, perforce, to be more restrained.

Nevertheless they had wrought valiantly. The ugly box pews had been torn out, the tottering three-decker pulpit had gone, the low, cramped galleries, dust-laden and used only at Christmas, were done away and such windows as had been converted to square-headed sashes were tastefully re-gothicised.

The desert within had been turned, by the happy availability of pitch-pine, into a miniature cathedral. Choir stalls choked the chancel. An organ chamber had been built to accommodate a pipe organ, the sanctuary had been railed off by a brass altar rail and such space as remained in it had been filled by a great Bishop's Chair on the North side and an over-large credence table on the South. The mean and undersized altar had been replaced by a solidly constructed oak table of correct dimensions and furnished with a cross and a pair of brass candlesticks, hefty rather than graceful.

The nave and both aisles had been pewed right across, leaving but a narrow centre aisle. The seating provided had always been more than the total population of the parish could ever have filled. A somewhat incongruously decorative stone pulpit stood at the head of the nave, on the North side, and a ferocious-looking brass eagle, with the Holy Bible nestling between its hunched wings, glared balefully at the congregation to the South.

John and Jane arrived five minutes before the Service began. They each collected from the table at the back of the church a dull red copy of *Hymns Ancient and Modern, Revised*, and a bright red pamphlet containing the words of the new Liturgy. Jane smiled and mouthed greetings discreetly while John put their weekly Free Will Offering envelope in the plate. Collections were not taken during services at St Mary's Fairloe.

In their normal places, and after their customary devotions, they sat back in their pew and looked about them.

Yes! There were unmistakable traces of a long-vanished rood screen on either side of the chancel arch.

"I must have imagined the wall paintings."

John looked glumly at the bare stone, neatly pointed, above the arcades and on either side of the chancel arch.

"Don't be silly, darling!" Jane whispered. "They always plastered the walls in the Middle Ages. Then the beastly Puritans whitewashed everything. And then the silly Victorians chipped it all off to make it look mediaeval! Of course it would have been painted. All the churches were."

Jane sounded more like Aunt Sarah every day – except when she was sounding more like Cecily every day.

"Nobody at the organ!" he whispered. "Are you going to volunteer?"

A look of the darkest blackness from Jane answered his question. Jane had volunteered once – and had been obliged to make an almost fighting withdrawal from an imposed permanent post as organist. That had been before Walter's day, but once bitten, twice shy!

"We sing much better without the bloody thing!" she whispered fiercely.

At that moment the vestry door opened and Walter appeared, vested in a green chasuble and preceded by the gangling figure of Harry, grandson of George the churchwarden. George's family had provided Churchwardens and, until almost within living memory, Parish Clerks for generations untold. His was the oldest of the two or three old-established Fairloe families.

The pair reverenced the altar, Harry swaying cheerfully, and then they proceeded to the chancel step.

Walter made a proper distinction between Word and Sacrament and preferred to conduct the first part of the Eucharist from the lectern. Harry, vested in a cassock too short and a surplice too long, was parked in the stall opposite to the Vicar's Stall in the chancel, from where he grinned amiably and looked vacant by turns.

"A proper yawny that un be!" Jane whispered to John. Dear Harry! He was a lovely lad but he was into the awkward stage with a vengeance!

John gave a start and turned to Jane. Her eyes suddenly opened wide.

"I wonder … ?" she whispered.

They sang lustily, unaccompanied, at a comfortable pitch and at a good pace. Yes! Jane was right. They sang much better without the organ.

As a kneeling John received the Body and Blood of Christ at the wobbling brass altar-rail he felt moved to make a conscious offering to God of the curious business of Hasfield and the *Dream* they seemed to have in common. He felt much better after that, and more relaxed than he had been all week.

"Walter! How far back do the current burial registers go? I was wondering if I could check up on someone who lived in The Court at the end of last century." John looked up from the hymn-book cupboard as Walter came in from the porch where he had been chatting up the departing congregation.

"Ten years, John. Sorry! All the rest are at County Records Office. They'll be only too happy to let you see them." He dropped his voice. "You could always ask George! He knoweth all things!"

As if summoned, George appeared from the vestry.

"I got the collection, Vicar!" (He pronounced it "klaxion".) He patted his jacket pocket. "I be a-takin of it 'ome, look. I be a-goin to the Bank in the mornin."

It was the invariable ritual, as was his next intelligence. "I bin a-writin of it up in the Register. Now! T'was the same this Sunday as t'was last year. And we be 'avin inflation, look!" His countenance showed concern, with a suggestion of rebuke.

Walter winked at John and turned to his henchman.

"George! You know just about everything that has ever happened here. Can you help John? He wants to know about a man who used to live in the Court. When was it, John?"

"He died in the eighteen nineties. Hasfield. James Hasfield."

"Ah now! 'asfield! James 'asfield! Friend o' my grandfather, 'im were. My old Dad used to go on about un. Right old funniosity, 'im did say! 'asfield wrote books and things, but nobody did buy 'em!" George chuckled to himself, his bright blue eyes twinkling merrily. "Solicitor 'im were. Turley and 'asfield o' Gloucester. Gone now o' course. 'im 'ad no children. T'was a nephew as took over the business and 'im were killed in the First War. Turley? Tis a Forest name, but weren't no Turleys left when young 'asfield were killed. Can't say as what 'appened to 'em."

Thanks, George! I came across one of his books the other day. Got me interested. Is he buried here?

"Top end, on the far side. Just by the flip-flap gate. 'im and 'is missus. 'er died and then 'im died. Mind ... !" He looked knowingly at Jane. "If you be a-goin up there to look at un, you watch your nylons my love! Tis a mass o' brambles!"

"Never mind, George! If I ladder them, John will just have to buy me another pair, won't he?"

She winked at George and looked saucily at John.

"Damned expensive to run, these women!" said John. "Worse than a motor car!"

" 'ave thou ever tried a-buyin of a new tractor?" George's voice took on a sombre tone. "Tis ruination! Tis a crime agin 'umanity! The prices they do charge!"

The awful inevitability of an hour-long lecture upon the subject of farming, its ruination and the coming apocalypse yawned in front of John like an abyss. But he was rescued by George's wife Gladys.

"Jarge!"

Her piercing voice sounded from the churchyard gate.

"I be a-comin! I be a-comin!"

"Jarge! Be thou a-comin 'ome? We got them things to see to!"

A look of harrassment settled on his amiable countenance.

" 'er do want I to be a-breakin o' the Sabbath, 'er do!" He grinned at John. "T'aint right! All them little jobs 'er's a-bothin on about. Tis a-profainin o' the Lord's Day! Tis!"

"Jarge!"

"I did tell ee as I be a-comin!" And with a broad wink to Jane, he went.

"Good old Gladys! I thought we were in for a long session." They watched the old couple set off down into the village, squabbling furiously.

"I love George! He's an old darling!" said Jane. "But I don't think I've got the right shoes on to go prancing about in the brambles. I suppose you are determined to find that grave?"

They found the grave without difficulty, exactly where George had said it was. It was overgrown with couch-grass and brambles but, after gingerly pushing away the undergrowth, the stone was partially uncovered and the top of its inscription was revealed:

*Sacred to the memory of Rebecca, beloved wife of James Hasfield of Fairloe Court. Died 1st March 1889.*

John read the inscription aloud. He brushed the brambles back further and revealed the rest:

*And of James Hasfield, Solicitor. Died 28th February 1894.*

"Bless them!" Jane felt touched and had to make an effort to stop tears from starting.

A very different emotion suddenly and quite unexpectedly assailed John. He recalled the speculations that had attended the discovery of Hasfield's photograph. Was he, perhaps, looking at his own grave?

"Bloody nonsense!" he said.

"What is?"

"All this business of me being the reincarnation of James Hasfield. Jolly business this! Discovering one's own last grave!"

"What was Rebecca like, darling? Can you remember?"

"Short, fat, blonde and brassy! Can't you remember what you looked like?"

"You're very naughty! I'm sure they were both quite delightful."

"Just like us!" John grinned. "And there is the famous flip-flap gate."

They both looked hard at an old kissing-gate in the churchyard wall. Jane turned to her husband.

"Do you think – you know – George's grandfather! The poem?"

"I'm sure of it! He and Hasfield knew each other. I can almost hear George saying that poem in the course of ordinary conversation."

"So the Proper Yawny was George's father and Molly Mawkins was his mother!" She giggled. "And George was the result. But is it possible? I'm thinking of his age."

"Perfectly! He was the youngest of four, by some years. He had an elder sister who died in childhood and his two elder brothers were killed in the First War. Their names are on the War Memorial."

"How long has his family been here? Does anyone know?"

"Hundreds of years, so he says. But how he knows, and what he knows – God knows! He's wearing well at any rate. He's quite as old as Cecily. Eighty if he's a day."

John looked at his wife's legs.

"You've laddered your tights! I'll buy you a new pair. Promised George I would."

"Damn! They were new on today!"


"Phone! I'll go!"

John rose up from his chair. He had been happy to sink into it after an

59

afternoon in the garden, but such was life! He went into the hall and picked up the reciever.

"John! My dear! I'm sitting in the dark, striking matches! Can you do something?"

It was Cecily.

"What's happened?"

"I just poked the fire. There was a bang and all the lights went out."

"Sit tight, dear. We'll be there straight away. *Don't do anything* whatever you do!"

"Well I can't just sit here in the dark! I'll get the car out and drive about."

"No darling! Don't do that! It isn't dark yet and we'll be there before it gets properly dark. OK?"

John looked round the drawing-room door. Jane looked up at him, one eyebrow raised in interrogation.

"Its your mother! She was just poking the fire and all the lights went out!"

"Don't be silly, darling! She hasn't got a fire. She's all electric."

"Precisely!"

"Oh my God!"

"I'll get some tools from the workshop. We'd better get a move on. She's threatening to drive round and round in the motor car until somebody arrives!"

John ransacked his workbench and put into a small toolbox everything that he could imagine might be of use. The list was comprehensive, but he was well experienced in his mother-in-law's capacity for comprehensive domestic catastrophe.

On a sudden afterthought he returned to the workshop for the plunger. It would be a miracle if her kitchen sink wasn't blocked as well.

Cecily Redmayne lived on the Evesham side of Bredon Hill. When Charlie had died she had sold up and was now comfortably settled in a beautiful half-timbered cottage, from which she made frequent expeditions to visit Barbara and her family in Sussex and a steadily diminishing number of her lifelong friends in all parts of the country and abroad.

It could not be said of her that she was predatory by nature, but she had always managed to get herself administered by an army of near neighbours and other acquaintances, all of whom ended up by feeling exclusively and anxiously responsible for her safety and wellbeing. She was not without domestic assistance. The good Mrs Edmunds, whom she affectionately referred to as "my horrible old woman," had done for her these twenty years past, and was twenty years her junior. Old Arthur Smith had looked after her garden for almost as long and, for her longer expeditions, drove her to and from the railway station in her own car. He enjoyed the description, "my little man."

Cecily was a perpetual traveller. She drove herself locally, and it was suggested, increasingly dangerously. Long journeys she made by train. The detailed administration of a house and its fittings and fixtures was something she had never felt the need to understand. There had always been someone else who would see to it. She was as innocent as a newborn child as to how anything worked and saw no point in bothering her head with such matters at her time of life. After all, she always had Jane and dear John to mend things when they ceased to function. John knew about things like that!

They drove, as fast as they could, through Tewkesbury and up to Bredon. Then they wove through Kemerton and Overbury, round by Conderton and on through the little lanes until Cecily's house came into view. There was still enough light to see by out of doors, but Cecily would be sitting in the dark by now.

"Striking matches!" thought John to himself.

"Darling! What have you been up to now?"

John kissed his mother-in-law, picked up his toolbox and a powerful flashlight and entered her drawing-room. Jane followed, carrying another flashlight and a box of candles.

"Its the fire, John dear! It was fizzing at me and I poked it with my stick to make it stop. And then there was a bang, and all the lights went out."

The inference in Cecily's voice was that things she didn't understand were engaged in an unkind conspiracy against her.

John played his flashlight on a large, ornate electric fire which sat in the chimneypiece. It was a "coal-effect" fire, like Sarah's, but older, and it had been much more expensive when bought. The elements, of which there were two, were of an old fashioned sort. The heating coils were zig-zagged through fireclay bricks, and one was broken and hung down across the metal frame of the fire.

"Doctor John has no difficulty with this diagnosis!" he joked, lamely, looking at his mother-in-law in gentle reproach. "You've bust it! What on earth did you poke it with?"

"My stick! The thing was making fizzing noises at me!"

John looked round for the stick. A walking stick lay by the armchair. It sported a big rubber ferrule.

"You're really quite lucky to be alive! You could easily have been electrocuted!"

"Absolute nonsense dear! I've never been electrocuted in my life!"

"Well don't start now, Cecily! This kind of fire doesn't like being poked – even if it is fizzing at you. You could get bitten!"

"But you can mend it, can't you!"

It was not a question, it was more like a statement.

"No Cecily, I can't! Not now at any rate. I'll take it home and see what I can do to it. It will need new elements and I'm not at all sure that I can get any of this sort. I don't think they make them now. I'll do what I can – as long as you make me a promise."

"What have I got to promise?"

Cecily's voice had a note of hesitation in it. Not that she would keep any promise she made a moment longer than she felt like it.

"You've got to promise me that you won't poke it again with your stick! Now are you going to be a good girl?"

"What if it fizzes at me?"

"Even if it fizzes at you. Sometimes it needs a good fizz, just like you!"

"All right! Guide's honour!"

With the injured fire unplugged and, with great labour, removed to the boot of John's car, electric light was soon restored. John was thankful that the trip-switch was as sensitive as it was. Jane brought down a smaller, safer and more efficient fire from a spare bedroom.

"How is the kitchen sink?" John asked.

"Making glugging noises at me!"

It took John twenty minutes to clear the sink. He had, of course, forgotten his big adjustable wrench and so he was reduced to vigorous exercise with the plunger.

"What the hell does she put down this thing?"

A noisesome and repellant brew had accumulated until, with a loud sucking noise and a final gurgle, it vanished from sight. He ran both taps to swill away unpleasant remains, then he filled the sink with cold water and pulled the plug to give the waste pipe a final deluge.

As he re-entered the drawing-room a tumbler was thrust into his hand. It was half-full of whisky.

"Thank you, John dear! You need a drink!"


A bright red Volkswagen was standing outside the front door of Fairloe Court.

"Aunt Sarah! Whose incarnation am I going to be today?" Well, at least he was forewarned. John put the company car in the garage and leaned over to the back seat to pick up his briefcase and a parcel which lay beside it.

A bit of luck! The day had begun inauspiciously with Jane displaying a marked reluctance to call at an electrical wholesaler in search of the obsolete elements which alone would make Cecily's electric fire serviceable again. She wouldn't know what to do, she had said. And electrical things were not her responsibility. And in any case she was too busy. It had been one of those breakfast times. In the event, a frenzied hunt through the Yellow Pages, half a dozen telephone calls and the despatch of the office boy on a private errand had produced the very last two elements, out of old and half forgotten stock, that probably existed anywhere. John was very pleased with himself. He could even face being an incarnation, as long as they gave him his tea first.

He put the parcel on his workbench, left his briefcase in the kitchen and, bracing his shoulders, advanced upon the drawing-room door.

"John dear! You're not Hasfield after all!"

Aunt Sarah's voice sounded determinedly reassuring.

"Who am I then? Genghis Khan?"

A merry laugh sounded from the settee. A second woman's face turned towards him. Something in John missed a beat. It was the Earth-Mother!

"Deirdre has seen the photograph and she says it isn't you. Cup of tea?" Jane's voice was as bright and as cheerful as her countenance.

"I'm not infallible, you know!" The voice from the settee was husky, very easy on the ear. "It just didn't say that to me. That's all."

She looked at John and gave him the shy smile of someone who hoped she was not intruding on something rather personal.

"No, it didn't say that to me either."

John heard his own reply with something like surprise. He didn't usually say things like that!

Jane furnished her husband with a cup of tea and a generous slice of cake. "This is magnificent! Been baking?"

"No darling. Mummy gave it to me last night. I think her conscience was troubling her."

"Cecily with a conscience!" John laughed. He turned to the Earth-Mother. "She doesn't know how anything works and won't be told, and God alone knows what she tries to flush down her kitchen sink! And the woman bakes cakes like this!"

"She used to win all the cakes and jams at the shows," said Aunt Sarah. "The only way they could stop her was to make her a judge!"

"You've been talking about me of course?"

"Of course! I've been telling Deirdre and Sarah all about the dreams you and Hasfield have been having – and your little adventure on Saturday morning!" Jane's tone was bright and politely defiant. She gave her husband the sweetest of smiles. "You frightened me to death, you chump! I thought you were having a coronary when I got home. You looked like death warmed up!"

A full description followed, plus a brief poetry reading to prove the point. Very little comment was made and John was rather relieved. He finished his tea and excused himself. He would change and then put the new elements into Cecily's old electric fire. He would run it over to her later on, all being well.

John surveyed the monster on his workbench with misgivings. It looked well enough in Cecily's great hearth, with its bogus firedogs and its great curved back. But John knew electrical appliances of old. To his mind they vied with each other for an International Award for Bad Design! One could get them apart – sometimes with difficulty – but getting them together again was all too often a nightmare. Patience and a judicious use of penetrating oil eventually laid the pieces of the monster on John's bench. No wonder it had been "fizzing!" One of the interior connections was loose and had been melting and re-welding by turns for months. John rummaged among his box of bits and pieces and found something that would serve as a replacement. He bent it in the vice, offered it up, drilled its ends and before long had both new elements in place and all the connections renewed and secure.

A sudden weariness assailed him. Was there any more tea in the pot? He would need to renew his strength before he tackled the hideous task of reassembly.

"I'll make some more, darling!" Jane slipped from the room, leaving John with Aunt Sarah and the Earth-Mother. The talk was of the sudden dash to the rescue of Cecily, and of the periodic sudden dashes in the same direction which were becoming a regular feature of their lives. And then Jane reappeared and tea cups were filled all round.

"I'd better go and put this brute together again."

John got up from his chair.

"Would you like another pair of hands?"

The Earth-Mother was looking up at him. "I know what these brutes are like! You need four hands at once and double-jointed fingers eight inches long!"

It was the voice of experience talking. John accepted the offer with alacrity and the two of them excused themselves and set off for the workshop. As they left the drawing-room, Aunt Sarah and Jane looked knowingly at each other and winked.


John kept a tidy workshop so oil, dust and wood shavings did not hazard the elegance of the Earth-Mother's attire.

And she was elegant too! John had met her only briefly, once or twice with Aunt Sarah. He knew her more by reputation than by acquaintance and it was her reputation that had earned her from him the *sobriquet*, Earth-Mother.

John found himself in close contact with a woman a very few years his senior, who had kept a remarkably trim figure and whose face was ... well, yes! The word was beautiful! It was the sort of beauty that Charlie Redmayne would have summed up nicely: "She'd have made a damned good-looking horse!"

Deirdre's was a very fine face and her iron-grey hair was beautifully arranged, exactly to suit it. But it was her eyes that made the most impression on John. They were dark, and they were very beautiful, and they saw right through him.

"Oh! What a brute! I had one once. I mended it, put it all together and blew all the fuses with it!" She giggled. A beautiful, husky, mischievous giggle that captivated John completely.

"It all has to go together in one go or it won't go at all! All the bendy bits of metal have to fit into those channels in the solid end bits – and stay there while I get the locating rods through and tightened up."

They worked together, fitting awkward shaped pieces into a precariously balanced pattern, all four hands fully occupied, both wishing for a few hands more.

"Can you get the rod through...? What do you make of your dream, John? That's it! Nearly! Oh damn! It's come apart!"

"Don't know what to make of it. If Hasfield hadn't had it too I would have put it down to too much cheese late at night! But I can't shrug it off that easily. And after Saturday… Can you push that bit back in there? Hold tight!"

"Got it! If you had to describe the experience, categorise it in some way, how would you do it?"

"Video-recording, I suppose. Of a sort … hold tight! Damn! Its come apart again! There now! Yes, video. Except for one thing."

"You're through! Can you get the nut on the end? What thing?"

"I wasn't watching it. I was taking part! Experiencing everything personally. And so was Hasfield, obviously. Good! That's one rod through. Now this next one!"

"And the church was different, wasn't it? The same church, but centuries back in time?"

"Yes. I was participating in a memory – or in the thing remembered. I can't work out which. Is that end through?"

"No, its fouling something. Jiggle it a bit. How does a scientist come to terms with it, John? The end's through now, by the way."

"With difficulty! Like this damned thing! The nut's cross-threaded and now its stuck! Damn! But I have been reminding myself that sub-atomic particles sometimes go backwards in time – or seem to –so no doubt there is a mechanism of sorts. I'm quite clear that this was no fantasy, no suggestion thing. Hold tight! I'll have to use two hands on this nut."

"Got it? Good! Yes, it is a matter of balancing reason and intuition, isn't it? Neither are really adequate on their own. You are very intuitive, aren't you John? I know you are, I can see it!"

"Yes, Deirdre, I know you can see it. You can see right through me, can't you, with those big X-ray eyes of yours!"

John looked up and their eyes met.

"Can you get the next rod through John? I hope I'm not as terrifying as you make me sound."

"You frighten me to death, Deirdre! But you do it quite delightfully, and I think its me I'm really frightened of. I'm not quite prepared for the intuition-explosion that seems to be going on, in me and all round me. I'm only a simple engineer!"

"Just as well, John, or we'd never get this contraption back together again would we? What did Cecily poke it with?"

"Her walking stick. Fortunately it has a big rubber ferrule on it. She says this thing was fizzing at her!"

Another beautiful, husky giggle sounded like music in John's ears. "There! Now there is a nut and bolt to locate the base-plate to the front assembly. This is going to be jolly!"

"I've got slimmer hands than you. I'll hold the nut over the hole and you poke the screw into it – if you can. Have you asked Sarah about the period – you know, the period of your church in the dream? She's a historian and it sounds like her period."

"Never thought of that! Am I getting anywhere with this screw? It seems to be going in."

"Yes, it's tickling the end of my finger! How old is this house, John? Late fifteenth century? It's a typical well-to-do yeoman's house and hall, afore un were rose up."

John was tickled by her use of the dialect term for enlarging a house.

"Yes. 'er were rose up!" He said, chuckling.

John set the body of the fire on to its bogus fire dogs, tightened the locating screws, replaced the red coal-effect bulbs with their little rotating fans, put the bogus glass coal back in place and looked at Deirdre.

"Well! Who is going to blow all the fuses this time?"

"It's your house, John!"

They found Jane and Aunt Sarah in the kitchen when they emerged from the workshop.

"Triumph!" said John. "Deirdre here is a jolly good electrician's mate!"

"I've just seen the time!" Aunt Sarah's voice betrayed its habitual surprise. "We'd better be going!"

"I'll fetch my handbag," said Deirdre. "I left it in the drawing room." She started towards the drawing-room door and then spotted the grand piano in the far corner of the long dining room. "Ooh! Can I have a look? What is it? Do you play?"

"Bechstein," said Jane. "I play a bit. Do you?"

"Badly! But I love it!"

The Earth Mother set off in the direction of the piano. In the middle of the floor she made an odd little detour round something and glanced back. Her eyes met Aunt Sarah's and what was obviously a little private joke was shared between them.

The piano was admired and the handbag fetched. John observed that the departure rituals were somewhat foreshortened and only ten minutes later Aunt Sarah's little Volkswagen disappeared from sight up the lane.

"What a woman!" John said, half to himself.

"Who? Deirdre?" Jane knew perfectly well who he meant. "Yes, the Earth-Mother! I used to think she was a witch, but she's a damned sight more potent than that!"

"Don't you like her?"

"Like her? I think she's terrifying! Yes, I like her very much indeed as a matter of fact. Wouldn't mind her as my Confessor!"

"Darling! What were you two up to in your workshop?"

"Magic, I think! We got Cecily's fire back together and working anyway. I'll run it over to her after supper."

John gazed after the now vanished Earth-Mother.

"I'm hungry!" he said. "When do we eat?"

# CHAPTER EIGHT

TWENTY-SIX is a good age for a man to marry, and when he is master of his own house and modest estates, a graduate of Oxford University and a lawyer with connections at Court – however tenuous – why, the very world lies at his feet. So it was with John Farelowe in the summer of 1526.

He was to be married, in his own parish church, to pretty Kate Archer, widow these two years of Walter Archer, a wealthy yeoman of Oxfordshire. Walter, an only son, had died within a year of their marriage, and had left no heir to succeed him. Kate therefore brought a tidy inheritance with her and she and her new husband were thus comfortably provided for. John would not have to wear himself out at the practise of law in order to keep them clothed and fed. Kate's father, William de Buforde, an Oxfordshire squire of the old school, would give his daughter away for the second time. He approved of her choice of husband and his only hope was that he would never have to perform the same task again.

John Farelowe had come into his inheritance these four years past. His father had died in 1522, the very year the Princess Mary was betrothed to the Holy Roman Emperor, Charles V, sixteen years her senior. Old Walter had been widowed and had no heart for going on after the loss of his beloved Meg. He had fulfilled his earthly pilgrimage, he made a holy death and was buried beside his wife in the churchyard barely two years after her.

Princess Mary was the only child of the marriage between King Harry and his brother's widow. Prince Arthur, never a fit man and not expected to live long, had been drowned in an accident. His father, himself then close to death, had made Prince Harry promise to marry his brother's widow and had set matters in motion for a Papal dispensation before he himself died in the February of 1509. Young King Harry, rising eighteen, promised well. He was learned, he was an accomplished musician, he was physically powerful, he was imperious of will and he was the most excellent company. In short, he looked every inch the King that England felt she needed after the rather bleak carefulness of the reign of his father which had followed the decades of bloodletting of the Wars of the Roses. He had fulfilled his father's wishes, though without enthusiasm. He married Princess Catherine of Aragon on St Barnabas' Day of 1509 and made her his Queen. She was five years his senior in age. She began at once the dreary succession of miscarriages and stillbirths that were to darken the young King's reign and have the most terrible consequences for Church and nation in years to come. For the King had no son, and as the years passed and he approached his forties, all manner of speculations and temptations assailed him. He was known to be anxious to be rid of his wife by the time she bore him their only child, the Princess Mary, in 1516.

Old Walter had set about his grand design for his house and hall in the Paschaltide of 1509. With a bright new King on the throne it was time to do brave things! So he had told a startled Meg at any rate, and immediately an army of workmen and carpenters had descended upon them to begin by tearing the roof off their hall.

A massive chimneypiece was installed in the middle of the back wall of the hall, with a chimney up which the smoke would now obediently rise, just as it did in the house adjoining.

There was no further need for a hole in the roof, or for a central hearth beneath it, so Walter took the roof off and built a second floor over his hall, with a third floor of small servants rooms in the roof-space above.

The floor joists protruded and overhung the outside walls in the time-honoured fashion, for the weight of the new walls to be built on their extremities, and the roof above, would counterbalance the weight of interior walls and furniture, and the very occupants themselves as they moved about. But the span of the beams was considerable and so prudence suggested a line of four stout oaken uprights to help bear the weight above. They served also to delineate a passage the length of the hall from the kitchen off-shut to the door of the house.

But the distinction between house and hall had now very largely disappeared. Walter had installed a fine oaken staircase, just inside the hall door. It led to the whole of the upper storey, and the old house ladder, connecting the upper room with the lower, was done away with altogether.

Meg had been overjoyed by the new splendours of which she was the mistress, but all her entreaties about the still ramshackle kitchens in leaky offshuts had fallen on deaf ears.

Kate was to be more fortunate. John had set about rebuilding the kitchen end of the house as soon as she had consented to marry him. The work was well in hand, though not yet completed. The two ends of the house would match each other. A great bread-oven had been built and a spacious bed-chamber for guests above the kitchen was just about ready for occupation in time for the wedding. It would accommodate John's three best friends, all as yet unmarried. Edward Carey, a Devonshire man from Exeter, had studied at the Abbey School at Glastonbury with John and they went up to Oxford together. There they met and befriended two others; Edmund Foster, son of a Norfolk yeoman and educated like themselves by the Benedictines, in his case at St Edmundsbury. Thomas Campion was the son of a London merchant and had become a light-hearted hanger-on to the Court of King Henry VIII.

Ned Carey was to be John's Best Man and the other two would gladly have robed themselves in surplices and held the nuptial pall over Bride and Groom as they prostrated themselves before the altar during the Sanctus. But Alas! there would be no nuptial pall at this wedding, for Kate was a widow. As St Ambrose had long ago explained:

"First marriages were instituted of the Lord, but second marriages were permitted."

"Now Tom, and what of King Harry?"

Tom Campion had just arrived, last of John's three friends and was, as usual, immediately pumped for news of the goings-on at Court, more in jest than in earnest for no-one really cared. And Tom knew what was expected of him by way of reply. "Harry is well pleased with his mistress if not with his wife! And rumour has it that he has begun to lust after the sister of his mistress too, so all should be merry for a month or so!"

"Now Tom!" A rich, musical voice, tinged with a trace of Devon, sounded from the far corner of the room. It came from a powerfully built man with sandy hair and a reddish face in which were set two eyes of the brightest blue.

"Now Tom! We be good Christian men here and care nothing for tales of bed-larking and alcove-chasing. And King Harry Defender of the Faith too! For shame!" He chuckled. "Tell us of Popes and Emperors. We be faithful subjects here!"

"God's Body! That's what Tom's about!"

Edmund, tall, thin and already beginning to stoop, had no illusions about folk in high places. He had tarried long enough at Court to know well what was the tone of the place.

"Well, Ned! I'll tell you a tale of Emperors and Princesses. Poor Princess Mary, ten years old, is jilted twice already!"

Tom shook his head. There was pity in his eyes. The three looked at him with raised eyebrows.

"Betrothed to the Dauphin of France at the age of two and jilted. Betrothed to the Holy Roman Emperor at the age of six, by the Treaty of Windsor no less … and he has just thrown her over and married a Portuguese Princess! Couldn't wait any longer! Poor little girl!"

"King Harry will have her married off soon enough. There must be more Kings for him to dangle her in front of."

John reached for the wine bottle and filled his friends' cups. "His sister Margaret is widowed of the King of Scotland, and France and the Empire are the only prize plums for the picking. He and the Emperor are dancing about like two prize cockerels, each outdoing the other. Last year was the undoing of France. Its King is still the Emperor's prisoner – so is the Pope, come to that!"

Tom settled back with his wine. He was glad to be away from Court. He had no illusions about it, he could keep his counsel there, and thus he kept his head. But he was among friends here. The talk turned to the wedding the following day, and of Ned's wedding later in the year, and of Edmund's growing sense of calling to the cloister. London and its doings soon faded from their minds; there were more real things to attend to.

And then, quite suddenly, John asked his friend:

"Tom! There is talk in Gloucester of them sending me to the next King's Parliament. Do I go, or not?"

The three looked at him. Tom spoke.

"Parliament is the King's creature, John. It is as free as a headless chicken, and as high-principled! If you care nothing for what you do or say, then go! But the John I know will be an unhappy man there. He will lose either his integrity or his head. Knowing John, it will be his head!"

There was a mutter of assent. John nodded thanks to his friend and went round again with the bottle.

"There is talk of the King summoning a Parliament before long to reform the Church. This year, next year, the year after. Parliament, I say! Not the Church's Convocations! Now it is but talk, but it is who is talking it that worries me."

"It cannot be, Tom!" Edmund's voice was quiet but firm. "Parliament has no power to reform the Church. God forbid it should try! Please God King Harry puts a stop to any such notion!"

"Why do we English always hate our clergy?" Ned's rich voice came out of its dark corner again. "They serve us better than any in Christendom and we are a good Mass-going nation. But we are always carping about the priests! Bitter, unkind carping too! And Parliament is full of it."

"So did His People hate our Saviour."

Edmund held out an empty cup, having delivered himself of the answer behind all other answers.

"There are grievances enough, Edmund." John filled up his friend's cup and opened more wine. "The Papacy is rotten to the core. The Church worships and ministers in spite of it! All the money it can grab goes to Rome and we are left with absentee Bishops, Prebendaries and what you will. No fault of our clergy, but the clergy feel all the force of our resentments. And the Church Courts are a shambles too!"

"Here speaks the lawyer!" laughed Ned.

"Thomas a-Becket died for them," said Edmund, gravely. "Yes, he died for them – and for other things we may never know about. But in his day they were a safeguard for the poor against the arbitrary will of the Barons. Not now! All they do now is multiply cost and play off against each other!"

"Tom Wolsey's Legatine Court was supposed to regulate it all, but his is the worst of the lot and he the biggest waster!"

"And the clergy are blamed for the lawyers' ills."

Edmund regarded his wine thoughtfully, and added:

"And the first year's purchase of every stipend goes to Rome in Annates. The clergy starve and are blamed for it!"

"And here we are, with learning reviving all about us, with books pouring from printing presses to teach us and to stimulate our thoughts – and none of us is allowed to think! God's Body indeed!" Tom had put his finger on the crux of the matter. The four fell silent. They were devout men and reverenced the Mass too profoundly to fall to easy debate. It was Ned who broke the silence.

"If I question the hows, and the whys of our Lord and His Mass, and make too much noise about it, I am hauled before the Bishop to be examined for heresy. Now the Bishop will fall over himself to save me from my error, but if I am stubborn and persist, through pride or lunacy, then I leave him no choice but to pronounce me a heretic."

Ned took a deep draught of his wine.

"But these two hundred years, Parliament – Parliament mind you! – has made heresy a capital offence, punishable by burning! And while the Bishop turns somersaults to save me, the Magistrates crowd about like devils to burn me! And the Bishop bears the rebuke! And the clergy with him!"

"Don't go to Parliament, dear John! You can change nothing in it and you would break your heart and damn your soul in the trying!" Wine had made Edmund fervent. Suddenly he laughed. "What dolours for a man's wedding eve! What Job's comforters we are for John. Come now! We'll sing him a song!" And the rest of the evening was spent in revelry, as it was in England before merriment was called a mortal sin, and good wine an invention of the devil.


If Tom Campion's complaint, and Ned Carey's commentary upon it are to be rightly understood, then some attention has to be paid to the historical background.

When Lotario de'Conti di Segni, a papal beaurocrat of noble birth, was made a Cardinal, while still in Deacon's orders, and at the age of thirty, it did not need abnormal prescience to predict his eventual election to higher office. He was still in deacon's orders eight years later, when his election to the Papacy came in 1198. He took the name Innocent III.

Innocent was anything but innocent. He was utterly sincere, but his unshakable determination was to enforce, extend and define the all-embracing authority of the Roman See. He was a diplomat and an opportunist. He was also subject to fits of depression. His immediate task was the establishment of authority over the Holy Roman Empire and he was successful in claiming the final say in approving whoever the Electors had elected to be the next Emperor. He launched the Fourth Crusade, but when it was diverted from its goal – the recovery of the Holy Land – and sacked Christian Byzantium instead, he used the opportunity to establish a temporary authority over the Eastern Church by putting in an Italian as its Patriarch.

In England, a quarrel over the appointment of the Archbishop of Canterbury ended with the submission of King John who recognized Innocent as his feudal overlord to the fury and contempt of his subjects.

In truth, there was very little that was innocent about Innocent III!

The Lateran Council of 1215 was the climax of his reign. Heretics, such as the Cathars (or Albigensians) were condemned and doctrines were defined. Innocent claimed for the Pope's exclusive use the title "Vicar of Christ." He went on to claim that "no king can rightly reign unless he devoutly serve Christ's vicar." And he defined, in a way which was to quickly become malignant, the functions of priest and prince, and all in relation to himself.

"Princes have power in earth, priests over the soul. As much as the soul is worthier than the body, so much worthier is the priesthood than the monarchy." And Innocent claimed, as Pope, to be Melchisedech, the priest-king, who would bring a centralised Christian society into being. Innocent died the following year at the age of fifty-six.

All the seeds of a future malignancy were sown during the Pontificate of Innocent III. It could be argued, with some cogency, that he was the father of the Reformation cataclysm, three centuries later.

Nothing that he did, however, exceeded in malignancy the declaration as *de fide* – central to the Faith – of a piece of very human, academic cleverness which sought to subject the very Mystery of Faith to the newly-discovered philosophy of Aristotle. The Mass is that Christ-given and ordained act of worship at which the Faithful meet together *to be the Church* and to re-enact the Lord's Supper as he commands. Priest and people have each their own liturgy to perform and it has ever been the understanding of the Church that Christ Himself is the true Celebrant, just as he is the Victim of the one, eternal Sacrifice, once-offered. The Mass is thus the expression of the Timeless and Eternal in Time.

The ultimate Mystery of the Faith is the Person of Christ, and the identity of the consecrated Elements at the Mass with Christ is part of that inexpressible Mystery. The "parts" of the Mystery are indivisible; the Mystery itself is incapable of definition. Such is the nature of Mystery.

Aristotle had recently been rediscovered, via the Arabs, and that formidable polymath Albertus Magnus had drawn his philosophy to the attention of his brilliant pupil Thomas Aquinas. Thomas had immediately and enthusiastically embarked upon his *Summa Theologica*, in which he sought to present the whole Christian Revelation in terms of the strictest Aristotelian philosophical exactitudes. Such was the spirit of the age.

The Fathers of the Lateran Council saw fit to tear the Consecration of the Elements at the Mass from its context and to seek to define the Mystery of the relationship of the Consecrated Elements with Christ in Aristotelian terms. The result was declared a doctrine, that of *Transubstantiation* – and proclaimed *de fide*. The effect of this was that anyone who questioned the definition, or indeed the propriety of seeking so to define the Mystery, was automatically guilty of heresy! The hierarchy and the priesthood had already been, in part, removed from their context within the whole company of the Faithful. The Church was by now almost automatically, though never formally, identified with its clergy. And the priest henceforth became, in some men's minds, a magical man with magical powers – such was the degradation wrought by that impious attempt to define The Mystery.

This was bad enough, but the condemnation of the Cathars as heretics encouraged the secular powers to outdo the spiritual in disordered zeal. The Holy Roman Emperor declared heresy to be a capital offence, punishable by burning. A hideous campaign of massacre then followed. Other secular powers followed the Emperor's lead, including England, and the very central act of the Mass, the indefinable Mystery of the Person of Christ, became practically impossible to mention without its degrading definition on the one hand or the fear of a hideous death on the other.

Some thirty years after the death of Innocent III, another ill-named Innocent, Pope Innocent IV, solemnly sanctioned the use of torture in order to break down the perversity of heretics and secure confessions.

John Farelowe and Kate Archer stood just outside the porch of the little church of our Lady Saint Mary. Kate's father supported her and John was surrounded by his friends with Ned Carey as his Best Man. It was a fine sunny day and it was made fresh by an intermittent light breeze.

They had intended to marry during Paschaltide but Kate had been taken ill and had not recovered until Rogationtide. It was not lawful to marry between *Quis Vestrum* and *Benedicta* and so they married on the first possible day: the Monday after the Feast of the Holy and Indivisible Trinity.

John stood at Kate's right hand, for, as Holy Scripture makes plain, Eve was made of a rib from Adam's left side. Kate, being a widow, stood quietly with her hands covered. Outside the churchyard a great crowd of villagers stood, whispering and excited. There was nothing like a wedding to get them all going and the worldly Tom Campion grinned at the thought that nine months hence there would be a goodly crop of Baptisms for the village priest to get on with! The good old Sir Richard had died not long since and his place had been taken by Sir Ralph, a fierce little priest with huge eyebrows and piercing blue eyes. But those same piercing eyes were capable of a very merry twinkle and he had quickly won the approval of his parishioners and was well on the way to winning their hearts as well.

Old Harry the Parish Clerk had also died not long since and he had been succeeded at once by Young Harry, for the office had been in the same family for generations.

Sir Ralph began by asking the Banns. No impediment being alleged, he solemnly addressed the gathering, not in Latin, but in the vulgar tongue which had long been used at Holy Matrimony in England. They were gathered, he told them, in the sight of God and his angels and his saints, and in the face of the Church, to join together two bodies, that henceforth they might be one body. And also that they might be two souls in the faith and law of God, to the end that, together, they might earn eternal life.

Still standing outside the church door, John declared that he would have Kate to his wedded wife, that he would love her and honour her, keep her and guard her in sickness and in health, as a husband should his wife. And he would forsake all others on account of her and would keep him only unto her so long as they both lived. For her part, Kate declared that she would take John to her wedded husband, that she would obey him and serve him, love honour and keep him in sickness and in health as a wife should a husband. And she declared that she would forsake all others on account of him and keep herself only unto him so long as they both lived. There was a sudden stirring of the breeze and, with it, a momentary pause in the proceedings. John felt an unexpected nervousness now the time had come for him to repeat after Sir Ralph his Marriage Vow.

"I John, take thee Kate to my weddyd wyf to have
et to holde fro this day wafort better for wurs for
richere, for porer; in sikenis se and in helte tyll
deth us depart, if holi chyrche wol it ordeyne: and
ther to I plycht thee my trouth."

Kate, trembling, made her Vow to John.

"I Kate take te John to my weddyd husbonde, to
have et to holde for thys day for bettur, for wurs,
for richere, for porer, in sykenesse and in helthe,
to be bonowre et buxom, in bed et at bord, tyll
deth us depart, if holy chirche wol it ordeyne:
et ther to I pliche te my throute."

John laid gold and silver, and a ring, upon a dish that Harry, the Parish Clerk, held out to him. Sir Ralph blessed the ring and John, taking it up, touched first Kate's thumb, then the first and second fingers before finally putting it on the third, saying as he did so:

"With thys ryng I the wedde and tys gold and silver
I the geue: and wythe my body I te worscype, and
wyth all my worldly catell I the honore. In the name
of the Father, and of the Son, and of the Holy Ghost."

Sir Ralph added a blessing:
"Be ye blessed of the Lord, who hath made the world out of nothing."
To which all present added their heartfelt "Amen!"

Prayers were said, after which the procession moved into the church and stood beneath the great Rood which screened off the Nave from the Chancel. Here solemn prayers were offered for them: that they might have the seed of eternal life sown within them; that they might live, grow and grow old in the Love of God; that they might see the sons of their sons and daughters to the third and fourth generation; that they might be joined together in the union and love of true affection and that, in all things, God would bless them. The Marriage Rite was complete, it remained for the Mass of the Holy Trinity to be celebrated. John and Kate were led through the screen into the Chancel and taken to the South side of the altar, with Kate on John's right, between him and the altar. After the Mass, and the feasting which followed it, John and Kate's bedchamber was blessed by the priest. And then their bed was blessed, and finally they were blessed in bed together. And then Sir Ralph departed, closing the door behind him and forbidding most sternly that they be disturbed.


Young William Farelowe was born in Paschaltide in 1527. John had long intended that his firstborn son should be named Walter, after his own father. But Kate's short-lived first husband had also been named Walter and so it was decided to call the boy William after William de Farlo, John's grandfather. By happy chance Kate's own father was a William and so all interests were served and everyone was happy.

Young Meg was born the following year, in the autumn. Kate had a hard time at the birth of her daughter and took many months to recover her strength. John was therefore able to use the excuse of his wife's continuing indisposition in resisting yet another attempt to return him to Parliament, for King Harry had summoned a Parliament for November of 1529 with a view to the reformation of certain Ecclesiastical abuses, beginning with the Church Courts. John had no intention of embroiling himself in the doings of Parliament for, as all men knew, it was but the King's creature and the means whereby most of its members could gain personal advantage in one form or another. Any serious resistance to the Royal will was likely to prove fatal for the outspoken member, for he would be informed upon and he would then be at once the subject of an indictment for High Treason.

Once indicted, the unfortunate fellow was a dead man, for where the King's interests were involved justice had no place whatsoever, however solemnly its outward trappings might be paraded. He might be tried in court, but as the years passed a more convenient method of disposal became increasingly common. Parliament would pass an Act of Attainder which declared him guilty of High Treason without the tedium of a trial. He was a Traitor by Act of Parliament! The Traitor, thus defined, would then be publicly hanged until he was half-dead. Still conscious he would he cut down and disembowelled, his intestines being burned on a brazier before his own eyes. His limbs would then be hacked off one by one and, at the very end, he would be decapitated. The skill of the executioners was such that he could well remain conscious for most of the proceedings. All things considered, therefore, John Farelowe was content to remain in the comparative obscurity of Gloucestershire. King Henry was in the twenty-first year of his reign. He was to be described in a later generation as a man of his times more completely than any other person in his realm:

"A man of force without grandeur: of great ability, but not of lofty intellect: punctilious and yet unscrupulous: centred in himself: greedy and profuse: cunning rather than sagacious: of fearful passions and intolerable pride, but destitute of ambition in the nobler sense of the word: a character of degraded magnificence."

As a young man, Henry could be charming and agreeable. Everyone, after all, had to agree with him! He was a sworn friend of the finest living Englishman, Sir Thomas More – until it suited his book to kill him! His Court shone with a superficial brilliance but as the years passed its tone became increasingly coarse, gross and intemperate. In this it reflected its Royal Master.

The old nobility had largely perished in the Wars of the Roses, or had been impoverished, or had simply been got rid of by King Henry the Seventh. Their place had been taken by a swarm of adventurers, many of whom could justly be described as the very worst men in the kingdom. It was into the hands of such men as these that the fortunes of the English Church were destined to fall. King Harry's first and closest confidant was a humble butcher's son who, in his way, was almost as typically a man of the times as the King himself.

Thomas Wolsey had done well for himself, and his rise had been spectacular, even meteoric. Born in 1474 he had become Chaplain to Henry Dean, Archbishop of Canterbury – that very Henry who had once been Prior of Llanthony St Mary in Gloucester. He had ingratiated himself with King Henry the Seventh who appointed him his own private Chaplain and, being a favourite of young Prince Harry, he had continued as the King's private Chaplain when the Prince succeeded his father to the throne of England. Tom was made Privy Counsellor in 1511. He was consecrated Bishop of Lincoln in 1514 and made Archbishop of York the very same year. He held the two Sees in plurality and found it unneccessary ever to go to York. Indeed he was seldom in Lincoln either as London was more congenial to him and a better stimulus to his energies.

Tom, now being a prelate of such substance, began to build himself a house worthy of his own magnificence. Hampton Court Palace was begun in 1514 and its opulence soon began to excite the envy even of the very King himself.

King Harry, still enamoured of his favourite, pulled Papal strings and Tom was made Cardinal in 1515. A month later he was Lord Chancellor of England, second only to the King. In 1518 he became Papal Legate and, in 1523 he missed being elected Pope by a whisker! Foreign policy was his forte. A celibate by solemn vows, he lived with his mistress at Hampton Court until a certain matter which had long been troubling the King began to overshadow Tom's relationship with his Royal patron and master. To keep King Harry sweet, Tom made him a present of Hampton Court in 1526, the very year John and Kate were wed.

The King must have a son! This was, arguably, his first duty to his people, and it was certainly the Queen's duty to present him with one. Queen Catherine had failed! There had been a succession of miscarriages and stillbirths and nothing to please the King but a daughter of a quiet and pious disposition, possessing a curious mixture of her mother's Spanish temperament and her father's obstinacy. It was a judgement! It was God's doing and it was all because he, Harry, had wed his brother's sister against the rules of Holy Church. The fact that the reigning Pope had given a dispensation only made it all the more the Pope's fault! Well, his successor could put matters right and declare the marriage null and void! It had been reported abroad as long ago as 1514 that "The King of England means to annul his marriage and obtain what he wants from the Pope as France did."

There were precedents among the Royalty of Europe. The thing had been done before. Only in 1499 had King Louis the Twelfth obtained a dispensation from Jeanne of France in order to marry Anne of Brittany. Kings were different!

In 1527, the year of William Farelowe's birth, matters came to a head. His Majesty was utterly besotted with a young lady in waiting, Anne Boleyn, sister of his current mistress, and he was determined to marry her and make her his Queen, come what may! Alas! For the King, for Tom Wolsey and for the English Church! In that very year the everlasting rivalry between the Holy Roman Emperors and the Popes provoked the Emperor Charles the Fifth to sack the Eternal City itself and make Pope Clement the Seventh his prisoner. And was not the Emperor none other than the favourite nephew of Queen Catherine?

How could the poor Pope declare the King of England's marriage null and void with the favourite nephew of the wronged Queen breathing down his neck and fingering the hilt of his sword? He prevaricated. He made objections that, in normal circumstances, would never have so much as entered his head.

Thomas, Cardinal Wolsey, became thoroughly alarmed. He suggested to His Holiness that the matter could be referred to his own Legatine Court and that His Holiness need not be troubled further. But even this was too dangerous for a Pope in thrall.

And so poor Tom failed his Royal master, and he fell. Only a month before Parliament assembled, Thomas Wolsey had pleaded guilty to a charge of Praemunire which was manifest nonsense to anyone but the enraged King. He had already been stripped of all his honours save that of the Archbishopric of York. In the Autumn of 1529 he made his first ever visit to the city and Diocese. He was going to have to begin to discover what it was to be a Bishop and a priest, and to minister to the poor and find Christ in them. If he was given time to do so.

It wouldn't last, of course. Someone would be paid to denounce him and there would be a charge of High Treason to answer with all its dreadful consequences.

There was one small crumb of comfort for him, however. The King, of the abundance of his mercy, would probably permit him to face the headsman's axe rather than suffer the indignities of a public disembowelling. The King was noted for little kindnesses of this sort towards fallen courtiers.

John Farelowe, a lawyer, happy in his rural obscurity, was broadly in sympathy with any well-intentioned move to reform the shambles into which the Ecclesiastical Courts had fallen. He had doubts, however, about the authority of Parliament to initiate Ecclesiastical reforms. The Church alone could reform her institutions and there was certainly a mind in the English Church to do it.

The Church Courts had at one time been the refuge of simple folk from the arbitrary justice of the barons. But times had changed and the whole apparatus had decayed into a hopeless tangle of bureaucracy and expense. Here, as in many other urgent concerns, Cardinal Wolsey had failed in his responsibilities. Parliament, as ever, was a hotbed of anti-clericalism and not the best forum for the discussion of much-needed but objective reform.

The Convocation of Canterbury, with that of York, the Church's own legislative body, was currently sitting in Old St Paul's. The agenda was full, for change was in the air. The eighty year old Archbishop Wareham had initiated a Visitation of all Monasteries and Religious houses some eighteen years before with a view to rationalisation and reform. The Religious Life was in decline, and had been for a century or more, but there was still much vigour in it and the Monasteries and Chantries fulfilled vital functions in society as a whole.

Most of the ecclesiastics in high office now, however, were from the ranks of the secular clergy and a new mind was abroad in the English Church. The Convocation sought to begin a process of gradual, faithful, wide-ranging but organic change.

It was never to be allowed to do anything of the kind. A great deal of the blame for what followed must be laid at the door of Thomas, Cardinal Wolsey, who had squandered the unique opportunities given to him and fostered, for his own ends, the malign development of Royal Absolutism both in matters secular and matters Ecclesiastical. John Farelowe, happy to spend time between his legal practise and his pretty Kate and their two children, was spared the torment of being an active participator in a process which was, in the course of his lifetime, to destroy almost everything he really believed in.

# CHAPTER NINE

IT HAD BEEN a pleasant morning. Jane enjoyed teaching and a part-time job was, in her view, just right. The Sixth Form had been in good order, they were enjoying their subject and Jane came home to her luncheon of slimming biscuits and fruit with a pleasing sense of fulfilment.

The afternoon presented itself with agreeable simplicity. The house was clean, supper was going to be a simple affair and a steady light rain made outdoor pursuits unattractive. Jane's mind was made up for her. She would light the drawing-room fire and settle down to a lazy afternoon with a good book.

A good book? Yes, but which good book? It occurred to Jane that, English teacher though she was, she had not yet looked seriously at the *Poetical Works* of James Hasfield. She had left that to John. Why? She asked herself the question and could find no answer. But Hasfield had impinged upon their lives. In a sense, they shared the house with him – with his memory and poems at any rate. It was probably not a very good book, but it was time she and Hasfield got better acquainted.

Jane took her time. Why hurry when there is nothing to hurry for? She was always feeling rushed when John was about. Men were like that. John was a stickler for the clock. It seemed to matter to him to arrive on the very dot! He could be relied upon to become tetchy and irritable if he thought she was going to make them late for something. As if it mattered!

Jane put a match to the drawing room fire, put the guard in front of it and went upstairs to change. Half way through changing she changed her mind and had a bath instead. Then, pleasantly relaxed and deliciously unhurried, she lingered before the mirror, re-doing her hair and touching up her make-up. Then she found a comfortable skirt she hadn't worn for months, spent a full twenty minutes trying on a selection of possible blouses and pullovers, and then she changed her mind and put on something different altogether. Eventually, looking very glamorous indeed, she descended the old oak staircase and made a graceful entrance into the drawing-room to renew acquaintance with James Hasfield, poet.

The drawing-room fire had blazed up and was now well-nigh burned out. Jane plucked the fire-screen away, seized poker and tongs and effected urgent repairs and refuellings. In the process she managed to streak one side of her face with charcoal. An observer, who knew her well, would have almost expected it. It was very much in the Jane tradition.

She picked up Hasfield's book from the occasional table by John's chair, settled down into the corner of the settee opposite the great chimneypiece, kicked off her shoes and tucked her feet up, pulling a cushion over them to keep them nice and warm. Then, fully prepared, relaxed and happy, she opened the book.

The first thing to do was to say "hello!" to its author, so she turned to the sepia photograph at the very beginning and looked at it long and thoughtfully.

Hasfield didn't seem to look as much like John as she had thought at first. Yes, there was a resemblance. They might have been cousins, perhaps. The main similarity was in the eyes. Hasfield was looking very directly at the camera when the photograph was being taken and he evidently had some urgent matter on his mind. The eyes were full of it. But somehow the shock that both Jane and Aunt Sarah had received when they first looked at the photograph had evaporated.

"Reincarnation?" Jane mused, remembering the speculations with Lucy. Well, it hadn't said that to Deirdre, and Jane was inclined to regard Deirdre as authoritative in matters of the intuition. And no! The photograph was not saying that to Jane either! Not now. She looked at it, puzzled. It was saying something! There was a connection somewhere. It wasn't just being a photograph.

"Dear Hasfield!" said Jane to the photograph. "I wonder what you are up to? You look a nice man!" And with that she turned to the Contents page and cast her eyes down it.

There were a number of sub-headings such as "Juvenilia" and "Industries and Artifacts in the Royal Forest of Dean." Jane found the Contents, as described, ponderous and suggestive of a massive tedium. But she remembered the little poem about the River Leadon, and the dialect poem about the "proper yawny" and trusted that the heavy titles would be found to conceal a lighter touch.

The Oxford Graduate and English Mistress in Jane found the volume very uneven indeed. Some of the "Juvenilia" was painfully juvenile and she wondered why he had included them. A poem of quite inordinate length, bearing the title, *St Mary's Church, Forthampton. The Restoration of 1849*, carried a footnote:

*"Composed for the amusement of the author's siblings and incurring the displeasure of their father."*

"I'm not surprised!" mused Jane. But she found herself warming to James Hasfield. It occurred to her that he had probably put in the bad as well as the good because he was simple and straightforward and it had just not occurred to him to do otherwise.

Jane Faversham, being very much a woman, wanted to know about Hasfield's love-life. Were there poems to his wife? To former girlfriends? Surely there must have been? She turned the pages, scanning urgently. She found it. *Rebecca!* Surely that was the name on the tombstone? Full of expectation and feeling delightfully nosey, she read the sonnet laid out before her.

O Chaste of Chaceley! Whither shall I wend ...

Jane had a fit of the giggles. She controlled herself with difficulty and continued.

80

My eager footsteps that we chance to meet?
Steadfast intent! With heart so quick to rend,
Its one desire: to cast down at thy feet!
Now chaperoned, attended in each place
We walk, polite, beside Sabrina's flood,
Exchange our pleasantries, glance at each face
Who both would be, shall be, one flesh, one blood!

Jane looked up from the page. The agony of young love, frustrated by parents or circumstances, ever chaperoned, never being allowed to be alone together, caught her powerfully. She felt tears coming and fought them back. Hasfield had got to her and her compassion was touched. But after all, they had become man and wife so there must have been a happy ending after all! She returned to the poem.

I, anguished, ache until that Day be come!
Until on high Love's banner be unfurled;
"Till chaste affections' holiday, the sum
Lend life and lightness to our weary world;
Until at length I come into thy bower,
Partaker with thee of thy Nuptial Hour!"

Poor Hasfield was ardent and no mistake! Jane reflected that, in this enlightened age, they would probably have gone casually to bed together ages ago. No waiting, no agony, no poetry! She thought, involuntarily, of her own daughter Rosemary, now graduated and at large in the wicked world. "I do hope she isn't ..." Jane shook the thought from her and noticed a footnote to Hasfield's Sonnet.

*"And Jacob served seven years for Rachel; and they seemed unto him but a few days for the love he had to her. (Genesis 29:20)"*

Jane sat quietly for several minutes. She had become very fond of James Hasfield. What did it matter that some of his poems were awful? Or that sometimes he sounded like Hasfield doing a skit on C. S. Calverley doing a skit on Hasfield?

And once in a while he could actually write poetry, amid all the versification. She returned to the book and read at random wherever the page fell open. This was Jane being Jane. The Graduate, the Schoolmistress, was having the afternoon off.

Twice Jane put the book down to put more logs on the fire. And twice she returned to the comfortable corner of the settee, curling up and putting her feet under the warm cushion. Yes! She was really very fond of James Hasfield! She knew him by now and it didn't matter that his *Poetical Works* were uneven, or sometimes really rather bad! The page fell open towards the very end of the book. A short poem of two verses caught her attention. It wasn't the last poem in the collection, but it was one of the last. The title was unusually short for Hasfield. A single word: *Nightfall*. She read the poem.

> The clouds are gathering, the darkness comes;
> I wear my melancholy as a cloak
> Deep-hooded and tight wrapped.
> Thus fast, it numbs Initiative and will, makes mind to choke.
> But yet – I cling to life – this is not me
> Nor is it mine, this all-enshrouding fog;
> But other, and another's. Thus is he
> Invigorate while I lie here, a log!

Jane felt a shiver run through her. The hair at the back of her neck was prickling. She closed the book quickly and then opened it again at the photograph of Hasfield.

The eyes were looking straight at her with a terrible urgency. At that moment the telephone began to ring in the hall. Jane closed the book, put it back on John's little table, slipped into her shoes and, still feeling very peculiar, left the drawing-room to answer it. "Eileen!" She shrieked! She plucked the telephone from its table and sat on the stairs. In a moment she was lost in chatter. Hasfield and his poems vanished from her mind as the minutes, the ten minutes, the half-hour and almost an hour slipped by. It was always like that when Eileen rang. They gossiped uninhibitedly, they giggled, they wallowed in tragedy, they prophesied doom, they revelled in scandal, they were outrageously suggestive, they told each other several times that they *must* stop talking because they both had *so* much to do, and they were only brought to an untidy halt by the sound of John's key in the front door.

Jane put the receiver down and put the telephone back on its table. She straightened her skirt and put both hands to her hair to make sure it was as pretty as it had been the last time she looked in a mirror.

The front door opened and Jane beamed at her husband. She was poised, relaxed and looking very, very attractive.

"Hello darling!"

He kissed her, and then stood back to get a better look.

"Been sweeping chimneys?" he asked.

# CHAPTER TEN

**A**MAN WITH LOCAL KNOWLEDGE could ford the River Leadon a little way upsteam from John Farelowe's house and hall. If he was on horseback and the river was low the matter was simplicity itself, although the river bed was muddy and could be treacherous if he chanced to stray to either hand. John knew it so well that he could have done it blindfold and as the water was low at the end of a warm May, he chose this short-cut at the beginning of his ride to Dene Abbey at Flaxley.

It was the Year of Grace 1532. Young William had just turned five years of age and little Meg was rising four. They were good, sturdy children and he adored them. He had kissed them and his pretty Kate, and had made a solemn promise that he would be away not more than three days – four at the most – and then he had set off on his way as merry as a cricket.

John Farelowe was a family man. He sat as lightly to the practise of law as he could afford and he had managed to avoid those dignities which puff a man's pride up like a bladder and multiply his sorrows at the same time. No! They would not ask him to represent Gloucester at the King's Parliament again! Of that he was right glad for its doings – and worse still, the tone of its doings –had grieved him more than he liked to admit.

And no! He did not care to be made a Magistrate and send his fellow men to the gallows, still less to supervise their hanging. John was no stranger to cruelty or to death. He was a man of his time and had become, to some degree at least, hardened to all of it. But it gave him no joy. He was never a casual spectator at an execution. He was a kindly fellow and, most of the time, a light-hearted and an easy-going one.

There was not a great deal to trouble John's mind this merry May morning. To be sure, King and Pope were at odds over the King's Matter, but at the distance from Court that he enjoyed he could take the thing as lightly as most other men were inclined to take it. Tom Campion kept him up-to-date with his lively letters and they met whenever they could find a good excuse to do so. The Pope would give way of course. King Harry would be rid of his gloomy Queen and, if Tom's whispered scandal was correct, England would shortly be rejoicing in a pretty English Queen Anne who would, of course, obediently present King Harry with a son and heir. John had never forgotten his father's passionate insistence that the King *must* have a son.

John thought of his three friends as he rode by the little old Norman church of St Oswald at Lassington, with its handful of cottages. Poor Tom! Still unmarried, and with a saucy mistress who had no more inclination to make the thing permanent than he had! Ned Carey was married four years since and he was now the father of two sons. Of all the three, Ned was closest to John's heart. They complemented each other and had done so ever since their very first meeting at the monastery school at Glastonbury.

Ned was a strong, solid fellow whereas John had always thought of himself as lightweight and wanting something of his father's ruggedness. This was John's opinion of himself, it was not necessarily the opinion of others. And Edmund? Dear Edmund was a monk at last, professed at Easter and soon to be ordained priest at St Edmundsbury, the very Monastery which had given him his schooling.

John rode down the mile-long lane from Lassington to Highnam Green. Now he was in the parish of Churcham and so he carried on down the lane some three more miles until he came to the village itself, on a little rise in the ground, with the church at the top of it. It pleased John to punctuate expeditions of this sort with brief halts at village churches, to offer a *Pater Noster* or an *Ave* before mounting his horse again and riding on. He had learned this habit from his father who had become deeply knowledgeable of the churches and villages within a thirty-mile radius of his house by the doing of it. So John dismounted, tied his horse to a convenient tree and attended to his prayers.

St Andrew's church at Churcham was a fine, broad-shouldered Norman building with a tower, topped by a wooden spire. John offered a prayer to the Mother of God and then, remounting, picked his way down the rough track, crossed the Long Brook and arrived at the next village of Minsterworth on the banks of the Severn. Minsterworth church was dedicated to St Peter, brother of St Andrew, and so John invoked the prayers of both Apostolic brothers for his family, his friends and himself before setting off once again upon his way.

John had connections with Flaxley Abbey, his destination, in more than one matter. As a lawyer he acted for them when necessary, but the Abbey also held the Great Tythe of Farelowe and appointed and paid its priest. The Abbot was Rector of the parish and Sir Ralph was his Vicar. John had long enjoyed the friendship and confidence of a holy monk who had not long since been installed as its Abbot. Abbot William had been mitred but four years before he died. Abbot Thomas Ware was now the father of the little Community. The Community was much reduced, there were but nine of them now and a fire had not long since gutted the church. But as Abbot Thomas would always remind him, John must not set too much store by numbers. If it pleased God to reduce the Community to one, then that one must keep the Rule and pray for his fellow-men! God alone was the giver of vocations and it must be taken for granted that He had good reason for witholding so many ever since the Great Plague had taken off a third of the population of England and men had ever since begun to fall away from the fulness of the One True Faith.

John rode the next five miles to Westbury with a silly tune going round and round inside his head. He had a fine tenor voice and loved nothing better than to share a song with his friends. But this one needed two voices if it was to be sung well. And poor John had but himself! The sun was shining and Spring was moving towards early Summer, and so John sang to his horse, bidding – albeit unsuccessfully – his horse to pick up the part and sing the song with him.

> Ah Robin! Gentle Robin,
> Tell me how thy leman doth
> And thou shalt know of mine:
> My lady is unkind, iwis,
> Alac! Why is she so?
> She loveth another better than me
> And yet she will say no!
> I cannot think such doubleness
> For I find women true;
> In faith my lady loveth me well;
> She will change for no new.

It was a sad and a most beautiful little song, and John sang it over and over again until it brought him almost to the brink of tears. So he laughed at himself, chided his horse for keeping silent, and found himself already at Westbury.

Westbury! Now here was a merry place and no mistake! The little riverside village possessed a feature that never failed to amuse John Farelowe. The church and its tower stood some fifty feet apart and it was as if they were no longer on speaking terms. He would chide them, gently, every time he rode past, but today he would make another halt and attempt a reconciliation by prayer.

Well, he would need a miracle to bring the two together but Heaven had a sense of humour too!

The old tower, a full century older than the church, had originally been built as a watch tower or garrison. The Welsh frontier had needed precautions such as this at one time. But then the church had been erected, hard by it, and the old tower had caught religion and grown a spire – A full 160 feet of it, from weather-vane to the ground.

John handed his horse to a young lad to hold, commanded that it be guarded with the boy's very life, and went into the church. There he invoked the prayers of St Peter and St Paul, who shared the dedication with God's Holy Mother whom he honoured with an *Ave*. He recovered his horse from a lad near-paralysed by the responsibility so suddenly thrust upon him, tossed him a coin, asked God's blessing upon him and rode on his way.

Some three miles of his journey remained before him and, soon after leaving the village, John turned up to the right towards that very line of tree-covered hills that his father had once pointed out to him. How long ago was that? Twenty-four years! But it was the same Forest of Dean and he was about to touch something of its darkness and its mystery, for Dene Abbey lay at its very foot. What would he and the good Abbot Thomas find to talk about on this occasion? His mind turned to matters ecclesiastical and his merry mood faded from him. King Harry was tweaking the noses of the clergy, aided and abetted by that very Parliament to which he, John Farelowe, was so glad not to have been returned. There was a viciously anticlerical spirit abroad. Not that this was any new thing, but it had taken on a new character of late. There was a vindictiveness, even a hatred in the very air and the clergy were the easiest and most visible targets for it. Most worrying of all to John was the fact that the King himself seemed to be indulging in caprices of this very nature.

Had King Harry not suddenly accused the total clergy of the English Church of the crime of *Praemunire?* Of the next worst thing to High Treason, indeed! And why? Because they had been so false as to recognise the Legatine Court of that very Cardinal Wolsey who had fallen from the King's favour and had only avoided the headsman's axe by dying at Leicester Abbey on his way to face it. But of course the clergy had recognised the Legatine Court! The King himself had required it! Had he not so pestered the Pope that Wolsey had been made, first of all a Cardinal and then, fourteen years ago, Papal Legate? Woe betide the clergy had they *not* recognised his Court!

John Farelowe, lawyer, rode more slowly. Kings were different, his father had told him. These were high matters of state. And had not King Harry been declared *Defender of the Faith* by the very Pope himself not many years since?

But it was all very confusing and not a little worrying. What was the use of law if it was to be enterprised, used with caprice, perverted … ? John shook himself out of his train of thought. It was dark and it was dangerous and he was powerless to do anything about it in any event. It was a troubled and heavy-hearted John Farelowe that topped the little rise to see, not far away now, the gaunt and gutted shell of the Abbey church of Flaxley confronting him.

John sat his horse and looked at the bare and smoke-stained gable-end of the Abbey church. At once there descended upon him a wholly unexpected and most terrible sense of premonition. He knew his soul to be in the greatest danger but why, and from what, was hidden from him. He resolved at once that, as soon as he arrived, he would make his confession.

And so it was a silent and thoughtful young lawyer who arrived at the gatehouse and knocked for admission.

Dene Abbey had been founded some four centuries before John Farelowe's arrival on that sunny, but so suddenly overshadowed May morning. Milo, Earl of Hereford had been killed in a hunting accident on Christmas Eve and his son, Roger, had immediately founded an abbey upon the very spot.

It was a Cistercian house. It had never been large and had for a long time been a daughter house of Bordesley. But it possessed one singular feature in that, ever since the reign of King Henry the Second, it had enjoyed Royal patronage and had been used as a Royal hunting lodge whenever the King went a-hunting in his Forest of Dean.

The lay-brothers' refectory had been turned into a magnificent guest-hall and King Edward the Third had rebuilt the Abbot's chamber for his own use. The Abbot was turned out of his chamber whenever the King rode abroad. This West Range was the only part of the monastery which was in good order, for many of the other buildings were ruinous. A temporary wooden structure had been erected inside the gutted church to allow the *Opus Dei* to be sung and the Mass to be celebrated.

The old guestmaster received John kindly and found him a favoured alcove in the guest hall which, most unusually, was bare of other guests. John's horse was comfortably stabled and would be well cared for. After a few quiet words of greeting John asked the Guestmaster if he might make his confession, for his conscience had smitten him grievously as he had been on his way. The guestmaster led him silently into the gutted church and bade him wait there. He looked about him, and the sense of dread foreboding returned. A monk appeared and silently beckoned him. So John Farelowe made his confession in a ruined chapel in the South transept. He made reference to the sense of impending calamity that had come upon him and he was comforted by the quiet, sane counsel of the old monk. "Beware of compromise, look always to your integrity!" the old man said. Then, shriven and given a token penance to perform, he rose from his knees and entered the temporary wooden church-within-the- church to offer his thanksgivings and his penance.

A dozen roughly made stalls were ranged, six on either side. A simple altar stood beyond with a fire-stained statue of God's holy Mother to one side of it. The Holy Sacrament hung over the altar in a pyx and there was an all-pervading atmosphere of peace and of profound prayer.

This extreme simplicity, enforced by circumstances, moved John Farelowe. It was with a real sadness that he recognised that, although this was everything that was needed, the sheer pressures of habit must surely cause the Community to beggar themselves by mortgaging the income of their lands for a hundred years in order to re-roof and re-adorn – even perhaps completely to rebuild – a church which bore no relation whatsoever to their lives, their numbers or their needs.

England was scattered with monastic follies of great beauty and quite inappropriate magnificence. The Cistercians were perhaps the biggest offenders in this, despite the extreme asceticism of their founder, St Bernard. They had become one of the wealthiest of the monastic orders and had developed estate management to a fine art. But at what cost to their life and vocation?

John Farelowe was at peace, being confessed and shriven. But he was sad and he was perplexed at the same time. He loved his England; it was a holy land and the holy land of Logres underlay it, never far from the surface. And he loved his Church because it was Christ's Church, but things were amiss and going further amiss, and he, John Farelowe, did not understand what was going on and did not know what he might be called upon to do about it.

"Well, Master John! 'tis the merry month of May and our Lady Saint Mary's own month too! But this year I fancy she will like it ill!"

John and the Abbot were sitting in the Abbot's sumptuous chamber. Vespers was over and there was an hour or two left before Compline ended the day and the Greater Silence began. John looked about him before replying. The Abbot was good at opening gambits, but John was fascinated, as ever, by the magnificence of a King's chamber. He knew that his friend found it a perpetual source of quiet amusement. Abbot Thomas was a true Cistercian and cared little for externals in any shape or form.

"Tis the King's Matter be a-troublin thou?" John, unlike his father, spoke the English of educated men, but he was thoroughly bi-lingual and enjoyed his native Gloucestershire tongue.

The Abbot gave a contemptuous snort.

"The King's Matter! When his Holiness wriggles out from under the Emperor's boot then King Harry shall have his will. And King and Pope will answer before the throne of God for it too. I thank God that I am but a poor monk and know nothing!"

Nothing pleases an informer more than the chance to inform. The King had his spies everywhere, but the two friends were safe here. They enjoyed each other's complete confidence. "No, Master John! Things nearer to hand. Things in our own Diocese of Worcester and not a week since!"

He saw the look of complete incomprehension on the younger man's face. He would have to enlighten him.

"What godly zeal! How pleasing to our dear Lord and to his most Holy Mother that a dead man should be thus burned at the stake for heresy!"

"A dead man? Burned at the stake … ?"

The Abbot was glad of a chance to unburden himself. "A fellow by the name of Tracey, of some small means. He died two years ago having written out his will in the form of a Gospeller's pamphlet. Full of half-digested pickings from that German fellow, Luther. Well, some hot-heads printed his will – Lollards and the like, you know the sort – and they have been brandishing it and raving about it as if t'were Holy Writ!"

The Abbot paused. John had seen some of the fevered and hate-filled pamphlets that were pouring into England from the Continent. They were stuffed with biblical quotations, usually torn from all context. Perhaps Tracey had been a friend of that renegade, Tyndale? John raised interested eyebrows at the Abbot.

"Tracey's silly pamphlet was thrust into the midst of Convocation and they were obliged to notice it. As if they had no better things to attend to! Like the silly fellows half of them are, they huffed and they puffed, and they decided they had to say something. So they said Tracey had been a heretic and unworthy of the Christian burial he had been given."

He gave a great snort of anger. John wondered what was coming next.

"So what does that jackass Thomas Parker do? You know the fellow? Vicar-General of our eternally absent Bishop. Well, he digs up Tracey's half-rotted corpse, and he ties it to a stake, and he publicly burns it for heresy! And not a week since!"

"Lunacy!"

John's face was that of a man who cannot believe the evidence of his own ears. But the fire in the Abbot's eyes and the fury in his gentle countenance was evidence enough for him.

"Aye, son John! Lunacy! And t'will do nothing but bitter ill to Christ and his poor Church. We are all tarred with Parker's brush in the minds of thinking men. There is hatred abroad, John! The monasteries are the target of every foul tale and evil report you can imagine – and folk are eager to believe them! And the secular clergy fare little better."

There was a long silence. For all her piety and Massgoing, England was seething with a bitter discontent with all things ecclesiastical. As ever, the clergy, both regular and secular, were the easy targets for popular hate. The really guilty, the Papacy and the absentee hierarchs it appointed to milk the English Church of its resources, and its people of their money, were too remote to be got at.

"We are too wealthy, son John! The monasteries have too much of the wealth of England in their endowments. There are too many great buildings and too few monks. The wealth is too much and at the same time it is not enough! And John! Prayer is out of fashion in our Church these days, and Contemplation altogether out of fashion!"

John nodded. He grasped only too well the Abbot's meaning.

"The head is taking the place of the heart in our holy religion, John. God help us if it does! Except that God cannot help us then!" There was another long silence. Now it was John's turn and he gave voice to a matter which was much on his own mind.

"Sir Thomas More has handed the Great Seal of England back to the King. He will be his Chancellor no longer. What make you of that, Sir Abbot?"

"What do you make of it, Master John?"

"The King's Matter? My father told me, many a time and oft –leave 'un to them as business 'tis! A man can lose his head – aye! And his arms, his legs and his entrails too – if he dares to show too much of an interest. And I have a wife and children!"

"The King's Matter? No! It goes deeper than that, son John. Whichever way the Pope rules in the business, More will accept and obey. But King Harry has bullied his Parliament to declare him *Supreme Head of the English Church and Clergy, so far as the law of Christ doth allow.* And More cannot allow it!"

"Tis but a dance of Kings and Popes!" John made a helpless gesture with his hand. "Since Saxon times the King of England has always been the *Vicar of Christ* – in England. That is what it is to be a Christian King of Christian men! What is all this but words?"

The Abbot reached out and laid his hand upon John's arm. "There is more in this than meets the eye, Master John! In times past the Kings of England have had to defend themselves against the worldliness of Papal power misused. But this time King Harry is emulating the German Princes. He is casting off the Pope altogether! But he is cleverer than the German Princes. We do not see his game until it is fully played out. And then it is too late!"

"The charge of *Praemunire* against the clergy is but a feint, then?"

"No feint at all, son John! There is enough hatred stirred up that, should the King wish it, the rabble would enjoy a massacre! The clergy have submitted to save themselves – but also to save Christ's Church."

"Submitted?"

"Yes! The Convocations have admitted *Praemunire* and will pay the King an immense fine. It will reduce many of the poor clergy to penury. The King has been bought off! And no more Canons will be enacted without the King's consent. And Canon Law will henceforth be revised by laymen as well as the clergy. Parliament has triumphed over Christ's Church! And Parliament is but the King's creature."

The Abbot paused and closed his eyes. There was a moment of profound silence. Then he continued.

"Archbishop Wareham presented the formal submission on the 15th of this very month. Sir Thomas More returned the Great Seal on the 16th. The King's mistress hates him and he can do no more. He sees what is happening and will have no part in it. It will cost him his head!"

"I think not!" John shook his head. "Thomas More has been the King's closest and best-loved friend since childhood. He cannot lose his head over this!"

"Wolsey was also the King's closest and most intimate friend, almost since childhood!"

The two men fell silent. John was much agitated. His generous and easy-going nature would always put the best interpretation upon affairs of state. King Harry was King of England! Could the King of England do such wrong? Hideous doubts assailed him and he felt threatened in the depths of his soul. It was as if Antichrist himself was abroad.

"What else of Convocation, then?"

John knew that the Abbot was not long since returned and more things than *Praemunire* had been discussed.

"Hugh Latimer recanted – again!" The Abbot laughed. His eyes twinkled. "He is a plausable rogue. Like Elihu the son of Barachel the Buzite, his wrath is kindled and he is full of matter!"

"I remember him! Rabid against the New Learning! Five minutes later he was full of it! A fine preacher with a wicked turn of phrase. People hang on his words. He was always in trouble when I knew him."

"He has been in trouble again, son John! But he has recanted again and he is restored again. Soon he will fly into more trouble, and then he will recant, find a suitable patron and get himself a Bishopric! After that, only God knows the story. I speculate no more."

The Abbot laughed.

"Come now, Master John! What about Hugh Latimer for Bishop of Worcester? He would have one advantage over Jerome de Ghinucci, our present Father-in-God; he would surely visit his Diocese, even if only once!"

"God forbid! Once would be too often!"

They both laughed heartily.

"Forgive me, John!"

The Abbot turned to him with a rueful smile.

"An Abbot is a lonely man and can seldom speak his mind freely. Enough of these dolours! Now tell me! How is sweet Kate? And young William? And little Miss Meg?"

The talk turned to family matters and the heaviness fell from both of them. And then there were some legal questions to be dealt with. It was a little before Compline that John ventured the question uppermost in his mind concerning the tiny Community at Dene Abbey.

"What of the church, Sir Abbot? What are your plans for putting the roof back on?"

The Abbot gave him a wry smile.

"I have no plans. None at all!"

John felt a curious sense of relief. It showed in his face. He raised an eyebrow at his host.

"John! We are better served for our prayers than we have ever been. I think we are closer to the mind of St Bernard too – and to the mind of Christ, I fancy. Our enforced simplicity reflects the poverty we profess. We have stalls enough for our present number and three to spare. We have an altar. What more do we need? No, dear John! I shall leave the new church to my successor – if I have a successor."

Their eyes met and the dread feeling of presentiment descended upon John Farelowe just as it had descended when he had first sighted the roofless church through the trees. He saw the same presentiment in the Abbot's eyes and he knew that the Abbot recognised it in his own.

Without a word the Abbot left his chair and searched among a pile of papers on a table. He found what he was looking for and returned to his chair. He gave John a look of the profoundest grief and began to read from the paper.

"At Rome, everything was bought and sold, so that benefices were given not for worth, but to the highest bidder ... and therefore when under the Old Covenant the priesthood was corrupted with venality, the three miracles ceased – namely the unquenchable fire of the priesthood, the sweet smell of sacrifice which offendeth not, the smoke which ever rises up – so I fear it will come to pass under the New Covenant, and methinks the danger stands daily knocking at the very doors of the Church."

"Who wrote that?"

John was smitten to the heart.

"Adam of Usk, in 1402. One hundred and thirty years ago!"

"What are we to do?"

"Pray without ceasing, as the holy Apostle said. Remember Sodom! Had there been but ten righteous men found in it ... I feel Judgement upon the Church, son John. We may yet live to see all that we love most dearly torn from us and burned before our very eyes."

"My father once told me to cling to Christ and to His Mass, and to our Lady Saint Mary and all the Saints, and to leave the rest to them as business 'tis."

"Do that and ye shall live! But whose business is it?"

"Is Antichrist abroad?"

"Oh yes! But which one is he? Or is he Legion? Resist not the evil, son John! Don't play Antichrist at his own game! Pray without ceasing and, who knows! God may repent Him of the evil, just as he did in olden times."

Abbot Thomas Ware stood up, and John did likewise. "Son John! I have a presentiment that I shall be the last Abbot of Flaxley and that I shall not be suffered to live out my days here. If that should come to pass, pray for me!"

The two men embraced each other. Tears were in the eyes of both of them.

"*Kyrie Eleison* is our prayer, John! And now Compline is upon us. And after that the Greater Silence, for which we may bless God!"

John took his leave and made his way through the guest chamber to the back of the temporary church. The Abbot met his brethren on *statio*, the little Community entered in procession and the Office of Compline was sung.

# CHAPTER ELEVEN

IT HAD BEEN a bad day! John Faversham sat at the wheel of his car, stationary in a traffic-jam. What the hell was going on up front! He turned on the car radio and immediately heavy static scratched and buzzed out whatever it was that Radio Three was attempting to offer. He flipped channels in irritation. Why the hell was it that only decent music seemed ever to be blared out by static? A young woman's voice broke upon him. She was delivering herself of a loud and tuneless caterwaul to the accompaniment of what it was now conventional to describe as a "backing." The "backing" was urgent and jangling and seemed unconnected, both as to time and as to tune, with the young woman in extremis. John flipped channels again.

A loud thudding assaulted his eardrums. He flipped again to hear an adenoidal young man prophesy heavy rain. He switched the damned thing off and sat, impotent, at the wheel of his stationary car, feeling himself diminishing relentlessly.

Depression crowded in upon John Faversham. He was fed up with work, he was fed up with driving a motor car, and he had become quite suddenly fed up with James Hasfield and the whole wretched business of "feelings" and "intuitions" that had so suddenly and uninvitedly broken in upon the secure little world that he had built up around himself.

John Faversham was beginning to feel very hard-done-by and not a little sorry for himself. Somewhere, towards the back of his mind, however, a part of himself was watching him and his depression, and it was grinning. The knowledge made him irritable. He turned on the radio again and the Six o'clock News assailed him with triumphalist politics. He switched it off in fury – and then he laughed. And at that moment the traffic began to move. Yes! He had been building up a secure little world around himself. He could no longer conceal that truth for now it was being assailed on more than one front at a time and, deep-down, John Faversham was beginning to feel more insecure than he had felt for as long as he could remember.

He couldn't wait to get home! He needed Jane! She was bossy, she was often difficult and sometimes she could be absolutely maddening, but he adored her and she was his security. He recognized it very clearly. John Faversham felt the need of a strong helping hand just now. It wasn't that anything very specific was threatening him – on any very specific front. But it had been a bad day on all kinds of levels and he felt thoroughly destabilised.

Maisemore! The bridge! Nearly home, thank God! John tried the car radio again and flipped back to Radio Three, his favourite and usual channel. A String Quartet was playing so relentlessly at odds with itself and so determinedly out of tune and tempo that it just had to be intentional! "Modern Music!" he sighed and, once again, turned the damned thing off.

Fairloe Court filled the windscreen. John felt better at once. His hostility towards James Hasfield evaporated. Jane – and something to eat – awaited him. Philomena would cover his business suit with affectionate cat hairs and all would soon – very soon – be right again with his little world. He scrambled wearily from the driving seat and reached for his briefcase.

"Darling! You look exhausted! Trouble at the office?"

"You might say so."

John embraced his wife. He felt better at once.

"Bloody awful day!" he said.

"Sit down beside Philomena and I'll make a nice cup of tea. The kettle's boiling. "Philomena!" Jane addressed the cat. "Make a fuss of Daddy. He's had a hell of a day at the office!" Philomena did not stir. She feigned unconcern but she allowed John to stroke her and she purred affectionately in return. John closed his eyes and he only opened them again at the sound of a teacup being rattled in front of his nose.

"Thanks darling."

"What was it all about this time?"

Jane could see strain all over John's face. It was very unlike him, he was usually very good at letting business stress flow off him like water off a duck's back. Not today. Something was worrying him.

"Do you want to live in Basingstoke?" he asked.

"Good God! You must be joking!"

Jane sat down suddenly on one of the kitchen chairs.

"They're not going to move you? They can't!"

John looked up at his wife and gave her a wan smile. "Oh! I don't suppose it will come to that, but Head Office is stirring things at the moment and all of a sudden nobody knows where they are. Everybody feels threatened, and the most unexpected people suddenly become nasty when they are threatened. Nothing is going right!"

He drained his cup and held it out for a refill.

"We are having far too much 'management' and not enough sound leadership these days. It does nothing for the morale of the chaps who are actually earning the money, I can tell you! We are doing very well just now, and we shall go on doing well as long as we are left to get on with it. Anything to eat?"

"We'll be eating in half an hour. But there is a bit of that fruit cake left."

Jane relented. This was not the time for wifely scolding. She rummaged among the cake tins and produced the end piece of a fruit cake. She filled John's cup again and she refilled her own. Basingstoke! She decided that if she ate half the remaining cake John would not be able to eat too much. She made her dispositions accordingly.

"Oh! I think we are probably safe enough," said a restored John. "It wouldn't be worth their while to move me now. What am I? Fifty-seven?

They might begin to phase me out in a year or two –you know, part-time. They call it Consultancy. I wouldn't mind that."

Tea, cake and Jane were restoring John Faversham. He found it in him to think beyond himself.

"Anything happen today?" he asked, almost brightly.

"Cecily phoned. She's off to Horsham, in a hurry."

"What is she sorting out now?"

Cecily spent quite a lot of her time with Barbara and Harold, and quite a lot of her still abundant energies went into unscrambling the effects of their excessive affluence and the clutch of essentially self-centred dispositions which they represented. At home she could be a drain on the resources of others; abroad she was magnificent!

"Tristram has been sent home from his public school."

"Expelled?" John's eyebrows were high on his head.

"I don't think it has come to that – yet! Cecily says they caught him smoking."

"Smoking what?"

"I think that's the trouble."

"Oh dear!"

John thought of his sister-in-law and her family. As relations he was honour-bound to love them, but he didn't like any of them very much. He felt sorry for Barbara and Harold, but he wasn't surprised. The boys were both thoroughly spoilt, arrogant and affected. But this was worrying. His dislikes faded with the awakening of compassion.

"Of course, we are not supposed to know!" Jane grinned.

"That is why Cecily phoned, of course!"

Barbara and Harold were an odd couple. Their first reaction would have been the maintenance of the image and the saving of face within the family. It would not have occurred to either of them that the immediate reaction of others might be compassion and a genuine concern rather than a smug and judgemental "I told you so!" John looked up at his wife. He had forgotten the office, Basingstoke and all the other nightmares of his day.

"Oh dear!" he said, again.

"You've just got time for a shower before we eat. Go on! You'll feel much fresher after that. And then I've had some thoughts about Hasfield. We'll talk about it later on."

"Hasfield!" John grunted. "I had almost chucked this Hasfield business altogether by the time I got home." He shrugged his shoulders and smiled wearily. "All right!"


"Darling!" John looked up at his wife from the depths of his arm-chair. Jane returned his glance and raised an eyebrow.

"Something doesn't add up. About Hasfield. It occurred to me while I was having my shower."

"What?"

"Hasfield died in 1894. According to George he was succeeded in the firm by his nephew. And the nephew was killed in the First World War. It doesn't add up."

"Why?"

Because to succeed his uncle as partner in a respected firm of solicitors he would have had to be – what? Thirty-ish? He might have been a year or two younger but hardly more."

"Well?"

Jane had a tendency towards the monosyllabic when challenged or dubious of an argument.

"The First World War didn't start for another twenty years. By 1914 he would have been too old for active service. I suppose he could have been killed by a Zeppelin!"

Jane laughed. "If I know Gloucester they would have a white marble statue in the Cathedral to any leading solicitor killed by a Zeppelin! Do you think George got his facts wrong?"

"No, I don't. The Georges of this world are seldom wrong on matters of fact. But he might not have all the facts. And he might not have thought it necessary to come out with all of them just then. I don't want to make a great thing of it with George. Not yet. We might ask the Law Society, but it would mean a trip to London."

"Where did Walter say the old parish registers are?"

"County Records Office."

Jane sat bolt upright and looked directly at John. It was plain to him that she had suddenly had a Bright Idea. He waited for it with a measure of apprehension. Jane's Bright Ideas usually involved him in extra work and endless complication. She was, after all, her mother's daughter!

"I'll spend the day there tomorrow. I'm not teaching."

John made a mental apology to his wife. Well, she was always catching him out, if not in one way then in another!

"Brilliant! We'll make a list of things to look up. What has stirred all this enthusiasm all of a sudden?"

"I spent a nice, relaxing afternoon reading Hasfield the other day. I've got rather fond of him, but there's something funny about it all. I just want to get to the bottom of it if I can."

John got up and collected a pad and a ballpoint pen from the little *escritoir* in the corner of the room. He sat down and wrote, repeating aloud as he did so:

"Fairloe Registers. Baptisms and burials relating to the house or to the Hasfields themselves." He looked up. "Where did they all come from? Any clue in the poems?"

"Forthampton. And Rebecca came from Chaceley, the next village." Jane giggled. "Do you know what he called her?"

John shook his head.

*"O Chaste of Chaceley!"*

"You're joking!" John chuckled. "Well, look up the Forthampton and Chaceley Registers too while you are at it. See how extensive a picture you can build up. Flirt with the County Archivist!"

Jane regarded her husband with a mixture of affection and resigned exasperation. She decided he needed teasing.

"Why did you never write poems to me when we were courting?" The tone was one of disappointment tinged with the slightest suggestion of reproach.

"I did."

"You never told me!"

Jane's teasing technique was immediately derailed. She was quite unprepared for this.

"I wrote one when we were first engaged. I like to think it is after Tennyson's *In Memoriam*. Only it is rather a long way after and there is only one verse. I recite it to myself quite often. I suppose Lucy would call it a *mantram*, it calms me down and brings me peace. Would you like to hear it?"

"Darling! After thirty years! Of course I would!"

John cleared his throat.

"Has anybody seen my darling Jane?
For I have hunted high and hunted low;
She promised to be here an hour ago.
She's late! Confound the wench! She's late again!"

There was a cry of "Oh!" from Jane. She leaped from her chair and rushed to her husband, flung her arms round his neck and kissed him.

"Darling!" she said.

She sat herself in John's lap and hugged him.

John laughed.

"Oh Chaste of Chaceley! The chump!"

# CHAPTER TWELVE

I F THE LIFE AND TIMES of King Henry VIII were ever to be given something by way of a tag, or sub-title, then a likely contender might be: "The Tale of Four Thomases."

It was the singular misfortune of four highly placed men, each bearing the name of the doubting Apostle, to be destroyed by their King. One was corrupted by him through human weakness thrust into impossible circumstances. Two revelled in their own corruption along with his. One retained his integrity. Two were judicially murdered by the King; one died of despair on his way to be so murdered and one survived to be the victim of an even more horrible judicial murder in a later reign.

One Thomas we have already disposed of. Thomas, Cardinal Wolsey, died at Leicester on his way to face trial and certain execution. But Wolsey had, some time previously, engaged his own namesake, one Thomas Crumwel, to be his own personal solicitor. This man had no formal legal qualifications whatsoever. He was the son of a Putney blacksmith. He had fought as a mercenary soldier in Italy and he had tried his hand at moneylending in London before coming to the notice of the opulent but already fading Cardinal. Tom Crumwel served his master as faithfully as the service of his own ambitions required. He accompanied the fallen star to York but then, like a rat leaving a sinking ship, he abandoned Wolsey and rode post haste to London, in his own phrase, "To make or mar!" Within a week he had secured a seat in the Parliament that had just assembled in the November of 1529. This he accomplished through the offices of an unsavoury but highly placed contact, Sir John Russell.

Russell then arranged for Tom Crumwel an interview with the King himself which the artful Tom put to the best possible use. Any man, whoever he might be, who could be of service in the resolution of the King's Matter was sure of the Royal favour, and to a very high degree.

"Why wait for the approbation of the Pope? Let the King follow the example of the German princes who had thrown off the yoke of the Pope. Let him, with the aid of Parliament, declare himself Head of the Church within his own realm. England was now a monster with two heads, but let the King assert the authority which was now usurped by the Pope and every difficulty would vanish. The clergy, holding their lives and goods at his disposal, would become *the obsequious ministers of his will!*" Such was the advice reputedly given by Tom Crumwel to his Monarch.

We have thus so far encountered two men called Thomas, both thoroughly corrupt and each revelling in his own corruption until the final nemesis. Another Thomas, as noble as the first two were ignoble, we shall encounter on a later page, together with the details of his martyrdom. It is now time to make the acquaintance of the fourth Thomas, in every respect the most tragic of them all, and perhaps, the most tragic personality of the whole of the period of the English Reformation.

Three years before Walter de Furlowe met and married his second wife, Meg, there was born, to Master and Mistress Cranmer of Asclaton in Nottinghamshire, a son. The boy was baptised in the name of the Apostle Thomas. His parents being of yeoman stock and of no great means, young Tom was educated very much as his younger contemporary, John Farelowe, was later to be educated. There were eleven years in age between them.

John was to go on to Oxford but Tom went to Cambridge, to St John's College, where he proved to be a more than usually gifted scholar.

At some stage during his young life Tom fell in love and married but, like Walter de Furlowe, he must have been widowed soon afterwards for he was elected to a Fellowship of his College, open only to celibates, and presupposing Holy Orders.

Tom Cranmer was ordained Priest in 1523 at the age of thirty-four. There, at Cambridge, he might well have remained as an obscure Don had he not made a chance remark to two of the King's advisers in that fateful year of 1529. Thomas had casually suggested that the King's Matter be referred to the great Universities for opinion, not only in England but on the Continent as well. A typically academic remark by a typical academic, remote from the scene of action, had an astonishing effect upon a King who was by this time angrily clutching at any possible straw. Tom was arbitrarily plucked from his comfortable chambers and press-ganged into the King's personal service. A strange but tragic irony then manifested itself. The monstrous King Harry developed a genuine fondness for this startled and apprehensive academic. It was reciprocated by a naturally fearful personality who, on the one hand knew that his life depended upon the Royal favour but who, on the other hand, had developed a genuine priestly compassion for the tormented man behind the monster.

And so it came to pass that Tom was sent by the King on an embassy to none other than the Holy Roman Emperor himself. This, and matters related to it, kept him out of England for some years and he used the opportunity to get to know, and to learn the minds of, a number of the leading Continental Reformers, among them the Lutheran Andreas Osiander who profoundly challenged and impressed him. Tom Cranmer was by now half-way to becoming a Lutheran himself.

Andreas and his associates may have been a powerful influence on Tom but there was one who influenced him more. This was Margaret Osiander, Andreas' niece. Tom Cranmer had fallen head over heels in love!

He was a long way from England. The vows of clerical celibacy had long been honoured as much in the breach as in the observance and Tom was a man who, if he was to break a vow, would do it properly! He would not dishonour his Margaret by taking her as his mistress. No! He would marry her! And so, in some secrecy, he did marry her, in that very year of 1533 in which John Farelowe rode to Flaxley with his premonition of doom, and the very year when, having submitted to the King, the clergy of England unwittingly made themselves the obsequious ministers of the Royal will. Tom was forty-three when he married for the second time. Margaret was quite a lot younger.

"What of the Court, You ask?"

Tom Campion looked across the fireside at John and Kate. The three of them were in the lower room of the old house, beside the great chimneypiece. A pile of logs was blazing merrily on the hearth. They had dined in the hall but now they were alone and free to talk, and it was clear that Tom had a great deal on his mind.

"Well! Treat what I have to say as the deadliest of secrets. It will kill the three of us if it gets abroad. Do I speak or not?"

He looked at John, and then at Kate. He trusted them absolutely and they him. John looked at his wife.

"Say on!" she said.

"We have a bigamist as our King!"

Tom paused, partly for effect, for he knew how to tell a tale, but partly also with the relief of having lanced a boil within him.

"A bigamist ... ?" John was puzzled.

"Yes! He married his mistress secretly, not long since, and now he is a man with two wives. And him Defender of the Faith!"

"But how?" Kate was nonplussed. The thing was impossible. It could not be done. No priest ...

"Some creature among the clergy did the thing – for fear of his head no doubt. There are whispers, but no more. The thing is so deadly a secret that all are in it! The Court is full of whispers. Why else would I chose a Gloucestershire Lent rather than the roisterous formalities of Hampton Court?"

"Does Wareham know? The Archbishop?"

John's mind was trying to cope with the implications of Tom's revelation but it was having little success.

"I doubt it. Wareham is a dying man. He is as near ninety as eighty, so they say. He will not last the year. He is a worried man too, and uttering great warnings and prophesies of doom. But I fear he is too late."

"What does the King think he is doing?" Kate was puzzled, and she was angry at the same time. Fornication was one thing – adultery was one thing – men and women were sinners when all was said and done; but bigamy! This shifted the very foundations!

"The King is doing his own will, as he always has done. He knows no higher law. He is the law! He is also Head of the English Church and Clergy!"

"So far as the law of Christ doth allow!"

100

John's interjection was emphatic, but it was also anxious, puzzled, uncertain.

Tom raised his eyebrows and shrugged his shoulders.

"He made his leman Anne Boleyn Marchioness of Pembroke before he did the deed. He filched one thousand pounds a year from the revenues of the Bishop of Durham and settled it upon her. Oh! A very pretty little Marchioness it made her too!"

John and Kate looked at each other and shook their heads, almost in disbelief. A darkness settled on their spirits.

"How will it end?" asked Kate.

"God knows!"

Tom shook his head and looked from one face to another.

"I've no right to burden you with all this. To know is to be in danger! But what are friends for? I have no illusions about Court or about affairs of state – or about the men who go about them. I thought I was as hardened a cynic as could be found the length and breadth of England. God knows, I'm no saint! But this frightens me. I don't know why it frightens me, but it does."

"It shakes the foundations," said Kate.

"Tom! Why do you stay at Court at all! Why don't you get as far away from it as you can. Pack up, man! Do something else with your life – while you have the chance!"

John was filled with a mixture of revulsion and fear for his friend's integrity – even his very life.

Tom smiled and shook his head.

"No, John! Court is the place where I belong. I know it, I am apart from all its factions, and known to be apart. I threaten no man and am respected – in a small way – by most." He gave a rueful smile. "I did not even trouble them by pursuing my own leman through their ranks when she began to extend her favours!"

"Oh Tom! I'm sorry!" Kate had never met Tom's saucy mistress and she did not approve of such long-term, loosely connected arrangements as an alternative to Holy Matrimony, but hers was a compassionate heart.

Tom smiled at her. There was sadness in his eyes.

"I'm as monkish as dear Edmund these days!" he said. "I go in mortal terror of the pox! It rampages through the Court, and the King and his courtiers spread it about with wild abandon!"

"Then it's true about the King, then?"

"I think so, John! The pox changes men's characters. Something does. I see it all the time. The Court is grown even more coarse, even more gross, even more treacherous. And it degenerates by the day! I'll say no more! I dare not!"

"Marry a wife, Tom." Kate looked at him with great compassion. She was very fond of him, and of all John's friends.

"Would you live with your wife at the King's Court, John?"

Both men shook their heads.

"No, sweet Kate! Not yet. Perhaps never. I tire of all this bedlarking and alcove-chasing! I'll join dear Edmund in his monastery!"

"Who is to succeed Wareham at Canterbury, Tom?"

John changed the subject. But the new subject seemed little better than the last if a bigamist – and thus an apostate and an excommunicate – was to choose a new Archbishop of Canterbury for the Pope's approval.

"Only God knows! But King Harry will choose one whom he can bend to his will. A pliant and obsequious prelate! A cypher!"


Not every man who has greatness thrust upon him is appreciative of it. Nothing could have caused Tom Cranmer more agitation and dismay than the news that broke upon him a year after his illicit marriage to Margaret Osiander. By command of the King, he was to succeed William Wareham as Archbishop of Canterbury! His protestations of unworthiness and incompetence fell on deaf ears. The King knew his man! He knew that it would be the simplest of matters to bend the compliant and timid Thomas Cranmer to his will.

The Pope was bombarded with demands and threats. Were the Bull authorising Cranmer's consecration not forthcoming, then certain monies due to the Papacy would not be forthcoming either. As soon as the Bull was received, the monies were put into the King's own pocket! So had Popes and Kings of England come to respect and to deal with each other.

The Cranmers returned, reluctantly, to England. Margaret Cranmer was immediately at pains to conceal her true status. As mistress to the Archbishop she would be unlikely to cause dangerous eyebrows to be raised. As his wife … !

Thomas himself must surely have been the most unwilling candidate ever to be presented for consecration to the Episcopate. He entered upon his high office at the age of 44. He was thereby exalted above the entire bench of Bishops, among whom he had never sat, and among whom were several men of greater ability, greater moral courage and possessed of far more coherently held convictions. Poor Tom was a threatened man throughout his Primacy. He was threatened by the King, threatened by his fellow Bishops, threatened by Traditionalists and threatened by the more extreme of the Reformers. He was a man who, freed from his threats, displayed great hospitality, considerable kindness and a notable charm. To those who excited his fears, however, he showed all the vindictiveness of the insecure. It was his perpetual fearfulness that developed in him a conviction that was to become as unalterable as it was essentially unfaithful: in ecclesiastical matters the State must always be supreme over the Church.

It was this one morbid principle, to which he clung ferociously, that allowed the remainder of his principles to manifest a sometimes astonishing degree of flexibility.

Tom Cranmer never wanted to be Archbishop of Canterbury. He begged to be passed over, he knew himself unequal to the task, and it was his tragedy to be thus frog-marched into office. Once enthroned, however, he entered into his responsibilities with both scholarship and vigour. He maintained discreet contacts with his Lutheran friends and continued to absorb much from them. In the back of his mind, probably from the very first, lay the beginnings of the reforms that he would introduce into the English Church, one day, if ever he was given the chance to do so.

Thomas Cranmer's first task, however, concerned the resolution of the King's Matter. He convened his own Court and tried the case himself. Not surprisingly he found in the King's favour. He was not alone in his view. University opinion had inclined in this direction as had a number of thoroughgoing traditionalists, including one Stephen Gardner, soon to be his most relentless adversary. The King's marriage with Catherine of Aragon was not lawful, ruled the new Archbishop. Nor had it ever been lawful for a man to marry the widow of his own brother. The marriage had been forced upon the King by his own father's wish, enabled by a Papal dispensation that should neither have been given nor applied for. The marriage was therefore null and void and the 23-year-old Lady Mary, daughter of this marriage-that-never-was, was solemnly declared a bastard.

The unseated Queen Catherine and her unhappy daughter were thereafter treated with a barbarity which shocked Europe. The following year, as if to add insult to injury, the suddenly bastardised Lady Mary was made nursery-governess to her infant step-sister Elizabeth.

That same Lady Mary, strange, brooding and deeply pious, a character fully as tragic as Cranmer himself, was in later years to show her episcopal tormentor great mercy and forgiveness in matters touching herself. She was to show him none at all in matters touching the Church and what she perceived as the fullness of its Faith.

# CHAPTER THIRTEEN

"**D**ARLING! This coffee is terribly strong! You're always so mean with the milk!"

Jane scowled into her cup, reached for the milk jug and attended to what John called the "fine tuning" of her coffee. It was an exercise of the utmost exactitude and it fascinated him.

There was a period of silent savouring and contemplation. The sun suddenly broke through upon the breakfast table. Jane's coffee was to her liking. John decided that it was his turn.

"Darling! Don't you think you might be going just a little bit over the top?"

John felt daunted by the array of new and curious substances, arrayed upon the breakfast table, with which Jane seemed determined to dose both herself and him.

He knew what must have happened. She had bought, and eagerly devoured, another of those little books on sale at the Health Food Shop. They were there, he was quite persuaded, in order to make one feel unhealthy and threatened, and thus all the more vulnerable to all the tubs, pots and potions displayed upon the shelves. Aunt Sarah was deeply into all this kind of thing. So was the Earth-Mother. Neither of them looked at all bad on it, John had to admit. And it wasn't doing any harm to Jane either. But John's home-life seemed to have been dominated by women ever since Steve left home and he sometimes felt outnumbered. A mild protest, once in a while, helped to keep his end up.

"Its good for you!"

Jane's tone was maternal and more than somewhat emphatic.

John felt like a small boy being given a lecture by Mummy.

"It helps to convert all the wrong sorts of fat into energy and it reduces the chance of coronary heart disease." She gave him a look which started chest pains in him at once. Pure suggestion of course. He shook them off.

"Why don't you try it, darling? I'm concerned about you!"

John's heart sank. If he refused outright he risked what the political commentators called a damaging confrontation. Jane could be highly confrontational at the breakfast table. He sighed inwardly, smiled at her, and nodded.

With a sweet smile of triumph Jane prepared a second bowl of her currently favoured muesli, sprinkled a teaspoonful of yellowish granules over it and set it before her husband. The naughty little boy had relented and was going to be good!

John regarded his muesli with an extraordinary feeling of distaste which stopped just short of actual revulsion. Now he knew what it was like to be a small boy in a Dickensian workhouse. Jane watched his every spoonful until it was all gone and the bowl was empty.

"Well?" she enquired.

"Wood chippings, monkey nuts and soft sand. I'll stick to toast and marmalade and die happy."

"You must have your zinc!"

Jane passed across to him a greyish pill in the bowl of a teaspoon.

John received it with raised eyebrows.

"You're bound to be deficient in zinc at your age. Now your Vitamin E!"

Another capsule came across to him in the bowl of the teaspoon.

It was gold in colour and seemed to be made of plastic.

"What's it for?"

He swallowed it obediently. This breakfast-time was Jane's turn. His turn would come tomorrow. Things usually worked out like that.

"It slows up the aging process."

John knew what was going on. Jane had woken up full of vigour and enthusiasm. In an hour or two she would hit the County Records Office like a whirlwind. He hoped they were up to it. John wished he could be a fly on the wall. It would be a lot more fun than driving to Birmingham for a Conference ...

John suddenly realised that he was not looking forward to going to work. This was a new and disturbing development and he didn't like it at all. He had derived immense satisfaction in his job for thirty years, but now ... ? For a horrid moment he found himself wondering why he had ever bothered!

"What's the matter, darling?"

Jane was looking at him with an anxious look on her face.

"Give me another Vitamin E. I'm feeling old this morning!"

"You're overdoing it, you know! You've been looking dreadfully tired for weeks. Could you take early retirement? Why don't you ask somebody? I'm worried about you."

"Early retirement? At fifty-seven? No, I'm not much looking forward to a boring day with Phillipson in Birmingham. It's as simple as that!"

He rose from his chair, picked up the coffee pot and the milk jug and, with great care, filled his wife's cup.

"Oh darling! No! You're always so heavy-handed with the milk!"

"I'll leave the fine tuning to you, darling!"

With an interlude of sipping, face-making, topping-up and savouring, the sun broke through again. Jane's coffee was once more to her liking.

"Darling! I'm going on to Aunt Sarah's after the Records Office. Could you come on there after Birmingham? It means coming home in two cars but I don't see the alternative."

John nodded, pushed his chair back and got up from the breakfast table.

"I'd better be off. I'll see you at Sarah's at about six. Earlier if I can finish with Phillipson in time. Good Hunting!"

He kissed his wife.

"Be a good girl, Sweetheart!"

This final exortation was addressed to the cat.

There was plenty of time. John didn't have to meet up with Phillipson until ten-thirty.

He backed his car out of the garage, rounded the front of the house and then nosed forward out of the drive, on to the lane leading up to the main road. The quickest way to Birmingham was by the motorway. That meant either braving the maelstrom around Gloucester or driving up towards Tewkesbury, turning for Cheltenham at Coombe Hill, and picking up the motorway at Junction 11. Plain sailing after that. Crowded and hair-raising, but plain sailing for all that. He would be at Brum in an hour. What for? It was half-past eight! He might as well enjoy the drive while he was at it.

John turned left up the A41 and headed due North. He liked this road. He loved this part of Gloucestershire, West of the river Severn, almost best of all. He glanced to his left and saw the great whale back of May Hill, crowned with its clump of trees, greeting him from some seven or eight miles away to the South-West.

"Dear old May Hill!"

John felt himself properly orientated and secure within himself every time he saw May Hill. He and Jane would climb it at least once a month, hooking round the back up Yartleton Lane, parking by the National Trust sign and labouring up through the woods, up on to the bare hillside and steeply up, through the gorse, on to the great whale-back and into the old plantation with its breathtaking views and its quite extraordinary peace.

They would usually find time for a pint of beer in the "Glasshouse," at the foot of the hill, on the way home too.

"Dear old May Hill!"

John had left Hartpury behind him now and he would soon have to make a decision. Should he go straight on, through Sniggs End and Pendock? What for? No! He would take the right fork through Corse Lawn, turn towards Tewkesbury at the cross-roads beyond Forthampton, cross the Severn by Telford's bridge and go up through the Mythe and Shuthongar. He would join the M50 from there, a mile and a half before it joined the M5 at Strensham. Forthampton! That was where Hasfield had come from. And Chaceley was just short of it, off down to the right of the road he was now turning into. Should he make a diversion … ? What for? No! Jane would come back from the Records Office with something this evening. Time for diversions later – if there was anything to divert for.

Damn! He had to meet up with her at Aunt Sarah's! He must remember not to forget. That would mess the evening up well and truly. They would probably eat there and they wouldn't get away before nine! And Jane would carry on alarming about drinking and driving, and they would go home in two cars.

It wasn't that John objected to going to Aunt Sarah's. He was very fond of her and enjoyed her company. But he had made other plans for this evening. It never occurred to Jane to ask him if he had other plans … It never, ever, occurred to her to ask! He had planned to strip down the motor mower, including its engine, and give the whole thing a thorough overhaul. It was the engine in particular – and the carburettor and all its linkage – that needed attention. Why they always put such flimsy bits and pieces into machinery that was bound to do such heavy duty he had never managed to fathom. Motor mower carburettors, in his experience, were almost universally unsatisfactory. He had hopes of being able to make some sensible modifications. There were always design faults …

He was at the cross-roads. He could go straight on, through Upton upon Severn. But was there a way on to the motorway from Upton? He turned right, after all, towards Tewkesbury and the Mythe Bridge. The mower would have to wait until Saturday morning. Jane would be safely out of the house, plunged happily into the thick of Sainsbury's. John felt a sense of relief. It was always much easier to get on with a job with Jane out of the house. There would be no interruptions with tins that wouldn't open, jars whose tops wouldn't screw off, vacuum cleaners that wouldn't work properly and things at the other end of the house that had, most urgently, to be shifted because they were too heavy for her to move.

Jane never interrupted of course. Because when she interrupted it wasn't interruption. And nothing *he* was doing could possibly be of the slightest consequence anyway. Men were always little boys, playing with their toys! Except when *she* wanted something done, and then it had to be done instantly – with arbitrary modifications, possible or impossible!

Tewkesbury, the Abbey, the flower mill and, closer to hand, the water-works, lay to John's right. He crossed the Severn by Telford's bridge, watched for a gap in the traffic and turned left up the hill to the Mythe.

Wasn't this where woad still grew? The stuff the Ancient Britons painted themselves with? John couldn't remember. Big, expensive houses lay to either side. The road would emerge from the trees in a moment, turn right at Shuthongar Manor and run rather messily up to the M50. He would be in Birmingham far too early, but that was better than being far too late.

Why was it, John wondered, that wives suddenly turned their husbands into small children as soon as the real children left the nest? Jane had always been bossy, but ever since Steve and Rosemary had left home it had been getting a bit much! He supposed that twenty-odd years of incessant correction, incessant instruction, incessant everything that goes with kids from the age of nought, established a pattern and the poor girl couldn't stop! Jane supervised him in every minute particular. Fortunately he took no notice most of the time, but sometimes he wondered if she had the slightest idea what she was doing. Or what the implications must be if this was anything other than conditioned reflex following twenty years of necessary incessance? Did she really consider him a helpless infant, he asked himself? Was he?

John turned round and up on to the M50. It was a pretty little motorway. But a mile and a half ahead it would run into the M5 and then, at this time of day, his wits would have to be about him and he would need eyes all round his head.

"Darling! You're early!"

Jane looked up, startled, from the depths of one of Aunt Sarah's armchairs. John came into the room, crossed over and kissed her. "Good day at the office?"

John nodded. He put his briefcase on the settee and sat down beside it. There was a rattle of cups and saucers from the kitchen. Aunt Sarah was busy making tea.

"For the first time in his life Phillipson didn't hold the job up. We got through in no time. Very satisfactory! I think the firm is going to make a tidy sum on that job – and I think they'll have me to thank for it. They won't thank me of course!"

John sat back and smiled. It was, Jane noticed, his well-fed-cat smile. It had obviously been a very good day. She felt a sense of relief; he had not seemed to have been having good days for a very long time.

"Any luck at the Records Office?"

Jane nodded. Her eyes sparkled. John knew at once that revelations would be forthcoming. He raised his eyebrows at her.

"I'll tell you over tea, when Sarah's back. I was just about to tell her when you arrived. Yes! I had a thoroughly good day too. Oh! And I bought myself a new dress on the strength of it. I'll put it on later. And a nice pullover! I found the pullover in the Charity Shop. You won't believe what I paid for it!"

There was a scrabbling at the door. John jumped up and opened it for Aunt Sarah. She was laden with an over-full tray from which cups, cakes and buttered scones were threatening to cascade at any moment.

There was a rapid exchange of comments, counter comments, apologetics and commentary by the two women as the tea-tray was stabilised on an occasional table and its contents redistributed about the room.

It was maintained, loudly and at length, that she really shouldn't have … that they couldn't possibly eat all that … that they really didn't need a cup of tea at all. That they really ought to be going home, and that she, their hostess, was terribly naughty going to all that trouble for them.

It was counter-protested, at equal length, that of course she would! That it was nothing at all! That poor John was starving and that she was just going to make a cup of tea anyway.

John was content to remain silent throughout the measure of this ritual dance. He helped himself to two thickly buttered scones, dripping with raspberry jam, accepted a cup of tea with thanks and smiled beatifically, and perhaps a little defiantly, at his wife.

"You've been to the Records Office!" Aunt Sarah's voice was breathless with animation.

"Yes!" Jane affected the studied nonchalance which, as John well knew, indicated a notable triumph. "I really got on quite well!" She took an elegant sip of tea, sat back and waited to be coaxed. She gave her husband a coy glance. Never, he thought, had she so resembled Philomena.

"What did you come up with, darling?"

"They were perfectly sweet. And they were so helpful. They seemed almost as interested as I was, and they kept on giving me cups of tea. They couldn't have been nicer! And – oh yes! – the loo was quite presentable as well!"

"All that tea!" Aunt Sarah began to giggle.

John said nothing. He knew it would be quicker that way.

"Well, James Hasfield was born in Forthampton, just as we thought…"

"Forthampton? Wasn't old Thingummy Vicar of Forthampton at one time? Oh! I'm sorry! Do go on."

Aunt Sarah reined in her interjection.

"Yes, Forthampton. And his father was Arthur Hasfield, and his mother was Matilda Turley, the sister of Benjamin Turley, his father's partner."

"Turley and 'asfield, Solicitors!"

John remembered George's verbal print-out.

"Arthur and Matilda had three children. James was born in 1829 …" Jane rummaged in her handbag for a notebook, opened it and refreshed her memory. "Matilda in 1833 and Charles in 1837."

"Anything on the Chaste of Chaceley?"

"Yes!" Jane consulted her notebook again. "Rebecca Jameson, born 1837, married James Hasfield in Chaceley Church in 1859. They must have come to live in our house almost straight away because a little boy, Arthur, was baptised at Fairloe in 1860 and buried the same year. And a little girl, Matilda, was baptised in 1862 and buried in 1864. Isn't it dreadfully sad!"

"George said they had no children." John was frowning.

"The Georges of this world don't count the ones who die in infancy," said Aunt Sarah, "unless they are their own, of course, but even then you don't always hear about them. I expect he meant they had no surviving children."

"Anything about the firm itself?"

Jane turned the pages of her notebook.

"Yes. There are all sorts of old directories and things and when they knew I was really interested a nice man spent ages fishing out all kinds of references for me. He knew where to look of course." She took a sip of tea and a bite out of a large scone, very liberally covered in jam. There was an intermission while she found a tissue with which to wipe her fingers and her countenance. A discussion followed as to the possible effects of raspberry jam upon her makeup. At length she resumed.

"Charles was a partner with big brother James. He seems to have vanished from the scene in about 1905. It was his son John who was the favourite nephew that George was talking about."

"And he was killed in 1915," said John. "End of story!" As he said it, John spotted a look on Jane's face which told him that it was far from being the end of the story.

"There is such a nice man at the Records Office," purred Jane. "I think he rather fancied me! Anyway – it seems that James Hasfield was a bit of a local historian and a naturalist. He wrote two books." Jane consulted her notebook and squinted at her own handwriting.

She looked up.

"*Flora and Fauna of the Royal Forest of Dean*, and another one. *A Memorial of the Hereford and Gloucester Canal*. They were both privately published. They are in the County Library somewhere."

John remembered another quotation from old George. "'im wrote books and things! George obviously didn't know about the poetry."

"I told the nice man at the Records Office that we had the *Poetical Works* and he was terribly interested. He didn't seem to know of it. But the real discovery came at the very end!"

John and Aunt Sarah both pricked up their ears and looked eagerly at Jane. They seemed to her like two little dogs who had just heard the magic word: "walkies!"

"Hasfield's nephew had planned to publish his uncle's "Remains". You know; letters, last poems and things, with a Memoir. They used to do things like that once upon a time. He never got round to it and all the papers were left with his daughter Katherine. She lived in Cheltenham, quite near Montpellier. She died last year and all the papers have come to the Records Office! They are sorting through them now."

Jane sat back in triumph.

"That calls for a gin!"

Aunt Sarah sprang to her feet, but noticing the hesitation on Jane's face, she added:

"A very little gin! I know you're both driving. I won't put you anywhere near The Limit! Just a sniff!"

"Just a sniff, then. All tonic and just a taste!"

Jane turned to her husband.

"And who's a clever girl, then?" she said.

# CHAPTER FOURTEEN

JOHN FARELOWE had incurred Kate's extreme displeasure. He had paid homage to the King and to his Queen Anne, and he could not for the life of him remember what the Queen had worn. King Harry had come to Gloucester with a great entourage, to receive the homage of its leading citizens and to be given presents of money towards the expense of maintaining his Court. The well established and respected young lawyer had been among those presented. John had been presented before, at Westminster, some twelve years earlier. Then he had met a powerful, commanding young man who had been possessed of great charm. John had been much taken by this talented patron of music and the arts. He had been somewhat less impressed by his Court, but the King himself had seemed everything that a King of England should be.

Now, in 1535, in his own Gloucester, John could scarcely believe the evidence of his own eyes. Here was a monster of a man, bloated, gross, ill-visaged and with eyes as baleful as he had ever seen. His homage was received with a contemptuous indifference, the chill of which was palpable. The King had clearly not remembered John Farelowe and of that John was right glad. He had no desire to be noticed – still less remembered – by those eyes.

Queen Anne, enthroned beside her Royal Master, had appeared to John as a most attractive young woman, small-boned and exquisite. Hers was an expensive, courtly style of beauty which did not appeal to him, but beautiful she undoubtedly was. She was most lavishly attired and adorned, but for all that there was something tragic about her which touched his heart.

No doubt Anne Boleyn had schemed and manoeuvred unashamedly to supplant her own sister as the King's mistress and to supplant Queen Catherine in her turn. No doubt she had achieved her ambition, but her eyes were not those of a happy woman. With such a husband, surely, John thought, her days must be spent on the edge of terror and her nights on the very threshold of revulsion! It was the look in the King's eyes, however, that had blotted out of John's remembrance all the niceties that Kate was waiting, urgently, to hear about. It proved very difficult to make her understand why that should be so.

The year 1535 was to prove one of unwelcome shocks for John and Kate Farelowe. There were no personal or family tragedies, indeed it was, in many respects, a good year for the family and for their modest estates. But there was a sense of unease that grew with every month that passed. After the encounter with King Harry, the next shock proved to be the enthronement of a new Bishop for the Diocese of Worcester in which the whole of Gloucestershire then lay.

The new Bishop was none other than that very Hugh Latimer of whom the Abbot of Flaxley had jested, a very few summers before. The Abbot's joke had proved to be unexpectedly prophetic.

"Well, John! At least he is an Englishman!"

Kate could not, for the moment, share her husband's sense of outrage. John responded with a snort of contempt.

"I have met him! I have heard him! He undermines everything he can – without actually losing his head in the process. Oh yes! And when he goes too far and is charged for it he grovels and recants! And then he creeps back into favour again."

"But John! There must be some good in the man. Is the King so befuddled as to appoint a fool to Worcester?"

"There is nothing befuddled about King Harry, Kate! His eyes are the eyes of a snake. He knows exactly what he is about and that is what frightens me. He knew what he was doing when he appointed Latimer. But I wish I knew what he was doing!"

"Now calm yourself, John! And tell me, quietly and calmly, what is wrong with our new Father-in-God. Heaven knows! The last one was no use at all. He never left his native Italy to come to Worcester. Master Latimer *must* be an improvement on that!"

John sighed and sat back on his stool by the fire. Then he leaned forward, hands on knees, and stared into it. Then he looked up at Kate and smiled at her. How could he not smile at her? She was beautiful, and as beautiful within as without. She was his whole life and his whole security, he adored her.

"Hugh Latimer is a remarkable preacher with a wonderful turn of phrase. People hang on his words. He knows it and I fancy it goes to his head. But he is destructive. He has about him something of the Lollard. He is a Gospeller at heart."

"But is that so bad, John? Won't the responsibility of his office make a sober man of him? Might he not grow into it?"

John shook his head. "He might. I pray that he does, but I doubt it. He is restless, unstable. I wonder how much of the True Faith he really holds and believes in. He is all for the New Learning and is heavily tarred with the Reformer's brush. But he will not build; Hugh Latimer is not a builder. He can only destroy."

"You will not send William to the Cathedral School at Worcester, then?"

Kate decided to tease John out of his dolours. His response was to spit in the fire. But then he laughed.

"No, sweet Kate! William shall go to Glastonbury at Michaelmas, just like his own father did."

Young Will was just turned eight. He knew smatterings of Latin, enough to answer the Mass and he could make sense of the words he was uttering too. Hugh Whiting, John's kinsman and his old schoolmaster, was now Abbot of Glastonbury, just as the old guestmaster had once prophesied. The Abbot was an old man now, but the school was flourishing and no alternative had ever been contemplated as the place for the boy's education.

Kate's thoughts came back to the Bishopric of Worcester and the curiosities surrounding it.

"The Italian fellow – the one Parliament has just deposed – 'tis said King Harry himself recommended him to the Pope for a Cardinal's hat. He must have been an admirable Bishop, never being in his diocese!"

John became agitated. His face reddened.

"Parliament has no right whatever to depose a Bishop!" He glanced, almost furtively, at the door to the hall. It was never safe to voice opinions unfavourable to Parliament, even in one's own house. For Parliament was the King's creature and its doings were the King's will, whatever huffings and puffings it might make in the process.

If the truth were to be told, John was a very unhappy man as far as matters of Church and State were concerned. The Supreme Head of the English Church and its Clergy had just appointed himself a Vicar-General, just as if he, King Harry, were the Pope! And he had chosen for this august responsibility a layman; none other than that son of a Putney blacksmith, Thomas Crumwel. And Tom Crumwel was set to order the affairs of the English Church over the head of its Convocations and in complete contempt of Thomas Cranmer, Archbishop of Canterbury.

"Parliament has no right whatever to depose a Bishop. The making and breaking of Bishops is not Parliament's business and never has been." John spoke urgently, with lowered voice. "The very law itself is degenerating into the King's whim. But what is to be done...?" He shrugged his shoulders and looked at his feet.

"Never mind, dear John! Even the King can't live for ever. The pox will carry him off before long!"

Kate added a few more stitches to her work. Poor John! He got so worked up about things he could do nothing about. It was better to just get on with life and cope with things as they happened. She gave her gloomy husband one of her prettiest smiles.

"And no son yet to succeed him!" He growled.

John's gloom was unrelieved. Queen Anne had presented the King with another daughter not long since, but a recent letter from Tom had hinted at miscarriages. It had also hinted at something even worse: the King was beginning to tire of his beautiful new Queen! Tom was a master at coded messages, nobody else would have guessed his meaning, but John knew full well what the apparently inconsequential hunting references were meant to convey. Tom would be in Gloucestershire soon and they would be brought up to date with affairs, but deep within himself John Farelowe knew that something was rotting at the very heart of England and tiny seeds of despair were beginning to sprout in the depths of his own soul.

Tom Campion's brief visit, at the beginning of August, added fresh burdens to John Farelowe's troubled mind. Tom was depressed and disillusioned. He, the cynical hanger-on at King Harry's Court all these years, now confessed himself disillusioned! John might have made sport about it, but there was no sport in him, for the two best men in England had just lost their heads and one of them, Sir Thomas More, had been a friend and a kindly patron to Tom Campion.

"Antichrist is stalking abroad, John! Men are being burned and quartered all over England. No man dare speak his mind for fear someone hear him. The King is hanging priests in their cassocks and monks in their habits! When was that ever done in a Christian country? Answer me that!"

"So Christ's Holy Order is hanged with the man?"

John would have flatly disbelieved such a report, had it come from any lips than those of his friend. Since time immemorial, if ever a cleric deserved death, he had been degraded from Holy Orders and dressed in lay attire before his execution. It was unthinkable …

"And Parliament extends the definition of High Treason practically every day, John! No man knows how to be safe from it. The courts of law are the King's creature as much as Parliament. Should the judges not condemn, they would face the axe within a week."

"But Tom! On what grounds did the King have More and Fisher condemned? How far did Parliament have to redefine High Treason to catch them?"

"Depriving the King of his rightful titles, John. Its High Treason now! They could not allow that he was Supreme Head of the English Church and Clergy. And for that, they were slaughtered like two bullocks at the butchers!"

"But that isn't all the definition, Tom. It has a proviso; So far as the law of Christ doth allow. That must surely have saved their consciences?"

"It wasn't enough, John. They didn't think the law of Christ could allow it in any circumstances. Its good enough for me and for most men, clerical or lay. It is but a jumble of words when all is said and done. But they preferred to lose their heads than risk losing their integrity. Little Queen Anne was delighted to see the end of both of them! She may be pretty but she is a scheming little bitch, and dangerous with it!"

"Get away from Court, Tom! Get away while you still can. I fear for you!"

Tom shook his head.

"No, John. I belong there. I belong there more than ever now, and I'll tell you why."

John looked at his friend's haggard face. The reliving of the past couple of months had aged him in an hour.

"Why, then? What can you achieve there – other than your own destruction?"

"John! Someone has got to love them all! Someone has got to pray for them! Someone has got to pick up the pieces, open a door here and there, bear the whole monstrous burden on his heart. It's what I'm for, John! Edmund is the monk in the monastery, praying for the world. I'm the monk, hidden in the depths of the world's corruption, unsuspected! And if I lose my head one day – what matter!"

John Farelowe crossed the room and embraced his friend. He could not speak.

It was mid-September and time for young Will to leave home and ride with his father to Glastonbury. There he must begin an education to bring him to manhood with the equipment that the modern world, with its explosion of New Learning, must increasingly demand of him. And John was anxious to reproduce for his son, as nearly as possible, the experience of his own first ride to Glastonbury, the magic of which had stayed with him ever since.

Harry, the Parish Clerk, asked leave of absence from Sir Ralph and would accompany them, just as he had accompanied John and his father, twenty-seven years before.

John and Harry relived the past as nearly as they could. They rode through Gloucester, pointing out everything old Walter had pointed out to the young John. They identified every church on the Bristol road. They rode up into the hills to Wotton and turned again South to arrive at last at the fine gatehouse of the Cistercian Abbey of the Blessed Virgin Mary at King's Wood where they received a kindly welcome and lodgings for the night.

It had been a joyful ride, Will had stood up well to it and they were in fine spirits. The Community at King's Wood had dwindled somewhat over the years and things were not quite as they had been. But it was his conversation with the guestmaster, just before Compline, that was to give John Farelowe as bad a night's sleep as he had endured for many a long year.

The King's Vicar General had just done an almost unimaginable thing. He had taken it upon himself to suspend the powers of the Bishops and had inhibited them from making visitations of religious houses in their dioceses. A great Visitation was now being made by the Vicar General himself, through Commissioners appointed by himself, and the Abbey at King's Wood had but recently bidden a glad farewell to the Commissioners sent to examine, most minutely, their life and their means.

"Them were no good! No good at all! Them 'ad minds like a bunged-up garderobe! I tell 'ee, Master Farelowe, Them was a-lookin' for a right Sodom and Gomorrah in this 'ouse o' Prayer. And right ill pleased they was, not a-findin' of it!"

John could not sleep. He tossed and he turned and he tried to think of other things, but darkness crowded in upon him from every side. Terrible things had happened and worse were threatening. What was the King up to with the Religious houses? And was he, John Farelowe, thrusting his young son into the middle of a hornet's nest by sending him to a monastery school in the present climate and with these goings-on? Should he turn back ... ? John thrust the matter out of his mind. But then Tom's account of the terrible deeds at Court came back to him. He tried to shut them out but failed, and the judicial murder of the Bishop of Rochester in all its hideous detail played about his imagination until he wanted to cry aloud.

115

Old Bishop Fisher had been starved, almost to the point of death, in the Tower of London. He then had to be carried to the scaffold on a chair. Before he died he had forgiven his executioner "with all my heart" and he had prayed for the King.

After his head had been struck off with an axe, his body was stripped naked and left on the scaffold all day. It was buried, at dead of night, still naked, in the churchyard of All Hallows, Barking, by the Tower.

Bishop Fisher's severed head had been stuck on London Bridge. The people had begun to venerate it as the head of a martyr, and so it was taken down and flung into the river Thames. Only thus could they be persuaded to desist.

This took place at the end of June. A fortnight later it was the turn of Sir Thomas More, and it was his death, added to that of Fisher, which sent shock waves of horror throughout Europe. It was now plain that a monster sat upon the throne of England. The Pope wrote out a Bull of excommunication, but he lacked the courage ever to publish it.

John Farelowe got up and walked about the guest-hall. But there were others sleeping and he did not want to wake them. He could not go out of doors for it was the Greater Silence and he must not take the risk of disturbing the monastery and thus abusing their hospitality. So he returned to his bed again, and once more the nightmares crowded about his sleepless head.

The trial of Fisher had been a mockery. That of More had been a farce! More had been obliged to guide Chancellor Audley on points of law and procedure throughout his own trial. When the inevitable sentence of death had been pronounced, More addressed his judges and his words were speedily reported the length and breadth of England.

"More have I not to say, my Lords, but like as the holy Apostle Saint Paul, as we read in the Acts of the Apostles, was present and consenting to the death of the protomartyr, Stephen, keeping their clothes that stoned him to death; and yet they be both twain Saints in heaven, and there shall continue friends together for ever: so I verily trust and shall therefore heartily pray that though your lordships have been on earth my judges to condemnation, yet we may hereafter meet in heaven merrily together to our everlasting salvation: and God preserve you all, and especially my sovereign lord the King; and grant him faithful counsellors."

Tom Campion had been present at More's execution, praying silently for his friend and patron. The scaffold had been a ramshackle structure, hastily erected. As he mounted the shaking steps, More had turned to the Constable with a smile.

"See me safe up. I will shift for myself in coming down!" As he laid his neck upon the block he had carefully moved his long beard aside.

"It were a pity to cut that. It never committed treason!" John wept as he remembered More's speech to his judges and Tom's moving description of his holy death. More had been Tom's inspiration, and it was the martyrdom of More that had shown Tom what his own, hidden and perilous vocation was to be. Still silently weeping, John Farelowe drifted into a troubled and fitful sleep. He woke drained and exhausted to face the second day's ride. Mass, and a distinctly autumnal nip in the air revived him, however, and their ride to the Augustinians at Keynsham was uneventful.

Not every Religious wore the habit as a result of a true vocation. A few were thrust into Religious houses by their families in order to get them out of the way, and some were quite unfitted for the life. In terms of numbers the Religious Orders had been in decline for two centuries, but during that period the Black Death had carried off one third of the population of England and the Wars of the Roses had spread death and destruction all over the country for decades on end. The Religious houses reflected to some degree at least the generally demoralised condition of the nation of which they were a part. It was not too difficult, therefore, for The Vicar General's carefully chosen and extensively briefed Commissioners to find, here and there, what they had been bidden to discover.

The Superior of the Praemonstratensian Canons at Langdon was surprised in bed with his "gentlewoman or damozel." The Commissioner wrote a highly coloured account of his discovery to a delighted Crumwel. This was just what they wanted! At Harwood in Bedfordshire, a tiny Community consisting of a prioress and five nuns revealed that one nun had two "fair children" and another had one. A Gilbertine Community, of both men and women Religious, produced two nuns "not barren," whose condition was traced to the sub-prior and a serving-man.

All was grist to the Commissioners' mill and all Religious houses were thus tarred with the same brush, without regard to realities whatsoever. The great Yorkshire Abbeys of Rivaulx and Fountains were claimed to be "the vilest abodes" of unnatural vice, but nobody would dare to ask the Commissioners for evidence to support the allegation and none was offered.

"'Twas as if them did think we all whoremongers and sodomites!" The guestmaster at Keynsham was indignant, but he spoke in a low whisper. One had to be very careful. He laid a finger to his lips and looked meaningfully at John Farelowe. "King's Commissioners indeed!" He snorted.

Abbot Hugh of Glastonbury received John and young Will with open arms, and the boy was delivered into the hands of the monk who was to be his schoolmaster. John and Harry then rode on into Devon, to stay two nights with Ned Carey, and then they returned to Glastonbury for the feast of the Apostle Saint Matthew, before starting off on the long ride home.

"Master John! The King, now! What be 'im a-doin?"

They were alone on the open road with no companions. It was safe to talk.

"Can't say as I da know, 'arry. But I byunt a-likin what I bin a-hearin." John shook his head grimly. "They Commissioners is a-bearin o' false witness, 'arry, and tis what they's a-payin of em ta do. Parliament'll sieze on every hint o' scandal like dogs at lump o' meat!"

"Them all 'ates Christ and 'is Church, don't a?"

It was not Harry's way to beat about the bush.

"'Tis their money and their lands, 'arry. The King's in debt!" Without doubt there were far too many Religious houses of all sizes and far too few Religious to fill them. And they had a quarter of the income of England tied up in their endowments. Change was long overdue, but how far would the King go in effecting it? The remarkably extensive educational system in England depended almost entirely on the Religious houses and the Chantries. Other than private tutors there was no other means of obtaining an education. And the monasteries were the only institutions who cared for the sick, especially the poor. And they also housed and fed, and often usefully employed, a multitude who would otherwise be begging in the streets.

"What'll 'im do, Master John? Will King be a-puttin of em together? A-fillin up o' the best Abbeys and a-closin down o' t'others?"

"Old Archbishop Wareham; 'im ad ideas o' that sort, 'arry, but 'im were too old and tis too late, look. King? All 'im's a-lookin for is a chance to be a-closin o' the lot! And 'im'll put the lot in 'im's own pocket! Just mark my words!"

John was shaken by what he had just come out with. But the premonition at Flaxley had stayed with him and now he knew what it was about. Vocations were few these days. Contemplation was out of fashion in a world full of the New Learning. The head was fighting for mastery over the heart, just as the Abbot of Flaxley had said.

They rode on in silence. And then Harry spoke.

"Well now, Master John! That old King o' Babylon; 'im as did carry off all them Jews. Now if 'im could be a minister o' God's wrath, and if th' eathen Cyrus as did let 'em all go agin could be a minister o' God's Grace – why! P'raps King and 'im's Vicar General byunt just out for their own. Even though them da think they be!" He gave a merry laugh. "Cheer up, Master John! Byunt th'end o' the world yet!" The arrived home at Michaelmas to a rapturous reception, the dolours of the journey were forgotten, for the time being at any rate.

The following year a Black Book of alleged monastic vice and corruption would be laid before a Parliament only too eager to receive it. It would be greeted with a great cry of "Away with them!" and legislation would ensue.

Among the loudest to shout, "Away with them!" would be John Farelowe's own Father-in-God, Hugh Latimer, Lord Bishop of Worcester.

# CHAPTER FIFTEEN

JOHN WATCHED his wife drive off to Sainsbury's with a sense of relief and satisfaction. Actually getting her out of the house took a great deal of time and energy – his energy. But she was safely out of the way now for a couple of hours and he could give his undivided attention to the motor mower.

He had brought it in the previous evening and hoisted it on to the bench. That had had to be done when Jane was on the telephone or there would have been a great fuss about it being too heavy for him to lift. He would be sure to rupture himself, she would have said. It was far too heavy for *her* to help him lift – in addition to which it was dirty – and why didn't he get a man in to see to it? He was so *silly* about things like that!

It depended of course upon Jane's mood at the time. If she was in what he called her "A" mood, she would have gladly volunteered assistance and helped him to get it on the bench. She would have made cups of tea and been full of encouragement and appreciation. "You are a clever old thing!" she would have said. But Jane had not been in her "A" mood, she had been very decidedly in one of her her "B" moods last night and John had made his dispositions accordingly.

John pulled out the telephone plug in the hall, and then he ran upstairs to pull out the plug of the bedside telephone. There were going to be no interruptions this morning!

He had an hour of sheer joy. The mower came apart with very little trouble and he laid out the components in order, on sheets of clean newspaper on the floor at the end of the workshop. The carburettor linkage and the Bowden cable to the lever, mounted flimsily on the mower handle proved, as usual, to be the most recalcitrant bits to shift. But he succeeded, and far sooner, and far more easily, than he had dared to expect, the carburettor was stripped down, the cylinder head was off the engine, and he, John Faversham, was in a kind of seventh mechanical heaven.

There was a loud, insistant ringing of the front door bell.

"Tough!" He said to himself. "I'm out! I'm deaf!"

The carillon was replayed angrily and at length. He was adamant, he would not hear! He began to measure, to offer up a piece from his box of spare bits. He could see that if he just … there was the sound of the back door opening! Who the hell was it? With a flash of real anger he turned and stormed out of his workshop, small pieces of carburettor in each hand.

"Oh! There you are, John dear. Couldn't you hear me ringing? I rang for ages."

"Sorry Cecily. I was up to my ears in the lawnmower. Didn't know it was you." He searched wildly for somewhere to put his bits and pieces down, settled for the end of the draining-board in the utility room, and smiled at his mother-in law.

"I'm covered in oil, darling. Do sit down. I'll clean myself up and put the kettle on. Jane will be back any minute now." John scrubbed his hands under the tap in the utility room, wiped most of the oil off on to the roller towel, and composed himself to be charming to his mother-in-law.

"I thought you were in Sussex."

"You're not supposed to know. You're very naughty."

"Yes dear, so are you. You rang and told Jane and you weren't supposed to. How are things in Horsham?"

"Oh John! They are *so silly*! I could bang all their heads together."

"Knowing you, darling, I expect you did. How is young Tristram?"

"Rusticated for a month. Or whatever they call it. In disgrace. One boy has been expelled and the police have been to the school. Of course that is what they pay those ridiculous fees for."

"Do you think he will have learned anything?"

"Shouldn't think so for a moment. I'm sorry to say so, but those two grandsons of mine are a couple of spoiled brats. They should have had their bottoms smacked when they were little. But I love them, of course."

Cecily really did love her grandchildren, and she had a unique *rapport* with all of them. She stood no nonsense and was both the co-conspirator and also the stern disciplinarian when discipline was required. Needless to say all her grandchildren adored her. She would have left young Tristram in no doubt as to her opinion of his escapade.

"How are Harold and Barbara?"

"Hysterical! And miffed at the same time. But they have managed to persuade themselves that it is really quite amusing and all the really smart people's children get into that sort of trouble. Sometimes I quite despair of them. But they are darlings really. I think Harold is more miffed with Justin than with Tristram." John called his eldest nephew to mind; tall, aloof, with a flop of blonde hair perpetually falling over one eye.

"What's he up to?"

"He's joined the Socialist Workers' Party – sports car and all! He's only done it to send up his father. Harold and Barbara are so True Blue its boring. And ever since the Election …"

"London School of Economics," mused John, "and never done a day's work in his life. It figures."

"I told Harold not to take any notice. This time next year the boy will be a Tory Prospective Candidate somewhere. Is that Jane arriving?"


"Sarah! How on earth did you get hold of this?"

John looked at the book in his hand, and looked up again at Aunt Sarah.

"Never mind! I just had a brainwave after you two left the other night. I phoned up some of my second-hand book men and one of them came up with it this morning."

James Hasfield's *Memorial of the Hereford and Gloucester Canal* had just been presented to John as a late birthday, or early Christmas present. He could decide which at his leisure.

"He is looking for the *Flora and Fauna* one, but he thinks that might take a bit longer." Aunt Sarah was looking very pleased with herself. Her well fed cat look was much in evidence. "I passed Cecily on my way here, I'm sure I did."

"Yes," said Jane. "She left about twenty minutes ago. She's been down to Sussex. Tristram has been sent home for a month – in disgrace. None of us are supposed to know of course!"

"Drugs." It was not a question, it was more of a statement.

"Yes. One boy was expelled and the police have been to the school. I think Tristram was just a silly ass. But Harold and Barbara are in a bit of a state, as you can imagine."

"Oh dear!"

Aunt Sarah let that simple comment suffice. There wasn't a lot more to be said, however long they might go on saying it. Cecily had stayed to lunch and Aunt Sarah stayed to tea. She could not be persuaded to stay longer. She had some function to go to with Lucy, the very idea of which induced feelings of anxiety in John. "A psychic Bring and Buy Sale?" He ventured.

"What a lovely idea! Just think of the possibilities! No, just a Vegetarian Coffee Evening – or something of the sort. I like to support poor Lucy and all her funny goings-on. She is such a dear."

"Do vegetarians drink coffee?"

"I've no idea! I'd never thought about it."

John and Jane waved farewell to the little red Volkswagen and closed the front door behind them.

"Isn't that just like her!"

John picked up Hasfield's canal book and idly turned the pages.

"She and Cecily have rather put paid to my plans for the day. I was hoping to persuade you to come and explore Forthampton and Chaceley with me. Too late now." Jane sank into her armchair.

"And I had just finished taking the motor mower to bits. The engine is all over the bench, and the carburettor ..." John's face was suddenly a picture of horror. "When I heard someone coming in through the back door I rushed out with half the carburettor in my hands. I put it down somewhere!"

Jane smiled the sweetest of smiles at him.

"On the draining-board darling. Its still there. I wouldn't dare touch it! And you wiped your oily hands all over the roller towel. You're a naughty boy!"

"Thank God for that!"

The matter of the roller towel never connected with John Faversham's consciousness. The bits of the carburettor were safe! That was what mattered!

"Darling, you are a clever old thing. But why didn't you ask me to give you a hand lifting the mower up on to your bench? You could have hurt yourself!"

John gave his wife a sheepish grin.

"It was a bit dirty," he said.

# CHAPTER SIXTEEN

T HE NIGHT of the 16th/17th of May 1536 was a sleepless one for many important people, and for a wide variety of reasons. A Scottish divine by the name of Alexander Aless, currently in London and staying at the Archbishop's palace at Lambeth, was quite unable to sleep that night. He rose from his bed in the very early hours and walked in the Archbishop's garden, hoping to relax enough to return to his bed in comfort.

To his surprise however, Alexander encountered another sleepless inhabitant, wandering in the garden in what appeared to be a state of utter torment. They met. The wanderer was none other than Thomas Cranmer, the Archbishop of Canterbury himself.

"What ails thee?" enquired Alexander.

The archbishop raised his eyes to heaven and said:

"She who has been Queen of England on earth, will this day become a Queen in heaven!"

And, so saying, he wept uncontrollably.

Thomas was weeping for pretty Queen Anne, but he was weeping no less for himself. The Abyss had opened up in front of him. He who had released the King from one marriage was now commanded to release him from another. To demur was to lose his own head, of that he had been left in no doubt whatsoever. Archbishop he might be, but he was now roughly ordered hither and yon at the whim of the King's own Vicar General.

Queen Anne, who had schemed herself into her present position, was already the victim of the schemers. She had given birth to a stillborn son and the King now despaired of her. This gave the Vicar General his opening, for he whispered to the King such a tale as his instincts told him His Majesty might not be altogether loth to hear. Was it not known that the Queen was as merry an adulteress as the Court had ever seen? Had she not entertained no fewer than four gentlemen of the King's Privy Chamber in her bed? And had she not compounded her iniquities by lying with her own brother? So whispered the unprincipled Crumwel. Was any of it true? No man knows and who cared anyway?

The Queen was arrested at once. On being assured of a trial as fair as that of the very lowliest of the King's subjects she responded with a roar of laughter. The four gentlemen were immediately tried and executed, as was her own brother George, and she herself was incarcerated in the Tower.

Thomas Cranmer, ignored by his King and treated with complete contempt by the King's Vicar General, had retired in a sulk to do the rounds of his country seats of Adlington, Ford and Otford. He was summoned from thence, in the most peremptory fashion, by Thomas Crumwel. He was to bide at Lambeth but on no account was he to presume to venture into the King's presence. He was then given his orders. He was to obey.

The Queen was tried on charges of adultery and incest. Cranmer visited her in the tower on the 16th of May. She told him, among other things, that while her sister Mary had been the King's mistress, she had been the mistress of the Earl of Northumberland. This seemed to provide the unhappy Archbishop with some slender grounds for a judgement in his own Court and he left her, a safer man but a tormented one.

On the 17th of May, after his night of wandering the garden in a torment of conscience, the Archbishop convened his Court. Within the space of two hours it found that "The marriage between the King and the most serene Lady Anne to be and always to have been null and void, without strength or effect, of no force or moment, and to be a thing of nought, invalid, vain and empty."

Two days later, on the 19th of May, the most serene Lady Anne was decapitated by sword in the Tower of London. Her infant daughter Elizabeth had already joined her nursery governess and stepsister Mary in bastardy.

King Harry waited to hear that his Queen was safely dead before arraying himself in a new suit of white clothes. The very next day, May 20th, he was married to her Lady in Waiting, Jane Seymour. The King and his new Queen made another visit to Gloucester later on in the year. John Farelowe contracted a diplomatic illness. What he had learned from Tom Campion about the death of Queen Anne, added to some disturbing events nearer home, had determined him never to set eyes on his Sovereign Lord again.


Dene Abbey at Flaxley was no more. The Commissioners who had enquired, suggestively and acquisitively, into its life and fortunes in 1535, had returned. Parliament had declared that all religious houses which had not above two hundred pounds in the year, or which contained fewer than twelve Religious, were abodes of "manifest sin, vicious, carnal, and abominable living." Dene Abbey qualified, having but nine Brethren. It was the Commissioners' Christian duty, therefore, to demand the surrender of the Abbey to the King that these scandals might cease forthwith.

John Farelowe, acting for the Abbey, employed all his legal wits in carefully concealed delaying tactics. It was five years before the Abbey, its manors and its granges could be given by the King to Sir William Kingston, Constable of the Tower of London, as a country estate. In such manner were large numbers of self-seeking and unprincipled men to be converted into country squires all over England. Abbot Thomas Ware and his monks were given pensions and dismissed from their Abbey. The dispossessed Abbot lived for some months with his young friend at Farelowe before going on to relatives at Aston Rowant, near Thame in Oxfordshire. Having been in vows of celibacy, he and his monks were naturally forbidden by a pious King ever to do anything so scandalous as to marry. John Farelowe found himself drawn into a business more mean, more barbaric, more driven by insensate greed than his imagination could ever have conceived. The treasury was ransacked and all the sacred vessels, vestments, and gifts of the pious were piled on to carts and taken away. This was pain and grief to John. But worse was to follow.

All the ancient, illuminated service books – works of art of the very highest order, and works of great love and devotion – were also removed. They were scraped of every speck of gold leaf and either burned on bonfires or sold as scrap to the highest bidder. This monstrous business was to continue all over England, throughout the reigns of both King Harry and his son, until practically nothing was left of a priceless national heritage and symbol of its Christian civilisation.

It would not do, however, for the common people to imagine that anything irreligious was afoot. Accordingly certain *Articles to Stablish Christian Quietness* were presented to the Convocations for their approval. They were nothing if not conservative in character and a man could be burned as merrily under the *Articles* for thinking for himself as he could under the former Papal dispensation, for the Papacy was finally repudiated. In addition to expounding the *Articles* twice a quarter, the clergy were commanded to preach every Sunday, for three whole months, against "the pretended power of the Pope."

John, the ex-Abbot and Sir Ralph, the Vicar, examined the *Articles* at length by the fireside in John's hall. In the main they were found to be reassuring, even admirable. And the requirement that a Holy Bible, in both Latin and English, be set up in the chancel of every church in the land seemed to be entirely admirable. John volunteered to purchase one, as soon as he could. At a time when so much seemed alarmingly negative and destructive it was a joy to feel able to do something – almost anything – that was positive and good.


That most respectful of rebellions, the *Pilgrimage of Grace*, did not touch John Farelowe at all. It was confined to the Northern Province of York and was an armed protest against the dissolution of the smaller monasteries. The King was surely being deceived and ill-served by false counsellors!

The *Pilgrimage* was quieted and reassured by deceit. It was then suppressed with the most ruthless judicial barbarism. But voices closer to hand were being raised in protest at the rampages of the Commissioners. Queen Jane herself, inclined more to Tradition than to the New Learning, made so bold as to petition her Lord and Master in the matter. She was silenced and threatened with instant decapitation should she ever again presume to meddle in matters of State.

What did touch John Farelowe, however, was the ever increasing number of vagrants crowding about his door, begging for alms. The entire Social Security system of the realm had been damaged and the homeless and the unemployable had fewer places to go now the smaller monasteries were closing down. Certain it was that the new landlords had no interest in caring for them.

The sick were turned out along with the vagrants, and – most menacingly of all to John – boys were beginning to return home from monastic schools. What would become of young Will's education? Would the larger monasteries follow the smaller into oblivion? The threat to the Religious Houses had ramifications that the King and his grasping counsellors may never even have considered.

In the Autumn of 1537, Queen Jane died in childbirth. She who had been Queen but fifteen months gave birth to a son, and the child lived. At the age of 46 King Harry had his long desired son and heir, but at the cost of three Queens. And the boy was sickly with a congenital disease. He was baptised in the name of Edward.

As if somehow to compensate for the assault upon the Church through its Religious Houses, the English Bishops drew up and issued a book which they called *Institutions of a Christian Man*. It gave an exposition of the Creeds, the Ten Commandments, the *Ave Maria* and the Lord's Prayer. It explained the Sacraments of the Church and it was intended to inform, and to edify, the growing number of literate and thinking men. It was an admirable publication for its time and was a reassurance to troubled Christians, such as John and Kate Farelowe. It was a marvellous aid to Sir Ralph, their Vicar, in his preaching too.

At the same time, this extraordinary creature King Harry, at once a monster of depravity and cynicism and a model of traditional piety, authorised for use in churches a passable translation of the Bible made by Miles Coverdale, an extreme Reformist agitator. It was to be used in default of a better.

# CHAPTER SEVENTEEN

"**H**ow was Frankfurt?"

Jane pounced boldly into the traffic stream. She blasted the dithering driver in front of her with her horn. At last she was clear of the railway station and able to drive and converse at the same time. "Big city, full of big, square office-blocks. Just like anywhere else really."

John tended to be a bit negative about business trips abroad when they allowed no time to see the sights.

"I had a brief stroll in the city centre, opposite the main railway station. Every third shop seemed to be a sex-shop and every fourth was Turkish. A bit depressing."

Jane laughed. The idea of her John let loose among the sex-shops tickled her not a little.

"Gloucester is going to seem a bit tame after that. How was Head Office?"

"As ever."

John did not elaborate. Head Office had never seemed to grasp the obvious fact that Research and Development was the very activity that gave the firm something to sell.

"They didn't threaten you with Basingstoke, then?"

Jane darted an anxious glance towards her husband. She was looking for tell-tale signs behind that poker-faced facade which he now put on whenever business was mentioned. He used not to be like that. It worried her.

"Nobody threatened me with anything. They were all terribly nice to me! I never trust Head Office when they are being nice." John grunted. It was time to change the subject. "Anything happen here?"

This was what Jane had been waiting for. She was doing her best to conceal a state of suppressed excitement. With the utmost difficulty she was restraining herself from planning her wedding outfit.

"Rosemary is coming home for the weekend. They'll be here by about eight. We're eating a bit later this evening."

"Rosemary? Oh good!"

John was animated. He and Rosemary adored each other. Then his eyebrow curled up and he look at his wife.

"They? Who are they?"

"She's bringing Bill home to meet us."

Jane's tone was matter-of-fact. She kept her eyes firmly on the road ahead.

"Who is Bill? The latest?"

"The ultimate, darling! We had over an hour on the phone the night before last. She is quite besotted!"

John winced. He could imagine the telephone bill …

"Who was phoning who?"

"She phoned me and then I phoned her back. She was in a phonebox in Croydon – the nicer bit of Croydon."

"Glad it was the nicer bit of Croydon."

There was a lull in their conversation. Both seemed to find it necessary to pause and regroup. They were clear of Gloucester by now and on the Causeway over Alney Island.

"What do we know about Bill? Anything?"

"He's a chartered surveyor and an estate agent. And Rosemary says he's doing terribly well just now."

"I should bloody well think so! Look at the house prices …" John bracketed together stockbrokers, estate agents and secondhand car dealers as a kind of unholy trinity. His instinct was to consign the whole lot to perdition.

"What else does he do?"

Jane, inwardly disposed to fall madly in love with Bill herself, whatever he did for a living, remembered:

"He plays rugger."

There was a grunt from John. It was not one of enthusiasm. "At least he did until the end of last season. Then he smashed up his knee and they won't let him play this season."

"Lucky it wasn't his neck!"

Team games had been a misery to John throughout his schooldays. He even found them tedious to watch.

They turned in to the drive of Fairloe Court. Jane looked anxiously at the dashboard clock.

"Two hours! I'll never get done in time!"

Getting done in time was, as John well knew, as arcane and as complicated a business as any devised by the mind of man. But it had not been devised by the mind of man at all; it had been devised by the mind of woman and so John wisely distanced himself from its progress and found other things with which to occupy himself. "Have we anything to drink?"

"Yes, darling. I got another bottle of gin and there are a couple of bottles of Sainsbury's White in the larder. And there is always your home-brew. Bill is bound to be a beer drinker, you can show off!"

"Hello Sweetheart! Have you been a good girl while I've been away?"

John swept Philomena from the settle and hugged her gently. He made a great fuss of her and sat down with her in his lap. She purred noisily. She was glad to see him back. She had wondered what he had been up to.

"Mummy has to get done in time," he confided to the cat in a stage whisper. "So I had better put the kettle on. Look, Sweetheart! She's winding up already!"

The next two hours passed very much as John knew they would. Jane flew about the house, from kitchen to dining-room and from bedroom to bathroom, in a state of the most intense concentration which he knew better than to break. And so he had a quick shower, changed from his crumpled business suit into one more comfortable, laid the dining table with the best silver, saw to the log fires in both rooms, checked the temperature of the wine and decided that twenty minutes in the refrigerator would be to its advantage, and laid a drinks tray ready for the Grand Welcoming Ceremony. At ten minutes to eight, Jane swept down the staircase into a dining-room which seemed to have altogether thrown off its usual melancholy. She was attired in her most expensive cocktail dress, she was discreetly jewelled and exquisitely perfumed. To John she looked – as indeed in his eyes she always looked – utterly beautiful! He advanced to the foot of the stairs and kissed his wife. Then, holding her hands in his, he stood back a little to better appreciate the vision before him.

"Gorgeous!" He said.

The vision responded with words that came right from the heart:

"Oh darling!" she said. "I'm dying for a gin!"

# CHAPTER EIGHTEEN

IT IS SAID that new brooms sweep clean. Hugh Latimer, Lord Bishop of Worcester, may well have found his Cathedral and Diocese festooned with ecclesiastical cobwebs after decades of absentee predecessors. Certain it is that he was noisy and zealous in his sweeping. He was in many ways a big-hearted fellow, but he was an intellectual of the New Learning. His centre of gravity was to be found in his head rather than in his heart and he had in the fullest measure that contempt for objects of simple piety that is not infrequently to be found among intellectuals.

In his Cathedral church at Worcester stood a ten-foot high statue of the holy Mother of God. It was elaborately vested after the fashion of the day and it was much venerated by the simple folk of Worcester. It excited Hugh Latimer to very different passions indeed.

"Tis the devil's instrument to bring many to eternal fire!" he raged. One day, in 1538, unable to contain himself any longer, he ordered "that great Sybil" to be stripped of all its vesture.

The astonishing discovery was then made that it was not a statue of the Blessed Virgin Mary after all. It was the statue of a beardless Bishop. It had simply done duty for Our Lady, for longer than anyone could remember, in default of a proper image of her! Hugh Latimer normally had a lively wit, but at this moment it failed him altogether. Heaven probably enjoyed the joke. No doubt the Blessed Virgin herself had long appreciated it. But Hugh Latimer did not. In righteous wrath – ever a dangerous commodity – he sent it immediately to London to be burned at Smithfield, the place of public execution!

Thereafter he raged against all images. He was incapable of understanding the needs of simple piety, or its operations. At his powerful insistence all the most notable shrines of the Mother of God throughout England were stripped of their images and most of them were burned, as if they were heretics, at Smithfield. The most loved and venerated image of them all, that of our Lady of Walsingham, adorned a bonfire specially lit for it at Chelsea by the King's own Vicar General himself.

It was in this same year, 1538, that all the great Shrines of the Saints in the land were plundered and broken up. Their treasures went straight into the King's own coffers. In the case of the greatest of all the Shrines, that of St Thomas of Canterbury, the pillage was crowned by a solemn trial for High Treason as bizarre as it was grotesque.

The bones of the Martyr, St Thomas, were solemnly tried before the King's judges. Had he not, in his lifetime, dared to defy King Henry the Second? St Thomas was found guilty of High Treason and his bones were burned, ground to powder, mixed with excrement and solemnly flung into the River Thames. Thus did the King triumph over his enemies!

"Master John! Master John!"

There was desperation in the cry. John, about to mount his horse to ride into Gloucester, turned to see one of the village lads run, stumbling, into the yard.

"Edwin! What ails thou?"

The boy, some thirteen years of age, panted and gasped for breath. "There's men in the church, Master John. They's a-pullin down of our Lady. Says tis King's orders. And they was a-knockin down of Sir Edward when he was a-stoppin of em."

A cold fury seized John Farelowe. He sprang on his horse and jerked his thumb to the boy.

"Up be'ind me, Edwin. And hold on for thy dear life!" They covered the half mile to the village at full gallop and, reining up sharp in the little square in front of the church, they scattered a handful of a crowd that had gathered there. The crowd was angry and their mood was ugly in the extreme. John sensed that blood would be shed at any moment if he did not prevent it. One of the magistrate's officers, a rough, ignorant fellow by the name of Perkin, was hemmed about by a crowd of furious villagers, both men and women. Several of the men were armed with knives, clubs and pitchforks.

Behind Perkin stood four of his men, violent, bullying fellows who attended him in his more unpleasant duties. Two of them carried between them the wooden statue of the Mother of God that had stood for two hundred years and more in the chancel of Farelowe church. They were intending to throw it into a cart that stood to hand, but now they dithered, fearful of the mob.

A half-dozen of the Chantry scholars had crept up behind them, large stones in their hands, ready to throw. Sir Edward, the Chantry priest stood between Perkin and his cart, his arms outstretched barring the way. Sir Edward's face was covered in blood. John jumped from his horse, thrust the reins in Edwin's hands and thrust himself through the crowd. In a voice loud enough to be heard by all, but still icily correct, he demanded of Master Perkin an account of himself.

"Tis King's Orders, Master Farelowe. Call thy rabble off or twill be the worse for 'em!"

"Be good enough, Master Perkin, to acquaint us with the King's Orders. We be simple men here, and faithful believers all of us."

"Tis Vicar General's *Injunctions*, Master Farelowe. All them idols is to be burned."

"I am well acquainted with the *Injunctions*, Master Perkin, for I am a lawyer as you well know. For the sake of these good people I will explain the *Injunctions* to them."

John turned to the crowd.

"The Injunctions command all idols to be burned. Now this is a godly thing and I will tell you what the King's Vicar General has in mind. There has been found, in Wales, an image of a warrior which the ignorant there

130

have been worshipping as a god. They call it, in their strange speech, *Darvel Gadern*. Now this is as idolatrous a thing as ever the Caananites bowed down to! Of course it is to be burned."

John felt the tension relax a little. He continued.

"And in some places, rascally men have made images of the Saints that move by clockwork or by strings and levers. They have done this to deceive the foolish and make a profit for themselves. Very rightly these are to be burned for they dishonour the Saints of God and are an occasion of sin for all who have to do with them. The *Injunctions* Master Perkin refers to concerns abominations such as these."

John turned to the Magistrate's officer.

"Now, Master Perkin! What hold these two good fellows of yours in their hands?"

"An idol, Master Farelowe! And tis to be burned for the witch tis!"

An ugly growl came from the crowd. They moved closer.

"Peace, good people!"

John raised his hand and smiled benevolently at the villagers. "Master Perkin here is dilligent in the service of our Lord the King, but Alas! In his zeal, he has fallen into error."

Perkin, an essentially stupid fellow, began to look unsure of himself. He knew he could not stand up to John in an argument and John's easy tone unnerved him.

"In error, Master Farelowe? How be I in error?"

"On several counts, my friend. The first: you have mistaken a lawful image for an idol. Second: You have confounded the *Injunctions* with the *Articles* issued not two years since, and you have nullified the *Articles* in your zeal to observe the *Injunctions*!"

Perkin, his face a picture of mystification, looked uncomprehendingly at John.

"Let me explain, Master Perkin. The *Articles* expressly permitted the right veneration of images, though not in superstition. The Injunctions deal with those likely to invite superstition. Perhaps you are not fully conversant with the King's quite clearly expressed will in the matter?"

John half turned to the crowd. He had to carry the mob with him or Perkin was a dead man. And if Perkin was lynched, most of them would be hanged – or worse. And so might he be.

"Third, Master Perkin: *The Bishops' Book*, issued not a year since – I am sure you are familiar with it and use it as the King intends that it shall be used – contains an exposition of the *Ave Maria*, that most Biblical of devotions, addressed by the Archangel Gabriel to her whose image your servants hold in their hands."

Perkin had barely heard of the *Bishops' Book*. He was a bully and a mobster by heart; Christian devotion was the very last thing that was likely to excite his interest. But he was caught off balance; the ground was shifting from under his feet. His four henchmen were also shifting uneasily, looking nervously from one to the other. Perkin began to feel that he was being made to look a fool. He reacted hastily, unthinkingly, just as John hoped that he would. "Tis all superstition, Master Farelowe! This idol thing! Tis a witch, and tis to be burned!"

Another angry growl came from the villagers of Farelowe.

"Superstition, Master Perkin?"

John's tone changed. He knew he now had the magistrate's bully where he wanted him.

"Aye! Rank superstition, all of it!"

"And this is an image of a witch?"

"Aye! And t'will be burned!"

John smiled at Master Perkin. It was a kindly, almost pitying smile. The smile of one who is trying to be kind to a condemned man. His voice took on a gentler tone.

"As to superstition, Master Perkin, there is not a man, woman or child here present who does not know full well that the image your men hold in their hands is but wood and paint! Wood and paint, Master Perkin! But Christ's holy Mother is not wood and paint! It is her we honour, as does our Lord the King himself as every man in England knows."

John checked himself. He was about to refer to the three pilgrimages King Harry had made to the Shrine of our Lady of Walsingham, earlier in his reign. But the Royal Pilgrim had just ransacked the shrine and allowed her image there to be burned! No! He would not give such reminders to his adversary. It was time to move in to the kill.

"On three counts you are in error, Master Perkin. But there is a fourth, and it is of a different order altogether. I fear for you, Master Perkin! I fear for you!"

Perkin sensed that, suddenly, everything had turned against him. He saw triumph on the faces of the villagers and revenge in their eyes. What had he said ... ?

John's voice became solemn, his countenance stern.

"In the presence of a lawyer, and before this multitude of witnesses, you have declared our Saviour to have been born of a witch! In this you have denied the Faith in the most explicit manner possible, for it is not possible that the eternal Son of God be born of one committed body and soul to the devil and all his works! Thus you deny the very Incarnation! This, Master Perkin, is heresy as black as any man was ever burned for. I fear for you. I fear for you, as I have already said. It is many a long year since there was a burning in Gloucester."

There was a chorus of assent from the villagers. Yes! They had all heard every word and would testify!

Behind Perkin's back, his henchmen were gesticulating frantically, distancing themselves from each other and from their doomed leader. Those carrying the image laid it on the ground and stood as far away from it as they could manage.

Perkin himself was aghast. He was speechless and was casting about to find a way of escape from the unthinkable abyss that had opened up in front of him.

John smiled and made a conciliatory gesture with his hand. "Come now, Master Perkin! I cannot believe it of you! What does it say in Holy Scripture? *The zeal of thine house hath eaten me up!* I tremble lest your zeal burn you up! It was never your mind to burn the Holy Mother of God as a witch?"

"No! No! Master Farelowe. T'was ill said on my part. I was but adoin of my duty as I did see it. P'raps I be mistook."

"Of course you were, my good man! And now you gladly acknowledge that this ancient and much loved image of God's Holy Mother is exactly as the King's Vicar General once described: *a book of unlearned men,* and a godly object of pious devotion?"

"Indeed, Master Farelowe! And I be right glad of your correction, for I byunt no scholar."

John turned to the Chantry priest whose eye was blackened but whose nose had ceased to bleed.

"Sir Edward! How came you by your injuries? Has some foul hand been laid upon God's own priest? The King shall hear of this!" One of Perkin's ruffians began to cringe and to grimace.

"No matter, Master John!" The priest's blackened eye had a merry twinkle in it. "I forgive my brother with all my heart. Why! In his godly zeal he mistook me for one who would defy our Lord, the King!" So saying, he made the sign of the cross towards his assailant who, in his turn, crossed himself repeatedly and made a series of absurd bobbings and genuflections in the direction of the Chantry priest as if to emphasise the extremity of his penitence. Sir Edward turned to John, and then to the crowd.

"And now we shall go in procession into the church, and Master Perkin and his men shall restore our Lady's image to its place. And they shall then join us in an *Ave,* and in a *Te Deum!* We have much to give thanks for, and we shall pray for our Lord, the King."

And so it was done. For a little while no more of these *books of unlearned men* – and tangible foci for their love and devotion – suffered at the impious hands of Master Perkin and his ruffians. And thereafter, and for several years, Master Perkin was uncommonly civil to Master Farelowe whenever their respective duties brought them into contact with one another.

It was, so Parliament had decided, High Treason to deny the King his titles. One of the titles King Harry had bestowed upon himself was *Supreme Head of the English Church,* and as the Papacy was now finally repudiated it became a matter of conscience in individuals as to how to interpret it.

Was it merely a jumble of words, a measure in the everlasting dance of Kings and Popes, the music of which was – as ever – power and money? Could it be nodded at for safety's sake and held privately as absurd and a temporary aberration? Beyond doubt the great mass of traditionalist believers thought so. A great number in the Reformist movement rejoiced and took it seriously, with a variety of mental reservations. Some, however, like the martyred Sir Thomas More, could have none of it at any price. One of these was a certain Friar Forest.

Friar Forest had brought himself to the notice of the authorities, a very dangerous thing for any man to do. But he became very careful what he said to any man and so informers were hired to pose as penitents. They were to make false confessions to him and lead him on in the counselling that followed.

The false penitents produced evidence enough to have Friar Forest hanged, drawn and quartered. Several had preceded him in this grisly exit from the world and more were to follow. But, for some reason, the authorities had it in for Forest and were determined to burn him instead. He was accordingly tried, not for High Treason, but for heresy.

Thomas Cranmer, the luckless Archbishop of Canterbury, was his examiner. Like every other bishop on the bench he went far out of his way to save the accused and, at last, obtained enough hint of a submission to save the good man's life.

In prison, however, Friar Forest had a change of heart and solemnly repudiated any suggestion of submission. The civil authorities, having been denied their victim, now had him restored to them and there was nothing more the Church could do to save him. The Civil Power therefore resolved to make Forest the subject of an experimental execution.

A large grandstand was erected by St Bartholomew's gate to seat the King's Council, the mayor and aldermen of London, and numerous other gentlemen, among whom – unexpectedly invited by the Vicar General himself – was an unhappy Tom Campion. A pulpit was also erected for it was an edifying thing to hear a sermon at a solemn execution. Another invitation went out from the Vicar General. The Lord Bishop of Worcester was invited to be the preacher. Hugh Latimer and Tom Campion had one thing in common; both knew that to decline their invitations would be dangerous in the highest degree. Latimer replied that he was content "to play the fool after my customary sort." He asked that the pulpit be so placed that the condemned man could hear him. Should the sermon persuade him to recant, the condemned man's life would be saved. Latimer could do no more.

Hugh Latimer preached what some at least of his hearers described as "a noble sermon." At its conclusion he asked the prisoner "what state he should die in?"

Friar Forest replied that, though an angel from heaven should appear and teach him differently, he would nevertheless die in the doctrine he had received, and believed in from his youth. Turning to the preacher, Forest fixed his eyes upon him and said:

"Master Latimer! Seven years ago thou durst not have made such a sermon for thy life!"

Hugh Latimer, driven by great passions and enthusiasms, had been vociferous in his support for the earlier burning to death of some Anabaptists for their heresy. He had not been present to witness the reality of it. Now he was to witness it in all its horror. Friar Forest was suspended from a gibbet by chains under his armpits and he was roasted to death over a fire. On the fire was also burned *Darvel Gadern*, the Welsh idol.

What Hugh Latimer's thoughts were, standing a prisoner in his pulpit, no man knows. He was to be the victim, fifteen short years later. But the officers of the Civil Power, seated upon their grandstand in all their finery, declared it a novel and excellent way of disposing of the King's enemies, and one to be repeated at an early date.

# CHAPTER NINETEEN

"**T**HEY'RE HERE!"

Jane jumped up from her chair. John followed.

"Quick!" she said. "Put these glasses in the kitchen. We don't want it to look as though we've been knocking it back all evening!" John grinned, took the glasses into the kitchen and was just in time to answer the doorbell and greet his daughter on the doorstep with their accustomed bear-hug.

"Daddy darling! This is Bill!"

John disengaged himself from his daughter and found himself confronted by a powerfully built young man with a cheerful round face. The cheerful round face was adorned with a moustache and it was topped with a reasonably well contained mop of curly dark hair. John extended his hand; it was seized with vigour.

"How do you do, sir?" said the cheerful round face. "I'm so pleased to meet you! Rosemary has told me an awful lot about you!" John made the sort of response that fathers of besotted daughters make on such occasions. He ushered the pair of them indoors and presented them to a Jane who appeared, slightly fluttering, almost as if she had been taken unawares by their sudden arrival.

"Darling!"

A kiss and a hug for her daughter, and then: "And this must be Bill!"

It was evident, after a very few moments, that Bill had made a big hit with Jane, and Jane had made an equally big hit with Bill. There then ensued a breathless tale from Rosemary, all about the journey down from London, and how they were sure they were going to be late – "*the traffic*, Mummy!" – and how she was sure that they really must be late, and how lovely it was to be home. Jane was talking hard at the same time, saying how terribly behind-hand she had been with everything all day, and wasn't it clever of them to arrive at exactly the right moment!

John found that he had slipped into a kind of observation mode. Mother and daughter were not having a conversation, they were singing a duet. This was a ritual! He glanced at Bill and, to his great delight, discovered that the young man was observing it just as he was, with a twinkle in his eyes. John warmed to young Bill. He was an ally! John realised that he had made his mind up about Bill on first sight.

There was a bringing in of suitcases and a showing of Bill to his room by a Jane who was being the very model of the welcoming mother to her daughter's new and favoured young man. The youngsters would need five or ten minutes in which to freshen up. Did Bill drink gin? One would be waiting for him in the drawing-room. Jane returned to the drawing-room, her eyes sparkling with delight.

"Poor Bill!" Said John.

"What do you mean: Poor Bill?"

"The poor bloke hasn't got a chance, has he? First of all Rosemary gets her claws into him and then her mother demonstrates, with reckless abandon, just how beautiful, slim and sexy Rosemary is going to look when she is fifty-two! You old baggage!"

"Darling! Don't be horrid! We women *know*! He is a nice young man and he will do very nicely for Rosemary. I like his manners too. Did you notice how he addressed you as sir? Not many young men do that nowadays."

John grinned. Yes, he had noticed.

"It makes me feel old! I'm old enough to remember how one was supposed to address one's father's friends and one's schoolmasters as sir. Tradespeople were Mister! It seems a very long time ago. Yes, he's a nice lad – so far!"


"Got any plans for the morning, you two?"

Dinner was over and coffee was being drunk in the drawing-room. John looked at his daughter. She was a pretty girl and she had inherited her mother's figure. Tonight she was radiant, a real beauty by anyone's standard. He regarded her, and her new boyfriend, with a comfortingly mellow benevolence.

Two large gins before dinner, a generous supply of wine with it, and an excellent brandy by a blazing log fire after it, had put John Faversham at peace with the entire Universe. Frankfurt, its Turks and its sex-shops, was forgotten. Head Office, with all its smiling menace, was a million miles away.

Rosemary looked coyly at Bill. Bill looked equally coyly at Rosemary.

"I think we are going to explore the Forest tomorrow, Daddy. The Autumn colours will be gorgeous, and Bill is mad about old mines and railway tracks and things. Aren't you Bill?"

Bill nodded.

"Industrial archeology. Its the surveyor in me trying to escape from the estate agent. I love snooping about in old mine workings and railway tunnels."

"You could have a look at the old Moseley Green Tunnel, if you can get to it these days. The old Mineral Loop Line. They took the rails up years ago, but I groped my way through it once, back in the 1960s. You'd need a torch."

The log fire and the brandy were taking him away. John found that engaging in conversation was like an excursion back from another world.

"We've got an Ordnance Survey map, haven't we, darling? One of the new ones, I think. They could borrow it."

Jane was eager to facilitate their every endeavour.

John smiled beatifically. They could borrow anything. They could have the lot! He was on the very threshold of unconsciousness. "Does Hasfield say anything about the Forest in his book?" Jane's voice was bright and a little louder than usual. She could see that they had all but lost John altogether.

"Has he written any poems about old mines and things?" Jane's voice was brighter and louder. John struggled back into the world.

"Who's Hasfield?" Rosemary looked puzzled.

"Ask your father. He discovered him."

With a superhuman effort John returned to the land of the living. He tried hard not to look as if he had been asleep.

"Local poet. Nineteenth century. Used to live in this house. Found him in a pile of old books at a sale. Any more coffee in the pot, darling?"

Jane filled her husband's cup, picked up Hasfield's book from the table and put it firmly in his hands.

"Fancy him living in this house!" Rosemary was full of interest. "Is he any good?"

"Not very!" John looked up from the depths of the Contents page. "He died in 1894. A few good poems but most of it is pretty awful!" John searched for a page, found it, and subjected the text to intensive scrutiny.

"Darlings! We shall have to wait at least half an hour, you know what your father is like! He has to read every word twice over before he lets us in on the secret!"

Rosemary giggled. She knew her father.

"Never mind, Daddy! We'll wait for you."

John looked up in triumph.

"He has a whole section on *Industries and Artifacts in the Royal Forest of Dean.*"

"Well, go on! Read something! Then Bill and Rosemary can go and explore it in the morning – if they like the sound of it."

John looked up, a twinkle in his eye. "What about *Ode to an Ironstone Mine?*"

There was another giggle from Rosemary. Bill grinned from ear to ear. "How does it go?" he asked.

John, fortified by a third cup of coffee, cleared his throat and addressed the text:

"Shakemantle!" An heroic name
For brigand or for Pimpernel!
But thine a more prosaic fame;
Set deep in Ruspidge rocky dell
With "Perseverance" for thy friend
And pick to sound thy stone-struck knell,
Through shafts and tunnels without end,
From depths most awful and alone,
Thou lift'st to light the ironstone!

"I'm not reading any more. It goes on for two whole pages."

"I love the bit about, Thou lift'st to light the ironstone," said Rosemary. "What did you think of it, Bill?"

Bill's amiable countenance was lit by a bright smile. "He's better than McGonagall!" he said.

Jane suddenly leapt to Hasfield's defence. "Yes, that one is a bit laboured, but some of his poems are lovely. There is a lovely one about the River Leadon."

"What is *Shakemantle*?" Bill was clearly fascinated.

"It was an Ironstone Mine in the Forest. And the name of the mine next-door was *Perseverance*. They gave mines the most wonderful names in the Forest. One of the old Coal Mines was called *Strip-and-get-at-it!*"

John was fully restored to his rightful mind by now. He thought of a possible excursion for the young couple. He turned to Rosemary. "If you went through Littledean and turned left, you could take in Soudley – pretty road that – and then you could turn up through Ruspidge. Can't tell you if anything is left of the old mines now though. But if you went on you would end upon the Speech House road." He turned to Bill. "Good pub that! Good for a lunch and near enough to Moseley Green and all the nice Forest Walks too." There was some discussion, with noddings and agreements. It was quite clear to John and Jane that if Bill wanted to explore every old mine from here to Land's End, Rosemary would be eager to accompany him all the way, looking gorgeous!

John's eye strayed back to the book. He turned a couple of pages and suddenly laughed out loud.

"How about this? It is only about a mile from Speech House. You could look in on this one."

"New Fancy" is a maiden's name!
Her own perhaps a strapping lad
All set to find in her the same,
To court her and to make her glad.

He looked up at his daughter. She was blushing, with just a hint of annoyance on her pretty face. Delighted, John continued.

But what is this? Two chimneys tall,
A headframe with two winding wheels
Set high above a giddy fall;
A coal mine to this name appeals!
Set high upon its Forest Shelf
And plunging down to deep "High Delf".

There was a merry laugh from Bill. Rosemary was still slightly ruffled about the feathers. One could not trust parents!

"What is High Delf, darling?" Jane was puzzled.

"It is one of the main Coal Seams under the Forest."

"What an extraordinary thing to write a poem about!"

"Oh! I don't know!" Bill looked up at her. "John Betjeman used to wax lyrical about encaustic tiles. He thought almost anything was a fit subject for poetry, if it spoke to you that way. I think I agree with him."

"Wordsworth was the same. He used to love starting with a name and an exclamation mark." Jane struggled to retrieve something from her memory.

*"Chatsworth! Thy stately mansion and the pride of thy domain."*

She grinned. "It wasn't one of his best either!"

The discovery that the rugged and rugger-playing Bill was also a lover of poetry further entranced his devoted Rosemary and also surprised and delighted her parents. Jane at once demanded that John read one or two of Hasfield's better efforts. It became clear that Bill was thoroughly intrigued by the book, and by the idea that its author had probably composed quite a lot of it by this very fireside.

"Might I borrow it to read in bed?" he asked.

The request was granted with enthusiasm but both John and Jane noticed Rosemary beginning to withdraw from what was going on about her. They knew the signs. Something would emerge from the withdrawal. Something unexpected.

"Daddy! Do you think this Hasfield sometimes haunts the house? Just a little bit?"

John and Jane exchanged startled glances. Bill raised an interested eyebrow.

"What makes you ask?" Something in John felt uncomfortably alerted.

"I don't know. Sometimes – only sometimes – it is almost as if someone else is about in the house. I've never mentioned it before. It hasn't really bothered me, and it is only sometimes."

John looked at Jane. Her eyes were as wide as saucers. "No idea, darling." John looked again at Jane. "It hasn't ever occurred to us – I think?"

Jane shook her head. But something had touched her.

"Oh Bill!" Rosemary turned to him. "Its all right! I haven't brought you to a haunted house, I promise! I must have had too much to drink! You know what a cheap drunk I am!"

"Cheap drunk?" Bill's eyes were wide open. "You must be joking!" He winked at John. "You drank us all under the table at the Rugger Club do!"

There was a shriek of protest from Rosemary, followed by an impassioned denial. She was playing to the parental gallery and Bill was enjoying the show.

"You play, then?" John ventured an interest.

"Used to. Smashed up my knee last season. Now I just drink for Blackheath."

It was time to retire to bed. Rosemary and Bill were dismissed to their respective rooms, Bill with Hasfield's book under his arm. John checked doors, windows and fireguards while Jane tidied away the last of the dinner things into the dishwasher. They met at the foot of the stairs.

"What did you make of Rosemary's thing about Hasfield haunting the house?"

"No idea," said John. "But he'll have his work cut out if he wants to haunt me tonight. I'm dead on my feet! Nice lad, Bill!"

"*Very* nice!" said Jane.

# CHAPTER TWENTY

I T WAS THE MISFORTUNE of John Farelowe to live at a time in history as uncongenial to his own make-up as any that could have been imagined. A great change was coming over European mankind, of which the Reforming movements of the Continent were the most obvious manifestations, but by no means the only ones. Men were thinking for themselves as never before. The Classics had been rediscovered, ancient Greece began to be the inspiration for art and literature and, slowly but inexorably, the mind of the King in matters of a nation's religion began to give place to the judgement of the individual. The immediate result was chaotic, and the chaos deepened with the passage of years.

It was a time when nations became conscious of their identity. It was also a time when the Old and New Testaments became widely available for ordinary people to read. The essential unity of Europe which a common acknowledgement of the Papal authority upheld – despite the warrings of princes – gave place to a fragmentation into increasingly self-conscious states.

Armies had hitherto owed their loyalties to individual leaders, mercenary armies to their immediate paymasters. Soldiers changed sides frequently; the prisoner of war became a turncoat and no man thought ill of him for it. Slowly, however, nationalism began to become a force in Europe. The unity of Europe, based upon a common religious allegiance, gave place to local and rival allegiances, inspired by lesser, political, sets of ideals. Soldiers now began to die for their countries, and for their own chosen forms of religious obedience within the one Christian Faith.

The very insularity of England made her nationalist before her time. It was still natural for the nation as a whole to follow its King in matters of religion. The repudiation of the Papacy seemed, to the vast majority, neither significant nor particularly important. It was yet another measure in the same old dance, the tune of which was money and power.

Nevertheless, men were beginning to think for themselves and the times were such that differences were violent and immoderately expressed. Christians were now beginning to be seen to hate each other, all over Europe.

Seven dark years had passed since John Farelowe had made his merry ride to Dene Abbey, there to be confronted with a premonition of disaster. Part of that premonition had come true. Dene Abbey was no more and he, the lawyer, was making haste, as slowly as he dared, to deliver it and all its estates into the grasping hands of the King.

John had seen the King and had suffered the destruction of all his illusions. His reason might come to terms with the suppression of the smaller Religious houses, but his conscience was outraged by the manner of it. His reason might see Divine Judgement falling upon the money-grubbing guardians of the great Shrines. The Old Testament taught him that God used Assyrians, Persians and Babylonians as his ministers of wrath, but the manner of the pillaging of the Shrines revolted him. Nothing good was taking the place of the corrupted and the bad. The tone of everything the King and his Commissioners did was entirely negative.

John, being an educated man, read as widely as he could. He was well acquainted with the New Learning, inclined to this bit and that, but otherwise he clung to the old. His security was being radically undermined, but he was innocent of any such concept as security. He could not objectify, nor could he become detached. He was doomed to suffer instead. Those small seeds of despair within him were beginning to shoot but as yet he was unaware of them. Apart from that alarming intrusion by Perkin and his ruffians, practically nothing of the upheavals of the past seven years had touched John personally. His estates prospered, his home life was tranquil, his practice of law was as profitable as he wanted it to be, his beloved Church was unchanged in either life or liturgy, and although he distrusted and disapproved of his own Diocesan Bishop personally, at least the man was an Englishman and present often enough in his Diocese to excite such emotions. That, at any rate, was a great improvement on everything that he had known before. It was at the age of thirty-nine that John began to feel the pressure of events impinge upon him and his household, for in the early summer of that year, his twelve-year-old son William returned suddenly from the monastery school at Glastonbury.


A second Act of Parliament, in 1539, decreed that all the remaining Religious houses should be closed and surrendered to the King. The Commissioners immediately set out upon their sordid errands and, with each closure, a fresh community of monks was dispersed on pension. The dispersals did not end with the monks, however. All the scholars were sent home and all the homeless, the dependent and the sick were also turned out. The land suddenly began to fill with beggars. They were to prove a growing and intractable problem throughout the Tudor period.

The Benedictine Abbey of St Edmund at St Edmundsbury was one of the first to be closed. The Community was dispersed and, in due course, the Abbey and its lands were sold by the King to a Master John Eyer. In this dispersal, Edmund Foster, priest and monk, was turned out on a pension. He had no home to go to for his parents had died and he had renounced all earthly possessions and inheritances. He therefore decided to visit his friends until such time as he could establish himself and think how best to live, in private, the life to which he was vowed. He acquired a horse from a well-wisher and set off in the direction of Gloucester.

William's homecoming was a sorrowful business for all the monasteries in which they had once stayed were closed or closing. By the end of the year the Augustinians had gone from Keynsham and their buildings were let to a Master John Panter for some commercial undertaking. King's Wood had gone already. Its roofless buildings were a quarry for building stone and a certain Sir John Thynne had been enriched by the Vicar General at the Community's expense. As the year wore on, disturbing stories began to circulate. The Abbots of Reading and Colchester had both been executed, as had certain of their monks. It did not do to show the slightest reluctance to comply with the King's lawful will.

But what was to be done with young Will Farelowe? The boy had showed promise as a scholar. Was his education now to be abandoned? John cast about for a solution and eventually sent him to a private tutor in Oxford, a former Friar who had begun to supplement his pension by educating the bright sons of such fathers as John.

What John did not know was that the good friar was an ardent, though discreet, enthusiast for the New Learning. Young Will took after his mother in temperament, was naturally open minded and was to imbibe all things new with such enthusiasm as to imperil his whole relationship with his father. This, however, lay unseen in the future.

It was towards the end of the year that the four friends met once more in John and Kate's house. Edmund had been staying a month or more already. Tom Campion had escaped from Court and had no mind to return until the New Year was well established. He could sense trouble ahead and wanted to be well out of its way when it came. But it was the quite unexpected arrival of Ned Carey that was to bring a blow to the very soul of John Farelowe from which he never fully recovered.


"John!" Ned looked up at his friend from his seat by the great chimneypiece in the hall at Farelowe. His ruddy countenance showed a mixture of emotions, none of them joyful. He had not long since arrived, the superficial greetings were done and it was time for him to tell his tale.

"John! I've a tale to tell such as you would give your right arm not to hear. But I'm bound to tell you. Its what I've come for."

The three men looked at him intently, John with that kind of apprehension that presupposes something already known at some deep level within. Kate looked first at Ned, and then at her husband.

"Say on, Ned! I would guess, but I dare not."

"Your kinsman, John: Sir Hugh, Abbot of Glastonbury and your schoolmaster and mine – he's dead!"

"He was an old man. God rest his soul."

"He was hanged, drawn and quartered for High Treason, John! Sacrificed to the devil himself on Glastonbury Tor!"

There was a full minute of stunned silence. Kate buried her face in her hands and wept silently.

"What happened Ned? High Treason? What could he have done to provoke that?" John's face was a picture of utter disbelief. Tom Campion grunted.

"He need have done no more than draw breath. If they had it in for him he was a dead man."

Edmund nodded, and added the other dimension:

"He was too Christ-like to be allowed to live! He will have become the focus of every hatred in the hearts of evil men for miles around. They will have used him as they used his Saviour."

Ned nodded. Tears were in his eyes. He waited until he had his emotions under command before he went on.

"Edmund is right, John! It was exactly that. And Tom is right too. They implicated him in some nonsense about concealed treasures, as if he cared for treasures! And they slaughtered two of his monks along with him to give substance to their story."

"But – sacrificed to the devil ... ?" John could not yet come to terms with what he was being told.

"As good as that, John. Or as bad. They dragged the three of them on hurdles through the streets of the town, with all the crowds screaming insults, and mocking, and throwing dirt at them. They dragged them to the top of the Tor – you know what a place that can be – and they made as barbarous a job of them as they knew how. Sir Hugh was soon dead. He was an old man. But the others ... !"

"All the devil-worshippers for miles about will have had a festival such as they haven't known since the first Good Friday! And it will have availed them as little!"

Edmund's voice was quiet and gentle, but he spoke with a great authority. The friends turned to him. "Would that we were all as closely identified with our Saviour as Abbot Hugh! He will have prayed for his persecutors and his prayers will have been heard."

"Edmund! Thank God we've got you with us!"

John embraced his friend. Then he turned to Ned.

"What a burden you've carried here, all the way from Devon! I can't thank you for the news, but I thank you with all my heart for bringing it."

John and Ned embraced each other, and they wept.

"I have an altar in the morning," said Edmund. "We shall pray for the soul of Abbot Hugh and his two companions. And for God's forgiveness for his murderers."

There was a murmur of assent. The friends sat silently, gazing at the fire. John got up without a word and threw on another log. Kate left her place and went out into the kitchen and the storerooms beyond. A cup of wine would do them all a power of good.

"What jackanapes is to be given Glastonbury to make a gentleman out of him?" Tom Campion's tone was one more of pity than of anger.

"The tale is that it's to be sold to the Duke of Somerset." Ned shrugged his shoulders. "He may be a fine gentleman, John, but he'll be no schoolmaster for our sons!"

"We'll pray for him too!" said Edmund.

# CHAPTER TWENTY ONE

"**D**ARLING! Is anything the matter?"
Jane groped in the dark for the bedside light switch. She was quite suddenly wide awake and full of alarm. Her fingers found the switch and she pressed it, urgently.

"Darling! Darling!"

John was obviously in distress, though still unconscious. Jane shook him.

"Darling! Wake up! Are you all right?"

There was a grunt from John, followed by incoherent mumblings. Jane shook him again. She was thoroughly frightened by now; something was terribly wrong. John's eyes opened. He blinked in complete disorientation.

"Oh my God!" he said.

"Darling! Are you all right?"

John blinked again and gave his head a violent shake as if he was trying to shake its contents into some kind of order.

"Yeah-Yes! I'm all right. Oh Lord!"

He gave his head another violent shake and struggled up into a sitting position. He looked utterly bewildered and was obviously in distress. Jane jumped out of bed and ran round to sit beside him. She kissed him, held him tightly and stroked his forehead.

"Darling! I thought you were dying – or something."

John managed a weak grin.

"Not dying. Just something!"

He blinked and shook himself again. Then he looked at her, his eyes full of trouble.

"I've just had that bloody dream again!" he said.

Jane's immediate reaction was to reach out and switch on John's bedside light. It suddenly seemed terribly important to get more light into the room. She felt frightened and she didn't know what to say or do.

"I'm so sorry," she said.

John seemed to be more in command of his own mind by now. He glanced round the room as if to fix himself in time and space.

"It was so vivid!" he said. "Absolutely vivid, and bits of it are still going on inside my head. I can't have woken up properly yet."

"Did you have the whole dream? You know; the cottages by the river, and the village, and the church – and everything?"

John nodded grimly. "The whole lot! In glorious technicolour! But it was something I saw in the church that is the crux of the matter. And it is the only thing I can't recall! I just felt as though I was going to go to hell by the most direct route. And then there was that deserted village business, and I ended up on our doorstep, peering towards Gloucester as if I was looking for something. And then I heard your voice and felt myself being shaken into another world altogether – thank God!"

"Oh dear!"

Jane was suddenly full of fears and anxieties. There was something dreadful behind all this. First of all the dream, and then that book, with the dream in it! And all this business of Hasfield. And now the dream again! She must talk to Aunt Sarah, and they must all talk it over with Deirdre …

And then Jane had a thoroughly practical bright idea. "I'm going down to make a nice pot of tea! Neither of us is going to go to sleep for a bit – not after this. I'll just get my dressing-gown and slippers and I'll go down and put the kettle on."

She kissed her husband and watch him relax, his eyes closed, but still very far from sleep.

John's mind slowly cleared. There had been real desperation in that dream. He had been dreaming it, but in some curious way *it had not been his own dream*. Something inside him had half-heard a cry for help. But from whom? And what about? And how did one respond? And to what?

Jane had slipped from the room and John heard her footsteps fading as she walked along the passage to the head of the stairs. He tried hard to think, but thoughts seemed reluctant to take coherent form inside his head.

"My brain isn't answering the helm!" he grunted. He glanced at the clock on his bedside table. It stood at ten minutes past two. A moment later Jane reappeared.

"That was quick work," said John. And then he saw her face.

"Darling!" She was pale and agitated. "I … I couldn't go downstairs!"

John was wide awake at once. He knew exactly what she meant and his skin began to tingle. But he still asked the question.

"Why?"

Jane looked at him. She was biting her lip.

"I got to the top of the stairs, and then I just couldn't go any further. The staircase looked like a bottomless pit! I'm sorry!"

John felt a surge of anger rise within him but he brought it quickly under control. Emotions were not going to help; total control and firm rationality were needed. He swung his legs out of bed, slipped into his bedroom slippers and reached for his dressing-gown. "Something is going on!" he said.

"What are you going to do?" Jane's voice was unsteady.

"I'm going to find out what the hell it is! And then I'm going to put the kettle on!"

"Do be careful!"

"Nothing can harm us. How can it?"

And with that assurance, as much for himself as for Jane, he opened the bedroom door and stepped into the straight corridor which led directly to the head of the staircase. The landing lights were on, so taking a deep breath and murmuring a prayer that came suddenly into his head, John marched determinedly to the head of the stairs.

Something seemed to be wanting to make John's heart jump right up into his mouth. Hairs prickled on the back of his neck. He stood at the head of the staircase and looked down. It was as if he was gazing directly into the Abyss. Not a glimmer of light seemed to be penetrating its utter blackness.

He took another deep breath and glanced back over his shoulder. Jane's slim figure was silhouetted against the light in the bedroom. She was holding tightly to the half-opened door.

"I'm going downstairs now. And I'm going to switch on the lights at the bottom of the stairs."

His voice sounded curiously hollow and not quite under his control. It didn't seem to want to be answering the helm either.

John Faversham made the sign of the cross, squared his shoulders and began, very deliberately, to descend the staircase. He seemed to be pushing against a strong headwind; it was like walking into a kind of electric storm. There was a tangible rise in pressure or something very like it – all about him.

After what seemed to have been an eternity he reached the bottom of the staircase and his hand found the light switches. He switched them all on; the light at the bottom of the staircase and the main lights in the dining-room. He paused and recollected himself afresh. His whole body was tingling and his hair felt as though it was standing up vertically on his head. He turned left into the dining-room and, to his great surprise, heard himself say:

"Lets say the Lord's Prayer, shall we?"

John said the Lord's Prayer, quietly but audibly. In an odd way he suddenly felt himself to be in control of the situation – whatever it was. The sense of pressure seemed to drop and his hair began to feel more normal on his head. Something seemed to need saying and so, in default of a better audience, he addressed the great chimneypiece on the far wall of the dining-room.

"Now look here, Hasfield – or whoever you are. If you've got problems I'll do my best to help you. But lay off the nightmares if you don't mind!"

John felt better at once. He was about to turn towards the kitchen door when something else came into his head. He made an odd little gesture towards the fireplace.

"The Peace of the Lord be always with you!" he said. And then he turned on his heel, went into a peaceful kitchen, put the kettle on and brewed a nice pot of tea. As he took the tray upstairs to the bedroom something told him, with an absolute certainty:

It wasn't Hasfield!

"What made you say that?"

Jane, still wide-eyed and awestruck, sat up in bed sipping her tea.

"Say what?"

"That bit from the New Service. The Peace of the Lord bit."

"Blowed if I know! It just came into my head. It seemed a friendly sort of gesture in the circumstances. The old fireplace looked quite touched! Bloody silly, isn't it?"

147

John shook his head. He laughed.

"I'll have to consult the Earth-Mother in the morning."

"Don't you think we ought to call in Walter? Mightn't it need exorcising, or whatever they do?"

John shook his head.

"I don't think so – not yet at any rate. I think the poor old thing was having its nightmare and I picked it up."

"Oh! The poor darling!"

Something in Jane wanted to rush downstairs and give It a big hug, and cuddle It until It was better.

"Why couldn't I go downstairs? I just couldn't! My legs wouldn't do what I told them to do!"

"I don't think you were supposed to. Its got nothing to do with Being Brave and all that – women are much more courageous than men anyway – its just that, in some odd sort of a way, its my problem. I'm the one who has to sort it out – if I can."

Jane put her arms round her husband. Something inside her knew he was right. She just hoped it wouldn't …

"Was it Hasfield?" Jane looked hard at John.

"No."

"Do you remember what Rosemary said – about a sense of there being someone else about? Well, It might just have been suggestion after what she said, but for the last week or so I have been thinking there is somebody else about too. A man. I thought it was probably Hasfield."

John shook his head.

"I'm sure it isn't Hasfield. Don't know why. God alone knows how these things work – if they work at all. This is such an old house it must be riddled with memories. Perhaps Aunt Sarah was right; perhaps I stumbled on one of its video-nasties!" He looked up at Jane.

"The place had calmed right down by the time the kettle boiled. I left the dining-room light on. Just in case!"

Jane glanced at the clock.

"Twenty past three! Do you think it's safe to go to sleep now?" John nodded. They kissed each other and put out their bedside lights.

They overslept and woke in great confusion. Philomena was howling at the front door, the back door having failed her. John was late at the office and Jane was late for school.

# CHAPTER TWENTY TWO

REGINALD POLE, son of the Countess of Salisbury, was a scholar and a theologian who spent most of his time abroad and devoted himself wholeheartedly to the service of the Papacy. He was connected by birth to the old royal house of York and, as befitted a man of royal blood, he was both an attractive person and not without a certain grandeur. His was an ardent disposition, though a gentle one. It has also to be said of him, however, that he was possessed of an obstinate and somewhat unreliable judgement.

Upon King Harry's formal break with Rome this latter trait was manifested in a formidable rebuke, delivered by letter, from Pole to his infuriated sovereign.

Pole was at once the subject of a Parliamentary Act of Attainder which declared him guilty of High Treason. As Pole was abroad and unlikely to return in order to be conveniently killed, the next best thing was therefore accomplished and his entire family, resident in England, was slaughtered instead. The last to die was the elderly Countess herself who fought her executioner on the scaffold and had to be felled with the axe before she could be satisfactorily decapitated. Pole's reaction to his mother's death was typical of him. "I am the son of a martyr!" he declared and redoubled the intensity of his service to the Papacy. Not surprisingly, a certain bitterness entered into his soul.

Hugh Latimer, Lord Bishop of Worcester, found it necessary to loudly applaud the slaughter of the Salisburys. His own fortunes were tending towards an eclipse and perhaps, by this loyal outburst, he sought to restore them. Early in 1540, however, the Vicar General suggested to Latimer that his health would best be served by a humble resignation of his see. He complied at once, spent a little time in restraint and was then a free man again and up to all his old tricks. He was, after all, a likeable fellow and a plausible rogue.

Thomas Crumwel, Henry's Vicar General and the cynical instrument of his rapacious will, had begun by now to suffer from delusions of grandeur. It was reported of him that he intended to seek the hand in marriage of none other than the Lady Mary, the King's eldest daughter. King Harry's health was on the wane, Prince Edward was congenitally sick and could not live long; what better for Crumwel and for England that King Harry be succeeded in due time by King Tom?

Alas! Tom's own star was beginning to set, though he may not have known it until it was too late. He had been involved in a full scale royal fiasco and was to bear the blame for it. For King Harry had been flirting with the Lutherans and had welcomed a number of their divines into the English Universities. What better, now Queen Jane had died, than for the King to marry Anne, daughter of the Lutheran Duke of Cleves? Tom Crumwel made all the arrangements. They were to prove his undoing.

The marriage was never consummated. Queen Anne was said to be singularly lacking in physical attractions, but it was also noised abroad that the King's drinking habits, his diet and the general state of his health had rendered him impotent. Be that as it may, the "Mare of Flanders" was released from her marriage bond and sent home, in unkind haste.

Earlier, this very year of 1540, Thomas Crumwel had been made an Earl for his loyal services to the crown. On June 10th, however, he was surprised by an arrest for High Treason, his days of usefulness being over. On July 28th he was decapitated in the Tower of London. His exit from the world was, alas, neither dignified nor particularly courageous.

"Well, Tom, and what of Court?"

Tom Campion sat warming himself in front of the fire in the house room. He looked first at John and then at Kate, and he gave a shrug of his shoulders and grinned a wry grin.

The question would not have been asked in the Hall. It was not safe now to mention Court, or even religion, in the hearing of others. It had been four long years since Tom had last been at Farelowe and much water had flowed under the bridges of England since then.

"I'll not pretend that life hasn't been a good deal more agreeable since Master Crumwel lost his head, but the matter of Queen Catherine set us all by the heels, as you can imagine."

"What was the truth of it? Does anyone know?"

Kate looked hard at Tom. To her, King Harry was the very embodiment of evil, but she kept her own counsel on that point.

"The truth? God knows! I don't think truth is a commodity anyone knows or cares about any more in England. Not in London anyway, and certainly not at Court. Queen Catherine was a silly young thing who had always slept with any man she fancied. She just carried on doing it, that's all! The King can have his mistresses of course, but the Queen her lovers? Oh dear no! That kind of thing is High Treason! The poor, silly thing just didn't believe what was happening to her until the axe took her head off!"

"They say the Archbishop betrayed her to the King."

John raised an eyebrow at Tom, hoping for enlightenment.

"Not really. Poor Tom Cranmer had the thankless task of handing all the papers to the King at Hampton Court – in the Chapel too. King Harry was at his prayers. The King is become a very model of piety these days – after his fashion!"

Kate shook herself involuntarily, in disgust. Tom glanced at her and grinned.

"What of this brave Archbishop of ours, Tom? Is he a man or is he just a shadow on the wall?"

"A bit of both, John! But there is more of him about now Crumwel is gone. He is a timid fellow at heart, that is why the King chose him. And Crumwel rode roughshod over him and everybody else while he was in power. In all fairness, had Tom Cranmer stood up for himself his head would have been off in a day, and some other cypher would have taken his place – one of Crumwel's friends no doubt! From that, God and Tom Cranmer's timidity delivered us!"

"Does he do anything? Does he stand for anything?" John liked his men to be men. He had been badly scarred by the abolition of the monasteries and the treatment of the Church in general by King, Parliament and the Vicar General. Truth – God's Truth – was involved in all this, and even the break with a corrupted and cynical Papacy was beginning to gnaw at John's conscience. Did it matter after all?

"Oh! Tom Cranmer does a great deal – quietly and on tip toes. 'Tis the only way. He was behind the foundation of the six new Dioceses. You have Tom Cranmer to thank that Gloucester has its own Bishop – John Wakeman, Abbot of Tewkesbury – and that the Abbey of St Peter is now the Cathedral of the Holy and Undivided Trinity and not a roofless ruin. Tom Cranmer *cares* for King Harry, John! He really does. He has the heart of a priest and he does his best for the poor demented wretch behind all the fat, the fury and the pox! He does his best for the Church too."

Tom Campion looked behind him, instinctively, as if to see if there was anyone who could have overheard him. He gave a cynical laugh and returned to his theme.

"And the King knows that Tom Cranmer cares. I think, in some funny sort of way, King Harry loves Tom Cranmer for it. He has certainly saved him from one attempt to get him attainted. Tom's at odds with his Cathedral Chapter, and they are at odds among themselves. Everyone has friends at Court and we have had a right merry carry-on ever since the *Six Articles* became law, with everyone denouncing everyone else for heresy in order to get rid of their rivals! I was nearly burned myself!"

"You! Nearly burned ... !"

John and Kate cried out in chorus.

"Nothing to do with religion, just petty jealousy. The King pardoned me – just as he has had to pardon half his Court or it would all go up in flames! They have had to alter the provisions of that Act now to stop all this nonsense."

"Was the Archbishop behind the *Six Articles*?"

"No, John. It was King Harry himself. He put the Duke of Norfolk up to it. Notice: it was *Parliament* that produced this Heresy Act! The Church had nothing to do with it! I think Tom Cranmer did his best to restrain the King from it, and that's why the King went behind his back to my Lord of Norfolk. The King is very Catholic these days; terribly Orthodox he is! I think he might just have a bad conscience!"

"Is that why he wrote a new preface for the *Bishop's Book*?"

"Yes, Kate. And now we have to call it the *King's Book* instead. I think Tom Cranmer is working on him, as best he can. I can tell you one thing about our Archbishop: he is working on the King to allow the English Language into the Liturgy! There is to be a Litany in English next year!"

"God bless Tom Cranmer!"

Kate sat up very straight and looked straight at her husband with, Tom thought, a mixture of defiance and triumph. John just looked puzzled and said nothing.

"We have had great disagreements in this house of late, Tom," said Kate. "John there, and our son William have nearly come to blows about it. And I am in bad odour because I agree with William!" She nodded defiantly at John, who scowled and looked uncomfortable. Tom looked from one to the other. He could guess the matters at issue. It would be the New Learning against the Old, the new, reforming generation against the old conservative one. It would be the murderous undercurrents of Court, writ small. John looked up.

"William, with all his Oxford ways, answers the Mass in English while the rest of us answer in the Latin of our forefathers. And folk hear him, and there is talk and dissention. And I have to answer for his Reformer's carry-on!"

"Joys of parenthood, John!"

"Aye, Tom. But he accuses Holy Church of magic! Says images and pictures are a poor substitute for the people hearing the Scriptures in their own tongue, and praying to God in their own tongue. He would strip our church out and whitewash it like a barn! And he would bring the Altar of God down into the nave and offer the Mass in English, and aloud, so that all could hear and understand – so he says!"

"Is he so wrong? This is a new age we are coming into, John. You and I are out of date. The world is changing such as it has never changed before and men are thinking for themselves now. All the Heresy Acts in creation will not stop them. Like it or not!"

"I grant you that I see sense in some of the things he says, but it is all the destruction that seems to go with it. If Mass were said in English – why! It is still the Mass. But have we to destroy everything beautiful, and loved, and hallowed by the prayers of our forefathers at the same time? Have we to abandon our hearts and pray to God with our heads only, like self-consciously clever men with no feelings? I'm a threatened man, Tom! Antichrist is abroad, of that I have no doubt. And it is mortal hard for any ordinary Christian man to discern the works of the Spirit when the works of Satan make such pious noises in the midst of the flames and brimstone!"

Kate's look of defiance softened. There had been angry scenes in the house. Young Meg, who adored both her father and her brother, had fled to her chamber weeping most days when young Will had been home. She herself had been worn out with it all. Will had been a typical sixteen-year-old know-all, full of revolution and quite insensitive to any other point of view. John had over-reacted more and more, and had been glad to see the back of his son. Will was now entered the University of Oxford, his tutor having served him more than well, in spite of his Reformer's influence. Kate decided that it was time to change the subject.

"And King Harry is wed again, they say?"

"Yes, we have another Queen Catherine, and unless she loses her head she will survive him. She is a good, and a wise woman. And she is a holy one too. I wish her well."

"And I!"

Kate gave an inward shudder at the thought of sharing a bed with that bloated, diseased and intemperate monster, the King! Queen Catherine should have her prayers, and no mistake!

"And what of Master Latimer, Tom?"

John was keen to change the subject too, but he could not help asking after his late, and unlamented Father-in God.

"Oh! About his tricks as usual. Preaching near-heresy when he thinks he can get away with it. Undermining all he can. Then happy to applaud the burning of any heretic that suffers in order to demonstrate what a champion of orthodoxy he is! He is splendid to listen to, I grant him that, and he is full of zeal. But he will never be a builder, he can only demolish."

John nodded. "The Abbot of Flaxley said exactly the same of him, ten or more years ago now. He will never change. I disapprove of him violently, but it is hard to dislike the wretch!"

Tom smiled. He had a very soft spot for Hugh Latimer as a man, but he would not trust him an inch.

"Its easier to dislike some of his hangers-on! There is one in particular, an ex-monk called John Hooper. He had been hanging about at Court with an eye to the main chance, and then he took fright at the *Six Articles* and is fled abroad somewhere. A big, opinionated, violent sort of fellow. Would tear down all the churches and invent a new religion, given half a chance! I was glad to see the back of him. I hope he stays abroad and never comes home! Not in my lifetime at any rate."

The talk moved on to more domestic things, and then the three of them retired to bed. But John and Kate Farelowe were to be reminded of Tom's last word. For John Hooper would not stay abroad. He would come home, and his would be a most terrible impact upon both their lives.


The closing years of the life of King Henry the Eighth were marked by a relative peace. It was as if all the violent storms of his reign, between the divorce of his first wife and his marriage to his sixth, had exhausted all the energies available.

Thomas Cranmer trod his tightrope with some skill and not a little cunning. He was obliged to suffer the Church's Convocations to be treated with contempt by a Parliament determined to order all things. Matters of ecclesiastical order and discipline were now enforced and punished by the civil magistrates, and the foundations were thus laid for the terrible upheavals of the reign that was to follow.

Tom Cranmer, unable to beat the system, had joined it. He had long persuaded himself that the Church should be subordinate to the State and increasingly, therefore, he exercised what influence he had through the secular authorities.

All was not ill, however. Religious and devotional books poured from the printing presses and, behind the scenes, the Archbishop made rough drafts of those translations, simplifications and adaptations of the Church's Liturgy which, given the slightest opportunity, he would introduce with all the benefits of the new technology of printing to aid him. It was Tom Cranmer's abiding and entirely admirable passion that England, like the Lutheran states in Germany, should one day worship Almighty God in her own mother tongue.

In 1546, Hugh Latimer was accused of heresy and committed to the Tower. As was usually the case in his brushes with authority the matter contained all the elements of tragi-comedy. Latimer defended himself with vigour, blaming all his misfortunes upon Stephen Gardner, Bishop of Winchester. Gardner was by far the ablest, and most clear-headed Bishop on the Bench. He was feared and hated by both the Archbishop and by Latimer, for they both knew themselves seen-through by a better and more principled man.

Eventually Heath, Latimer's successor at Worcester, together with sundry other divines, visited Latimer in prison, at the King's command, "to talk friendly with him, to fish out the bottom of his stomach, that the King might see further into him!"

Their friendly talk and their "fishing" resulted in Hugh Latimer being released into private life. It was impossible not to like the fellow, and he was a plausible rogue.

Also in 1546, Thomas Ware, one-time Abbot of Flaxley, died. He had lived out the Cistercian life alone, to the very end. On the 28th of January 1547, King Harry died in his fifty-sixth year. He was given a funeral of unparalleled extravagance – some said vulgarity – and he was laid to rest beside Jane Seymour, the mother of his only son.

The son was nine years old and congenitally ill. The dying King had made careful dispositions regarding the succession, and also regarding the minority of young King Edward. It was always doubtful that the new King would ever reach his majority.

# CHAPTER TWENTY THREE

"I AM BARKING up the wrong tree!"

John Faversham sat back in his chair and gazed across the office to the watercolour of the Langdale Pikes on the opposite wall. It was a day full of bits and pieces, a lull between one sudden panic and the shock that must ensue when Head Office suddenly grasped the implications of what he had been trying to tell them about the Turkish contract. That would produce the mother and father of all panics!

"Coffee, Mr Faversham."

"Thank you, Vera."

He looked up and smiled. It was a daily ritual. The words never changed and he always looked up and smiled. He was very fond of Vera and, as Jane had spotted at once, she was very fond of him. Theirs was an old-fashioned, formal relationship; they held each other in great respect and their mutual loyalty was, at times, almost ferocious. They had hardly ever met socially, other than at gatherings organised by the Firm, but they knew every detail of each other's circumstances and cared profoundly about them, and about each other.

Vera wore spectacles in fashionable frames that were a touch too big for her. Her fair hair was sensibly cut – for easy maintenance, John thought – and she adorned her not unattractive figure as one who had never quite mastered the art of making the best of it. She was in her mid-forties and was exceedingly efficient. She was also a very good and kindly woman.

"How is Lorraine getting on with her O-Levels?"

Vera raised her eyes to the ceiling.

"She'll be doing her mocks in a week or two. She's in an awful state about them. But she's quite bright really; she'll be all right."

John grinned at her. Daughters seemed to take exams much more to heart than sons. It was the same with homework. Sons just wanted to get the damned stuff over and get on with something else. Daughters wanted to get it right!

"You'll need gin when she does her A-levels! You mark my words!"

Vera gave a despairing laugh, smiled sweetly, but very properly, at John, and vanished back into her own den.

"If somebody took that girl in hand, did her hair nicely and dressed her properly, she could be quite stunning!" John gazed affectionately at the closed door. This too was something of a ritual. Poor Vera! Her Stanley had died when Lorraine was quite small. She was bringing up the kid single-handed, and looking after a difficult old mother at the same time. Salt of the Earth, he thought, as he did, every day.

John stirred his coffee and took a sip. It was too hot. He put the cup down, sat back and addressed the painting of the Langdale Pikes.

"I'm barking up the wrong tree!" he said, again.

He had been completely taken up with Hasfield, the Victorian poet. Hasfield's book; Hasfield, the former occupant of the house; Hasfield, the dreamer of the same nightmare dream that he had dreamed – yes, but it hadn't been Hasfield's dream either!

At that moment, John became vividly aware that someone, on another level altogether, was trying to communicate with him. What the hell was going on? John concentrated his mind and tried to discover what indeed was going on.

It was all inside his own head of course; where else could it be? And yet it wasn't just inside his own head, any more than Vera had just been inside his own head when she brought in the coffee. It was simply that the levels, the planes, the dimensions, the wavelengths or some damned thing or other were different.

Someone was "there," quite unmistakably, but John didn't know where "there" was! But he knew full well who it was. It was Hasfield! What was being communicated? It was a sense of urgency, a concern, almost an anxiety.

"OK old son! I think that's enough!"

John made a conscious break with whatever it was. He was not alarmed by it, merely slightly surprised. He took a sip of very hot coffee, burned his mouth and came down to earth with a bump. He looked up at the Langdale Pikes again.

"What the hell was all that about?" he asked.

At that moment the telephone on his desk gave a discreet ring.

He picked up the receiver. Vera's voice said:

"Mr Thompson from Head Office for you, Mr Faversham." With a sense of grim satisfaction John knew that this could mean only one thing: Head Office had suddenly got the message on that Turkish Contract.

They had.


"This is most interesting. It is *Karmic* of course; will John be able to accept that?"

Lucy fixed Jane with one of her intense looks. Jane began to wonder how wise she had been to mention John's second dream in Lucy's hearing, but it was too late now.

"Well, everything is Karmic I suppose, but it rather depends what you mean by Karma, doesn't it?"

Aunt Sarah poured out the tea and tried to exercise a modicum of restraint on Lucy at the same time. Lucy was rather inclined to seize upon things and dogmatise.

"What do you mean, Lucy?"

Jane was quite ready to hear Lucy out, whatever reservations she might have about her Oriental-sounding notions. There were no experts in this kind of field and anybody's theories might have a grain of truth in them.

"John will have left something unresolved in a former incarnation," explained Lucy, with great confidence. "In fact it sounds like more than one incarnation. He did something, or failed to do something, a long time ago – perhaps several lives ago. He had the chance to fulfil his Karma as Hasfield, but he obviously failed to complete whatever it was. Now, as John Faversham, he must try again. I think it is important."

"And if he does?" Jane asked.

"He will have fulfilled his Karma – that part of it at least – and he will be closer to *Moksha*!" Lucy smiled benevolently.

"Closer to what?" Jane had not heard that word before. Aunt Sarah had, and she supplied the answer.

"*Moksha*. It means 'release,' doesn't it, Lucy?"

Lucy nodded.

"Release from *Samsara*, release into the All."

"You and your funny words!" Jane laughed. "Well, I'll keep an open mind on that one."

"Like John?" Lucy's eyes twinkled with mischief.

"Lucy, I'm not being critical or anything like that ..." Aunt Sarah was frowning slightly. It was a thoughtful frown rather than a critical one. "Its just that ... Well, if you structure everything round one framework – reincarnation, Karma and all that – it does rather foreclose your options doesn't it? John's dream-thing doesn't quite feel like that to me. No doubt I'm wrong, but ... your explanation is wonderfully logical, but ..."

"Well, at least it is one possible explanation."

Jane didn't want to antagonise Lucy. Lucy could withdraw from a conversation in something of a huff if too strongly disagreed with. She was very committed to her theories and all the funny Sanskrit words that went with them and she was easily hurt.

"I'm only outlining a framework," said Lucy, quietly. "What happens within that framework is not my business – not my Karma. But it works for me. It makes sense of my life."

"In terms of my framework," said Jane, "I am beginning to think we have a ghost in the house. Not Hasfield; someone else. And it looks as though Hasfield realised it too, and tried to help, but didn't quite make it. And now it is rather as though Hasfield – or at least his poems – are prodding us to have a go."

"Three separate people, Lucy, rather than three incarnations of one person," said Aunt Sarah. "We'll know which one of us is right when we get to heaven! A piece of cake?"

"I can't resist, Sarah!"

Lucy, bright eyed, helped herself to a large slice of sponge cake. She turned back towards Jane.

"One thing I am certain about, though: it is John's Karma rather than yours. You are in this together of course, so it is your Karma too, to some degree, but the real task – whatever it is – belongs to John."

Jane glanced at Aunt Sarah, then she turned to Lucy. "Yes, Lucy. I am quite sure of that too, and so is John. I just hope ... I don't know what I hope but I just hope he doesn't get hurt or damaged ... or something."

Jane bit her lip, took firm control of herself and turned to Aunt Sarah.

"You might have offered me a slice of cake too!" she said.

"If Lucy is to be believed I've been hanging round this house for centuries!" John made a face and grinned. "I think I would rather be involved in helping some other poor chap than in endlessly polishing up the me-ness of me!"

"Deirdre is away for a few days. I had rather hoped we could have talked it over with her. I just feel she – sort of – knows about these things."

Jane sighed and bit her thumb. John wondered if, as a schoolgirl, she used to do that in exams, or if the hockey team looked like losing. Jane had a number of what John called her schoolgirl habits. He found them very endearing. He was, of course, quite unconscious of his own schoolboy habits, some of which Jane found maddening.

"Let's ask Philomena," said John. "She and Deirdre have a lot in common. They are both Wise!"

He turned to the cat.

"Come on, little Sweetheart! Tell us what the score is!"

Philomena responded with a stretch, a yawn and a look of crushing disdain. If it was really true that they didn't know, how on earth did they expect her to tell them! She went to sleep again.

"She knows! The little devil! I swear she does!" John laughed and gazed adoringly at her.

"Darling! That business at the office; you know – Hasfield trying to chat you up. Was it like the other night?"

John shook his head.

"No! Not a bit. How shall I put it? Qualitatively different. On another level altogether. All the difference between order and disorder. But I had a feeling that if I paid too much attention it would disorder me! So I thanked him kindly and switched off. Then Thompson phoned from Head Office, so that switched Hasfield off well and truly!"

"Was he trying to tell you something?"

"There was nothing verbal. Just a sort of communication of moods or emotions. Urgency. Anxiety. But not for himself, I'm sure about that. God knows how I'm sure, but I am."

Jane gave a sudden gasp, clapped her hand to her mouth, jumped up from the kitchen table and dashed from the room. John followed her departure with raised eyebrows. He turned to Philomena. "Mummy has had a sudden inspiration!" he said.

Philomena opened one eye, looked at him wearily, and closed it again.

At that moment Jane reappeared with Hasfield's book in her hand.

"I just remembered a poem I read, near the end of the book ... ."

She searched frantically. Her fingers seemed to be all thumbs.

"There!" She thrust the book into John's hands. "Read that!" she said.

John looked at the two-verse poem, cleared his throat and read it aloud:

The clouds are gathering, the darkness comes
I wear my melancholy as a cloak
Deep-hooded and tight wrapped.
Thus fast, it numbs Initiative and will, makes mind to choke.
But yet – I cling to life – this is not me
Nor is it mine, this all-enshrouding fog;
But other, and another's. Thus is he
Invigorate while I lie here, a log!

John looked up. Their eyes met. Jane's eyes were full of anxiety.

"It sounds as if he was on to something, doesn't it?"

John read the poem through again.

"Darling! I don't like it! It frightens me!"

John reached out and took his wife's hand.

"I'm sure we are not supposed to be frightened. I don't think its about that. Forewarned is forearmed anyway. Hasfield is giving us clues, through his poems and unless I'm completely crackers – directly from wherever he is. We are in it together. Hasfield and I have the job of rescuing a Third Party. Now I have met the Third Party, the other night, in the dining-room. Hasfield and I have both shared in his nightmare. We both *nearly* know what it is about. As soon as I find out *who he is* I reckon we shall have cracked it!"

"Don't you think you ought to go and see Walter? Might it not need exorcising, or whatever they do?"

"No! Not yet. Later on perhaps. But I'm quite sure there is nothing to be frightened of. We'd better give a name to the Third Party. It might help to get him in from the cold and make him feel human again. What shall we call him?"

"Horace," said Jane. "Or Jack."

She grinned and squeezed John's hand.

"We'll call him Jack," said John. "He might not take too kindly to Horace. Well, now he has got a name we can cope with him, can't we?"

John turned towards the dining-room door. Raising his voice, he said:

"No more nightmares, Jack!"

# CHAPTER TWENTY FOUR

KING HENRY was scarcely in his grave before the careful arrangements he had made for an orderly and conservative Regency fell to pieces. A scandalous exercise in manipulation, misrepresentation and falsehood resulted in the appearance of a Regency Council made up entirely of the reforming party and headed by the Earl of Hertford as Lord Protector.

The Lord Protector then announced a series of ennoblements, intended by his late and deeply lamented Majesty, with all necessary money and estates to be taken from the Church. The Lord Protector ennobled himself to a higher degree and proclaimed himself Duke of Somerset. The whole of the estates of the former Abbey of Glastonbury passed into his hands.

It was an age of widespread nominal Christianity and formal, though not always committed, churchgoing. The wealthy, the powerful and the ambitious jumped on the reformer's bandwagon, as much in hope of personal gain as of any conviction whatsoever. It was clear at the outset of King Edward's reign that whatever merits the reformer's views might or might not have, the remaining wealth of the Church was best extracted under their aegis.

The reform movement was, as almost always, an urban phenomenon and an academic concern. The townsmen were, as ever, determined to foist their up-to-date opinions upon their country cousins, aided by a vulgar, *nouveau riche* squirearchy already fat on plundered monastic wealth. The mob, ever fickle, caring little for religion in any event and always ready for an affray, was only too glad to go along for the ride.

The nine-year-old monarch, precocious, degenerate and ailing, was put into the charge of Chaplains of extreme reforming views and was brought up in hatred of all that had gone before. The curates and Churchwardens of St Martin's Church, Ironmonger Lane, in London, then set the trend that was to prevail by tearing out all the statues of the Saints, ripping the Crucifix from the rood-loft and replacing it with a great board painted with the royal coat of arms, and covering all the wall-paintings with whitewash. The newly consecrated Bishop of Rochester, one Nicholas Ridley, a former chaplain to the Archbishop, then preached a sermon in his Cathedral denouncing all images. A sermon was preached at Court denouncing the observance of Lent.

Parliament, more determined than ever to keep the Church under its thumb, repealed the harshest of King Henry's legislation and opened the door to free religious debate. Mindful of its own vulnerability it also reduced the definition of High Treason to reasonable proportions, but it altogether failed to put an end to the hideous civil penalty for heresy, that of burning at the stake. Tom Campion, seeing only too clearly the way the wind was blowing, was mightily relieved to inherit – somewhat unexpectedly – a modest estate in Oxfordshire. He slipped quietly away from Court and settled at Chipping Norton, not an impossible distance away from his lifelong friend John Farelowe.

The clean country air put new life into Tom. He made the acquaintance of a handsome widow, his near neighbour, and at the age of forty-seven, he married her.

At the same time that Tom was settling into his new home and paying court to his neighbour, all the Bishops and Archdeacons of the English Church were inhibited from administering their dioceses until further notice. They were, in fact, forbidden by the civil power to fulfil their proper functions.

A new set of Injunctions was issued, concerning the worship in churches and cathedrals. These were enlarged by decree in September, and Commissioners were appointed for every Diocese, armed with sweeping powers and commissioned to ride roughshod over Bishops, Archdeacons or anyone else who got in their way. Those appointed to enforce the Injunctions upon the newly created Diocese of Gloucester were the Deans of St Pauls and of Exeter, one Sir Walter Buckler, a reformist preacher by the name of Cotisford and John Redman, a Registrar.

Bishop John Wakeman was obliged to stand back and watch this band of official marauders wreak what havoc they would all over his diocese that Autumn. There was nothing he could do about it.


In the tiny Chantry, in the North aisle of the Church of our Lady Saint Mary at Farelowe, the old chantry priest was teaching a dozen village lads to read and to write. Old Sir Edward was a good schoolmaster, he worked them as hard as he could and some showed promise. He had started a few on careers beyond their parents' imaginings during his time there, and he had a couple of promising lads in his present class.

It was October, a fine sunny morning with the beginnings of a nip in the air. The autumn colours, one of the glories of Gloucestershire, were at their most sumptuous. There was the sound of voices, and of shouted commands. A commotion was beginning outside in the village square. The old priest looked up and peered through the traceries of the wooden screen that divided his chantry from the nave of the church. He was just in time to see the church door fly open and armed men pour through it.

Perkin, the magistrate's officer, had never forgiven the village of Farelowe for his ignominious defeat a few years since. Now he had his chance for revenge, for the King's Commissioners were in Gloucester, abolishing the chantries, destroying images and leaving a trail of vandalism, alienation and distress wherever they went. A few words in the proper ear and their wrath could be turned upon Farelowe as the den of iniquity and idolatry that Perkin now denounced it to be.

John and Kate Farelowe were away, visiting Tom Campion and his new wife. It was, perhaps, as well for them that they were. Almost before old Sir

Edward could gather his wits, his chantry was invaded by men-at-arms. An ill-visaged cleric was at their head and Perkin announced him as the King's Commissioner and bade Sir Edward hear him and obey.

The old chantry-priest was then informed that, in the name of the King, his chantry was abolished forthwith. Its tiny endowment, his livelihood, was to be taken from him, he was to surrender all that pertained to his office at once and he was to be gone from the village before nightfall.

The chantry scholars were driven from the chapel. One who protested was sent sprawling for his impertinence.

A shocked and bewildered Sir Edward surrendered his books, his vestments and the sacred vessels that belonged to the chantry. He was like a man in a daze. The Commissioner snatched a vestment from his hands and ripped it in two.

"Filthy rag of popery!" he shouted in the old man's face. There was a commotion at the door. Armed men brought in Sir Ralph, the Vicar, and Harry, his Parish Clerk. They were at once subjected to a blistering harangue as to the evils of their religion and the base idolatry to which their church bore such eloquent witness. They were forced to watch while Perkin and his men tore the statue of the Mother of God from its plinth. Perkin put its head on the floor and, with much stamping and jumping, smashed it off, with much else besides. The remains were carried outside to the cart.

The Holy Rood itself was next. The great crucifix was torn down, together with its flanking figures. They were broken up with axes and the remains went to the cart. Ladders were fetched, and such frescoes as most offended the Commissioner were daubed with whitewash, and the eyes of the picture of the Blessed Virgin, enthroned in heaven, were picked out with the point of a dagger. Attention was then turned to the altar in the chapel of the Holy Trinity in the South aisle upon whose floor old Walter and the young Harry had knelt, praying for Master John's safe delivery into the world, forty-seven years before. There was a fine stone reredos to this altar, with figures cut in relief and beautifully coloured. The reredos was attacked with hammers until nothing remained save smashed stone and flakings of pigment.

Almost sated, but not quite, the Commissioner turned and saw the one, fine piece of painted glass in the church. It depicted the Assumption of our Lady Saint Mary, the Mother of God and patron of the little church. It was smashed to fragments, for it was an idol, leading men to perdition!

After what he was pleased to describe as "this godly cleansing of an Augean Stable of Popish Idolatry," the King's Commissioner turned his attention to the reading of solemn instructions to the Vicar, white-faced with shock, and to his sullen and enraged clerk. In a voice heavy with sanctimony and self-importance he informed them that the Lessons at the Divine Offices, and the Epistle and Gospel at Mass, were henceforth to be read or sung in English! He went on to tell them that the English Litany – which they already used – was henceforth to be sung kneeling; there were to be no more glad processions about church and churchyard, as there had been ever since Saint Augustine had set foot in Kent. Religion was a serious business; it was not a thing to be enjoyed! Reading from his paper, the Commissioner ended by telling Sir Ralph – who by this time thought the man was raving mad – that he was to "suffer from henceforth no torches nor candles, tapers or images of wax to be set before any image or picture, but only two lights upon the high altar, before the Sacrament; which, for the signification that Christ is the very true light of the world, he shall suffer to remain still."

The King's Luminary, with his men-at-arms, then departed, with Perkin smirking with satisfaction, only regretting that Master Farelowe had not been present to watch his beloved church being smashed up. The cart-load of statues, books, vestments and all else repugnant to the Commissioner's tender and most Christian conscience, was burned on a great bonfire in Gloucester.

The sacred vessels and certain other valuables were retained, however. The Farelowe chantry chalice found its way into the sideboard of an Oxfordshire Squire's house. Chalices were made for drinking out of when all was said and done.

John and Kate, returning a few days later, wept with a mixture of grief and rage at the ruin they beheld. The merriment went out of John, never completely to return. The forces of Antichrist were surely running riot all over England! He remembered his father's words. Hold fast to our Lady Saint Mary and all the Saints; only the devil would try to corrupt, pervert, destroy … Well, this was the devil's work and no mistake! But how could a man be sure where lines were to be drawn … ?

It was Harry who voiced the same perplexity.

"Master John! When 'im was done a-smashin up o' th'ouse o' God, why! 'Im did turn to Sir Ralth and I and 'im did say as we was to sing th'Epistle and Gospel in English! Now, Master John! That were well said! But why be I a-'earin of 'un from the lips o' Antichrist? Why do 'im act like the very devil 'isself one minute and talk sense the next?"

Harry shook his head. He looked up at John.

"Master John! Whatever they reformers *think* they be a-doin, I'll tell ee what they *really* be a-doin! They be a-turnin o' the Gospel o' Love into a religion o' 'atred!"


When King Henry had turned the monks out of their monasteries he had made adequate provision for them in the way of pensions. No such provision was made for the chantry priests, some of whom ended up by swelling the growing ranks of beggars and vagabonds. So serious did the vagabond problem become that the persistently homeless were ordered to be branded with a "V". Upon a second offence they were to be branded again with an "S", after which they were to become the slaves of their mutilator who might do what he wished with them.

Nobody ever knew what happened to old Sir Edward. In this, and in a second Visitation the following year, two hundred Grammar Schools and unnumbered tiny village schools were destroyed by the Commissioners. The entire educational system of England was thus destroyed, for what King Harry had begun his son completed. A pathetic handful of "King Edward the Sixth" Grammar schools were founded, here and there, but at Farelowe, as in most of the villages of England, it would be almost three hundred years before the lads had any kind of schooling again.

One who would have much enjoyed the Commissioner's sport at Farelowe was still abroad, and it was to be another eighteen months before the unsmiling countenance and the chilling personality of John Hooper, the ex-monk, were found in England again. He had settled in Zurich and had become a close associate of the extremist reformer Bullinger, upon whom the mantle of the formidable Zwingli had fallen. These three were birds of a feather and no mistake, and John Hooper looked forward to the day when he should turn England, or at least a part of it – into as close a copy of Zurich as he could manage. In Zurich, Catholic Christians were herded, Sunday by Sunday, into the churches they had loved. There, surrounded by bleakness, whitewash and devastation, they were compelled to listen to interminable sermons denouncing them and everything they had loved and believed in. They were then obliged to take part in a liturgy carefully devised to deny *The Mystery* and to repudiate any objective reality in the Sacraments of the Christian Church.

# CHAPTER TWENTY FIVE

**W**ALTER CLOSED the door of Church House behind him and emerged into the late autumn greyness of College Green. Well, there was a patch of green in the middle of it, even though it was entirely surrounded by parked motor-cars. He glanced about him. The fine old houses in the great square were all old friends. He had known their exteriors all his life and, at various times and in various circumstances, he had acquired a knowledge of the interiors of most of them as well.

Walter was a Gloucestershire man, through and through. Before his ordination, in middle life, he had served the Diocese well as a layman on the Synod and as a member of this Diocesan Board, or that one, and the Cathedral and its precincts were like a second home to him.

"Good morning, Walter!"

"Good morning, Margaret!"

He gazed affectionately at her retreating form. Pert, slim as a tape-measure, as pretty as a picture and eighty years old if she was a day! He had taken many a glass of sherry wine in her enchanting drawing-room.

"Barchester!" He grinned. "Why not? What is wrong with Barchester?"

Walter looked at his watch. Yes, he had time. He would have to get back to Cheltenham by lunchtime though. He glanced across at his car, nosed in – almost squeezed in – by connivance with the Cathedral's car-park attendant who acted like a circus ringmaster from his little hut round the corner opposite the South Porch. He would leave the car here. Half an hour wouldn't be cheating too disgracefully.

Five minutes in the Cathedral first though.

Walter glanced up at the great list of forthcoming preachers, displayed outside the porch. He wondered why it was necessary to advertise like that. The Church of England did not go in for personality cults or "personal ministries," and he was profoundly glad of it. He doubted if his own name would attract great crowds. It had been up on that board once and he had felt a bit silly and self-conscious about it. The crowd had been average.

"Mornin' Walter! 'ow be the Dook o' Fairloe, then?"

"Fair to middlin' Tom! 'ow bist thou?"

There was an exchange of banter, and the other priest left in search of wife and motor-car. Good old Tom! He was retired now of course, but he had been a great support to Walter in years past, and had encouraged him to offer for ordination.

When Walter had been offered the living of Fairloe, Tom had misheard him and thought at first it was Etloe, some miles down river towards Lydney. The land about Etloe was, for some obscure reason, called "Etloe Duchy" and Tom had dubbed Walter "Duke of Fairloe" ever since. The title appealed to Walter, it was delightfully absurd.

The whole Church of England was delightfully absurd, come to that! Supremely fallible! Walter was deeply grateful for it. There was something chilling, something not quite Godly about the very idea of infallibility. Heaven had far too much of a sense of humour for that kind of thing.

Walter knelt at the back of the great nave of Gloucester and offered his prayers. Then he sat for a minute or two and recalled his ordination. He had been made Deacon and, a year later, ordained Priest at that great Nave Altar. And by good Bishop Basil, of blessed memory!

Walter looked round him. Tewkesbury had the edge on it, though. The two great Norman naves were almost identical; they bore the same mason's marks too. But Tewkesbury had a certain something that Gloucester never quite had. Gloucester was glorious, but Walter could say his prayers better in Tewkesbury! Never mind! He loved them both.

He looked at his watch again, got up from his place, left by the great South porch, nodded and pointed to his watch for the benefit of the car-park attendant who nodded back, and walked briskly out of the Cathedral Precincts into Westgate.

Turning right, down the hill, he crossed over and before long came to a fine, half-timbered building which housed the Folk Museum. There was a room in there he wanted to have another look at, and to check some of the names on the old documents on display there. Twenty minutes later, Walter emerged, much interested. He had found something which, when he had time, he must certainly follow up. He would have to consult old George! But right now he must get back to the office; he had played truant long enough!

"This is such a pretty cottage!" Jane sat back and looked about her. She and John had map-read their way from the Forthampton cross-roads and, having negotiated little lanes they had never explored before, they had stumbled upon Deirdre's cottage more by luck than by good judgement. It was an ancient cottage, half-timbered and deeply thatched. The walls were hung with old-fashioned rambler roses and honeysuckle surrounded the door. It looked the very picture book image of "Olde England," even in late November. What it must look like in summer Jane could hardly imagine.

"Yes, I'm very lucky. It's just right for me, but it does get a bit crowded when Sally and the family descend on me." John gave an involuntary start. He had never connected the Earth-Mother with anything so ordinary as a daughter, a son-in-law and grandchildren! His eyes suddenly took in the framed photograph on the bookcase. A pretty young woman looked out of it. Hers was very much the sort of face found in *The Tatler* or *Country Life*. The Honourable Miss Somebody, who has just become engaged to the Honourable Mr Somebody-Else.

John glanced further and saw another family group, framed upon Deirdre's writing-desk. He found himself wondering what had become of the Earth-Father?

As if she had read his thoughts, Deirdre volunteered the answer. "Yes, I was married once, you know. But poor Charles ran away thirty years ago. I don't really blame him – I used to of course, but not now. I must have been very difficult to live with!" John saw a great sadness in her eyes, but a great compassion as well.

"You've forgiven him?"

"Oh yes! Somebody once said, 'to understand is to forgive.' As I began to understand – on all sorts of levels – it became easier. And if we won't forgive we destroy ourselves. I learned that too!"

It was time to get to work.

"Now tell me all about your adventures," she said.

John and Jane told Deirdre about John's second nightmare, about Jane's inability to go down the stairs, about John's experiences in doing so and his encounter in the dining-room.

"It was rather like walking into an electric storm," he said. "It was as if I was walking into an energy-field of some kind. But it was personal. It was *somebody*, if you know what I mean?"

Deirdre listened to everything very intently. The ghost of a smile came and went. "Where was the centre of the energy-field?" she asked.

"By the big chimney-piece in the dining-room."

John was slightly surprised to hear himself say it; he had not consciously asked himself the question before.

"Was it Hasfield?"

"No!"

"No, I didn't think it was Hasfield either."

Deirdre smiled her impish smile. Her eyes twinkled.

"There's an open hearth in the middle of the floor in your dining-room," she said. "And the smoke goes out through a hole in the roof. I had to walk round it when I was in your house a few weeks ago."

"So that's what you were doing?" Jane remembered Deirdre's little detour. "I saw you and Sarah exchange glances."

"Yes. Sarah loves your open hearth. She loves the dog too."

"The dog?" Jane and John looked at each other, wide-eyed.

"Sarah has often seen a dog lying beside the hearth. She thinks it is a Talbot, but it might not be quite pedigree!" The Earth-Mother's eyes were twinkling like stars. "Don't worry, dears! It may be just a doggy place-memory. How does Philomena react to it?"

"She doesn't like the dining-room!" Jane was surprised to hear herself say it. "She always darts straight through it without stopping!"

The Earth-Mother got up from her chair.

"The kettle will be boiling by now," she said.

John and Jane drove home in silence. Both had a great deal to think about. They decided to go home through Tewkesbury for a change but they had almost got to the Mythe Bridge before either of them spoke.

167

"What did you make of Deirdre telling me that Hasfield doesn't know as much as I do?" John asked. "Desperate to help but in danger of getting in the way!"

"I think she might be right." Jane looked at her husband's face. "You have suddenly started to become yourself, darling. You are showing your true colours suddenly after fifty-something years of trying to pretend you were nothing but a scientific rationalist! I think you are as potent as Deirdre! Potentially at any rate."

"Do you think she knows what the trouble is?"

"In a way, yes, I think she does. But perhaps not all of it. And she certainly agreed with Lucy. It's your job!"

They were turning round the Cross and into Church Street. The Abbey would soon appear, round the bend to their left. "Fancy her telling us to go to Evensong more often!"

John laughed.

"I always thought she was a witch! But witches don't usually exhort one to go to Evensong!"

The Abbey gates slid past to their left. The great bulk of the Abbey itself loomed in the darkness beyond.

"That is where she goes." Jane looked back as the Abbey vanished behind some houses. "She has been going there for years."

"I believe in the Communion of Saints." John nodded to himself. "Funny how we keep saying these things and then can't cope when their reality hits us! Good old Hasfield! Chatting me up within the Communion of Saints! I like that!"

"And Jack?" Jane had a terrible compassion for Jack, whoever he was, or whatever he had done.

"Doing Seven Days Confined to Barracks or something."

"Deirdre thinks he might have confined himself."

There was a long silence. It broke as they waited for the lights to change at Coombe Hill.

"I'm sure we have to find out who he is."

"How do we do that?"

Jane had an instinct that John was right, but couldn't for the life of her see how they could set about it.

"No idea! No idea at all! But if we are supposed to, no doubt we will!"

There was another long silence. As they passed Bishop's Norton church, up on its hill, John spoke again.

"What a *lovely* woman she is!"

"So is her daughter. Did you see the photograph?"

"Yes. Pretty girl. Very English. Very County. Not in the same class as her old mum though!"

Jane laughed and squeezed her husband's arm.

"You just wait till she's sixty!" she said.

# CHAPTER TWENTY SIX

Thomas Cranmer, Archbishop of Canterbury, was released by King Henry's death from the ever-present dread of a sudden Royal Displeasure which would bring him to the block, the gallows or the stake. The succession of the nine-year-old King Edward, surrounded by a Council of Regency, brought with it only the realisation that he had achieved little more than an escape from the frying-pan into the fire.

Cranmer was surrounded by characters stronger than his own, both among the grasping and unprincipled Council and also among the very reforming clerics in whom he now put his trust. His onetime chaplain, Nicholas Ridley, was now Bishop of Rochester. Ridley, an austere man and a determined Reformer, was a far stronger character than his Archbishop and his influence began to be seen in much that the Archbishop now did.

Both Nick Ridley and Tom Cranmer were nevertheless in fear of a man of greater stature and profounder learning than either of them. Stephen Gardner, Bishop of Winchester, was a traditionalist whose eagle eye saw through all that was false or superficial in the Reformers' arguments. There was much that was indeed false and superficial, for the Reformers were men in a great hurry. Nothing could be done, therefore, with Gardner at liberty at Winchester. A discreditable intrigue ensued and it resulted in Gardner being imprisoned and thus put out of their way.

Tom Cranmer had his own very clear intention and he had done much preparatory work towards its fulfilment already. The entire Liturgy of the English Church had been simplified and translated most beautifully into the vulgar tongue. A work of quite outstanding liturgical genius awaited approval by the Convocations of the Church and by Parliament. The new technology of printing would then enable every Englishman to have his Church's Liturgy for all occasions in his hand between the covers of one book. In the circumstances, therefore, it was a pity that the cause of national literacy had just been put back by some three hundred years. Tom Cranmer's defence mechanism against stronger characters was lethargy and inaction.

"This Thomas has fallen into so heavy a slumber, that we entertain but a very cold hope that he will be aroused even by your most learned letter." So wrote one John ab Ulmis to the Swiss reformer, Bullinger.

"Canterbury conducts himself in such a way that the people do not think much of him, and the nobility regard him as lukewarm." This, another complaint to Bullinger, probably paints an accurate enough picture of the Archbishop's timid and lack-lustre personality. The Convocations of Canterbury and York met in 1548 and, of their own initiative, presented a Bill to Parliament. It was the only initiative they were to be allowed to make during the entire reign of King Edward and it proposed the abolition of the vows of clerical celibacy.

Universal clerical celibacy was a peculiarly Western phenomenon, owing not a little to St Augustine of Hippo and his later disciples, and arising very largely out of a too ready identification of sex with sin. The Eastern Church, perhaps closer to the origins of the Faith, required of its clergy that they commit themselves either to monastic vows or to the married state before ordination. Clerical celibacy, therefore, however exalted and romanticised in the writings of celibates, belonged to Church discipline and not to Church order. The Convocations, well aware that vows were honoured as much in the breach as in the observance, arrived at a decision of surprising enlightenment.

The clergy were henceforth to be free to marry, or not marry, as their individual consciences dictated.

The House of Commons passed the bill in 1548 but it was too late to be included in the programme for the Lords. Their Lordships passed it in the early part of 1549 and it was stipulated that such clerics as wished to marry must do so according to the Marriage Rite of the new *Book of Common Prayer*.

The zeal of the Archbishop had already been displayed by the removal of the obligation for intending Communicants to make their confession before receiving the Sacrament. The effect of this obligation had long been that of reducing frequency of communion to an absolute minimum, save for the very devout. In 1548 an English *Order of Communion* became effective, to be incorporated into the Latin Mass of Sarum, by which a Corporate Confession and a General Absolution replaced the individual's confessions to a priest. All this was admirable, but Tom Cranmer's best efforts were to be perpetually doomed to ruination by the company they were forced to keep. The second *Visitation* of 1548, by which all the parish churches with chantries were assaulted as Fairlowe had been the previous year, raised such a storm of hatred, resentment and alienation, nationwide, that no liturgical innovation, however admirable in itself, was likely to be well received by the bruised, hurt and insulted churchgoers of England.

The most ardent advocate of the first, and still the best, *Book of Common Prayer*, could never claim with hand on heart that it represented the considered mind of the English Church. It is uncertain that it was ever submitted to the Convocation of Canterbury for approval, and it is quite certain that it was not submitted to the Convocation of York. It was thrust, quite arbitrarily, upon the Cathedrals and Parish Churches of England by the Archbishop himself, through the agency of the secular authority, Parliament. It was to be used on Whitsunday 1549 under pain of dire civil penalties for deviation.

Once again, Tom Cranmer's best effort – in this case his life's work and his work of true genius – was to be ruined by the company it was obliged to keep. The *Book of Common Prayer* was introduced in the context of yet another accursed *Visitation*, the Articles of which were positively calculated to offend, to distress and to alienate. They were the work of a Lutheran friend of Thomas Cranmer, one Martin Bucer, and they prohibited – with penal sanctions – practically every known gesture of traditional Christian devotional respect. One of many grotesques in this list was the prohibition of the use of the Holy Rosary in private prayer, upon pain of instant excommunication! It was all too much. Riots broke out all over England. An insurrection, connected also with other grievances, took place in Norfolk, and the counties of Devon and Cornwall rose in open, armed rebellion.

"What are we to do, Master John? There will be a riot!"

Sir Ralph, Vicar of Farelowe, was a worried man. He was also a profoundly disturbed man, for he was about to be required to do things that seemed to run clean contrary to his beliefs. Like many others in the same situation, he was far from clear where lines should be drawn; where did truth end and falsehood begin?

"We'll forget all about the *Articles of Visitation* just now, I think," said John Farelowe. "They never came from the hand of an Englishman and we can be a bit slow in hearing about them in any event."

John's lawyer's mind was calculating just what might be got away with in the way of disobedience, and for how long.

"Sufficient unto the day is the evil thereof," he added. It was Ascensiontide, 1549. The new *Book of Common Prayer* was to be taken into use from Whitsunday. It lay on the table in John's hall and he, the Vicar and Harry the Parish Clerk were looking at it, wondering what to do. Kate sat by the fire, sewing and listening. She had her own ideas.

"What are the problems?" she asked.

Sir Ralph turned to her, hopefully. He had a great respect for Mistress Kate. John was no longer the man he had once been, the devastation that Perkin and the King's Commissioner had wrought in the church had affected him badly; the spark was gone out of him.

"Tis the Mass, Mistress Kate," he said. "Tis all in English and it do seem different. Maybe t'isn't, but it do seem like it and I fear trouble!"

"Does it say different things?" she asked.

The three men looked at each other. John turned to the *Canon*, the great prayer of consecration and read it through again.

"Not in essentials," he said. "It follows the old pattern; it misses out the Pope and makes great play of the King and those in authority under him instead. It has no great lists of the Saints by name, but it still remembers them, and our Lady Saint Mary in particular. No, it is much as it was, but it will *seem* different, and we have had too much change and too much hurt to cope with any more."

"We can't be a-singin of it, Mistress Kate," said Harry. "The English words and the Latin – they's different."

"You got your tongue round the Epistle in English, and Sir Ralph managed to sing the Gospel in the proper tones. Why can't you make the plainsong fit the English words? Have you tried?"

Again the three men looked at each other. No, they had not tried.

The hurt and demoralisation of the last two years had defeated them.

Again, John turned pages and began to sing, quietly, to himself.

"John! You and James, the Cantors, surely you can get together and sing the Mass as it has always been sung, but in English? Make it seem as little changed as possible and folk might even like it!"

Kate returned to her sewing, darting glances at the three men round the table. She was thoroughly in favour of using the English language in worship. She grieved like John over the assault on the church and upon the devotional tradition of its people, but Kate was a realist. The King would soon die! The Lady Mary would succeed, and everyone knew what a traditionalist she was! A balance would be struck in a year or two. Some things would have gone for good, but others would return because of their innate merits. Meantime the sensible thing was to make the new things feel as much like the old things as possible, then people would not be roused to a dangerous degree of fury.

"Can we do it, Master John?" Harry saw Kate's point.

Sir Ralph was crooning little bits of the Mass to himself. He paused from time to time, re-phrased and crooned again. John was doing the same with the Kyries, the Gloria and the Credo.

"I think we can!" A light came into John's dull eyes. "I've got to be a-shoutin o' the Canon as if I was a-sellin apples in Gloucester Market!"

Sir Ralph glared at the command to "saye or syng, playnly and distinctly."

"A nice change from mumbling silently in your beard, Sir Priest!" Kate's tone was one of reverent impertinence.

The Vicar gave her a pained look and then smiled. She was doing a good work, sitting by the fire, prodding the demoralised menfolk. And she was right! They would have to use this new Liturgy in any event so why not use it with a good grace and make it seem as consistent with the old one as possible? He turned back to the book and carried on crooning to himself.

James was sent for and presently arrived. The problems and their possible solution were explained to him and before long the four men were singing their parts of the Mass, in the traditional plainsong but in English, round the table in John's hall. Kate startled them with a round of applause.

"Well, Mistress Kate," said Harry. "It may be a bad job, but we'll be a-makin the best of it!" He nodded gravely, gazed at his boots and looked up again.

"T'wouldn't do, else!" he said.


On Whit Monday, the 10th of June 1549, the parish priest of Sampford Courtenay in Devon left his parsonage in order to go to church to say Mass. He was met by a number of his parishioners among whom was Ned Carey, a devout member of his congregation. A brief but heated discussion ensued and full agreement was reached. He entered his church and, discarding the *Book of Common Prayer* with contempt, celebrated the Mass in Latin according to the old Sarum Missal, with full ceremonies.

The news went round the county like wildfire. On Tuesday 11th June, the Feast of Saint Barnabas, four Justices arrived, with a company of armed men, to investigate this flagrant disobedience and restore order. They were surrounded by armed villagers and forced to run for their lives. News then came of an armed rising in Cornwall and within a few days both counties were in open rebellion. Somerset, the Lord Protector, dithered – but his Council acted. Two Devonshire gentlemen, Sir Peter and Sir Gawain Carew, were sent from London with armed mercenaries to put down the revolt. The English Army was made up almost exclusively of foreign mercenaries. German, Spanish, Italian and Flemish Captains, soldiers of fortune, each with their own regiments of well trained and equipped fighting men, were to be employed to extinguish a rebellion of simple English churchgoers, whose bills, bows and matchlocks were almost useless against them.

The first battle was fought at Crediton. The Sampford men, Ned Carey and his two sons among them, joined forces with those of Crediton and erected an earthwork which the mercenaries failed to carry. A heavy fire was opened upon the Royal Army from the cover of barns along the road and the rebels were only dislodged when the barns were set ablaze.

A few days later the village of St Mary Clyst became the scene of a second engagement. A local gentleman, one Walter Raleigh – father of a more famous son – met an old woman telling her beads on her way to church. He treated her roughly and threatened her, and all like her, with "gentlemen burning them and all their houses!" There was immediate uproar. Earthworks were constructed and cannon were taken from the ships on the river. The Carews and their mercenaries made a half-hearted attempt to take the village and then withdrew to await reinforcements. Within days every village was defended with earthworks, roads were cut and bridges broken. The insurgent army by this time numbered some ten thousand and began organising under officers found from among both gentry and commoners.

The Devon and Cornwall insurgents then conferred and discovered a common mind. The King and his Council must leave religion in the same state that King Henry left it and they would have no changes until King Edward was come of age.

A number of Articles were drawn up and were sent to the King and Council. They wanted the Six Articles of King Henry revived, the Mass in Latin, the Bible in Latin, Communion in one kind and at Easter only, the Pyx containing the Reserved Sacrament hung over the Altar as had formerly been the case and the restoration of all the ancient ceremonies.

They went on to demand that their children be confirmed by the Bishop – an indication of serious pastoral breakdown in all the reforming zeal – and they would have no married priests.

The insurgents went further. They demanded that half the abbey or chantry lands in any man's possession be restored to the Church's use and they required that gentlemen be restricted in the number of their servants. However the Council and Parliament might react to their religious demands, the rebels were perhaps unwise in linking them to a demand that the very persons addressed should give up their very own ill-gotten gains!

"We will have God's service said or sung in the choir, as heretofore; and not God's service set forth like a Christmas play!"

The boy-King, the Lord Protector and the Archbishop all answered these Articles. Cranmer's response was immoderate to the point of absurdity. It was the petulant raving of a weak man in authority whose authority is questioned. It can have advanced his beloved – and essentially admirable – cause not at all.

The City of Exeter was then invested by the rebels and mining and countermining began. Food began to run short in the city and the population, most of whom were in strong sympathy with the rebels, began to agitate for the surrender of the city in defiance of its Mayor.

# CHAPTER TWENTY SEVEN

"**P**OOR STEVE! What a pity he couldn't be here after all!" Aunt Sarah gave a sigh and laid down her knife and fork. So did Jane and so did Rosemary. The three of them looked wistful and bereft, they were gazing into the middle distance and John had a sudden horror that one of them would produce a tiny handkerchief and dab her eye with it. Then it would be tears all round.

"Never mind, dears!" Cecily sounded determinedly bright. "He'll be home for Easter instead. Won't he, John?"

"Yes. Or so he says. He did volunteer for this extra stint after all. It's summer in the Falklands now and he says it isn't too bad, given decent weather."

John looked round anxiously. The last thing he wanted was all his womenfolk in tears, weeping into their Christmas dinner.

"When does he go to Staff College?" Aunt Sarah adored Steve. She had great hopes for his future career, his knapsack being stuffed full of Field-Marshals' batons in her eyes.

"Next year, he hopes."

"Dear Steve!"

Aunt Sarah picked up her knife and fork again, and so did Jane and Rosemary. Cecily had been steadily devouring roast turkey throughout the brief emotional hiatus.

"Daddy! You're sure he will be home for Easter?"

Rosemary, who adored her elder brother, seemed more than naturally anxious to see him. John noticed it, and so did Jane.

"Rosemary dear! When am I going to be allowed to meet this young man of yours?"

Cecily had picked up the same vibrations and had decided to allow the energies to flow.

"Tomorrow, Granny darling! He is arriving in time for lunch!" Rosemary looked about her in a mixture of triumph and slight apprehension. Then she toyed with the remaining slice of turkey on her plate with an obviously suppressed excitement. Jane discovered her mind dwelling on a gorgeous hat she had seen in that wickedly expensive little shop in Cheltenham. It would be just right …

"I do love Fairloe Church!"

Aunt Sarah put down her knife and fork and relaxed into a faraway look which was, John thought, as much the product of roast turkey and white wine as of romantic attachment to old buildings. "I should have loved to have seen … I'm so glad he doesn't use a kitchen table!"

"Yes," said John. "So am I!"

Slightly to his astonishment, John realised that he was following Aunt Sarah's mental processes almost as quickly as they were happening.

"Those lovely Baroque churches! It was horrid!"

"Sarah dear! What are you talking about!"

Cecily, her knife and fork still firmly grasped, looked at Sarah with what John could only describe as a glare of amusement.

"All those gorgeous Bavarian churches with their wonderful extravaganza altarpieces and ceilings painted to look like Heaven! And a beastly little kitchen table in front of the congregation for the poor priest to say Mass on!"

Aunt Sarah made a face.

"Bishop Hooper would have loved it! But of course he would have smashed up all the lovely statues and whitewashed Heaven out of sight."

She sighed. "Poor Bishop Hooper!" she said.


Bill arrived in triumph, or so it seemed to John. His car had hardly stopped in the drive before Rosemary and Jane were rushing as if to embrace it. Aunt Sarah lingered, just outside the front door, and Cecily stood beside John on the front doorstep.

"Look at 'em!" she said, jerking her head towards her daughter and granddaughter. John laughed.

There were noisy greetings with everybody talking at once. There were introductions. Bill made a great hit with Aunt Sarah, who was already well disposed in that direction, and Cecily was charming. When everyone else was busy talking at once she caught John's eye and gave a curt nod of approval. Bill had passed muster. The whole *menage* moved inexorably into the kitchen and coffee was drunk out of mugs. Towards the end of the second mug of coffee, Bill gave Rosemary a look charged with meaning and then he turned to John.

"Could I possibly have a brief word with you, sir?" he asked. The two of them got up and, as they slipped out of the kitchen, Rosemary began to engage her mother, her aunt and her grandmother in urgent, and rather loud, conversation.

"Drawing-room," John muttered to Bill. "Away from the racket!" They entered the drawing-room and John closed the door behind them. There was a moment of awkwardness. Both men knew what was to follow and neither of them quite knew how one set about it.

"Well, sir ..." Bill made the first move. "I know some people think it a bit old-fashioned these days, but I am a bit old-fashioned ... I would like to ask you for your daughter's hand in marriage ... if you know what I mean."

Yes, John did know what he meant. He found himself, quite suddenly, very moved. He took a firm hold on himself. But what was he supposed to say? What were his 'lines'? How did a father properly respond?

What John Faversham heard himself say was:

"Absolutely delighted, my dear chap! Let's have a drink for God's sake!"

Fortified with whisky and hugely relieved that the formalities were over, John and Bill looked first at each other and then at the door. "I suppose we had better tell 'em!" said John.

He opened the door and shouted in the direction of the kitchen.

"Darling! We've got something to tell you!"

John could not help taking note of the ritual expressions of surprise and the set-piece lookings at each other that Rosemary, Jane and Aunt Sarah indulged in. Whatever could it be?

They fluttered into the drawing-room and stood, bursting with expectation. Cecily, her eyes twinkling, stood slightly apart. It was time for a bit of theatre and she was the appreciative audience, waiting for a well-loved show to begin.

John addressed his wife, almost theatrically:

"My dear! Bill has asked me for the hand of our daughter in marriage and I have given my consent!"

Pandemonium broke out at once.

Taking advantage of a lull in the huggings, kissings and general euphoria, John reached for more glasses. The move was observed. "Good idea, John!" said Cecily.

"Had you thought about … ?" Jane was probing.

"We had thought of Easter," said Rosemary.

"Daffodils!" cried Aunt Sarah. "I adore Spring weddings!"

"We don't want anything elaborate, do we Bill? Just a nice, quiet family wedding."

John found a shadowed part of his mind saying to him: "Not more than five hundred guests at twenty pounds a piece!" But he did his heroic best to dismiss the thought.

"You'll have to see Walter and choose hymns and things, and see about the Banns."

Jane was beginning to organise her daughter. The hat in that shop in Cheltenham suddenly returned to mind and a part of Jane was planning an outfit round it. She mustn't outshine the bride of course, but she was going to upstage every other bride's mother in Gloucestershire. She was, after all, her mother's daughter!

Aunt Sarah's mind was full of daffodils. She was mentally arranging them all over the church, with the utmost attention to detail. Bill was now the centre of attention, with John, his moment of glory over, entirely forgotten. Come the wedding, Bill would have been stepped down to the status of the groom that a bride must of necessity produce to justify this most feminine of all extravagances.

John felt grateful that he and Bill were human beings and not bees.

"It must be a bit grim being nothing more than a disposable drone!" he thought.

177

"You will have the Old Service of course?"

Jane, entirely happy with the new Liturgy, found herself curiously traditional now that her daughter was to be married.

"Oh I don't know!" said John from his armchair. "Its a bit agricultural. All that stuff about brute beasts and fornication. Do we really want that?" He for one, did not.

"Thats the *Old* Old Service," said Aunt Sarah who knew about these things. "Jane was thinking about the *Not-So-Old* Old Service. Nobody has actually used the Prayer-Book Service since 1928. They just talk about it as if they did. And brides carry nice little white Prayer Books with the wrong Service in it and never open them."

"Bill and I will talk to Walter before we decide."

Rosemary, who knew her mother only too well, was determined to keep control of what was, after all, her wedding.

"When's lunch?"

John believed in putting first things first. The wedding was at the very least three or four months off and he was feeling hungry.

"Any time you like."

Jane was uncharacteristically accommodating.

"What about now? Bill must be starving. You must have made a quick getaway from Croydon to get here by eleven?"

"Well, I had a bit of business to see to!"

"Poor Bill!" said Aunt Sarah. She had altogether fallen for him.

# CHAPTER TWENTY EIGHT

ROBERT KET, a tanner of Wymondham in Norfolk, suddenly found himself the leader of a popular uprising. Two grievances, coming together, had goaded the peasantry beyond endurance. The first was the hedging and enclosing of land by the gentry, to their own enrichment and the further impoverishment of the peasantry. The second was the final, intolerable, interference with the practice of their religion in the shape of the *Book of Common Prayer* and the *Visitation* that accompanied it.

The County of Norfolk was in rebel hands for seven weeks and it was July before the Council sent a force of Italian mercenaries, under their Captain, Malatesta, to put the rebellion down. This he failed to do, although accompanied by several members of the Council with troops loyal to themselves.

The Royal Army was invested in Norwich. The rebels then proceeded to carry the city by assault and the Royal Army fled in disorder. It became plain to the Lord Protector and other members of the Council that an adequate force, under the command of a competent general, would be needed to put down Ket's rebellion and prevent the rest of England from rising in its support. England and Scotland were at war and a larger mercenary army was in the north. The fighting was broken off at once, the parts of Southern Scotland in English hands were abandoned and all the English garrisons marched south. The Army thus gathered proceeded by forced marches to join up with the Earl of Warwick, their newly appointed Commander-in-Chief.

Warwick was anxious to seize the initiative. He gathered together a force of newly levied troops, took under command the defeated levies of the Marquis of Northampton, and struck at Norwich. After an attempt at negotiation he forced his way into the city and, in savage street fighting, one hundred and thirty rebels were killed and some thirty or forty rebels, or suspected rebels, were seized and held prisoner. Without examination or trial, they were hanged in the marketplace forthwith.

One of those thus summarily executed was a one-time monk of St Edmundsbury, one Edmund Foster, a priest who had been concerned to minister to the needs of rebel and royalist alike and had been seized in the street while doing so.

In the midst of the tragedy there was a moment of farce, for Warwick's military train, his artillery and his supply wagons, passed right through the city in the confusion and was taken entire by the rebel army on the far side of it. A series of furious assaults were then made upon the city in an unsuccessful attempt to re-take it. For nearly a week the Royal cause was a desperate case, but on the 26th of August the German mercenaries arrived from Scotland. The rebels, some fifteen thousand men, then retreated from their camp on Mousehold Hill into Dussindale, a deep and narrow valley which they proceeded to fortify.

It was all in vain. Captain Drurie's arquebusiers fired volley after volley into the rebels' packed and disordered ranks. A charge of pikemen and an assault by cavalry broke the rebel front and, in the battle and in the pursuit that followed, three thousand five hundred peasants were killed and some seven thousand wounded. The hard core of the rebel force, with all their artillery, resolved to stand and fight to the last. Warwick, an honourable man and a merciful, rode into their midst and pledged his word for their lives if they laid down their arms. This they did, but as is usually the case the vindictiveness of the politician overruled the mercy of the soldier. No fewer than four hundred were executed, including the redoubtable Robert Ket himself. He was hanged in chains in Norwich Castle.

Thus was the *Book of Common Prayer* made secure in East Anglia, together with the vested interests of that very squirarchy through whose influence in Parliament it had pleased the Archbishop to impose it upon the English Church.

The Counties of Oxfordshire, Berkshire, Buckinghamshire and Northants, already goaded to the limits of endurance, also rose in rebellion against the imposition of the *Book of Common Prayer*. Their insurrection was, however, sporadic, disorganised and incoherent and a force of thirteen hundred men, under Lord Grey of Wilton, was despatched to put it down.

With great speed and efficiency the revolt was stamped out and a number of recalcitrant clergy were hanged from their church towers. Lord Grey did not hesitate to hang a goodly number of laymen along with them, and the *Book of Common Prayer* was thus enforced in those four Counties with little further trouble.

One of the priests who vacated his living in this manner was the Vicar of Chipping Campden who was hanged from his church steeple. A devout layman of his congregation, one Thomas Campion, was saved from summary execution only by being recognized as having been a member of King Henry's Court. He was taken to London under arrest and committed to prison to await trial.

There was no trial. Friends pulled strings and all charges were dropped. The string-pulling was not enough to release him however, and he remained in custody for the rest of King Edward's reign.


While Robert Ket and his followers were still victorious in Norfolk, Lord Russell advanced upon Devon and Cornwall with a mercenary army to put down the rebellion in the south-west. His advance was blocked at Taunton and so he camped and awaited the return of the Carew brothers from London with reinforcements. As soon as he was reinforced, Russell advanced again and established his headquarters at Honiton. Hardly was he encamped there when a force of rebels was reported at Fenington Bridge, some three miles distant. Battle was joined and the bridge was carried by Russell's men. The main body of the rebel force then formed up beyond the bridge but with "a good store of blows and bloodshed" they were driven off.

The Royal troops began looting and terrorising the villagers, but they were surprised by a force of three hundred Cornishmen, led by one Robert Smith, a gentleman of St Germains. A savage fight followed and it resulted in the Cornish assault being repulsed. The rebels were pursued for some three miles and a total of three hundred rebel dead were counted at the end of the battle. This was an early indication of the futility of half-armed villagers taking on fully armed and trained professional soldiers in pitched battle. Russell, his front secure, was then joined by Lord Grey, fresh from his punitive campaign in the Midlands. Grey's reinforcements included Hanoverian cavalry and Genoese arquebusiers. They were accompanied by a reformist licenced preacher, one Miles Coverdale, famous as a translator of the Bible and whose translations of the psalms were to become permanently associated with the *Book of Common Prayer*. He was shortly to be rewarded with the See of Exeter for his pains.

Russell's first task was the relief of the City of Exeter which was in imminent danger of being surrendered to the rebels. He marched to its relief by a somewhat circuitous route and camped not far from the village of St Mary Clyst, making his headquarters in a windmill belonging to a gentleman by the name of Cary, a distant kinsman of Ned Carey.

No sooner was he camped than his lines were attacked with great ferocity by the villagers of St Mary Clyst. Once again the training, discipline and superior weaponry of the professionals told against the courage of the half-armed and untrained peasantry. So steady was the fire of the Genoese arquebusiers that the attackers were shot down in heaps, the survivors retiring in disorder behind the village barricades.

Never one to miss a chance for the promotion of the reform of religion, Master Coverdale then stood in the midst of the stiffening corpses of his countrymen and preached an improving sermon upon the subject.

The Battle of Cary's Mill was fought upon a Saturday. On Sunday morning the Royal Army assaulted the village of St Mary Clyst which was defended by six thousand men. The attack was three-pronged. Two were repulsed but the third penetrated the defences. The villagers then counter-attacked with such vigour that the assailants were tumbled out of the village and chased off the battlefield in disorder. The counter-attack took a number of guns and penetrated to the Royal wagon lines.

On the Monday morning the assault was renewed. It was met by a hail of stones, the villagers being out of ammunition. The defences were overrun, the village was set on fire and the confused defenders were slaughtered wholesale. Over one thousand Englishmen perished in the battle, besides a multitude of women, children and wounded men who were burned to death in their blazing cottages, or who were drowned while attempting to swim to safety. Lord Grey, scouting beyond the village, then spotted the approach of what appeared to be a large body of rebels. At once the order was given to kill all prisoners and within a very few minutes another thousand had perished.

The rebels mounted a furious counter-attack on the Tuesday morning but, failing to dislodge the Royal Army, fell back in disorder, suffering an immense loss in killed and wounded. The way was then opened for the relief of Exeter. The very day the city was relieved the Royal Army was reinforced by Sir William Herbert with a thousand men from Wales. A further three hundred followed a few days later.

Russell remained in the city for twelve days, hanging everyone who gave any indication of having supported the rebellion. Those summarily executed included nine parish priests, one of whom – Parson Welsh, the vicar of St Thomas' church in the city – was hanged in full Mass vestments from a gallows erected on the top of his church tower.

Ned Carey and both his sons, Ralph and Roger, fought with the rebels at St Mary Clyst. Ned and Ralph escaped but Roger was missing. It was learned soon afterwards that he had been among the prisoners slaughtered after the village had fallen. Ned and his remaining son returned home to Sampford Courtney where a rebel force was attempting to re-group.

On the Feast of the Assumption, August 15th 1549, a Royal Army of ten thousand men marched on Crediton and the following morning engaged the scouts and pickets of the rebels. Such was the resistance that the Royalists only reached the village of Sampford Courtney on Sunday the 17th. Grey and Herbert led the assault and full battle was joined.

The rebels fought with the utmost desperation, using sticks, stones and agricultural implements to supplement what few matchlocks and bills they possessed. A savage counter-attack turned the flank of the Royal assault and for some time the issue was in doubt. Superior training, discipline and weaponry won the day, however, and the rebels broke and fled. Six hundred died in the village itself and a further seven hundred in the pursuit. Ned Carey fell in the battle, and Ralph was killed trying to defend his parents' home in which were hiding Ned's wife and their daughter Mary.

The Royal army suffered a mere twelve killed, but a great number were wounded. The village was ransacked and left in ruins as Russell continued his advance into Cornwall.

Vengeance and summary execution were now the main aims of the Royalists, and Russell was ably assisted in his endeavours by a man whom, had he lived four centuries later, might have served the S.S. admirably as a hangman in occupied Poland.

This gentleman was none other than the Provost Marshall, Sir Anthony Kingston, who had succeeded his father as squire of the lands formerly belonging to Flaxley Abbey and who was, among other things, patron and lay rector of the living of Fairlowe in the County of Gloucester.

The news of Tom Campion's arrest and of the martyrdom of his parish priest smote John Farelowe with all the force of a thunderbolt. As more news came from the immediately neighbouring counties, his sense of shock deepened and with it an intense feeling of personal guilt and despair.

What of his own integrity now? To what unfaithfulness might he himself have been a party? What was going on in England that devout Christian men could be arbitrarily hanged and imprisoned for doing what they and their forefathers had faithfully done from time immemorial?

John, though a clever man and a good if not over energetic lawyer, belonged emotionally to his father's generation. His religion was of the heart. The Church's Liturgy conveyed to him *The Mystery* and it was quite unnecessary to him to indulge in intellectual argument or speculation about this thing or that. He was secure in his Faith; his mind had long learned to abide in his heart. John had been as well aware as any man that a great many things needed improving and that there were not a few corruptions within the institutions of Holy Church. But Christ and His Mass he had always clung to, as his father had bidden him. And our Lady Saint Mary and the Saints he had always clung to and known them as his own very real friends. He was a simple man at heart and Heaven was very close to his simple heart.

But now he was heart-broken, and full of guilt and of self-accusation. For surely these precise verities were now being, almost explicitly, denied! Had he betrayed the True Faith by not inviting imprisonment or death … ? But for what specifically? He had been largely instrumental in the new Liturgy being received by the villagers, if not with enthusiasm then at least without open riot and disorder. He had saved lives … ! But should he have done? Would it not have been better to have died defending a principle?

But exactly what principle? Rome was utterly corrupt, that every man knew. The King and his advisers had been utterly corrupt too, but although they had destroyed the monasteries, the chantries, the education system, the care of the sick and all effective charities, they had been careful to preserve the integrity of religion… The integrity of religion! What was that if not the care of the sick, the education of the ignorant, the life of contemplation in the midst of the world … ? John's mind was in utter confusion. The seeds of despair, sown long since within him, were sprouting and growing apace. His light heart and easy-going nature were gone from him and Kate, tormented as well but with a realism and a clearer head than her husband, was distracted with anxiety about him.

And then came the news of the rebellion in the south-west, and of Ned Carey's death, fighting for his Faith, and of the death of both his sons. And of his wife and daughter Mary raped by foreign mercenaries, hired to kill Christian Englishmen for worshipping as their forefathers had worshipped!

And then came the news of Edmund Foster, priest and the saintliest of them all, having been strung up summarily for being seen in the street, hearing the confession of a dying rebel.

In a later century, men would talk about Clinical Depression and Nervous Breakdown. At the end of the year of Grace 1549, John Faversham succumbed to the Melancholy and lay for weeks, utterly prostrated by grief, guilt and confusion.

Deep down within him a growing despair produced its bitter fruit. His light hearted and loving personality began to nurture an all-consuming hatred. Antichrist was abroad! All John Farelowe awaited, did he but know it, was a suitable candidate upon whom to project his hate-filled obsessions.

John Wakeman, last Abbot of Tewkesbury and first Bishop of Gloucester, died. During the course of the year 1550, the Council decided upon a successor, and the ex-monk and extreme Zwinglian reformer John Hooper was informed that it was His Majesty's pleasure that he should be consecrated Bishop and succeed to the See of Gloucester.

# CHAPTER TWENTY NINE

JOHN FAVERSHAM regained his office and closed the door behind him. He crossed to his desk, rounded the end of it and stood behind it. He remained standing behind it because, all of a sudden, there seemed no point in sitting down any more.

He looked at the top of his desk and he found that he couldn't relate to it at all. It didn't seem to be a desk any more. It didn't seem to be anything any more. He wasn't at all sure if he was himself any more. He wondered, for an instant, if he really existed at all.

He was calm, he was rational and he was clear-headed. He was surprised to observe that he felt no emotions. They would come later; shock had probably anaesthetised them.

The whole thing had taken two minutes, probably less. He had been called on the office phone to go and see Thompson straight away in the Board Room. It was important! It just had to be the Turkish contract! Trouble was brewing without a doubt. John remembered thinking that he wouldn't mind a trip to Istanbul. He had been shown straight in. There was obviously a hell of a panic on about something. Thompson had been sitting there looking, John thought, even more like a dung-beetle than usual. And Wilkinson from Head Office had been there, and Broadhurst, another Head Office type he didn't know so well. The three of them had looked pale and stressed up to the eyeballs.

And then they had told him.

The Company was undergoing a major restructuring. All Research and Development would be concentrated in Basingstoke and they were obliged to tell him that he was now redundant.

They would get in touch within a few days about redundancy terms and he could have the use of the company car until the end of the month.

And now would he please clear his desk and be clear of the premises by noon.

Someone, standing by the door, had showed him out. John could not remember his walk back to the office at all. He could not remember having uttered a word. How did one clear a desk?

After standing there for a full minute, John decided that he couldn't be bothered. He picked up the framed photograph of Jane that stood on one end of his desk and put it in his briefcase. Then he picked up the other folding photo-frame, with its photograph of Steve in uniform and its other photograph of Rosemary at her graduation. That went into his briefcase too.

He looked round his office with eyes that didn't seem to want to register anything. That watercolour of the Langdale Pikes … how long had it hung there? Years and years! He would leave it for Vera.

Vera! Would she like it? In his mind he heard her say: "Yass!" He felt a sudden surge of affection and inexpressible gratitude. Vera? No! He couldn't cope, and neither could she.

John took a sheet of paper from a drawer of the desk that was no longer his, sat down on the very edge of what was now a borrowed chair, and wrote her a note.

Vera,

I've just been made redundant. Be an angel and clear my desk for me. If there is anything you think I really ought to have, then please hang on to it. I will be in touch in a day or two; I'll phone you at home. And please keep the Langdale picture as a reminder of old times. And thanks for everything. God bless!

John Faversham

John left the note in the middle of his desk, picked up his briefcase, retrieved his hat and coat from the little cupboard in the corner of the office, and slipped out of the building practically unnoticed. As he settled into the driving seat of his borrowed car he looked at his watch.

"Noon be damned!" he said. "Twenty minutes!"

He was home at Fairloe Court by a quarter past ten. Jane's car was missing. She was obviously out somewhere.

As he climbed awkwardly out of the car John knew that he had been in no condition to drive home. He had no recollection of the journey at all and the anaesthetic was beginning to wear off. He pushed open the kitchen door. Philomena sat bolt upright on the settle. She emitted a little growl of anxiety and looked at John fixedly as he went through the motions of putting the kettle on the Aga and making a pot of tea.

He sat down beside Philomena with a mug of tea in his hand. His automatic pilot then switched off. Its batteries were dead. John Faversham sat gazing straight ahead of him but seeing nothing. Into the back of his mind crept the realisation that thirty years of loyalty, devoted and indeed distinguished service with the Firm had meant nothing to them whatsoever. Absolutely nothing! He, John Faversham, had no value, either as a scientist or as a human being. He had been discarded in under two minutes as if he was a used paper handkerchief.

Yes! And like a paper handkerchief he had the advantage of being biodegradable!

Two hours later, Jane found him, still sitting on the settle, still staring into nowhere, almost totally oblivious of Philomena who was firmly and protectively established upon his lap.

# CHAPTER THIRTY

THE SHORT AND INGLORIOUS reign of King Edward the Sixth was dominated by two classes of men in an extreme hurry. The time available to them was short, for the boy-King could not live long and his elder half-sister Mary would succeed him when he died. She was known to be devoutly and determinedly traditionalist in matters of religion, she had inherited her father's stubbornness in fullest measure, but in every other way she was as Spanish as her mother. She was also, not unreasonably, an angry and embittered woman. The reformist clergy must therefore drive their cause forward relentlessly while opportunity offered. The Council and Parliament, as much the Council's creature as ever it had been King Henry's, must loot and plunder the English Church of its remaining wealth while they were still free to do so. Both groups, the sacred and the secular, used each other with the utmost cynicism in order to effect their very different aims.

Thomas Cranmer was a man in a great hurry whose own intentions were, for the most part, admirable. But he was a weak man and he was threatened and hustled along by stronger, more extreme characters than his own. More and more Bishops were imprisoned in order to get them out of the way. Bonner of London, Heath of Worcester and Day of Chichester joined Gardiner of Winchester to make the Fleet prison a place of rare learning and conservative study. Tom Campion was also imprisoned in the Fleet. He had met all his episcopal fellow-residents at various times and their presence and friendship were a comfort to him.

Nicholas Ridley engineered his own translation from Rochester to London. Almost his first act upon being enthroned on Old St Paul's was the demolition of its High Altar! He was anticipating an Act then going through Parliament which ordered the destruction of all stone altars and their replacement by wooden tables. John Hooper, not long returned from Zurich, had put himself at the head of the most extreme reformist party who styled themselves the Gospellers. He pushed himself forward, secured the post of chaplain to Somerset, the Lord Protector, and was in time to be appointed one of the Lent preachers before the King.

Hooper has been described as a man of strong body and perfect health. His mind was powerful but unimaginative. He was essentially an intellectual and, like many others of an intellectual makeup, had an antipathy towards anything resembling mysticism and had no sense whatever of *The Mystery* in his religion. Hooper was not incapable of humility but he was in the highest degree self-sufficient and entirely confident of the exclusive rectitude of his own position. He was a tireless worker and he could show a considerable degree of benevolence. Alas, it was not a benevolence which always made its recipient a happier man. For John Hooper suffered from a severe personality defect which was to do no service whatever to the cause in which he so passionately believed. Even Fox, Hooper's hagiographer and anything but an unbiased witness, was obliged to acknowledge him as being so sour and forbidding as to be virtually unapproachable.

Hooper's fortunes at Court fluctuated somewhat when he explicitly denied any Sacramental objectivity to the office and ministry of a Bishop in the Church of God. In spite of this, however, he was appointed Bishop of Gloucester by Letters Patent of the Crown. John Hooper objected. He objected to everything, but in particular he objected to being consecrated while wearing the vestments traditional to the office. A situation then arose as ludicrous as it was monstrous. The Church was allowed no say in the matter. Merely to save the face of the Lord Protector and the Council, Hooper was ordered to be consecrated Bishop, willy-nilly! He was also committed to the Fleet prison to cool his heels until he submitted. He gave in and was consecrated in the chapel at Lambeth Palace on the 8th of March 1551. Cranmer was his unwilling consecrator, assisted by Ponet of Rochester and Ridley of London who hated him. The troublesome Hooper consented to attire himself correctly for the occasion but thereafter discarded all his vestments, putting them on only when required to preach before the King.

In one extraordinary and quite lamentable particular, however, he got his own way. He consented to be consecrated Bishop provided that all reference to angels and saints was omitted from the service.

Hooper thus became Bishop of Gloucester but, in an extraordinary exercise in pluralism the following year, he also became Bishop of Heath's vacant See of Worcester. He then reduced Gloucester to the status of an Archdeaconry and gave all its endowments and possessions to the King! Gloucester was to be restored to its proper dignity in the next reign.

Hooper has been called "the father of nonconformity," and with some justice, but once in office he imposed a relentless conformity with his own views and requirements. He ruled his extended See with tireless energy and great diligence. He was unremittingly austere with his clergy who, for the most part, regarded him with a fearful loathing. He was even-handed in punishments, severe with heretics and faithful at all times to the peremptory demands of his own, fiercely Zwinglian, conscience.

John Hooper's first year at Gloucester saw a colourful demonstration of his even-handedness in administering godly disciplines to those in his pastoral care. He administered a stinging rebuke in public to no less a person than Sir Anthony Kingston, the Provost Marshall. Kingston was roundly upbraided for his adultery and for the general and notorious viciousness of his life.

The outraged Provost Marshall, in his turn, administered a stinging blow with the back of his hand to the Bishop's unsmiling countenance. For this, the Bishop had him brought before his own Consistory Court and fined him the then colossal sum of five hundred pounds. The Provost Marshall swore a terrible revenge. It was to be granted to him within a very few years.

# CHAPTER THIRTY ONE

"HE's TERRIBLY depressed and withdrawn. I've never seen him like this, I'm very worried about him."

Tears were not far away. Jane looked up at Aunt Sarah, and then looked quickly down again.

"Its absolutely barbaric!" Aunt Sarah was shocked and she was angry. "He was the best man they had! He knew it and so did everybody else!"

"Yes darling, but he is nearly fifty-eight. They probably didn't think it worth their while to move him."

"Ageism!" snorted Aunt Sarah. "And what a way to reward thirty years of loyalty and exemplary service! What a way to treat a human being! Not even a 'thank-you!' Just chucked out in two minutes flat like a ... like a ..."

Aunt Sarah didn't know what it was like! She knew of course that men and women were made redundant, just like that, every day all over the country. But this was different. This was her beloved John!

The two women sat defeated and outraged. An assault had been made on the very "nest" itself. All their instincts screamed within them for a bloody revenge. Reason prevailed however and practicalities came back into focus.

"They'll have to give him a fat redundancy cheque!"

If blood was not readily available, money would have to do instead.

"Oh! I think we will be all right, Sarah. And I think I could go full-time if I really had to. We'll be able to see off what's left of the mortgage, that's one good thing. We were lucky to buy when we did, before all the house prices went mad. But it's not that. It's John!"

John Faversham had, quite suddenly, lost all his confidence. He felt ashamed to go out and to be seen in public. He had begun to wonder if his whole life had been wasted; if there had ever been any point in having done any of the things he had done in his life. Had he had been nothing but a deluded fool all his working life? Giving himself, giving the firm all his loyalty, serving it and defending it; doing his level best for it, and for thirty years?

Something of John was left within him to observe all this going on inside with something like detachment. Something of him knew that this was, for the most part, merely the result of the shock of being so peremptorily discarded. That same something also knew that, had he survived in the firm for another seven years, he would have been given a retirement luncheon, a cheque, a presentation clock and a couple of fulsome speeches from the Managing Director. He would have hated it! It would have been like attending his own funeral. It had had that effect on most of the recipients too; most of his retired ex-colleagues had died within two years. Well! He had been spared that piece of ritualistic humbug – if it really was the humbug it now seemed to him to be.

The observer within was only there intermittently however. Most of the time John was entirely identified with his depression. He could do nothing. He could not even bear to enter his beloved little workshop any more. All Jane's bright suggestions for "little jobs" and "useful projects" met with no more than a silent shrug of his shoulders.

And John had taken, unthinkingly and for the first time, to sitting by the big chimneypiece in the dining-room. He would sit there all morning and all afternoon too, indeed whenever Jane was out and not trying to move him somewhere else. For the first time since they had come to live at Fairloe Court, he felt completely at home in that room. He was identifying with it, and it was identifying with him.

It took Jane a heroic effort to get them both to church on the Sunday following the redundancy. John had insisted upon going by car, and at the last minute, and rushing out as soon as the service was over. It was all very unlike him.

The same pattern was repeated the following Sunday, but by the end of the service, this time, John had relaxed a little and was inclined to linger and chat.

There was a reason for it although he was not conscious of it until later. John had somehow found it in him to pile all his depression and humiliation on to the altar when he had come to receive the Holy Communion. He felt lighter after that. Still devalued, still reduced to nothing, but – for all that – lighter.

Walter had been round during that first week, when he had been told the news. That had been helpful. Walter hadn't said much, but he had been there and that was the thing that had mattered. They now exchanged their usual Sunday morning pleasantries and were, as usual, interrupted by George.

"Now Vicar! 'tis the clecshun, look! We's a bit up on this same Sunday last year!"

George's countenance revealed satisfaction, even benevolence.

"You'll not be making me redundant then?" said Walter. He winked at John.

"Mind," said George. "T'aint in line wi' th'inflation!"

He too winked at John.

Something quite unexpected then came into the back of John's mind. To his surprise he heard himself ask a question of the Parish Oracle that, as far as he knew, had never occurred to him until the instant it was asked.

"George. You know that James Hasfield who used to live in our house – the man your grandfather knew. What did he die of?"

"Asfield?"

George's face lit up. His memory spun into top gear. He liked nothing better than having his vast memory-bank stimulated and called upon. "Can't say as 'im did die o' anythin much. Them was just a-findin of 'un jud one mornin. By the big fireplace in that 'all o' yourn. In im's chair. 'im adn't bin bad. 'im were just jud!"

"Thanks George."

"Jarge!" A shrill call came from the churchyard gate.

"I be a-comin!"

And with hurried farewells to Walter, to John and to Jane, he went.

John opened the driver's door for Jane. He was the passenger just now. He had lost all his confidence at the wheel ever since he had "come to" after that last, semi-conscious, drive back from the office.

"Darling?"

Jane backed round, changed gear and turned down into the little square, away from the church.

"Yes?"

"Why did you ask George about Hasfield's death?"

John's brow furrowed, he looked puzzled.

"I haven't the faintest idea!" he said.

# CHAPTER THIRTY TWO

JOHN FARELOWE emerged from the depths of his melancholy much altered both in mind and in manner. He was consumed by a nagging guilt at being still alive and he was resolved to be determinedly careless of his life thereafter where matters of the Faith were concerned. Young Meg was married in the Paschaltide of 1552. Apart from an Introduction that told her that her marriage was "a remedie agaynst sinne, and to auoide fornicacion," the Marriage Rite was very little changed from that which had joined her father and mother twenty-six years before. Another maddening injunction, forbidding the placing of lighted candles on the altar, was ignored however, and something in John was almost hoping that he would be arrested for it!

Young Will had mellowed. His reformist zeal was much modified for he had been aghast at the bloodshed that had attended the imposition of the first *Book of Common Prayer*, the actual contents of which he had thoroughly approved. He had long sat at the feet of the extreme Reformer, Peter Martyr, and was thought by many at Oxford to be his disciple, but Will had inherited his mother's common sense in good measure and had by now distanced himself from the frenzied band of fanatics who crowded to their hero's lectures. He was moving towards a very English middle ground in the matter of reform.

Father and son, though not in agreement, were at least reconciled. Will had been offered a Fellowship of his College and was contemplating the entry into Holy Orders that was a condition of it. And in a way very different from his father's, he was equally disturbed by the excesses of the current occupant in plurality of the Sees of Gloucester and Worcester.

To Will, John Hooper was a Zwinglian heretic and had no business to be a Bishop. To his father, Hooper was the very incarnation of Antichrist himself.

John Hooper's unswerving intention was to force the Dioceses of Gloucester and Worcester into as faithful a representation of the theocracy of Zwingli's Zurich as could possibly be achieved. His whole See was currently, in his eyes, a sink of ignorance and base superstition and he intended to make this plain to the entire world.

Hooper was so displeased with the essential traditionalism of the Liturgy of 1549 that he came close to refusing to use it at all. Prudence suggested that he made an accommodation with it, however, and he did so by reducing its actual celebration to a shambles. Everything previously traditional was forbidden or turned on its head. The people were forbidden to sit to hear the reading of the Epistle, and they were forbidden to stand out of respect for the words of Christ in the Gospel. He regarded kneeling to receive the Sacrament "grievous and damnable idolatry" and sought to impose his will in the matter through the civil magistrates. He required every intending communicant to recite aloud the Creed, the Lord's Prayer and the Ten Commandments, individually like a child in school, before actually receiving. The effect of all this was, not unnaturally, to alienate most Churchgoers in his Diocese and to discourage them from ever receiving the Sacrament at all.

To impose his will more effectively upon his parishes, Hooper ignored the traditional disciplinary structure of Archdeacons and Rural Deans and appointed his own henchmen as Superintendents through whom he bore down heavily, and incessantly, upon his unhappy parish priests.

Sir Ralph, Vicar of Farelowe, was a not untypical English clergyman of any generation. He was jealous of his own responsibilities and was inclined to take interference from even lawful authority exceedingly ill. He ran his own parish in his own way, very much as he had been taught as a younger man. He disliked innovations and in particular any which required of him that he do things differently. He was also quite decided in his opinions about what was right and wrong, faithful or heretical. Sir Ralph had had altogether too much to contend with during the last five years, and a Zwinglian heretic as Father-in-God was the last straw!

He refused, point-blank, to talk to the Superintendant when he came. The fellow might harangue to his heart's content, but Sir Ralph would not hear him. He dared not actually throw the man out but he came as close to doing so as he could get away with. When the pestilent fellow was in church, nobody received the Sacraments. Nobody would speak to him and John Farelowe turned his back on him without a word. If the Superintendant decided to preach, the congregation would leave after the reading of the Gospel. Nevertheless, the village was not united as it had always been hitherto. Factions were beginning to show themselves, and the hate-ridden atmosphere of Bishop Hooper's episcopacy was already threatening to tear many whole communities apart.

Hooper's Visitation of his Diocese, therefore, was an ominous and unwelcome event. He administered to his clergy a body of fifty Articles of Religion, many of which tortured their consciences. This was accompanied by a rigorous programme of Interrogations and Inquisitions. At the same time he required of the laity of each parish that they submit to Interrogations and Examinations concerning the life and conversation of their clergy. The good villagers of Fairlowe were thus hectored and bullied in the expectation that they would inform upon their good and faithful priest, and to his discredit. The result of this infamous Visitation is alleged to have revealed that out of three hundred priests, one hundred and sixty-eight were unable to repeat the Ten Commandments, of whom thirty-one could not tell where in the Scriptures they might be found. Forty did not know where, in Holy Scripture, the Lord's Prayer was written and thirty-one did not know who was the author of it!

The good Sir Ralph, a man of prayer, a lover of Holy Scripture and a tireless teacher of his people, was obliged to actually speak to the Superintendent for the purpose of this Interrogation. In a fury of anger, contempt and resentment he said he supposed the Lord's Prayer to be so described because it was commanded by my Lord the King! This was solemnly written down, with all his other contemptuous answers, and deposited against him.

Hooper's Visitation has been cited ever since, and quite uncritically, as revealing the mass ignorance and corruption of the parish clergy before the heroic efforts of the reformers improved matters. It was undoubtedly Hooper's intention to cause such an effect. If a new broom is to sweep so heroically and publicly clean it is politic first of all to magnify the dirt! The sheer improbability of this ever having been an honest and objective exercise seems to have escaped succeeding generations. Nothing else was objective and unpartisan in that tormented reign and it is improbable in the highest degree that this could have been the sole exception.

Whatever shortcomings there were, and there are many in any generation, the alleged findings of Hooper's Visitation constitute one of the foulest calumnies ever perpetrated upon the long-suffering parish clergy of England.

The calumny did not stop at the parish clergy, however. It extended to include Hooper's predecessors as Diocesan Bishops. The integrity of John Wakeman, first Bishop of Gloucester, of Heath of Worcester and of Hooper's fellow-reformer Latimer were also impugned. However cynical or careless the new patrons might have been in presenting men to the livings in their gift, they could in fact only present them to the Bishop in the first instance. The Bishop's personal responsibility in the matter was to satisfy himself that the candidates were fit in all respects to be admitted to Holy Orders, and fit in due time to be instituted to the cure of souls which, as the Bishop would remind each one, "is both mine and thine."


The year of Grace 1552 had begun in very much the way in which it was to continue. Somerset, the Lord Protector, had been deposed in a palace revolution. He had come off the worst in a series of mutual murder plots and was solemnly beheaded on Tower Hill on January 22nd. He was succeeded as Lord Protector by Northumberland, a man even more cynical and grasping than himself. King Edward's health had by now begun to deteriorate visibly. It became clear that he could not live much longer. The looters and the extremists must therefore make haste and it has to be said that the haste that both made, each using the other, was indecent in the extreme.

The New Lord Protector ordered a new and special Visitation. In every shire, city, bishopric and town, a body of local gentry was named to list all goods, plate, jewels, bells, vestments and other ornaments belonging to every church and chapel in the land. They were invested with powers to commit to prison any who resisted their demands. A second Commission was issued to a number of London officials to receive the inventories thus taken.

John Farelowe had early warning of this. He guessed at once what was afoot. The monasteries had gone, so had the shrines and the chantries. Only the parish churches had escaped the loss of their treasures. He had heard not long since that the King was ailing, so the churches must be plundered now or it would be too late! The Lady Mary would succeed before long and everything would then be thrown into reverse!

John, Harry the Parish Clerk and Sir Ralph the Vicar met to decide upon a plan. The church, like most parish churches, was well supplied with plate, vestments and linen. There were two copies of the Sarum Missal and there were duplicates of a great many things, including the hanging pyx which was now forbidden. At dead of night certain dispositions were made with the utmost secrecy, for lives could depend upon it. All they then had to do was endure what was left of the dying King's short life. All would surely then be restored.

The Commissioners arrived and took a convincing enough inventory. They then took everything on the inventory away with them in the name of the King.

The Commissioners were allowed to leave, at their discretion, a chalice, a linen cloth or two for the altar and a surplice, only for the priest and one for any assistant he might have. These meagre remnants were described as gracious gifts, bestowed "to the intent that churches and chapels might be furnished of convenient and comely things meet for the administration of Holy Communion" and for "the honest and comely furniture of coverings for the Communion table, and surplices for the minister or ministers."

John Farelowe watched this plundering with a mixture of hatred and grim satisfaction within him. The best was safely hidden! Soon it would all be restored. In the meantime he prayed piously for the King to die soon, and he longed urgently to see with his own eyes the destruction of that Antichrist who sat where he should not, like the Abomination of Desolation spoken of in the Gospels, upon the Episcopal Throne in the Cathedral Churches of Gloucester and of Worcester.

This wholesale robbery occupied most of 1552 and the first few months of 1553. London was the last Diocese to be ransacked and Ridley, its Bishop, summoned all the Churchwardens of his Diocese to the Guildhall, bringing their inventories with them. The vultures then descended upon their unhappy churches and everything was taken. Ridley's own Cathedral of Old St Paul's was ransacked last by the Lord Mayor, the Chief Justice and sundry other Commissioners on May 2nd 1553.

The intention was to line the King's coffers, but such was the avarice of the local gentry that "parlours appeared hung with altarcloths; tables and beds were covered with copes; fair large cushions reposed in windows and chairs; and many a chalice entered the taproom or the pantry as a parcel gift goblet."


While this wholesale looting of the parish churches of England was in full flood a second *Book of Common Prayer* was compiled to replace the first. In every respect it represented a diminishment of the genius of the first and reflected the current doctrinal and liturgical fads and fancies of the most extreme among the reformers. To this day it is uncertain to what extent it was the work of Thomas Cranmer. The main – and extreme – change was in the Eucharistic Liturgy which, subjected to alterations and second-thoughts even while with the printers, represented the doctrines of reformers as extreme and as bleak as John Hooper of Gloucester. It was intended as a deliberate and conscious repudiation of all that had gone before. It has been aptly described as "the perfect liturgical expression of Zwinglianism."

No attempt was made to present this second *Book of Common Prayer* to the Church's Convocations. It was thrust upon the Church by Parliament and ordered to be taken into use on All Saints Day 1552. The confusion surrounding its compilation and printing was such, however, that copies were not available in time and it is doubtful if it ever reached the provinces at all.


The looters and the liturgists, each using the other to facilitate their aims, were just in time. The King died on the 6th of July 1553. On his deathbed however, well prompted by Northumberland, he required his Council to sign a deed altering the Law of Succession to the Throne made by his father, King Henry the Eighth. Northumberland had married his fourth son to Jane, the eldest daughter of the new Duke of Suffolk. The King, utterly determined to prevent his half-sister Mary succeeding, drew up a preposterous scheme by which the Crown should go to the male heirs of the Duke of Suffolk. But the Duke of Suffolk had no male heirs, and so it should go instead to the Lady Jane Grey and her heirs male, thus confirming Northumberland's position as the holder of the real power in the land.

With great hesitation, all necessary dignitaries complied and put their signatures to this monstrous document. First among those signing was Thomas Cranmer, Archbishop of Canterbury.

# CHAPTER THIRTY THREE

"**B**ISHOP HOOPER!"

Aunt Sarah, who had been bending over a mixing bowl on her kitchen table, suddenly straightened up.

"Bishop Hooper!" she said again.

"Oh! Golly!" she added. "February the 9th! It all adds up!"

Aunt Sarah gazed into space.

"Except that it doesn't!"

She sat down, rather heavily, on a kitchen chair which was set against the wall conveniently behind where she had been standing. She sat bolt upright, her eyes wide open in astonishment, looking at nothing in particular and seeing less.

"February the 9th," she said. "That's why he is redundant! Oh dear! Poor Hasfield!"

A bolt from the blue of Aunt Sarah's powerful intuition had landed, all unexpectedly, in the middle of her baking. It usually happened like that. She wasn't thinking, she was baking and so it didn't have to shout to make itself heard.

And now her reason, rudely awakened, was struggling to make sense of the shock-waves.

"Lighten our darkness we beseech thee, O Lord!" said Aunt Sarah to the Almighty. "Oh! Golly!"

February! Hooper on the 9th, Hasfield …? She struggled to collect a bundle of loose ends that seemed to belong together but she didn't know why.

"When did Hasfield die?" said Aunt Sarah, if not to the Almighty in person, then certainly in His general direction.

The answer came instantly. She had a vivid mental image of Hasfield's tombstone in Fairloe churchyard. She had made her own little pilgrimage to it after John and Jane had discovered it, and there it was, brambles and all, vivid in her mind. She read off the inscription.

And of James Hasfield, Solicitor. Died 28th February 1894.

"Thanks!" said Aunt Sarah. "Poor Hasfield!"

She breathed in a huge breath, breathed it out again all at once and, in her own expression, "flumped."

After a moment or two of total inertia Aunt Sarah returned to the fray, all her faculties now in top gear.

Bishop Hooper! So he was mixed up in all this, was he? The thought briefly occurred to her that it might be Hooper who was haunting Fairloe Court. She dismissed the thought at once. No! He wouldn't have looked at her like that, standing on his monument, if he had been a ghost.

"He's mellowed! Heaven is obviously doing him good!"

197

But there was a connection! Hooper on the 9th of February, Hasfield on the 28th. It was February now and John was redundant – a kind of death, in a way. It all added up, at least to Aunt Sarah's intuition if not to her reason. But there was a vital ingredient missing, and that vital ingredient was the real problem. "A classic case of the missing link!" she muttered.

If only Deirdre was at home! But Aunt Sarah knew she was away for the day. There was nothing for it; she would have to ring the Court and hope that John would be able to take in what she was trying to tell him. It might just make sense, if not now, then later. She reached for the kitchen extension of the telephone.

Five minutes later she put it down, anxious and frustrated. John had been patient with her, he had obviously struggled to be attentive, but it was like talking to a ghost!

Tears started to her eyes. Aunt Sarah knew at once that, slowly but inexorably, her beloved John Faversham was dying.


Walter unlocked the door from the vestry to the chancel. He opened it, passed through it, bowed to the altar and then, switching on the lights, looked about him.

The place was cluttered! It had never been intended for all this furniture. The choir stalls were redundant for a start. There had never been a proper choir, even in Victorian times. Like most of the seating in most of the churches, they were there in happy anticipation of people that had never existed but might exist one day! Left to his own devices Walter would have thrown all the pews out and started all over again.

But Walter was not likely to be left to his own devices. The Faculty Jurisdiction Measure and the Diocesan Advisory Committee lay between him and the realisation of his own private preferences. Added to this, a marked tendency towards conservatism in the parish meant that he would have to make haste slowly whatever he did. He looked at the altar. No! It could not be pulled forward for him to get behind it and celebrate facing the people. To do that in a seemly fashion, the whole chancel would have to be re-ordered and the altar moved more than half-way towards the chancel step. It could be done. But something in Walter told him that a small thirteenth century building was usually better left the way it was. But it would be the better for being purged of redundant Victorian pews, stalls and general clutter.

Walter sensed that the mood in the parish now was right for a modest re-ordering of the interior of the church. He had to get his own mind clear before he embarked upon the business of persuading – and of necessity enthusing – the Parochial Church Council. He must win George over first! Walter loved his tiny parish. He was a good parish priest, even though he was non-stipendiary and only "a weekend parson" as someone had unkindly described him. And he loved the little church in which he served. Its history, unremarkable though it probably was, had begun to fascinate him. History itself had become a favourite study in recent years. And there was plenty of it in Gloucestershire. Walter wandered, thoughtfully, to the back of the church. By the door hung a board with the names of former Vicars of Fairloe inscribed upon it. Walter had glanced at it often enough. He glanced at it again.

Ranulf ... circa 1247

Walter's eyes followed the list down. About half-way he stopped. His eyebrows went up in surprise. He remembered a note he had taken down in the folk museum in Gloucester a couple of months earlier. He had not looked at it since.

"I wonder ... ?" he said.

Walter retraced his steps. Whatever else they did they must clear the side aisles of all this perfectly useless seating. Nobody could see the altar from there and nobody ever sat there. Nobody ever had, according to George.

Walter had a mental picture of the chancel, cleared of all its useless choir stalls and decently carpeted from the chancel step to the altar. Well, they would have to ask their architect first if they decided to do anything at all. And then they would have to face all the bureaucracy ...

Walter settled into his stall in the chancel and read Evening Prayer. He spent a few minutes in silence and then returned to the vestry, having first of all switched off the lights.

He thought of the list of former Vicars and he shook his head. "Funny how you can look at a thing for years and years and never see it!" he said.

# CHAPTER THIRTY FOUR

NORTHUMBERLAND's desperate attempt to change the succession ended in fiasco. He brought Lady Jane and her husband, his own son, to the Tower of London and proclaimed her Queen, placing the Crown of England on her head. She responded by making it clear beyond doubt that she would indeed be Queen, and that she denied to the husband foisted upon her any royal rank whatsoever! The Lady Mary was in Suffolk, in the meantime. At once there was a great rallying to her, the whole country seemed to be taking arms on her behalf. Northumberland, greatly alarmed, rode out with all the forces he could muster. He then learned that, as soon as his back had been turned, the very Council itself had broken into the Tower and proclaimed Mary to be Queen, to the wild rejoicing of the entire populace.

Within days, Northumberland, three of his sons and all of his co-conspirators were in the Tower. They were joined by Ridley, Bishop of London, who had preached against Queen Mary in the most intemperate terms and had then sought to go and make his peace with her by any means possible.

There was a great issuing forth of Bishops from the prisons of London. Gardiner of Winchester, Heath of Worcester and Day of Chichester emerged in triumph from the Tower to which they had been transferred from the Fleet. Tunstall of Durham came out to daylight from the prison of King's Bench, and Bonner of London processed with great solemnity from the Marshalsea prison to Old St Paul's.

Tom Campion emerged from the Fleet and was united with his wife who had taken rooms in London. They remained in the capital for several weeks, Tom renewing his acquaintance with the Court and rejoicing in what seemed at first to be a very reasonable and enlightened return to normality.

Gardiner was immediately made Lord Chancellor in place of Goodrich of Ely, who had devastated his cathedral even more thoroughly than had Hooper of Gloucester.

The funeral of the boy-King was the first problem that Queen Mary faced. Was he to be buried according to the Latin rites which Mary loved but which he had been brought up to hate? Or was he to be buried according to the rites of the thoroughly unsatisfactory second *Book of Common Prayer* as one who had died a heretic? The Holy Roman Emperor had already written to her strongly advising that she adhere to the reformed rites for the time being and make haste slowly, and with sensitivity.

In the event, Gardiner celebrated a Requiem Mass in Latin for the boy-King, attended by the Queen and her Council. At the same time Cranmer buried him at Westminster according to the rites of the *Book of Common Prayer*. Day of Chichester preached at the funeral and, for a time, it seemed that sensitivity and common sense would prevail and the various warring factions would soon be reconciled.

It was not to be. Queen Mary, a frail and pious spinster of thirty-seven, had inherited all her father's stubbornness but everything else from her mother. There was very little about her that was English at all. All her reactions were Spanish, and thus alien to her subjects. She simply did not understand the English people over whom she was to reign.

Queen Mary was at heart a good, kindly and deeply devout woman. She was merciful and forgiving towards those who had wronged her personally, but quite unable to contemplate compromise in matter of religion. She was constitutionally incapable of taking the Holy Roman Emperor's advice and her most urgent and overriding aim was to bring England back under the Papal obedience, and on terms never admitted by any English monarch before her.


Latimer was arrested, the first of many of the leading reformers to lose his liberty. He was given the opportunity to escape abroad but declined to take it. Hooper of Gloucester and Coverdale of Exeter were committed to the Fleet prison, though not for heresy. They were committed for debt, for they owed large sums of money to the Crown, as did a number of other Bishops, Deans and Chapters. Thomas Cranmer was committed to the Tower for High Treason, along with others in the succession conspiracy including the unfortunate Jane herself. Northumberland and a few others paid for their adventure with their heads, but all the others, including Jane and Thomas Cranmer were pardoned. They remained in custody, their pardons notwithstanding.

In October of 1553 the Convocations of the Church were restored to their proper dignity. While they debated matters of theology Parliament repealed all the Statutes of King Edward concerning religion, including the permission of the clergy to marry. During the eighteen months following, a number of the Bishops and perhaps a fifth of the parish clergy were deprived of their livings as a result. Some took the option of separating from their wives instead.

Parliament shrank from one suggested course of action however. The chantries and the extinct monasteries did not have their former lands and possessions restored to them as was proposed. Members of Parliament had all been enriched at the Church's expense; were they now to be impoverished? The thing was impracticable in any event but one Member, Sir Anthony Kingston, became so agitated at the thought of losing the former lands of Flaxley Abbey that he seized the keys of the House of Commons from the serjeant to prevent the House sitting. He was committed to the Tower at once but, professing abject penitence, was soon released.

The country was beginning to slide into liturgical confusion. It was well known that the Queen heard Mass in Latin and the old Use began to be restored all over the country In Oxford the old Mass was restored almost at once and the reformers began, with some urgency, to pack their bags.

In September, Peter Martyr fled from Oxford to London, fearing persecution. An embittered traditionalist, who had been worsted in a debate by Will Farelowe, laid charges against him that he was a disciple of Peter Martyr and a heretic in consequence. He was given the opportunity to escape abroad and fled to Holland. Parliament set December 20th as the day upon which the Latin Mass was to be restored and the whole state of religion was restored, legally, to what it had been in the last year of King Henry the Eighth. As soon as the Great Antichrist, Hooper, was safely in prison, the Latin Mass was restored at the church of our Lady Saint Mary at Farelowe. From John Farelowe's carefully chosen hiding places, from Harry's hayloft and from a half dozen other places, emerged altar frontals and vestments, silver plate, the hanging pyx for the Sacrament and the best and newest copy of the Sarum Missal. The village stonemason rebuilt the altar and with great care the whitewash was removed from those wall paintings that had been obscured. In lieu of a proper carved rood, a wooden cross was erected on the screen, bearing a painted figure of the Crucified. Most of the village wept with joy and relief, though some were resentful. After a few Sundays it became clear that the younger generation were in some difficulty for, with the collapse of the educational system, few of them knew any Latin words with which to answer the Mass.


While England was shaking itself with relief and near disbelief at the end of the nightmare reign of King Edward, the Papacy was not being idle. A Congregation of Cardinals was held on July the 29th and England was high on the agenda. The disposition of Queen Mary was well known and it was decided to appoint a good Englishman of Royal Blood as legate in order to effect the reconciliation. He was, of course, none other than the Cardinal Deacon, Reginald Pole.

Pole, whose entire family had been slaughtered in his stead by King Henry, had narrowly avoided being elected Pope three years before. Pope Paul the Third had died at the end of 1549 and, in the behind-the-scenes negotiations which tend to precede the actual elections with all their mystique and ponderous secrecy, he was the preferred candidate and seems to have been elected by an unofficial ballot late one evening.

A number of his supporters came to his room to wake him up with the news. He had retired early and had been working on his speech of acceptance and his first sermon as Supreme Pontiff. To their immense surprise, however, Pole greeted them with a sad smile and a shake of the head. "Judge not only by night, but by day!" he said. He was not the right man and, in the preparation of his speech and his sermon, he had come to acknowledge the fact. Cardinal del Monte was elected in his stead and ascended the Papal throne as Julius the Third.

Pole narrowly missed having another kind of greatness thrust upon him for, with the dawn of 1554 and the still popular Queen Mary in her thirty-eighth year, Parliament began to enquire as to her intentions regarding Holy Matrimony and a son and heir for the throne of England.

Among the possible candidates was Reginald Pole the Cardinal Deacon and legate-elect!

The thing was not as absurd as it might appear for he was of the Blood Royal and without doubt he would have been dispensed from the Diaconate and his vows of celibacy by the Pope had this notion been proceeded with. Queen Mary, however, was in awe of his Cardinalate and of all that went with it. He did not seem the right sort of person to go to bed with, and so his name was struck off the list.

The Queen then displayed, in fullest measure, the total political ineptitude that was to characterise the rest of her tragic reign. She chose the very man least acceptable to Englishmen and most certain of any to stir their latent xenophobia into a fury. She announced her betrothal to King Philip the Second of Spain, her own kinsman on her mother's side.

At a stroke, Queen Mary dissipated her popularity with her subjects. Thereafter, everything she did, and everything done in her name, was seen as the work of hated foreigners. Risings took place in Kent, in the West Country and in the Midlands. Once again foreign mercenaries were employed to put down the protests of native-born Englishmen.

The executions which inevitably followed the risings were surprisingly few and the pardons surprisingly many. But the rebels claimed the support of Lady Jane Grey in their rebellion – probably quite falsely – and the unhappy young woman and her husband suffered for it with their heads. An attempt was made to implicate the Queen's half-sister Elizabeth and relations between the two were strained until the Queen summoned her tearful sibling, put a ring on her finger, embraced her and said, "Innocent or guilty, I forgive you!"


"Tom! What's gone wrong?"

John Farelowe stared at his old friend with pain all over his countenance. His prayers had been answered. His beloved Church had regained its integrity. Things were returning to the way he had known when he was younger, and much happier, than he was now. He ought to be happy, but he was not, and neither was England.

"The Queen's a fool, John!"

Tom kicked a log back into the fire and looked up again at his friend.

"No. That isn't fair. She's no fool and she has a good and kind heart. But she is a Spaniard like her mother. She thinks differently, reacts differently. And she has married that ... that ..."

Tom shrugged his shoulders and gave up. "She might as well have married the Grand Turk!" he added. "And she has sold England to the Papacy, lock, stock and barrel. That is her crime, John!"

Queen Mary having been too frail to travel to Spain, King Philip had arrived in England instead with a glittering retinue and they had been married on St James' Day 1554, the feast of the Patron Saint of Spain. That in itself had been felt as an insult by most Englishmen. What was wrong with Saint George?

Worse had followed. Cardinal Pole had arrived as Papal Ambassador on November the 20th. He assumed the functions of legate by letters patent soon afterwards and on November 30th, following a Supplication made by Parliament to King Philip and Queen Mary for a Reconciliation with Rome, Pole formally received England's submission to the Holy See and pronounced Absolution over the penitent Kingdom.

John Farelowe scowled as he thought about it. Traditionalist he might be, but this had gone altogether too far. Since when had England – his England – ever *submitted* to a foreigner! Tom leant forward in his chair.

"John! We are trying to make the sun go backwards! Things don't stand still in nature. There was reform in the air in the days of old Archbishop Wareham. It has just gone too far and too fast, and done too much damage. We've been hurt so much all we want to do is pretend the last twenty years haven't happened. But they have, John! And we can't put them back!"

"Tom! I longed for the day when all that I loved would be restored. I wept for joy the day it was restored. But I take small joy in it now."

John, had he been any longer capable of tears, would have wept.

But the despair within him had deprived him of the ability to weep. He had, apparently, all that he had sought – save of course the restoration of the chantry and its school, and of the old monasteries which he had loved. But England was an altered land, and it had grown away from him – or he from it. He remembered one source of bitterness, however, and he looked at Tom, his face hard and his eyes blazing.

"That Antichrist who pretended to be a Bishop – No! I'll not say his name! I just hope that I am there when he comes to his just deserts!"

John Farelowe was shaking as he said it. Tom looked at him, his eyes betraying to anyone who could see it a hideous memory behind them.

"No John! I fear for what might begin, any day now. If John Hooper comes to the deserts that I greatly fear, I pray to God that you are not within a thousand miles of it! I know you too well, John. It would destroy you!"

He shook his head. "If Hooper – and others – get the deserts that some that I know have in mind for them, then their destruction will destroy with it everything that you and I have ever loved!"

# CHAPTER THIRTY FIVE

IT HAD GONE ON for days on end, and she was driving him mad! From the very moment when John Faversham had arrived home, ill with the sudden shock of being made redundant after thirty devoted years with the Firm, Philomena had not let him out of her sight.

As soon as he sat on the settle by the kitchen window she would appear on his lap. If he went into the drawing-room she was there, and if he took it into his head to lie down on his bed for a little while she would immediately curl up beside him.

Whenever John washed his hands or his face, or attempted to shave, Philomena would be there, rubbing against his legs and purring deliciously. The little cat showered affection upon her man. She purred, she licked his hand, she snuggled up close. Never had Little Sweetheart lived up so magnificently to the nickname he had bestowed upon her.

And, it must be said, she was an immense source of comfort to him for, feeling within himself to be one totally devalued, he was left in no doubt that at least Philomena valued him to an infinite degree. To his tangled and bruised emotional state she was a powerful, if diminutive, healing agent.

Why, therefore, did she now seem hell-bent on driving him insane?

John had taken to sitting by the great chimneypiece in the dining-room. He had never sat there before but now he felt powerfully drawn to the place. Its sombre quietness matched his mood for he was in a low state and getting lower, and something within him knew it but seemed powerless to do anything about it. John Faversham could not take decisions any more, he felt little or no motivation to do the smallest thing. Jane, who was sick with worry about him, had suggested seeing the doctor but he would not hear of it. John had always had a horror of anti-depressants. Something in him knew that merely tinkering with symptoms would not help to deal with the cause. Not in this case at any rate. All he asked was to be allowed to sit in peace in his newly-found corner and let the world go by.

Jane hated it and tried to move him about. But Jane was doing an extra day's teaching this term. It was Philomena who took the matter in hand, and in her own inimitable manner.

She would have nothing to do with him if he chose to sit there! She would crouch by this door or that and howl to have it opened for her. John would be driven to oblige, but no sooner would he be settled in his chair than she would howl piteously to be let in again. Whenever John sat in the dining-room Philomena would be at the utmost pains to disturb him. She would rush up the staircase and wail. If this had no effect she would pat small ornaments until they fell from their places with a thud on the carpet. John would have to rouse himself suddenly, go upstairs and restore order. Philomena would crouch meaningfully by the front door and mew plaintively to be let out.

As soon as John got up to open it for her she would suddenly dart upstairs again and hide under a bed. There would then be an exhausting business of coaxing and poking her out with whatever was to hand before she would consent to be caught and put out – only immediately to scream to be let back in. John decided that he would take no notice whatsoever. The immediate result was a spreading puddle by the front door which he had to mop up. When he remonstrated with Philomena she spat at him and then refused point-blank to eat her dinner.

There was nothing for it. After more than a week of torment, with Jane out most days and John at the mercy of Philomena, he finally gave in. He surrendered unconditionally to his cat. John transferred himself to the settle in the kitchen instead. Immediately Little Sweetheart was all affection and attention. She was the soul of comfort and completely undemanding. John Faversham looked down with affectionate exasperation at the little bundle of fur on his lap. For the first time for a fortnight, he laughed.

At that moment the telephone on the window-sill behind him rang.


"John! I've been worried sick about you! Are you all right?"

It was Cecily, telephoning from darkest Sussex.

"Yes darling. I think so. Why?"

"I woke up at five o'clock this morning and they told me you were dying!"

"Who told you?" John was fascinated.

"I've no idea. No idea at all!"

"Well, I don't think I'm dead yet, dear."

"Good! Keep it up! But I got a horrid shock."

It occurred to John that she must indeed have received a horrid shock. This was Cecily in deadly earnest. It was not Cecily being capricious, or naughty.

"I'll do my best, Cecily. Philomena is taking me in hand!"

"And the angels and the wild beasts ministered unto him." Cecily was quoting Scripture. She did, sometimes, and always the most unlikely bits at the most unexpected moments.

"I don't know much about angels," she added, "but wild beasts are damned good! Do what Philomena tells you!"

"Yes, darling. How is Sussex?"

"Opulent and self-satisfied. A bit of redundancy would do Harold good. Do they ever make stockbrokers redundant?"

Cecily sounded hopeful on the subject.

"No, darling. They get hammered or something instead."

"I'll have to hang up now, I can hear someone coming. Now you just look after yourself, John. We are all worried silly about you! And do what the cat tells you!" she added by way of a Parthian shot.

John replaced the receiver and looked thoughtfully at his cat. What in the world had the little thing been up to? If ever there had been a determined, single-minded effort, pursued for days on end, John had seen it, and been on the receiving end of it.

"What do you know that I don't know?" he asked.

And at that moment the answer hit him like a thunderbolt.


John picked Philomena up and put her on the settle beside him.

He stood up and addressed the cat.

"I'll be back in a minute. Don't get anxious!"

She sat up, looked at him and emitted a soft, low growl. John strode purposefully out of the kitchen, straight to the door of the drawing-room with Philomena in hot pursuit. He picked up Hasfield's book from the occasional table which seemed to have been its home ever since it had arrived in the house, and he opened it towards the end, turning pages, searching for something. He found it, and he read it aloud to Philomena.

The clouds are gathering, the darkness comes;
I wear my melancholy as a cloak
Deep-hooded and tight wrapped. Thus fast, it numbs
Initiative and will, makes mind to choke.
But yet – I cling to life – this is not me
Nor is it mine, this all-enshrouding fog;
But other, and another's. Thus is he
Invigorate while I lie here, a log!

John felt himself tingle all over. The hair at the back of his neck felt as if it was trying to stand on end. He shut the book and he and the cat looked at each other. Quite suddenly she turned, trotted back to the kitchen and jumped up on to the settle, leaving him, book in hand, in the drawing-room.

"Little Devil! I bet she's fast asleep already!"

John turned to the photograph of Hasfield and looked at it. "Well, Hasfield!" he said. "That is another experience that you and I have shared!"

And then he remembered Aunt Sarah's extraordinary telephone call the other day. All about Bishop Hooper, and Hasfield, and why he, John Faversham was redundant. She didn't know why he was redundant, but she was sure there was a connection. He had seriously wondered at the time if she was, perhaps, going a bit funny in the head.

Hooper on the 9th of February, Hasfield on the 28th. What was it now? Friday the 19th. And Cecily thought *he* was dying. Was it Hooper who was spooking the house? Something within John dismissed the idea. But was there a connection?

At that moment he heard the front door open. Jane of course. He put the book down, walked quickly to the door and surprised his astonished wife with a bear-hug embrace and a kiss. "Good God!" she said. "What's happened to you? You've come alive again!"

Walter looked from John to Jane, and then he looked from Jane to John. "What an extraordinary business!" he said.

"Could there be any connection between Bishop Hooper and Fairloe Court?"

Jane was leaning forward, desperate for any clues she could gather. Walter rummaged in a file and produced a sheet of notepaper covered in his own, nearly indecipherable scribble.

"Yes! I'm pretty sure of it. I spent a rather gruesome half an hour in the Bishop Hooper Room at the Folk Museum a couple of months ago," he said. "And I spotted a John Farelowe among those involved in that horrid business. I wondered if there was a connection at the time, so I asked George. He said there was. John Farelowe used to live in your house."

"Like Hasfield," said John Faversham.

"I'll tell you another thing," said Walter, triumphant. "His son William was Vicar of this parish from 1559 unto 1598! I suddenly made the connection a couple of nights ago when I had another look at the list of former vicars at the back of the church."

"Good God!" John looked round at Jane, his eyes wide open, his hand half-covering his mouth. "Now I know what *The Dream* is all about! I remember, vividly!"

And he told them.

# CHAPTER THIRTY SIX

THE REIGN OF QUEEN MARY entered a new and darker phase with the dawning of the new year, 1555. Parliament was dissolved on the 18th of January and two days later all the political prisoners in the Tower were released at the request of King Philip.

Religious prisoners were not released, however, for on that very same day there came into effect once more all the barbarous old laws which Parliament had just seen fit to revive "for the punishment of heretics."

However forgiving Queen Mary might be towards those who wronged her personally, it was not in her make-up to be merciful towards those, who by their malicious errors, rotted the souls of their fellow men and sent them to perdition. She was a Spaniard, married to that very Spanish King under whom the Inquisition was to earn its most gruesome reputation in Spain.

King Philip was an austere, pious man, but everything was black or white to him. England was a land where everything has been seen, historically, in subtle shades of grey. There was no meeting of minds whatsoever between the Spanish King and Queen and their English subjects.

By Act of Parliament it now became incumbent upon the Bishops to begin once more the hateful task of examining for heresy. The best of them, such as Gardiner, were at pains either to warn such reformers as were still at liberty to flee the country or by any means to arrive at some statement from the accused which would support their orthodoxy and save them from the stake.

There were others who were of a different mind, however. Bonner of London proved to be an embittered, spiteful man and one only too glad to see the heretics who had imprisoned him burn for their impertinence, if not for their heresy.

The examinations of Cranmer, Latimer, Ridley and Hooper revealed them to be determined and unrepentant heretics according to law. But Cranmer then recanted and there was, for a while, some chance that he might be released into private life to end his tormented days in peace.

The other three were condemned, however, and delivered to the secular authorities. Ridley and Latimer were to suffer at Oxford, Hooper was to be burned alive at Gloucester.

John Hooper was degraded from Holy Orders and delivered into the tender care of Sir Anthony Kingston, the Provost Marshall, and six armed guards. They were to proceed to Gloucester where they would be met by the Mayor and Magistrates, among whom was one by the name of John Farelowe.


Kate saw her husband depart for Gloucester on the 8th of February with a terrible foreboding of doom weighing upon her. John's face was set and he rode away without a word. He would be staying two nights in Gloucester as there was to be a grand celebratory dinner following the burning of the Bishop.

John was totally at odds with himself. His heart and his head were pulling him in different directions at once. He was a traditionalist, but he had found certain of the reforms wise and beneficial and had come to value them. But he had been outraged by the relentless insensitivity, the excesses and the cruelties that had accompanied them.

He was also tormented by guilt. His best friends had died or been imprisoned. He had not suffered at all! Emotion played havoc with his reason and he had plunged into a bitter reactionary stance, far more reactionary than either his Vicar or the Parish Clerk, and quite alien to his much more level headed wife. It was alien, indeed, to his own true character, as well she knew.

And now his bitter prayer that he be present when Hooper received his just deserts was to be granted! John could not think about it. He could only function as an automaton until the thing was over.

"Will they put him out of his misery?" Kate had asked as they had both lain sleepless.

"That depends upon the will of the Commissioner."

And John had remembered who the Commissioner was, and the dire revenge he had sworn upon Bishop Hooper not four years since. The condemned at the stake were not infrequently put out of their misery in one way or another. Another victim, a priest by the name of Roland Taylor, was to be burned at Hadley in Suffolk on the same day that Hooper was to suffer at Gloucester. In his case the fire was not long lit when a long-armed blow from a halberd put his suffering to an end. But he did not have Kingston for his Commissioner.

In company with the Mayor and his fellow magistrates, John met The Provost Marshall, his armed guards and their prisoner upon their arrival at Gloucester on the 8th of February. Fox, Hooper's hagiographer, later claimed that Hooper's conversation on the journey had won all their hearts, but of this John Farelowe saw no sign at all.

They conveyed Hooper to lodgings at the foot of Westgate Street. There he addressed himself to one of the sheriffs, desiring but one thing: "A quick fire, shortly to make end."

John spent a terrible night in Gloucester, tormented with nightmares and was almost glad when it was time to dress and accompany Kingston, Lord Chandos and others, with a party of men-at-arms, to Hooper's lodging in order to escort him to the stake.

The prisoner received them with a grim courtesy:

"You needed not to make such a business to bring me," he said. "I am no traitor. I would have gone alone to the stake!" The commission which his captors held described Hooper as "a vain-glorious person who delighted in his tongue." He was therefore to be forbidden to address the crowd. He might only make such protestations as he saw fit as he walked to the place of his execution. John Farelowe, more desolate and empty within than he had ever felt in his life, could not look his former and deeply hated father-in-God in the face. But, glancing out of the corner of his eye he saw that, as they rounded the ancient church of St Mary de Lode and the stake came into view, a smile played upon Hooper's usually unsmiling countenance and he knelt in prayer.

It was John's task to place before the condemned man a box containing a pardon on the condition that he recanted. It was his last chance to save himself.

With a great shout, Hooper turned furiously on John Farelowe. "If you love my soul, away with it! If you love my soul, away with it!"

Turning again in prayer he prayed aloud that: "In the fire I might not break the rules of patience."

John, feeling like one stabbed to the heart and at the same time kicked in the stomach, turned from the scene. He longed to vomit but nothing came. It was only when he pulled himself together and turned to see Hooper being fastened to the stake by one of the three iron hoops provided that he saw – and at the same time took in the significance of it – that the wood provided for the fire was meagre to the point of absurdity.

Hooper was not merely to be burned. He was to be tortured to death!

A bladder of gunpowder was hung round Hooper's body. This was now the accepted means of limiting a victim's sufferings, for a spark, let alone a flame, would end the martyrdom immediately and spectacularly. It also had the advantage of being popular with the mobs that gathered, like ghouls, to watch.

The fire was kindled and, the wind being violent, the flames played cruelly upon the victim but without exploding the powder. The powder was never to explode. It was eventually to splutter and flare and so reveal itself as having been thoroughly wetted in advance! As a State execution the thing was a mockery. The fire went out and had to be re-lit three times; Hooper's nether extremities were reduced to ashes before any vital organ was touched. Blood, fat and water hissed out of his fingers and one arm dropped off while the other continued to beat his breast.

Forty-five minutes elapsed before John Hooper's terrible martyrdom was at an end.


John Farelowe, gathered up by Lord Chandos, Kingston and the others, was taken from the immediate scene at an early stage. They repaired to a little room over the Great Gate of the old Monastery, the windows of which provided a convenient viewpoint. There, while Hooper burned, they drank wine and made jokes about it. The three Stewards of the City of Gloucester, in account with the city, were afterwards to make certain application for expenses involved that day:

*"... And the same accomptantes also asketh allowance of Eleven Shillings in money given in reward to the King and Queen's servants at the bringing down of Master Hooper to be brent by the commandment of Master Maire and his brethren.*

*Also in money by them paid for a dinner made and given to the Lord Chandos and other gentlemen at Mr. Maire's house that day that Master Hooper was brent, as by a bill of particulars made by the aforesaid Master Maire, and upon his accompte shewed, proved and examined more at large appeareth Thirteen Shillings and Eight Pence.*

*And more in money paid to Agnes Ingram for wine by Master Kingston and others expended the same day in the morning by commandment of Master Maire, Five Shillings and Eight Pence."*


John Farelowe rode home to his house and hall in the early hours of the morning of the 10th of February. He had stopped several times on his journey and had vomited until there was nothing left in him.

He did not go to bed. Kate came down on hearing him enter the house, but he could not speak to her. He sat by the fire in the hall, shivering as much inwardly as outwardly for an hour or two. And then, at the first light of dawn, he went out again.

John stood for a moment on his step, hoping that the cold air would bring his mind under control. But still deeply in shock he set off down the lane to where the two or three cottages marked the turn towards the village.

Very little registered with him but a few, absurd, details were vivid. The door to Harry's hayloft hung open, and he wondered why.

In the village square, John turned up towards the church. He was going to pray but he did not know what to pray. For a terrible instant he wondered if there was a God to pray to after all, but his feet took him inside and, in the dim light of dawn the long-loved and familiar little place seemed utterly alien to him. It was as if he had no place there any more.

He looked up at the rood, the painted crucifix which he himself had paid for to serve until such time as they could replace the beautifully carved crucifix that Perkin and his gang had destroyed. John looked up at the rood, but what his eyes saw in place of the Crucified was a half-burned man, charred but still alive. As John looked on in horror, one arm dropped off while the other beat his breast.

And the words of the Crucified burst like a thunderclap inside John Farelowe's head:

"Inasmuch as ye have done it unto one of the least of these my brethren, ye have done it unto me."

There was a split-second available to John Farelowe and a choice to be made within it. Just sufficient of him was aware and for just long enough.

He could cast himself on the floor, at the feet of the Crucified, or he could turn and flee in despair.

He fled. He ran from the church and half-ran, half-stumbled through the deserted village until he arrived, breathless and staring with horror, at his own doorstep. He clung to the door-jamb, panting, and then he turned and he looked towards Gloucester. At that moment a shaft of pale, early sunlight played upon the great tower of the Cathedral but John did not see it. All he saw – or thought he saw – was a wisp of smoke trailing upwards from before the Great Gate.

His mind recalled another passage from the Gospels:

"Depart from me, ye cursed, into everlasting fire, prepared for the devil and his angels."

John Farelowe stumbled through the door. Kate ran towards him and then, seeing the look on his face, stopped dead in her stride.

"I am damned!" he said.

# CHAPTER THIRTY SEVEN

*T*HE *KING AND THE KINGDOM: TEMPTATION.* John Faversham peered at the table of Sunday Themes in his prayer book and then turned to the lessons for the First Sunday in Lent. He read through the Gospel for the day; St Luke's account of the temptations of Christ in the wilderness. Predictable enough, he thought, given the season and the theme.

And then he began to think, as he had been thinking half the night, about poor John Farelowe. It occurred to him that he had made a good guess about the ghost's name. He and Jane had referred to him as Jack. Once named he had ceased to frighten or to alarm. In an odd sort of a way he had become one of the family. It occurred to John that he and Jane had become really quite fond of Jack.

Well, Jack was a John, like himself. Whatever temptations had he fallen for? What had made him a candidate for ghosthood? It was the Bishop Hooper business of course, but what had he had to do with it specifically?

John Faversham decided that he didn't really want to know. Solemnly, judicially, burning a man alive on a bonfire just because he thought the wrong things was beyond his imagination. The idea that the Christian Faith might have served, in some pathological way, as a justification was acutely painful to him, even though the real reason was probably spite and politics. Or was it? He didn't know and he didn't really want to know.

John sat in his pew, ten minutes before the service began, and he recalled *The Dream* vividly, but without any trace of nightmare, just with a terrible sense of tragedy. Momentarily – blessedly only momentarily – he had actually seen … No! He would pass that over and put it on the altar where it belonged. He didn't have to recall it any more. *The Dream* had fulfilled its object; he knew, and now he and Jane – and Walter – could put it all before the Lord and invoke Heaven to sort it all out. And Heaven would sort it out, of that John had no doubt whatsoever.

Odd that it had needed two other men in two different generations to sort it out! Hasfield had come close to it. He had had *The Dream*, but he hadn't somehow got beyond it. In fact the whole thing had been a bit too much for him. He had been taken over by it. Chronic depression, getting slowly worse, fatally worse, just as it had been with John Faversham himself. Ah! But Hasfield had not had Philomena to look after him! Yes, and he, John Faversham, had had Hasfield's experience, faithfully recorded in verse, to guide him. And Hasfield had taken to dithering, urgently, at the edge of John's intuitive awareness. Warning? Drawing attention to something? Funny business! It was just as well he had not talked about it at the office! They would have called in the psychiatrists and got rid of him even sooner!

"There's Walter, doing a Hezekiah!"

Jane nudged her husband. Their eyes met. They both grinned. Walter, with five minutes to go before the service began, was doing something up at the altar. George had performed his churchwardenly duties and had lit the two candles before going to the back of the Church to perform his final Obligato on the bell. Walter was arranging the corporal, the small cloth upon which the chalice stood, and he was covering the sacred vessels with the pall. But as John and Jane both knew, he was also putting a piece of paper on the altar. He turned to return to the vestry and his eyes met theirs, just for a moment.

"I'll do a Hezekiah!" he had said. "When King Hezekiah received a letter he couldn't answer he took it to the Temple and spread it before the Lord. Whenever I am completely stumped, or really don't know what to do about something, I write it all down and put it on the altar; I spread it before the Lord. And then I say Mass on top of it!"

Walter had had no idea what to do. He had begun to suggest calling in the Diocesan exorcist but John had been adamant against it, and Walter had sensed that he was right. He had decided, therefore, to offer the Sunday Mass for the peace and reconciliation of Fairloe Court, of John Farelowe and of any other unquiet souls therein. And he had written it all out on a piece of his notepaper, adding the names of James Hasfield and John and Jane Faversham for good measure, and he had put it on the altar, spreading the corporal over it and putting the sacred vessels on top of it. And he had confessed to the Lord his ignorance and his inability to fathom the thing out, and also his complete bewilderment as to what should properly be done.

And then he had returned to the vestry supremely confident that all would be well. Heaven would sort it out! Heaven always did, if you trusted them.

He remembered one of his clerical colleagues telling him how, in the terrible inflation days of the 1970s, when prices doubled, trebled and quadrupled and clerical stipends had more or less stood still, the household bills had ended up on the altar, often and often. "But you have to be defeated first!" he had been reminded.

They were without an organist again, and so they sang the Lenten Hymns lustily, unaccompanied.

*Forty days and forty nights*
*Thou wast fasting in the wild ...*
If ever there was an inevitability about anything, John thought, surely this was it! Was there ever a Lent that had not started with that hymn?

"George, do you know anything about a John Farelowe who used to live in our house in the sixteenth century?"

"'im as brent Bishop 'ooper?"

"Yes. What happened to him? Does anybody know?"

George composed himself and put an expression upon his countenance appropriate to one who is Custodian of the Corporate Memory.

"'im died o' shame."

"What happened?"

"'im come 'ome after 'im were a-burnin o' the Bishop and 'im did say, 'I be damned!' And 'im never spoke agin. 'im were jud in three weeks. Some say t'was more like a fortnight. 'im was just a-sittin in 'im's chair and one mornin, they da find un jud!"

"George! How do you know all this?"

George gave John a look which combined pity with just the faintest trace of contempt for the kind of in-comer who found the need to ask a question of quite that degree of silliness.

"Tis allus bin known in Fairloe," said he.

# CHAPTER THIRTY EIGHT

SIR ANTHONY KINGSTON had intended to remain in Gloucestershire for a little while after he had settled his score with Bishop Hooper but his sabbatical was suddenly, and rudely, disturbed. A plot had been uncovered to rob the Exchequer of fifty thousand pounds and, with the money, to raise a rebellion. It became clear from the outset that Sir Anthony was implicated up to the hilt and he was summoned to London to stand trial.

All his fellow conspirators were found guilty and executed but Sir Anthony, patron of the living of Farelowe, managed to escape the executioner by the simple expedient of dying on his way to London. Nicholas Ridley and Hugh Latimer had been excommunicated and deposed the previous year. Further examinations of them were carried out throughout 1555 but, on their final refusal to bow down before Aristotle's definition of an undefinable Mystery, they were sentenced to be burned alive at the same stake, at Oxford, on the 16th of October.

It was the faith and the heroism of these austere and not always attractive Reformers, contrasted with the meanness, the cruelty and the spite of their persecutors which, as much as anything else, turned their fellow-countrymen decisively towards their own reforming cause.

The night before Ridley was burned he invited his hostess and friends to his marriage for, said he, "tomorrow I must be married." And to calm the distress of his friends he said to them, "Quiet yourselves! Though my breakfast shall be somewhat sharp and painful, yet I am sure my supper shall be more pleasant and sweet." When he was brought to the stake, Ridley, like Hooper before him, was given a last opportunity to recant and save himself. He replied: "So long as the breath is in my body I will never deny my Lord Christ and His known truth: God's will be done in me."

Hugh Latimer suffered at the same stake with him. As the fire was lit he called to his friend: "Be of good comfort, Master Ridley and play the man. We shall this day light such a candle, by God's grace, in England, as I trust shall never be put out!"

As in the case of the burning of John Hooper, the fire was devised as much to torture as to burn, but in the cases of Ridley and Latimer the gunpowder hung round their necks had not been made damp and their agonies were therefore somewhat foreshortened. Their martyrdom, combined with the martyrdom of others the length and breadth of England, made the alienation of the great mass of Englishmen from Queen Mary and the Papacy inexorable. Latimer's last words were to prove prophetic indeed.

Thomas Cranmer followed his reforming colleagues to the stake, also at Oxford, the following year on the 21st of May. The final months of Cranmer's life were pathetic in the extreme for, in mortal fear of death by burning, he had signed one recantation after another before regaining his integrity and renouncing them all. His writings at this period betray a profound inner confusion and convey more than a hint of mental breakdown but, at the very end, this most timid and vulnerable of men met his death with all the courage of a true Martyr.

King Philip of Spain had by this time returned home without his Queen. The marriage had been a disaster, Queen Mary had suffered a false pregnancy and it was clear, not only that there would be no children from the marriage, but also that her health, always frail, was deteriorating steadily.

The luckless Queen, whose accession had been greeted with almost universal rejoicing so very few years ago, had alienated her subjects by her marriage, had lost the affections – such as they had ever been – of her husband, and had no child to succeed her. The revival of the Heresy laws was also rapidly alienating her subjects from the Roman obedience to which she had so abjectly committed them.

Her humiliation was completed by her involvement in her estranged husband's war with France in 1557. An English Army was sent to France at Philip's request and initially the French suffered reverses, being defeated at the battle of St Quentin. In 1558 however, the tide of war turned against her and Calais, England's last toe-hold upon the Continent, fell to the French.

The loss of Calais was a death-blow to the isolated and demoralised Queen Mary. Her health took a sudden turn for the worse and she died at St James' Palace on 17th November.

Reginald Pole, described as a man of the purest morals, the sincerest piety, of ascetic life and of remarkable singleness of purpose, was ordained priest at the Greyfriars at Greenwich on 20th of May 1557, the day before Thomas Cranmer was burned at the stake. Two days later, Cranmer having vacated his office by death, Pole succeeded him and was consecrated Archbishop of Canterbury. Gardiner had died in 1555 and by now most of the old English hierarchy were either dead or dying; confinement in prison had not improved the health of any of them. Both Pole and his Queen were now surrounded by mediocrities and, to make matters worse, hardly had Pole been consecrated when he found himself totally out of favour with the Pope!

King Philip's war against France had put him at enmity with the Papacy with which France was allied. England, being allied to Spain, was also now the Pope's political enemy and Pope Paul IVth's reaction was swift. Reginald Pole had his legation cancelled at once and he himself was accused of doctrinal unsoundness.

The same depression and conviction of utter failure that killed the Queen killed her Archbishop at the same time, and on the same day. He died twelve hours after the Queen who – had she been less in awe of his Cardinalate – might have been his wife.


Kate Farelowe lived some fifteen years after John's death. For a while she left Farelowe and lived with Meg and her family, but then Will returned from his self-imposed exile and Tom Campion's remaining influence at Court succeeded in obtaining him the living of Farelowe. Like Tom Cranmer, Will had married while abroad, and he and his Dutch wife settled in to the old family house upon their return. Kate then came home, got on well enough with her new daughter-in law and lived to hear of Queen Elizabeth's excommunication by the Pope in 1570. By this time, devout woman though she was, she cared not a fig for it, one way or the other.

Will related well to the Elizabethan Settlement. He had inherited much of his mother's plain common sense but with a touch of his father's romanticism to lighten it. He lived to rejoice in the defeat of the Armada sent by Queen Elizabeth's brother-in-law, now a royal recluse cloistered in his monastery-palace of the Escorial. Will lived a full ten years after the Armada, battling against the encroaching tide of Calvinism and leaving two sons and a daughter to succeed him.

Fairlowe Court remained in the hands of the family until just after the Royal Siege of Gloucester in the Civil War.

# CHAPTER THIRTY NINE

JOHN FAVERSHAM woke on the Monday morning knowing, with the utmost clarity, what he had to do.

He didn't trouble Jane with it. Monday was not usually one of her better mornings, she usually started her working week in ominous silence. Breakfast, on a Monday, was usually fraught with menace. Jane would scowl into her muesli, looking up only to glare, her eyes darting about the kitchen, finding fault with everything they saw. She would storm from the house trailing, John swore, small spirals of brimstone behind her, and she would invariably reappear at tea-time radiant and loving, at peace with the world. John prepared the breakfast as usual and was pleased to see a smiling, Saturday-morning Jane appear at the table, two or three envelopes in her hand.

"Post's early," she said. "Two for me, one for you!"

Muesli and coffee waited as Jane opened her envelopes. Coffee, toast and marmalade waited as John opened his.

"Mummy is inviting herself for lunch on Sunday," said Jane. "She says Rosemary and Bill will be here and she rather fancies Bill!" Jane slit the second envelope and drew out a piece of paper. She made a face at it.

"Monthly account from Cavendish House," she said, putting it back in its envelope, John thought rather hurriedly. "What's yours?"

The question was asked by a mouth full of muesli.

"Hmm!" said John, and then again, "Hmm!"

"Looks interesting. One of these short-term government research projects. They had asked the Firm to second me but as I'm redundant they are approaching me direct."

"You mean a Quango?" Jane's eyes lit up.

"Quasi-autonomous Government Organisation? Yes, I suppose it is. I shall probably have to go to London rather a lot but I shan't mind that. I'll get a letter off today. Might give them a ring later on."

Jane did a very un-Mondayish thing. She jumped up from her chair, ran round the table, sat herself on John's lap and hugged him.

All in all, John thought, it was a good start to the week.


John tidied the breakfast things away, loaded the dishwasher and addressed the cat.

"I'm going into the dining-room, Sweetheart," he said, "and it will be quite all right; I don't want to be rescued. Not this time!" Philomena, fast asleep on the settle, did not so much as twitch an ear.

John walked across to the chair by the big chimneypiece where he had sat for days on end, diminishing inexorably, until Philomena had tormented him back into the land of the living. He made the sign of the cross – it seemed the right thing to do – and he sat down, made himself comfortable, and composed himself to prayer. John Farelowe and the Bishop Hooper tragedy; and the James Hasfield tragedy too. It had nearly been the John Faversham tragedy to complete the hat-trick, but the danger was past, John knew that. Now it was time for compassion, a holding of it all up before the Lord. Well, he would do his best.

There were no words that had to be said; the Almighty knew all about it when all was said and done. John was aware that he was entering into a stillness which, once or twice in his prayers, he had known before. The stillness became timeless and it became spaceless as well. John was conscious, supremely conscious, conscious as he had never been conscious before. He did not know if he was outside of himself, or utterly deep within and beyond himself. All he knew was that he WAS, and that he was filled with the profoundest peace and an immeasurable joy.

He also knew that, down there, or up there, or wherever his body was, it was weeping. Tears were streaming down the face that others knew as John Faversham.

Somewhere, after ages of ages, lost in the depths of Eternity, John began to know that he was returning to himself. He became aware of his body. He could move his hands, wriggle his toes and discover that he was wearing shoes. And then he found that he had been weeping and his shirt collar and the lapels of his jacket were soaked with tears. He fished a handkerchief from his pocket and mopped his face. And then he sat back and discovered himself to be laughing; laughing with relief, with joy and with an unutterable compassion. "Thanks!" he said.

And then, still sitting in his chair, he fell fast asleep.

Jane was only working a half-day this Monday and she arrived home at about a quarter to one. She opened the front door and something made her glance into the dining-room.

Jane's heart leapt into her mouth. For one terrible moment she was paralysed with horror.

John was slumped in that chair by the chimneypiece, and he was dead! Dead! And Philomena was curled up asleep on his lap.

The corpse looked up at her.

"Hello darling!" it said.


Walter sat back in his chair and looked hard at John.

"There is something called The Grace of Holy Tears." he said, "but it's all a bit beyond me! But I wouldn't be surprised if you haven't done the trick. It has that feel to it. I've got a funny feeling poor old John Farelowe is off the hook now."

John nodded.

"I'm sure he is, but I don't know why I am sure."

"You know because you *know*! You are probably one of those folk who do. I have met a few. Sometimes they frighten me, but I don't think you do, John!"

"Deirdre used to frighten me. She *knows*! I used to call her the Earth-Mother. I was sure she was a witch."

"I'd love to meet this Deirdre woman one day."

Walter looked hopefully at John and then got up and, crossing to a bookcase, pulled from the bottom of it a large, black leather-bound book, and returned to his chair.

"What about tidying this up with a Mass next Saturday?" he said. "Handing it all over to the Lord. We'll round up John Farelowe, Bishop Hooper, James Hasfield, you and Jane and say 'Thank you very much!' Early in the morning, nice and private; just the 'Dramatis Personae' there – in their various dimensions!"

"Marvellous idea! I'll get Aunt Sarah and the Earth-Mother along as well, and we'll all have a jolly breakfast afterwards at our place. What time? Half-past seven? Eight?"

"Eight! We might as well be civilised about it."

Walter opened the great book and turned its pages. He shook his head, frowned, seized another book from a nearer bookcase and consulted it and then he looked up in triumph.

"We want to do it properly, don't we?" he said. "Pity we can't do the old Sarum Mass for old John Farelowe, he'd like that! But we'll use the Propers from Sarum with good old, modern language, Rite "A" instead. Mass of Our Lady on Saturday, just like we always used to do at Tewkesbury Abbey when I was a lad and old Brian was the Vicar."

He laughed.

"Mind! Old Hooper might not like it! And he won't like my new vestments either! Rabid old thing, he was!"

John smiled.

"Perhaps Heaven has mellowed him a bit?" he said.

# CHAPTER FORTY

"THERE WERE an awful lot of people about!"

Aunt Sarah put down her coffee-cup and gave Jane a look which was charged with meaning.

"Jane dear! You are a love to lay on this wonderful breakfast!" Deirdre was enjoying herself, she had been deep in conversation with Walter; they were obviously very taken with each other. "I love nice, noisy breakfasts!" she said. "But it is a bit difficult to be jolly at breakfast-time when you live on your own."

"I was just saying to Jane," Aunt Sarah abandoned her *sotto voce*, "We seemed to have an awful lot of congregation this morning – in one way or another!"

Walter looked up with a start.

"Funny you should say that! I seemed to be getting glimpses of people out of the corner of my eye all through Mass. I thought I was seeing things!"

Aunt Sarah caught Deirdre's eye and the eyes of both of them twinkled.

"I thought the boy read very well." Deirdre turned to Walter. "Ecclesiasticus, out of the old Bible too! Not the easiest thing for modern youth to get its tongue round. Who is he?"

Walter grinned and glanced at John.

"Young Harry. Old George's grandson. George is one of the churchwardens. His family have been churchwardens at Fairloe ever since Noah's Ark. They used to be Parish Clerks too, when we had such things. Parish Clerks always had the duty of reading the Epistle, so reading will be in young Harry's blood."

"I always get a sense of centuries of continuity whenever I come here," said Aunt Sarah. "I'm glad Gloucestershire hasn't lost it all – not yet at any rate."

She relaxed into what John called her well-fed cat look and then sighed.

"I'm *so* looking forward to the wedding!" she said.

"When do they arrive?" John looked at Jane.

"In time for lunch," she said.

"They are seeing me at six," said Walter. "I got the Banns Certificate from Croydon the other day. I'm starting to read their Banns here tomorrow."

Breakfast was over and the guests were departing. As John opened Deirdre's car door for her, he asked:

"Deirdre! Who was it who was doing all the weeping the other day? Was it me, or was it John Farelowe?"

"Both of you, dear! You had a lot of hurt and anger to get out of your system, and you did. I can see it in your eyes. And poor John Farelowe – Heaven alone knows what he had to get out of his system! He must be very grateful to you for the loan of your eyes to weep with."

She gave him a smile of quite astonishing radiance.

"I had a very strong sense of John Farelowe in church this morning. And James Hasfield too. It was lovely! Two Johns and a James! Three lovely men!"

And with that she kissed him and got into her car.

"Thanks Walter!"

"My duty and my Joy – as the new book says. Pure Joy too, and a privilege. And a lovely breakfast too! Thanks, Jane!"

Jane gave her parish priest a hug and a kiss, and then she vanished indoors, into the kitchen. She didn't want to speak any more. She just wanted a few minutes alone with herself.

"What a woman Deirdre is!" Walter was clearly smitten. "I wish I had her as my Confessor! She sees right through you; you get away with nothing! But what a compassion the woman has! She must have done a bit of suffering in her time?"

John watched the cloaked figure of his Vicar stride off down the lane. Yes, he was grateful for Walter. He turned and, closing the front door behind him, joined Jane in the kitchen.

"Any more coffee in the pot?" he asked.


"John!"

John Faversham turned to find the tall, almost scraggy figure of Lucy bearing down upon him.

"Hello Lucy!"

"Congratulations, John! Sarah tells me you have fulfilled rather an important bit of Karma. I'm so glad!"

John smiled at her. He was fond of Lucy.

"Don't congratulate me, dear. I don't think I've done anything very much. But something worthwhile seems to have happened, and that's what matters."

Lucy looked at him with mock severity.

"You did promise to keep an open mind you know."

"Yes, and I honestly think I did. I certainly tried. But – well, in terms of former incarnations and all that, it just didn't *present* like that, as the doctors would say. Your theory might fit another situation but I honestly don't think it was right for this one."

Lucy's countenance assumed its slightly Himalayan look. "It is not easy to correctly interpret experiences within the constraints of *Maya*," she said.

"I grant you that!"

Lucy shook her head at him and smiled an impish smile. "We are just going to have to agree to differ on some things, aren't we John?"

"Perhaps! But when we get to Heaven we shall know the answers, won't we? Some of them at any rate."

"When we are released from *Samsara*," she replied.

Jane appeared at the front door as John got out of his car.

"How did you get on?"

"Fine! A three-year contract but, privately, it is expected to last for five."

John kissed his wife.

"That will take me to sixty-three. I think I might be quite content to be retired by then."

They went indoors.

"I bumped into Lucy in Cheltenham," he said. "She congratulated me on fulfilling my Karma and cleaning up my former incarnations and things. We agreed to differ. I like her!"

Jane giggled. "So do I," she said.

"Well, Little Sweetheart! Daddy has a job again!"

Philomena stretched herself, extended her claws, yawned and then rearranged herself on the settle in a manner which suggested interest and attention.

John sat down beside her. He picked her up and put her on his lap. And while Jane put the kettle on the Aga, he stroked her and tickled her behind the ears.

"Little Sweetheart!" he said.

Philomena purred with an extravagance of satisfaction. And then, for good measure, she bit him.